STARS OVER SUNSET BOULEVARD

Center Point
Large Print

Also by Susan Meissner and available from
Center Point Large Print:

Secrets of a Charmed Life

**This Large Print Book carries the
Seal of Approval of N.A.V.H.**

STARS OVER SUNSET BOULEVARD

Susan Meissner

CENTER POINT LARGE PRINT
THORNDIKE, MAINE

This Center Point Large Print edition
is published in the year 2016 by arrangement with
New American Library, an imprint of Penguin Publishing
Group, a division of Penguin Random House LLC.

This is a work of fiction. Names, characters,
places, and incidents either are the product of the author's
imagination or are used fictitiously, and any resemblance
to actual persons, living or dead, business establishments,
events, or locales is entirely coincidental.

The text of this Large Print edition is unabridged.
In other aspects, this book may vary
from the original edition.
Printed in the United States of America
on permanent paper.
Set in 16-point Times New Roman type.

ISBN: 978-1-62899-901-3

Library of Congress Cataloging-in-Publication Data

Names: Meissner, Susan, 1961– author.
Title: Stars over Sunset Boulevard / Susan Meissner.
Description: Center Point Large Print edition. | Thorndike, Maine :
Center Point Large Print, 2016. | ©2016
Identifiers: LCCN 2015046449 | ISBN 9781628999013
        (hardcover : alk. paper)
Subjects: LCSH: Large type books.
Classification: LCC PS3613.E435 S73 2016b | DDC 813/.6—dc23
LC record available at http://lccn.loc.gov/2015046449

For Raechyl and Nicole,
two talented young women who possess
old souls, artistic minds,
and a love for nostalgia

That star-enchanted song falls through the air
From lawn to lawn down terraces of sound,
Darts in white arrows on the shadowed ground;
And all the night you sing.

—Harold Monro,
"Nightingale Near the House"

Hollywood
March 9, 2012

C hristine unfolds the tissue paper inside the pink-striped hatbox and the odor of lost years floats upward. She is well acquainted with the fragrance of antiquity. Her vintage-clothing boutique off West Sunset overflows with stylish remnants from golden years long since passed.

"I thought you were going to hold off estimating that lot until this afternoon," her business partner, Stella, says as she joins Christine in the shop's back room. The two friends are surrounded on all sides by the wearable miscellany of spent lives.

"Mr. Garceau, the man who brought this stuff in last night, just called. There's apparently a hat in one of these boxes that wasn't supposed to be included. He told me what it looks like. I guess the family is anxious to have it back."

Christine withdraws a paper-wrapped lump from inside the box, revealing at first just a flash of moss green and shimmers of gold. Then she pulls away the rest of the layers. The Robin Hood–style hat in folds of soft velvet, amber-hued fringe, and iridescent feathers feels ghostly in her hands, as though if she put it to her ear, it might whisper a litany of old secrets.

She has seen this hat somewhere before, a long time ago.

"Is that it?" Stella asks.

"I think so. He said it was green with gold fringe and feathers."

Stella moves closer, brow furrowed. "That hat looks familiar to me."

"It does to me, too." Christine turns the hat over to inspect its underside for signs of its designer—a label, a signature, a date. She sees only a single name in faded ink on a yellowed tag:

Scarlett #13

———⟫·◇·⟪———

1938

ONE

December 1938

A brilliant California sun bathed Violet Mayfield in indulgent light as she neared the soaring palm tree and the woman seated on a bench underneath it. Legs crossed at the ankles, the woman rested her back lazily against the skinny trunk. She held a cigarette in her right hand, and it was as if the thin white tube were a part of her and the stylish smoke that swirled from it an extension of her body. The woman's fingernails, satin red and glistening, were perfectly shaped. Toenails visible to Violet through peep-toes winked the same shade of crimson. The woman wore a form-fitting sheath of celery green with a scoop neckline. A magazine lay open on her lap, but her tortoise-shell sunglasses hid her eyes, so Violet couldn't tell whether the woman was reading the article on the left page or gazing at handsome Cary Grant, whose photograph graced the right. A wad of wax paper lay crumpled on the bench beside her handbag and a bit of bread crust poked out of it. She sat in front of the Mansion at Selznick International Studios, the stunning white edifice that movie-maker Thomas Ince had built back in the twenties to look like George Washington's Mount Vernon.

The woman under the tree didn't look at all like a fellow studio secretary, but rather a highly paid actress catching a few quiet moments of solitude between takes on the back lot. Violet glanced around to see whether there was someone else sitting outside the Mansion on her noon break. But the woman in front of her was the only one eating her lunch under a palm tree, and that was where Violet had been told she'd find Audrey Duvall. She suddenly looked familiar to Violet, which made no sense at all. Violet was two thousand miles away from anything remotely connected to home.

"Miss Duvall?" Violet said.

The woman looked up drowsily, as though Violet had awakened her from sleep. She cocked her head and pulled her sunglasses down slightly to peer at Violet over the rims. Her luminous eyes, beautiful and doelike, were fringed with long lashes she couldn't have been born with. The casual glance was the wordless reply that she was indeed Audrey Duvall.

"My name's Violet Mayfield. I'm new to the secretary pool. Millie in accounts payable told me you are looking for a roommate. I was wondering if you'd found one yet."

Audrey smiled and her painted lips parted to reveal moon-white teeth. "Good Lord," she exclaimed, her voice rich and resonant, almost as deep as a man's. "Where are you from?"

"Pardon me?"

"You're not from around here."

"Um. No. I'm from Alabama. Originally."

Audrey's smile deepened. "Alabama. Never been to Alabama."

Violet didn't know what to say. Had the woman not heard what she asked?

Audrey patted the empty space next to her. "Have a seat. What did you say your name was?"

"Violet Mayfield." She sat down, and the cement beneath her was warm from the sun despite it being early December.

Audrey lifted the cigarette gently to her mouth and its end glowed red as she inhaled. When she tipped her head back and released the smoke it wafted over her head like a feathery length of gauze.

"Want one?" She nodded toward the pack of cigarettes peeking out of her handbag.

"No, thanks."

"Don't smoke?" Audrey puffed again on the cigarette and smiled as the smoke drifted past her lips.

Violet shook her head.

"My last roommate didn't, either. She was always leaving the windows open to let the smoke out."

"Did you not like it when she left the windows open? Is that why you need a new roommate?"

Audrey laughed. "You're kidding, right?"

Violet said nothing.

"She got married."

"Oh."

Audrey pushed the sunglasses up onto her head, fully revealing shining tea-brown eyes that complemented her shimmering brunette hair. She seemed to study for a moment Violet's navy blue dress with its plain white collar. Violet's mousy brown hair—far less wavy than Audrey's—was pulled back into a beaded barrette she had bought in a five-and-dime on the day she started heading west.

"So you just moved, then? From Alabama?"

"I came by way of Shreveport, actually. I've been working for my uncle the past year. He's an accountant."

"And how long have you been here?" Audrey asked.

"Two weeks."

"And you found a job that quickly?" Her tone held a faint edge of sly admiration. "Good for you!"

"I've worked in an office before," Violet said quickly. "And I went to secretary school."

"I've heard there's a school for what we do," Audrey said, amused. "What are you? Nineteen? Twenty?"

"Twenty-two."

"That will come in handy here, looking younger

14

than you really are," Audrey murmured. "I'm thirty and can still pass for a twenty-year-old if I need to."

"Why would you need to do that?"

Audrey tossed back her head and laughed. Even her laugh was low and rich. "You seem to have a knack for humor, Violet from Alabama." She arched one penciled eyebrow. "So. Did you come to Hollywood to be a movie star?"

Violet startled at the question. "No!"

"That's why most girls your age come here."

The thought of performing in front of people didn't interest Violet in the least. Hollywood had beckoned her for a different reason. "That's not why I moved here."

"No?"

Her motivation for coming to California apparently mattered to Audrey Duvall. "I met one of Mr. Selznick's talent scouts at an audition in Shreveport. He said he'd put in a good word for me if I wanted a secretarial job at the studio."

"You went to that audition?" Audrey's eyes widened in measurable interest.

"Only because my cousin Lucinda insisted I come with her. She found out people from Hollywood were coming to Shreveport to search for a young woman to play Scarlett O'Hara. I let her talk me into being interviewed along with everyone else. I think by the time Mr. Arnow got to me he was just relieved to talk to someone who had actually read Margaret Mitchell's book and wasn't fawning all over him."

"You don't say!"

"I told him I was a much better secretary than I was an actress and that I knew stenography, and that I'd lived in the South all my life. He told me if I wanted a job at Selznick International in Hollywood, he'd put in a good word for me. He said it would be handy to have a Southerner in the secretary pool during the filming. So I came."

"Just like that?" Audrey seemed both intrigued and dubious.

Violet nodded.

"You have a family back there missing you right now?"

"Just my parents. And my two brothers, Jackson and Truman. They're both married now and raising families. I doubt they think about me much."

"But your parents?"

Violet's thoughts somersaulted back to the strained phone call she had placed from Shreveport, telling her parents she'd been offered a job in Los Angeles and was taking it. They had begged her to reconsider.

"Come back home to Montgomery!" her mother had pleaded.

"Come back home to what?" Violet had responded. "There's nothing for me there."

Daddy had asked what California had that

Alabama didn't. She hadn't known how to express that Hollywood didn't have expectations of her.

Or sad memories of what might have been.

"I suppose they miss me," Violet answered.

Audrey cocked her head. "So, what made you come all this way, if you don't want to be a star?"

But Violet's reason was too personal to share with a virtual stranger. She was not going to tell someone she'd only just met that fully realizing she could never have the life she'd been raised to live and wanted to live had sent her scrabbling for a new foothold on a meaningful existence.

"I was ready for a different life with new opportunities," Violet said, with a slight shrug of her left shoulder.

For a stretched moment Audrey stared at her. "Then you came to the right place," she finally said. "Are you allergic to cats?" She took a long pull on her cigarette.

Violet shook her head.

"You don't have any furniture, do you?"

"Just a suitcase. I've been staying at a hotel."

"The rent is sixty dollars a month. Plus half of the utilities." Audrey dropped the stub of the cigarette to the pavement and ground it out with her shoe. "My place is a bit out of the way. Eight miles by way of bus and the red car. It's a very pretty neighborhood, though. Close to the hills and the Hollywoodland sign. It was my aunt's house. But now it's mine."

"The red car?"

"The trolley. The streetcar. It's a good thirty minutes getting there in the morning and just as long or more at night. Still interested?"

"Yes. Yes, I am."

Audrey smiled. "I'm on loan to one of the assistant art directors the next few days, so how about you meet me out front at quitting time? We can take the red car together so you can see the place and decide." She rose from the bench, clutching the magazine and the handbag. "C'mon. You don't want to be late getting back."

Audrey strolled confidently to toss the wax paper into a trash can some yards away and Violet had to quicken her step to catch up. Audrey's attention was fixed on the people they passed, some wearing elaborate costumes, some street clothes, some moving leisurely, some rushing as though desperate to catch a departing train. A few of these people Audrey greeted by name; some she did not. But everyone was given a look.

At a few minutes after five, Violet was at the front gate, waiting for Audrey to join her. When fifteen minutes had passed and there was still no sign of her, Violet was ready to assume she'd been forgotten. She had just decided to head back to her hotel when she saw Audrey walking slowly toward the gate, in the company of a man in a suit. They were laughing as they sauntered in her direction. He broke away before they reached the gate to head to one of the sound stages.

"Sorry about that," Audrey said easily when she reached Violet. "But that fellow is not one to rush away from. Ready?"

They set out toward the Pacific Electric trolley stop, alighting onto a Venice Line car seconds before it set off east toward the Hollywood foothills. The streetcar had made a few stops before the two women were able to find two seats together. They sank into the last double seat at the rear.

"So, have you lived here a long time?" Violet asked as they settled more comfortably.

Audrey looked out the window at the passing scenery. "I suppose I have. I came when I was sixteen to live with my aunt." She turned with a half grin on her lips toward Violet. "I'm not from here, either. I was raised four hours north on a plum farm. I'm a farm girl."

The image of stunning Audrey Duvall as a pigtailed tomboy in dungarees made Violet smile for only a second. Sixteen seemed a young age to have left home. Violet's own parents had been distraught when she told them she was heading to Hollywood, and she was a grown woman.

"And your parents let you come?" Violet asked.

Audrey laughed lightly. "My father pretty much insisted on it."

Sorrow and disappointment laced Audrey's

words despite the grin. Violet was instantly curious to know what had happened between Audrey and her father. But it would have been rude to ask.

"And your mother?" Violet said instead.

Again Audrey's gaze turned to the passing sights on the street. They were leaving the dull and drab neighborhoods of Culver City, where the studio was located, and entering the charm and glamour of Hollywood. "She died when I was ten."

"I'm so sorry."

Audrey was quiet for a moment. "I don't have any regrets about coming to Hollywood, but I do wonder sometimes where I would be right now if my mother had lived." She turned her head to face Violet again. "Do you ever wonder what your life would be like if different things had happened to you?"

Violet thought of her childhood friends back home who were all engaged, married, or pregnant, blissfully enjoying the existence she had always pictured herself living. It was such an ordinary life, but she had wanted it. She still wanted it.

"All the time," Violet answered.

The streetcar stopped and a dozen passengers around them maneuvered their way off the trolley. A few others boarded.

"So . . . you never wanted to go back home?" Violet asked, hoping she wasn't prying. But she needed to know. She had left home, too, and she wanted to know what made a person decide to remain so far from it.

"I had my reasons for staying here," Audrey said after a pause. "First of all, Aunt Jo was happy to have me, and second, my father remarried and his new wife was a complete stranger to me. And third, I got discovered."

"Discovered?"

She turned to Violet and a look of sweet reverie swept across her face.

"I almost starred in a movie when I was eighteen. I would have, if silent films hadn't died away."

"Really?"

Audrey leaned her head against the back of the seat. "I was working at a coffee shop on Vine, and one morning I was waiting on a man who was a Hollywood talent scout. He told me I looked just like Lillian Gish, and he asked me if I had ever thought of being in the movies."

"You do look like Lillian Gish!" Violet said. "I knew you looked familiar to me."

Audrey smiled. "Well, I hadn't to that point imagined being a professional actress, but I knew I could be one if I wanted to. And the thought of being a sought-after star sure beat pouring coffee and taking orders for pancakes. Aunt Jo wasn't overly in favor of it. She had lived in this town all her adult life and she wasn't too keen on me getting sucked into the movie industry, but she knew it was my decision. I signed a contract to be represented by Mr. Stiles. He paid for acting lessons and a new hairstyle. And he bought me fancy clothes so that when he arranged for screen tests, the casting directors wouldn't see some girl from the Central Valley they didn't know; they'd see Lillian Gish. He got me a few bit parts, but finally, after a year, and after all the money Mr. Stiles had spent on me, I was cast in the lead for a movie based on the life of Pocahontas."

She paused a moment and Violet could tell something bad had happened.

"But," Audrey went on, "before they even started filming, *The Jazz Singer* came out. Do you remember that movie?"

Violet shook her head. She wasn't sure she did.

"It was the first movie with sound," Audrey went on. "Suddenly, all the movie producers wanted to make talking pictures. The director of the Pocahontas movie quit to make a talking picture with someone else. The financial backers left the movie, too, to put their money into productions with sound. The movie was scrapped. Mr. Stiles tried to get screen tests for me for other pictures, but I had such a deep voice, no one wanted me. Stiles finally let me go, and that was that."

The streetcar rumbled on for a few moments before either one of them spoke.

"But you stayed here," Violet said.

"I wanted to get back what had been taken from me. For a very short while I had been treated like a queen. It's intoxicating to be treated like you're a rare gem. There's no other feeling in the world like it. I tried for a couple of years to get another agent and another part in a movie. It was . . . It was not a great time for me. And I'll just leave it at that." Audrey shook her head as if to dislodge a cobweb that had fallen onto her. "Then my sweet Aunt Jo got sick and died. She left me the bungalow, so it was even easier to just stay. By this time I'd figured out that I wasn't getting anywhere with my career and I was going to have to do something different. I decided to get a job at a studio, so that I could be visible to all those men who had the power to change my life. Those people all have secretaries. And they are all fiercely dependent on their secretaries. So I taught myself typing and stenography and got a job at MGM, and then when Mr. Selznick left MGM to start his own studio, I came with him."

"And?" Violet said.

"And what?"

"Has it worked? Being around all those studio people?"

Audrey frowned slightly. "You mean, is it working?"

The streetcar squealed to a stop and a host of passengers jostled around them as they got off.

"I guess."

"Of course it's working. Do you think I would still be there if I didn't think it was?"

Violet wished she hadn't asked. Words escaped her as she wondered if she had just blown her chance of rooming with this woman. And she liked Audrey. Something about her made Violet think old hopes could be given new shapes.

Audrey looked intently into Violet's eyes. "You don't just throw in the towel after a couple years here. This is not the kind of town to be in if you're going to give up easily."

Violet felt her face bloom crimson. "Sorry. I didn't mean to insinuate—"

"No, I know what you meant. You want to know if working as a studio secretary for the past seven years has paid off for me. You're thinking it should have by now."

"No, I just—"

"And I want you to know that you can't give in too soon here. You have to be smart. Clever. Patient. Do you hear what I'm saying?"

Violet nodded in assent even though she wasn't sure what she was saying yes to.

Audrey took Violet's hand and squeezed it. "Don't forget I told you this. This is the city where everything is possible if you are patient. Don't forget it."

She sounded like a wise old sage giving counsel to a pilgrim preparing to embark on a difficult and harrowing journey.

"I won't," Violet said, and she knew she would not.

The streetcar lurched forward toward the foothills and the Hollywoodland sign as the first two stars of the night sky pierced the lavender horizon.

TWO

D usk had settled over the hills as Audrey and her potential roommate stepped off the bus. A chilling wind had also crept over Hollywood. They started down Franklin Avenue to walk the four blocks to Audrey's bungalow, and pulled their lightweight coats tight around their middles.

Audrey glanced at the woman who walked beside her. Violet Mayfield seemed nice enough. A bit naïve, but in a sweet, comical way. Pretty but not beautiful. Charming but not alluring. Funny without trying to be. And a bit of a risk taker to have come so far from home without knowing a soul. Audrey found that reassuring. And though Violet was a good eight years younger, she had hinted that she was hungry for success in life, just like Audrey was. Yet unlike Audrey, she had no desire to be an actress, and this, too, was comforting. Most of the single women in Hollywood looking for a room to rent wanted exactly what Audrey wanted. A fellow aspiring actress would surely make for a terrible roommate.

Her previous renter, a former script girl at Selznick named Dinah, had gotten married in July to a dentist she'd met at the Cocoanut Grove. Audrey had been with Dinah the night her roommate met the man she would marry. Audrey and Dinah had gone to the fashionable nightclub—in satin and sequins—because Audrey knew that a certain assistant producer from Warner was a regular there on Friday nights. Audrey had met the dentist first and then had introduced him to Dinah so that she could subtly work the room without him on her arm. But the producer hadn't made a showing that night. Afterward, and as the months wore on, Dinah had been almost apologetic that she'd won the well-to-do dentist when Audrey had "had him first."

Dinah had never quite understood that Audrey wasn't looking for a husband. She was looking for the man who would discover her the way Stiles had.

Audrey hadn't been in a great rush to replace Dinah. The rent checks had been nice, but since Audrey owned the bungalow free and clear—the nicest thing Aunt Jo had ever done for her, among a string of nice things, was will her the little house—the extra money wasn't essential. But it was a bit lonely out on the edge of the city. All the clubs, theaters, and restaurants were a good ten blocks away. Aunt Jo's cat, Valentino, was only so much company. And while Audrey invited friends over often enough, it was too quiet and subdued when everyone left, and there was no one to talk to in the morning or sit next to on the bus and streetcar.

She liked having companionship in the house.

Her closest friend, Bert, whom she had known since her earliest days at MGM and who had also come over to Selznick International when she did, would have been the perfect roommate choice if only he wasn't a man. Not only was he polite and decent, but he would've also been able to tackle all the spiders, trim the bushes in the yard, fix the perpetually leaky faucet in the bathroom, and scare away would-be Peeping Toms. And since he worked in wardrobe at Selznick, he could have ridden the bus and streetcar with her. Bert was the most genuinely thoughtful person she knew in Hollywood, probably because, like her, he wasn't from there. He'd been born and raised in Santa Barbara. But a male roommate was out of the question.

If only appearances didn't matter.

She laughed out loud at the thought of steady Bert Redmond, the bighearted little brother she never had, explaining to his widowed mother that he'd moved to a new house and had a new roommate and her name was Audrey.

At the sound of her giggle, Violet looked over

at her, surely wondering what she had missed.

"Sorry," Audrey said. "Just thought of something funny. It's nothing."

They walked in silence for a few steps.

"It's nice out here," Violet said, taking in the lay of the quaint shops, the older couples walking their dogs, the grocers bringing in their sidewalk displays for the night, the teenagers on bicycles heading home for dinner. "Even if it is a bit out of the way."

"You can almost forget that just a mile behind us are streets that never sleep," Audrey said, nodding toward the lights of Sunset and Hollywood boulevards off in the distance.

They turned up a side street with stucco houses on either side. A mother stood on the doorstep of one of the homes with a toddler on her hip and a dish towel over her shoulder, calling out into the twilight for an older child to come in.

Violet's gaze seemed to linger on the mother, and then on the place where the woman had stood after she'd stepped back inside her house.

"So, did your aunt work in the movie business, too?" Violet asked when the house and the mother with her children were behind them.

"Not hardly," Audrey answered. "She married a man from Los Angeles who was a professional gambler, for lack of a better word. She met him at a casino before I was even born. I think her job was keeping him out of trouble."

"Oh."

"Apparently Uncle Freddy habitually made a lot of money and habitually lost it. I never met him. He got himself killed when I was still little. Luckily for Aunt Jo, it was after he had just made a lot of money. She bought the bungalow with what he had hidden in their apartment and lived off the rest so she didn't have to worry about taking a job at the library that barely paid her anything. My father wasn't too impressed with whom his older sister had married. He's always resented the fact that when he expected me to come back home to him, I didn't. I stayed with Aunt Jo."

"So why did he send you to live with her, then?"

"Let's just say it was convenient for him."

Violet opened her mouth to say something else, but they had arrived at the bungalow and Audrey filled the momentary silence. They could have that conversation later, if they had it at all.

"Well, here's the house," she said.

The bungalow, like many of the other houses on the street, was Spanish themed, one of the three architecture styles allowed in the bedroom community of Hollywoodland, with white stucco walls, a red tile roof, arched doorways, and terra-cotta pots of geraniums happily blooming on the porch, even though it was December. She slipped her key into the lock and they stepped inside.

Audrey hadn't replaced any of the furniture

since Aunt Jo's death six years earlier. There had been no need. Jo had bought only quality pieces with the money she had found hidden in the floorboards of the apartment. There was a long sofa, coffee table, two armchairs, a Victrola, and a dining room set Audrey never used. The yellow-and-white-tile, eat-in kitchen had a door that opened onto a shaded patio and a laundry closet in the corner with an electric clothes washer. Two bedrooms, a bathroom, and the ten-year-old tabby cat completed the interior.

"This would be where you would sleep," Audrey said as she showed Violet the room that had been hers before Aunt Jo died. There was a bed, a dresser, and vanity inside. Lacy blue curtains hung at the windows. A hooked oval rug lay in the middle of the floor. A painting of the ocean decorated the longest wall. "It's fully furnished, as you can see, so it's a good thing you've only got a suitcase."

"It's perfect," Violet said, almost breathlessly.

"Not as big as your Southern plantation back home, though, right?"

Violet laughed. "I didn't live on a plantation. We lived in the city."

"In a big house?"

Violet hesitated before nodding. "It was. But . . . but I don't live there anymore."

Audrey sensed for a second time Violet's desire for something that for the moment was out of reach. This young woman from Alabama by way of Shreveport wanted something that life back home couldn't give her. She had come to the land of dreams to find it. "Do you have any bad habits I should know about?" Audrey said.

"Why? Do you?" Violet asked, and a tiny current of dread rippled across her face.

Audrey smiled. Violet didn't appear to be like any of the other Hollywood women she knew. Audrey liked her. "I tend to leave my shoes and clothes lying around. You?"

Violet smiled back at her. "I tend to put things away."

"Do you want to think on it?"

"I don't need to think about it. I would like very much to rent from you if you'll have me."

"Well, then. Shall we go get your suitcase?"

"Right now?"

"Why not right now? Do you want to go back to your hotel to sleep tonight?"

Violet shook her head.

Audrey moved away from the bedroom door. "C'mon. We'll catch a cab on Franklin and take the bus back."

A moment later, the two women were heading west toward the glittering lights of the city.

Audrey awakened the next morning to the aromas of coffee, cinnamon, and toasted bread. For a moment she could almost believe she was a little girl again and it was Christmas morning and her mother had made sticky buns.

She closed her eyes to hold the image captive for just a few seconds longer, but Valentino had noticed she'd stirred. He now rose from where he had been sleeping curled up at her elbow and nuzzled his feline face into hers—his way of communicating that he wanted his breakfast.

Audrey pushed the cat away gently and sat up. Dinah hadn't been a coffee drinker. Audrey couldn't remember the last time she had awakened to the fragrance of a freshly brewed pot. She reached for a silky robe on the armchair next to her bed and slipped it on. Valentino jumped down and meowed at the door. Audrey opened it, yawning as she tied the sash around her waist. After a quick stop in the bathroom, she walked into the kitchen, where her new room-mate was sitting at the kitchen table in her night-gown with a cup of coffee, two slices of cinnamon toast, and Audrey's latest copy of *Variety* magazine open to the middle. The dirty dishes that had been piling up in the sink over the past few days had been washed and the countertops wiped clean of smudges, dried spills, and crumbs.

"I hope you don't mind that I made coffee for us. I found some Hills Bros. in the cupboard," Violet said, her thick Southern drawl elongating every syllable.

"Mind?" Audrey grabbed a coffee cup from the

dish drainer and poured a cup. "Smelling it was like waking up in paradise."

Audrey pulled out a chair and sat down across from Violet. Valentino began to wind himself in and out her legs, meowing a reminder that he had not yet been fed. "I can't remember the last time I had cinnamon toast."

Violet pushed the plate toward her. "Have one. It's your cinnamon. Your bread. I promise I'll get my own groceries today."

"Don't worry about it." Audrey lifted one of the pieces of toast off the plate, brought it to her mouth, and took a bite. Violet had been liberal with both the butter and the cinnamon sugar. It was divine.

"I am in awe of how great this is. I usually skip breakfast. You might have noticed there's hardly much to make a meal with here."

"I like to cook," Violet said. "I can make us breakfast in the mornings. I don't mind."

Audrey took another bite. "You know how to make biscuits and gravy?" she asked as she chewed. "I've always wanted to try that."

Her roommate smiled wide. "Of course. Mama taught me how to make everything."

Audrey broke off a piece of the crust and tossed it down to Valentino. "Word gets out among the single men at the studio that you can cook, and I'll be looking for another roommate."

Violet laughed lightly.

Audrey looked up from the cat. "You think I'm kidding?"

Her new roommate shrugged. "I think men want more in a wife than just someone who can cook."

Audrey arched an eyebrow playfully. "And it's a good thing they do! Can you imagine how terrible it would be if all a man wanted was someone to be his maid?"

Violet shrugged. "I don't know."

"You don't know?" Audrey half laughed.

Her roommate chewed on her bottom lip for a second. "I don't think too much about stuff like that."

"Stuff like what?" Audrey laughed fully now.

"You know. Stuff about . . . men."

A new thought stole across Audrey and she gasped slightly. "Violet! Do you . . . do you prefer other women?"

Violet's face went crimson and a half bite of toast catapulted out of her mouth as she nearly choked on it. "What? No! No, I don't. I'm not . . . No!"

"All right! Okay!" Audrey said in a reassuring tone. "I just thought for a second that maybe, you know. . . . Most women *do* think about stuff like that, Violet. You can't fault me for wondering."

Violet brought a hand up to her right cheek, as though to cool her discomfort with her palm. She exhaled heavily, forcing any remnant of toast from her windpipe. Her breath was feathery with alarm and embarrassment. "All I meant was I don't like to think about that *right now,*" she said.

There was a trailing hint of sadness in Violet's words. Audrey felt a tug of kinship toward her. Violet had been hurt. Recently, perhaps. It was why she had come to Hollywood for a fresh start. Audrey understood that unspoken thought perfectly.

"What happened to you?" Audrey asked softly. Respectfully.

Violet studied the empty plate in front of her for a moment. "I'd really rather not talk about it." She rose from her chair. "I'll make some more toast."

Audrey knew as well as anyone that some wounds simply could not be spoken of easily. She would not press the matter. Not yet, anyway.

She stood as well and reached down to the floor for the cat's dish.

THREE

The last of the day's warmth had disappeared when Violet and Audrey arrived at the far end of the studio's property, a dirt-covered expanse known as the Forty Acres, even though it measured closer to twenty-three acres. Studio employees called it simply the Forty. Violet could see her breath in white puffs, and her hands were already numb despite having been plunged into her pockets from the moment she'd stepped off the streetcar. She hadn't thought it got this cold in Southern California, and she wished she had stayed in the warm bungalow instead of dashing out on a second's notice. She had planned to use that Saturday evening to wash and set her hair, but Audrey had arrived home breathless after being away all day and told her to put on something warm. They were going out.

"Out to do what?" Violet had asked.

And Audrey had turned to her, eyes gleaming. "Do you want to go to a fire?"

"Like a bonfire?"

Audrey had laughed. "Like no other fire you've ever seen. Come on. Get your coat."

On the way to the studio, half by cab, half by streetcar, Audrey had told Violet that her friend Bert knew someone who worked on the technical crew who could get the three of them onto the Forty for the filming spectacle of the decade.

"The what?" Violet had asked.

Audrey had leaned forward to whisper, lest any of the other streetcar passengers hear her. "They're going to film the burning of Atlanta tonight."

Many minutes later they found themselves joining a crowd of maybe two hundred people whose collective attention was riveted by a towering row of old sets at the edge of the back lot. A man of medium build, with a kind, clean-shaven face and dark curly hair under his cap, waved them over to where he stood just on the other side of a cordon.

"There's Bert." Audrey nodded toward the man.

They closed the distance to him. Bert looked to Violet to be about her age, maybe a little older, with pleasant features. Audrey had told her on the way over that Bert was her oldest friend in Hollywood. She had met him when they were both working at MGM. Bert Redmond had moved over to Selznick International not long after Audrey had. He was a wardrobe assistant, though he dreamed of one day being on the camera crew. He had grown up in Santa Barbara and he liked the outdoors—particularly hiking, fishing, and bird-watching.

Bert also apparently liked Audrey; at least that was how it appeared to Violet. His eyes had lit up as they neared him. Even in the shadowed light of dusk, Violet could see that Bert fancied Audrey. But, then, who wouldn't? Audrey was beautiful and enchanting.

"Bert, this is Violet Mayfield, my new room-mate," Audrey said as soon as they were at his side. "Violet, this is Bert Redmond. The nicest guy you'll ever meet."

Bert seemed embarrassed by Audrey's compliment. "Pleased to meet you, Miss Mayfield," he said.

"Please, call me Violet."

His mouth broke into a smile when she spoke, and Violet found herself feeling warmer, even though it had to be close to thirty degrees. Her accent had amused him.

"Audrey tells me you're a long way from home," Bert said.

Audrey put an arm around Violet. "Home is just where you hang your hat, Bert."

"Well. Welcome to California, Violet." Bert tipped the brim of his cap.

"See what I mean? Nicest guy you'll ever meet." Audrey dropped her arm from across Violet's shoulders. "So, do we have to stand right here or can we get closer?"

"Jim said if we stay put he will be able to vouch for us if anyone asks why we're here." Bert pointed to a group of men huddled around one of the seven Technicolor cameras set up beyond the cordon. "He's right over there." One of the men turned toward them and waved. Audrey waved back.

"Are all these people here to watch the fire?" Violet asked, looking around at the groups of people, all waiting with their hands in their pockets.

"Of course," Audrey answered. "It's going to be the talk of the town tomorrow. I can't believe a million secret memos didn't go out yesterday about it. You know how Mr. Selznick is about his memos."

The day before, Violet had been stuck taking dictation for one of the accountants in another building. She had learned in just a few weeks at Selznick International that everyone in management had something to say, and everyone needed someone from the secretary pool to say it. Selznick himself, whom Violet hadn't yet met face-to-face, apparently dictated memos morning, noon, and night.

"I wasn't in the pool yesterday," Violet answered.

"I wonder what they're waiting for," Bert said, looking toward the imposing facades from *The Gardens of Allah*, *King Kong*, and other completed Selznick and RKO films. The old sets, which had been taking up space needed to build the *Gone With the Wind* exteriors of Tara and Twelve Oaks, had been hastily repainted to look like an antebellum downtown. "It was supposed to start already. I was afraid you gals were going to miss it."

"We had to find someone to hitch a ride with from the Mansion. There's no chance we could have walked all the way out here in high heels," Audrey said.

Minutes later, a man got onto a portable public address system and its speakers squawked in protest. A few introductory remarks were made and then the crowd was told that absolute quiet was required once the fire started burning and the cameras started rolling. No one was to make a sound.

Bert leaned toward Audrey and Violet. "They've only got one chance to do this," he said quietly. "There's no way they can stage another shot like this one."

Fire engines that had been idling off to the side now moved into place, and men with hoses positioned themselves at the ready should the blaze get out of hand. Smoke machines were primed and the sweet, pungent odor of a flame accelerant tinged Violet's nose.

One of the three stunt doubles for Clark Gable stood well past earshot, but he was listening intently to instructions being given him by another man, who pointed to the facades, then to a waiting wagon, and then to the bank of cameras. A horse hitched to a wagon whinnied and the man holding its reins reached up to pat the animal's flank.

"I never would have guessed moviemakers would start a film with a scene from the story's middle," Violet said as a tractor was driven into position. "The burning of Atlanta doesn't happen until nearly halfway through the book."

"It will be like this the whole time they shoot," Audrey replied, never taking her eyes off the elements of the spectacle that was about to transpire. "Selznick could very well film Scarlett and Ashley kissing in the paddock tomorrow— if they had a Scarlett."

"And to start shooting before you have the entire cast in place? That just seems backward. How will Scarlett even be in this scene?"

Bert turned to Violet. "Scarlett's double in the wagon won't be filmed in close-up. The camera will never show that woman's face. Then when there *is* a Scarlett, production can take scenes shot elsewhere and layer them on top of what's already in the can."

"In the can?"

Audrey smiled and took a step forward. "Finished. Done. Let's get closer."

She advanced toward more of the hubbub in front of them. Bert hung back a moment before he joined her. Somewhat reluctantly, Violet followed.

After moving up twenty yards or so, Audrey eased her way into a larger group of spectators. No one seemed to notice. Everyone's gaze was trained on the facades.

Someone shouted, "Action," and for a second there was no sound or movement. And then the jets supplying the gas flared to life. As if bewitched, the storefronts and warehouses burst into flame. The stunt doubles in the wagon began to make several passes in front of the massive wall of fire. The indigo sky was suddenly swathed in orange and rose and yellow. Thick smoke started to rise and wander, and the heat and roar of the flames reached those who watched. Violet was astounded by the hellish tableau in front of her.

41

She would learn later that the local fire department had been flooded with calls from people who were sure all of Culver City was on fire.

The cameras kept rolling as the fire reached its zenith, and then the tractor at the edge of the burning sets began to move slowly forward, dragging chains behind it, which elongated and then grew taut. The engulfed facades began to tumble to the ground like a defeated dragon as the tractor slowly yanked them down. A few minutes later a director yelled, "Cut!"

Clusters of people began to cheer and applaud. The burning of Atlanta seemed to have been a success. The gas jets were switched off and the smoldering sets were allowed to be further consumed before the water trucks were at last released.

"I wish I could have brought my camera to this," Bert said, in awe. "I've never seen anything like that before in my life."

"Me, either," Violet replied.

She and Bert both looked to Audrey, but she seemed not to have heard them. Her gaze was fixed tightly on a small group of people closer to the platform on which David Selznick had been standing.

"Do you know those people or something?" Bert asked Audrey, and Violet could tell he was concerned that she was about to abandon him and Violet to go speak with them.

"That man over there is Laurence Olivier." Audrey nodded toward a man off in the distance. "I have no idea why he's here."

Violet craned her neck to catch a glimpse of the British stage star but the man stood too far away to be seen clearly.

"And that's David Selznick's brother, Myron," Audrey continued, pointing to a gentleman in a hat and overcoat not as far away as Mr. Olivier, but still not close enough for Violet to make out any facial features. "But I can't see who that is with him."

The woman next to Myron Selznick was also wearing a hat, and the light from the fires was mostly gone now. It was far too dark and she stood many yards away.

After a few seconds of silence Violet suggested they go back to the place where Jim had told them to wait. Bert seemed immediately amenable but Audrey hesitated and so did he.

"Audrey?" Bert said.

But Audrey seemed lost in thought as she stared at the woman in the hat.

"I'm going back to where we were," Violet announced. She didn't like not being where they'd been told to wait.

Bert, obviously torn between wanting to stay with Audrey and wanting her to come with them, paused midstep before following Violet.

Several minutes passed before Audrey made

her way back to Violet and Bert. She seemed to have recovered from the disappointment of not knowing who the woman in the hat was.

When tall, redheaded Jim joined them at the cordon, he suggested they go out for drinks and dancing and fun. Audrey turned to Violet and said, "Shall we?" but she didn't wait for Violet to respond before facing Jim again. "We're not exactly dressed for the Trocadero, you know."

Jim grimaced. "Good thing you're not. I'd much rather we go to a place where you don't need to worry if your butler polished the underside of your shoe." He laughed at his joke and poked Bert, who also laughed but with less vigor.

Audrey seemed to thoughtfully consider her response for a moment. "You have a better place in mind?" Her tone was coy and challenging.

"You bet I do."

Jim led them to his car, a rusting ten-year-old Packard, and opened the front door for Audrey, leaving Bert to open the back door of the aging sedan for Violet and to share the backseat with her.

Jim talked the whole way down to the coast, giving the three of them a running commentary on how successful the evening's shoot had been. Twenty minutes later they were stepping inside a seaside nightclub in nearby Venice, where couples danced in bare feet on a wooden floor dusted here and there with sand that had been tracked in off the beach. The four-piece band consisted of a man on an upright piano, a second on a bass fiddle, a third on a clarinet, and the last seated at a set of snare drums he played with brushes instead of sticks.

They chose a table near the sandy dance floor, and Audrey quickly ordered a round of Orange Blossoms, and then another. The vermouth-and–orange juice concoction was both refreshing and bracing on Violet's tongue.

Jim, obviously attracted to Audrey, turned out to be adept on his feet, and he and Audrey spent dance after dance on the floor while Bert and Violet watched.

After five or six numbers, Violet finally asked Bert if he'd care to dance.

"Sure." He smiled uncomfortably, as though he knew a true gentleman should have asked her first.

Bert's hand was firm on her back and his palm, sandwiched with hers, was cool and strong. Violet hadn't danced with a man since a friend's wedding more than a year ago. She had been in Franklin's arms that night and had been blissfully unaware of the dark enemy inside her body, nibbling away at her insides. She hadn't yet felt the searing malice of the tumor; that would come a few weeks later when she collapsed into a puddle of her own blood and woke up hours later, emptied of purpose. Violet could smell Bert's aftershave, woodsy and enticing, as they moved. The effect of the cocktails tempted her to rest her head on his shoulder and remember what it had been like to feel Franklin's kisses on her neck.

A few feet away, Jim said something to Audrey. She tipped her head back and laughed like a starlet on a rich man's yacht.

Bert watched them as they spun away.

"So, Audrey tells me you like to go bird-watching," Violet said, eager to sweep away the memory of Franklin's kisses and to get Bert to take his eyes off Audrey so that she might have a chance of having a good time.

He turned to her. "She told you that?"

"Is it a secret?"

"No," Bert said quickly. "I guess I'm surprised she found that interesting enough to mention."

"Have you always liked birds?"

Violet could sense Bert relaxing more as his attention was being diverted to something he enjoyed. "It was my father's hobby before it was mine. He took it up after he got home from the war. When I was a kid, he and I would go out to the mountains and deserts with binoculars to look for certain birds, and we kept a little notebook of all the ones we found. It was like hunting, but without having to kill anything."

"Sounds nice. Do you still go with him some-times?"

"Not with him. He died when I was eighteen. I go on my own now, when I go."

"Oh. I'm so sorry."

"He had some lingering health issues from the war. They finally caught up with him."

They danced in silence for a few seconds, and Violet wrestled mentally to come up with something else to talk about. Something that didn't make her dance partner sad. She didn't want to stop dancing. It felt so wonderful to be in his arms.

"So, I guess there aren't many birds to go looking for in Hollywood," she ventured.

"Actually there are all kinds of birds close by. Just up the road where you live with Audrey are the foothills and there are lots of different kinds of finches and black phoebes, mockingbirds, jays, and starlings that live there. But you're right. On the city streets, there are mostly just sparrows, crows, and pigeons. Although one time I heard a nightingale. On Sunset Boulevard, of all places."

He paused in expectation. She apparently waited too long to respond with, "Oh?"

"Nightingales aren't indigenous to the United States. They're European." He seemed both wildly pleased and slightly disappointed that he had to tell her this.

"So somebody had one in a cage? You heard it through an open window?"

"I heard it in the fronds of a palm tree."

"But how could that have been possible if nightingales don't live in America?"

"Precisely," he said. "I've gone back to the same place a few times but I haven't heard it again. I've been tempted to ask Audrey to come with me for good luck. She was with me the first time I heard it."

"And she heard it, too?"

Bert frowned slightly. "No."

The song was coming to a close. The dance was ending.

"I'll go with you sometime. If you want company," Violet offered, casually shrugging her left shoulder. She liked the thought of strolling down glittering Sunset Boulevard with Bert.

He blinked at her as the last notes of the music drifted away and the dancers stopped.

"Oh," he finally said as he drew his arm away from her back. "Sure."

They walked back to the table and Violet realized Bert didn't want just any company while listening for some unexplainable nightingale. He wanted Audrey's.

Hours later, as Violet was brushing her teeth before bed, Audrey appeared at the open bathroom door.

"I've finally figured out who that woman was at the fire tonight."

Violet stopped brushing. She'd had too much

alcohol and was too tired to comprehend what Audrey was talking about. "What?"

"With Myron Selznick. The woman in the hat. She was talking with Mr. Selznick after the fire. I figured out who she is."

"You did?"

"It was Vivien Leigh! She was there with Laurence Olivier, although I'm sure she was pretending she wasn't."

Violet blinked at her. "Why?"

"Because she's having an affair with him, even though she's already married and has a family back in England. That's why *he* was there tonight."

"How do you know all this?"

"When you pay attention to the details in this town you can learn a lot, Violet. What do you bet she's here to test for Scarlett?"

Violet frowned. "But she's English."

Audrey stepped into the bathroom and reached for her own toothbrush. "So are Leslie Howard and Olivia de Havilland. I'll bet you five dollars I'm right."

Violet turned on the tap and washed the remnants of tooth powder off the bristles of her toothbrush. "I don't have five dollars to lose to you."

Audrey sprinkled the powder onto her own brush. "You wait and see, then. I'll bet we haven't seen the last of her. English or not."

Violet put her toothbrush in the drinking cup

they used as a holder and moved away so that Audrey could have the sink.

"Did you have a good time tonight?" Audrey asked, and then stuck the toothbrush in her mouth.

"I did."

Audrey stopped brushing for a second. "I'm glad you were there so Bert had someone to dance with. Jim was a rather insistent partner. He wouldn't take no for an answer. Good dancer, though."

"I am glad I was there, too. Bert's very nice."

"He's a gem. Did you tell him all about Alabama?"

"We actually didn't talk about me all that much," Violet said, wanting to add that Bert had been a little preoccupied. "We did talk about his bird-watching."

"I bet that made him happy."

"He told me about the nightingale he heard."

Audrey looked at Violet's reflection in the mirror over the sink. White foam rimmed the corners of her lips. "He did? He is nuts about finding that bird again. Like a little kid."

"He said you were with him that night. But you didn't hear it?"

Audrey spit into the sink. "No. But, then, I don't have an ear trained to hear birdsong like he does. And we were walking down Sunset Boulevard on a Saturday night. It wasn't exactly quiet."

"I think he likes you, Audrey," Violet said, the words tumbling out of her mouth before she could even decide if she wanted to say them.

Audrey cupped her hands into the water running at the tap. "I know he does," she said a second later, not looking up. She bent down and sipped water from her hands and then turned off the tap. "But I'm five years older than he is. And the last thing I need right now in my life is a romance. I need to focus on my career." The words fell weightless from Audrey's lips, as though they weren't her words at all, but lines from a script. She wiped her chin on a towel and dropped her toothbrush into the cup holder next to Violet's.

Audrey turned toward Violet and the open bathroom doorway. "Bert is too nice a guy for someone like me," she said, her voice now her own. She wished Violet good night and walked past her and into her bedroom, closing the door softly behind her.

FOUR

Christmas Eve 1938

The afternoon train from Los Angeles began to slow as it neared the Visalia city limits. Audrey cast a glance at Violet sitting across from her with her gaze glued to the passing cotton fields outside the window. It had taken no convincing to get her roommate to join her on the overnight trip to the farm. This would be Violet's first

Christmas away from her family, and she'd been blue the past few days because of it. A package had arrived from Alabama a few days earlier and its contents—pearl earrings, a leather hand-bag, sugared pecans, and a snow globe—had led to tears of home-sickness and a burned roast, both of which Violet had apologized plentifully for.

Audrey leaned back against the seat and allowed herself to remember her own first Christmas away from home. She and Aunt Jo had taken the train down to San Diego and they had stayed at a beach house and eaten lobster for dinner. A potted jasmine that Jo had dragged in from the porch served as their Christmas tree. Her aunt had given Audrey pink satin bedroom slippers, perfume, and rhinestone earrings that looked like diamonds so that Audrey would still feel like she was pretty. There had been a crèche set up on the tiny lawn of the beach cottage next to theirs. The baby Jesus had looked so perfect, and the Virgin so at peace as she smiled down on her child, while Joseph stood just inches away. . . .

But that had been a long time ago.

She had been home only a handful of holidays since moving to Hollywood. Three years had passed since she'd been there for Christmas; two since she had been home at all. Her stepmother, Cora, had asked that she make an effort to come this year. Her father had been asking about her, wondering how she was.

"He misses you, Audrey," Cora had said when she'd called Audrey a few days after the filming of the burning of Atlanta. "I know he has an odd way of showing it, but he does."

He doesn't show it at all had been the words Audrey had wanted to say.

"Does he know you're inviting me?" she had asked instead.

"Of course he does. He wants you to come. So do I. We all do."

Audrey had started to say she would think about it, even though she knew she would decline, but then she had remembered Violet wasn't going home to Alabama for the holidays. If Audrey brought a friend, all the conversations would be on the level of polite pretense, a much nicer way to spend the Christmas hours, even if it was genteel artifice. If Violet came, there would be no awkward silences that reminded Audrey of what she was and what she had done. Audrey had answered that she could come, but she wanted to bring her roommate.

"I can't come without her," Audrey had continued, when Cora said nothing. "She doesn't have any family in California. It would be unkind to leave her here by herself."

Cora had finally said that would be fine and they'd be happy to have them both.

The train now pulled into the platform at the station, the rails whining a high-pitched welcome.

"I just can't get over how flat this part of California is." Violet turned at last from the window. "It's like Kansas. There are cotton fields! I know you told me you were raised on a farm, but I just couldn't picture it. All I know of California is Hollywood. This part is very different."

"Yes, this part is very different."

They stood to reach for their overnight bags on the shelf above their seats.

"By the way," Audrey said, "my last name used to be Kluge. I changed it to Duvall a long time ago. Mr. Stiles didn't think Kluge sounded melodic enough for a screen name. So, whatever you do, don't call my dad Mr. Duvall."

Violet looked at her a bit wide-eyed and nodded. "All right."

They stepped off the train and onto a platform crowded with other holiday travelers. The station's railings were festooned with evergreen garlands that were turning brown from having swayed for too many days in the ample San Joaquin Valley sun. Audrey spied Cora in a clutch of people at the far end of the platform. She waved.

"There's my stepmother." Audrey nodded toward Cora and they made their way toward her.

Cora, only twelve years older than Audrey, greeted her with a cordial hug, not deeply expressive. Audrey returned the embrace with the same courteous restraint. They were like coworkers, next-door neighbors, or seatmates who rode the same bus every morning. They didn't like or dislike each other. They respected each other's choices. This was the balance the two of them had wordlessly struck at Aunt Jo's funeral minutes after Audrey's father had asked that she at least give Cora a chance.

"So, we're giving each other chances now?" Audrey had replied on that long-ago day. She and her father had been standing at the Los Angeles cemetery where Jo was to be buried next to Uncle Freddy. Audrey had just laid a handful of jonquils on top of the casket. Jo's favorite flower. Cora and the rest of the funeral party were waiting for them at the cars.

"What is that supposed to mean?" her father had replied.

Audrey had been too tired to elaborate on what seemed so obvious to her. Grief was exhausting. "I barely know Cora."

"That's what I'm talking about. I'm afraid she thinks you don't like her. She came all this way. It would have been easier for her if she and the boys stayed at the farm. She's making an effort, Audrey. I don't think it would hurt you to do the same."

"You don't have any idea what hurts me," Audrey had murmured, loud enough for him to hear, had he been standing a little closer.

"What was that?"

She looked up from the casket to face him. "I

said, I'll be sure to let her know how much her coming meant to me."

He'd studied her then, as if needing to familiarize himself with her features, even though she knew he likely saw her face on troubled nights when sleep eluded him. She looked just like her mother. When he spoke, a mix of resentment and disbelief strung his words together.

"For the love of God, Audrey. It's been nearly a decade. Are you honestly still angry with me? I did what was best for you."

Fresh tears had pooled in her eyes and she had willed them back to the deep well from which they had sprung. "Are you honestly still angry with *me?*"

Even from a few feet away she had felt him stiffen. "You really want to talk about where you'd be right now if I hadn't sent you here?"

"Yes," she had whispered. "I do."

She had waited for him to respond even though she knew his question had been posed to end a conversation, not begin one. He had looked away, off to the north, where his home and life waited for him. He said nothing else.

Audrey had touched him on the shoulder, the closest she could come to embracing him. "I'm glad you came. Aunt Jo was wonderful to me." She then started toward the cars. Cora was leaning against the long Cadillac that Audrey's father had driven down from Visalia, fanning herself with a

California road map. Audrey's half brothers, six-year-old twins Sam and Gordon, were slapping each other in the backseat and laughing.

"Thank you so much for coming, Cora," Audrey had said when she reached the Cadillac.

"It was our pleasure to be here for you, of course," her stepmother had said, matching Audrey's gracious tone.

"I mean it. I'm glad you came."

She had said good-bye to the boys and then had turned for the car, driven by one of Aunt Jo's longtime friends, that was waiting for her. She hadn't looked back to see whether her father was watching her go.

Now inside that same Cadillac as Cora drove away from the train station, the talk was general, easy, and nonspecific. Leon, Audrey's father, was doing well. The farm had had a good year. The twins were happy and healthy. In due time, they pulled off the highway onto a two-lane road, and then onto a single lane marked KLUGE FARMS—PRIVATE DRIVEWAY. Plum trees as far as the eye could see lined the road, tall and confident even though the picking season was over and no fruit clung to their branches. They passed several acres of trees before the house and farm buildings came into view, and an old ache rose within Audrey at the sight of them. From the outside the house looked the same as when her mother was alive. Three dogs of various pedigree roused themselves from the shade of a massive sycamore and scampered, tails wagging, toward the car as it pulled forward. Audrey recognized two of them from previous trips home.

"You've got a new dog," she said to Cora.

"Oh. You mean the black one? That's Orion. We've actually had him for a while."

Audrey said nothing else as Cora pulled into the empty carport.

The women got out of the vehicle and Cora opened the trunk. The dogs regarded Audrey and Violet with joyful curiosity. Audrey looked past the animals to the house, watching the side door and then the front door.

"Your father and the boys are finishing up at Merle's," Cora said, as if answering a question that Audrey had spoken aloud.

"Working on Christmas Eve?" Audrey murmured as she reached into the trunk for her bag.

"You know your father," Cora replied, and then she looked away quickly, as though she wished she had thought of something different to say just then.

Violet lifted her bag out of the back as well, and Audrey shut the trunk with a gentle thwack. "Merle is my uncle," Audrey said to Violet. "He farms, too."

"You gals don't mind sharing your old room, do you?" Cora asked as she turned toward the house. "The twins each have their own room now, so I've lost a guest room."

"Is that what you still call it? My old room?"

Cora offered a half smile that was difficult to read. Audrey wondered if it meant *No offense, but we actually don't call it anything.*

"We'll be fine anywhere," Audrey said.

Inside, Cora led them past the big kitchen that had been Audrey's mother's favorite room in the house, past the dining area, through the living room that now sported a magnificent Christmas tree, and then down a central hallway that led to all the bedrooms. They passed several closed doors before Cora stopped at one and pushed it open. Inside the room a new four-poster bed with matching nightstands dominated the space. Where Audrey's childhood dresser had been were two padded armchairs with a table between them. Slate blue accented with white made up every thread of fabric in the room, from the bedspread to the rug and the draperies.

"I like what you've done with this room," Audrey said as she surveyed the decor.

"Oh?" The single word was clothed in doubt.

Audrey turned to her stepmother. "I really do."

The two women stared at each other for a moment before Cora seemed to accept Audrey's words as truth. She thanked Audrey for the compliment.

"What can Violet and I do to help you with

dinner?" Audrey set her bags on the bed. Violet followed suit.

"I've only to put the ham in the oven. Everything else is done," Cora said. "Why don't you and Violet take a walk in the orchards? It's a beautiful afternoon. Be a shame to waste it sitting indoors. I told your father to be home by five. You've plenty of time for a nice stroll before then."

Audrey and Violet made their way back outside. The dogs, eager to be anywhere with anyone, pranced ahead of them as the two women walked across the gravel to the closest row of trees.

"Sorry about the awkwardness. Inside, I mean," Audrey said. "Most of the time Cora and I get along all right."

"You two aren't close?"

"She and my dad had just met when I moved to Hollywood and I don't get back here very often. I really don't know her well."

"Oh," Violet said, obviously unsure what to say next.

"I'm actually okay with that, Vi. And she is, too. She's taken over my mother's house and we both know she has. Cordial distance is how we deal with that. Don't worry about it."

They entered the orchard.

Violet scoped the endless rows as they walked. "I've never seen so many plum trees all in one place."

"When they're in bloom, it's as though you've been transported to Eden. I used to put the blossoms in my hair." Audrey breathed in deep. "I loved playing in these rows. I could pretend to be anything I wanted to out here."

They walked in silence for a few moments. It was so nice having Violet there, but the hours between now and when they were to get back on the train already seemed long and complicated.

"Are you wishing you didn't come?" Violet asked, as if she had read Audrey's thoughts.

Audrey's laugh was slight. "Maybe. It wasn't always like this for me. Before my mother died, I was happy here. But when she got sick . . . I don't know. My father became one of those people who stop learning how to handle great disappointments. Life is full of them, as I am sure you know."

"Yes. I know," Violet said.

"My mother's death wasn't the only big disappointment to come his way. There were other ones. And when they came, he just stopped trying to find a way to live with them."

"He remarried, though."

"Yes."

"But you don't like Cora?"

Another few moments of silence followed as they walked. "I don't dislike her," Audrey finally continued. "It's just . . . women have a way of making a house their own. Everything that was my mother's or that reminded me of her was taken down and given away or put away when Dad married Cora. I can't even feel my mother here anymore."

Audrey and Violet emerged from the orchard and into a clearing. A long, skinny building with repeating doors and windows met their gaze. One of the dogs trotted to a door, sniffed its edges, and then scampered away.

"What is that?" Violet asked.

Audrey stared at the building. "A bunkhouse. For the fruit pickers. They come from Mexico and they go from farm to farm during picking season. They sleep there at night. It's empty right now."

"Oh. Like a dormitory. How long do they usually stay?"

Audrey closed her eyes for a moment as a flood of memories began to crowd in around her: The aroma of corn tortillas sizzling on outdoor brick ovens. The rapid and beautiful language of the workers. Checked shirts drying on makeshift clotheslines and their raven black hair and straw hats. Hearing their laughter at night when the workday was done, and the sweet notes of someone playing a guitar and singing . . .

"Audrey?"

She opened her eyes. "They stay until it's time to move on." She turned from the building. Violet took a step forward to peer through a dust-covered window, wondering what the bunkhouse rooms looked like inside.

Audrey was suddenly filled with a strange need to be understood, to have a confidant. Especially there at home. "My father sent me away because I was pregnant," she said.

Violet turned to look at her.

"I had fallen in love with one of the pickers. His name was Rafael. I wanted to run away with him."

Violet blinked. "What happened?"

Audrey shrugged, as if such a languid movement could ease away the weight of old sorrows. "My father found out and had Rafael deported to Mexico. He told Rafael that if he ever returned to the United States or tried to contact me again, he'd have him sent to prison for what he had done to me."

Violet sucked in her breath. "Oh, Audrey!" she murmured.

"I never saw Rafael again. I didn't know how to even look for him. Aunt Jo said it would be best if I let him go, just like I had to let the baby go. I had a little boy, Violet. With black hair. I saw him before they took him away."

Violet's eyelashes were now silver with tears. "I can't even imagine how hard that must have been."

Audrey had never had anyone say such words of consolation to her and a wave of emotion swept across her. Not even Aunt Jo had said what Violet had just spoken.

"It was terrible."

They stood in silence for a moment.

"I was young and stupid, I know. But I thought I was in love."

Another stretch of silent seconds passed.

"And that's why you never went back home, isn't it?" Violet said after a pause. "Because of what your father did?"

Two tears began to slide down Audrey's cheeks. She let them fall as she shook her head. "In the beginning, yes, I was mad at him. But I was too young to marry and be a mother. I was little more than a child myself. And I didn't love Rafael as much as I loved the feeling of being wanted. He never would have slept with me if I hadn't encouraged him to. He was starving for affection just like I was. After a while I understood this. Having Rafael taken from me wasn't the only reason I stayed away."

"Then . . . why did you?"

"My father didn't really want me to come back, Violet. He still doesn't."

Violet shook her head, lost in bewilderment. "But why? Why wouldn't he want you to come home?"

Audrey looked down at the ground, peppered here and there with pickers' footprints from the last harvest. "Aside from the fact that I disappointed him, I think I remind him too much of my mother."

"But if he loved her, how can that be a bad thing?" Violet pressed.

Audrey inhaled heavily, preparing herself to say the words she hardly ever said. "Yes. If he loved her."

"You . . . don't think he did?"

"I think it was complicated, his love for her."

Violet stood speechless beside her for several seconds, and Audrey felt as if she had ruined the Christmas mood. She was about to apologize when Violet filled the silence.

"But even if that's true, what does that have to do with you?"

Audrey turned from the bunkhouse. The relaxing atmosphere of the orchard was morphing into a fog of old wounds. She reentered the plum trees so that they could head back. "Anytime I came here for a visit I would ask myself that.And that's why I stay away. It's easier for us both."

Violet fell in step with her. "You've never asked him?"

"He refuses to talk to me about my mother."

"Make him!"

Audrey grinned at Violet's naïve vehemence. "Well. You can lead a horse to water, you know."

"Make the horse thirsty and then he'll drink!"

The tension in the air around her seemed to dissipate and Audrey laughed despite the subject matter. She laced her arm through Violet's. "And to think I wanted you here with me so that I wouldn't have to think about any of this."

They started to walk back through the bower of overhead branches, and the dogs raced ahead, as if they knew Christmas Eve dinner was not far off. Audrey could tell Violet was contemplating what she had told her and was ruminating on the wrongness of it, but she said nothing else and Audrey was glad for the silence as they walked. The two women emerged from the orchard as a truck was pulling into the carport next to the Cadillac. Her twin stepbrothers hopped out and the dogs ran to meet them. Her father got out on the driver's side.

"That him?" Violet asked.

"Yes."

Leon Kluge had started to reach into the backof the truck, but then he caught a glimpse of Audrey and Violet moving toward him. He stopped for a moment, and pulled out two lengths of pipe as long as his arm from the truck bed. The twins also saw her and Violet. They stood up straight from patting the dogs to watch them approach.

Sam and Gordon both said hello when the two women were close enough to speak. Of the two fraternal twins, Sam looked the most like Cora. Gordon was very much the image of Audrey's father. At twelve the boys already stood a head taller than her. They seemed glad to see her.

She greeted them both and then turned to her

father. He stood near the back of the truck with the two lengths of pipe in a loose grip with one hand.

"Merry Christmas, Dad."

He fumbled with what he carried and then he stepped forward to kiss her on the cheek, holding the tubes at an awkward angle. The metal pipes clanked against each other.

When he stepped back, Audrey introduced Violet to him.

"So good to see you, Audrey," he said then. "How was the ride up?" He hoisted the pipes into a better grasp.

"It was very pleasant," Audrey answered. "Thanks."

"Nice afternoon for a walk in the orchard." He walked forward a few steps to set the pipes against the exterior wall of a small shed next to the carport.

"It was."

He turned back to Violet. "So. You're from Alabama, then? And what brought you all the way out to California?"

The weight of all the words Audrey and her father needed to say to each other and didn't seemed to hang between them like one of the movie sets on the back lot that pretended to be something it wasn't.

Violet began to tell Audrey's father about meeting Mr. Arnow at the audition for the role of Scarlett O'Hara as the five of them walked to the house, the dogs skipping toward the kitchen door.

Hollywood
March 9, 2012

C hristine runs her fingertips across the hat's brim. A thin line of discoloration circles the wired fabric, evidence that the last person to wear it had done so under the exacting heat of a bright light.

"Scarlett number thirteen? Are you thinking what I am thinking?" Stella, standing next to her, gapes at the hat in Christine's hands.

"Sure looks like it."

"How in the world did this family end up with a hat from *Gone With the Wind*? Shouldn't it be in a museum or something?"

Christine turns the hat back over, marveling at her sudden desire to eat macaroons with a glass of milk. "Old movie props get bought up all the time by private collectors."

"But to have something as valuable as this just sitting in a hatbox, where silverfish and moths could have their way with it. Who would do that?"

"I've seen this hat before," Christine says absently.

"Everyone who has seen *Gone With the Wind* has seen it before."

A wave of nostalgia, hazy and undefined, falls

across her and Christine brings the hat close to her face to breathe in its musky scent. "I mean, I have held this hat before."

The memory is stronger now. In her mind's eye Christine sees the hat sitting on a chenille bedspread, along with umbrellas, stacks of books, holiday decorations, and other attic treasures. A TV is on in another room set to KTLA, and she hears the scattered dialogue between Major Nelson and Dr. Bellows. In the hallway, stairs have been lowered from a hole in the ceiling, and a man in a uniform is ascending them. She was afraid of the man because he was there to kill a nest of rats in the attic.

"I was watching a rerun of *I Dream of Jeannie*, and there was a man in the attic laying down rat poison," Christine says.

"What?"

The memory begins to fade but not before she recalls there had been someone with her. The elderly next-door neighbor who had been her babysitter the year she was in first grade.

"Do you want to try it on, Chrissy? You can if you want. Just this once."

And she sees her small hands reaching for it.

⇒●◇●⇐

1939

FIVE

Mid-January 1939

Violet looked up from the pages of shorthand on her desk and massaged the back of her neck while sneaking in a yawn. All around her the others in the secretary pool were busily tapping away at their typewriters, including Audrey in the far corner by the window. The cacophony of hundreds of keys striking their cylinders seemed louder today. She and Audrey had stayed up too late the night before, drinking and playing Pitch with Bert, Jim, and a script girl named Louise, who won nearly every hand. Violet wasn't used to entertaining on weeknights the way Audrey was. Getting up in the mornings after crawling into bed at midnight was taking a toll. "You're only going to be young once," Audrey had said, when Violet had commented about their eventful social calendar. If Audrey wasn't asking friends over to the bungalow, she was going out with them and taking Violet with her, partly for the camaraderie but more so for the connections she wanted to make with industry insiders who frequented the same nightclubs and restaurants. Being visible was how a person got noticed, she said.

She and Audrey had been out on the town or

entertaining at the house nearly every night since they'd returned from Christmas at the farm. And what a strange holiday it had been. There had been words between Audrey and her father; that much had been clear. Violet had awakened Christmas morning to the sound of raised voices. But by the time she had gotten out of bed and grabbed a robe, Audrey was in the kitchen alone and her father was visible through the window above the sink, striding purposefully toward a farm building outside. Audrey and she had stayed only for breakfast and presents, then left on the noon train, instead of on the four o'clock. When Violet had asked Audrey if she wanted to talk about what had happened earlier that morning, she had shaken her head.

Violet couldn't help but assume that Audrey's current busy schedule left little time for dwelling on the situation with her father back home. Who could blame her? Violet's parents didn't dote on her, but she was sure of their love and affection. They still hoped she would tire of Hollywood and return home.

Audrey had not spoken further about what she'd told Violet out by the Kluge bunkhouse, either; it seemed a thing that aspiring actress Audrey Duvall had not experienced. Violet didn't know if even Bert knew. And, truth be told, Violet had her own reasons for not wanting to bring up the bunkhouse conversation now that they were back home. She had no desire to talk about the baby Audrey had borne all those years ago and given away.

Violet pulled her hand away from her neck and repositioned herself in her chair. She had a mountain of dictation to get through.

She'd just set her fingers to the keys when she heard the supervisor of the secretary pool call her name. Mrs. Pope was walking toward her with Miss Rabwin, David Selznick's executive assistant, whom Violet had not yet met in person. Marcella Rabwin, who looked to be about Audrey's age, moved quickly and decisively. Violet's immediate thought was that she had forgotten to attend to something important and Selznick was upset with her.

"This is Violet Mayfield," Mrs. Pope said when they arrived at her desk. "Violet, this is Marcella Rabwin."

Violet rose unsteadily to her feet. "How do you do, Miss Rabwin?" Her unease must have been obvious.

"Don't worry—no one is angry with you," Mrs. Pope said. "Miss Rabwin is in need of an assistant for our new technical advisor and she wants to talk to you."

"Oh?"

"I hear you were born and raised in the South," Miss Rabwin said. "And you graduated from secretarial school?"

"Yes, ma'am. That's correct."

"We need someone from the pool who can assist Miss Myrick every hour that she's at the studio, for the duration of the shooting of *Gone With the Wind*."

"Miss Myrick?"

"Susan Myrick is a Georgia native and journalist as well as a personal friend of Peggy Marsh. She's the official technical advisor, so it's important to Mr. Selznick that she have whatever she needs."

Peggy Marsh? Another name Violet did not know. She would ask later who this woman was. Surely Audrey would know. "I see," she said.

"The secretary who assists her will be following her around with a notepad and taking down all her dictation, and then typing and sending out her memoranda and correspondence. There will be some long days ahead; maybe some late nights and surely some weekends. Do you think you can manage that? You will be compensated for your overtime."

The other secretaries in the room had all raised their heads from their typewriters. Violet felt their envy as easy as a breeze through an open window. "Uh, yes. Yes, of course."

"Good. Very good." Miss Rabwin seemed very relieved. "Tomorrow morning you will report to the office Miss Myrick will be using. Mrs. Pope can show you where it is later. At the end of every day you will ask Miss Myrick where she wants you to go the following morning. If she leaves the studio for a meeting or for dialogue coaching, you come back here. That will be your time to get her dictation done and her correspondence out. If you are unsure of anything, don't hesitate to ask someone, all right? Miss Myrick's being here is very important to Mr. Selznick and to Mr. Cukor, the director. We don't want there to be any problems that we could have warded off if we'd known about them. Do you have any questions, Miss Mayfield?"

"No, I don't think so. Thank you very much. I . . . I am honored."

"Remember what I said. If you have a question, ask."

"I will."

Miss Rabwin turned to head back out. Mrs. Pope nodded toward Violet's stack of dictation. "Finish what you're working on and then come find me. I'll show you where Miss Myrick will be."

"Thank you for thinking of me, Mrs. Pope."

The supervisor tipped her head to let the compliment slide off. "You should thank Audrey Duvall. She's the one who recommended you."

Violet spun around to face the far wall. Audrey was sitting at her typewriter, clacking away, but a wide smile curved her lips.

Violet waited until Mrs. Pope returned to her

little office and then she hurried over to Audrey's desk.

"Congratulations on your new job, Miss Mayfield," Audrey said softly, mindful of the others in the room.

"Audrey! Why did you put my name forward? You should have asked for this job," Violet replied in a hushed tone.

"Because you're perfect for it. You are the fastest typist in the room. You take the best dictation. You're from the South, for Pete's sake. You were meant for this job. And I will be remembered as the one who knew you were. Don't you worry about me."

"I don't know how to thank you."

"Well, you might want to save your thanks until you find out how busy you're going to be. It can get pretty crazy around here during filming."

Violet looked to see if Mrs. Pope was still inside her office and then she grabbed a chair from an unclaimed desk. "So who's Peggy Marsh?"

Audrey pulled out the typed letter she had been working on and inserted a fresh piece of paper. "Peggy Marsh is Margaret Mitchell. Your Susan Myrick is chums with the author of the book, Vi."

"Oh my goodness."

"I hear Miss Myrick is nice, though. Funny, but doesn't take nonsense. She's probably in her forties and single."

"Single?" The notion filled Violet with a strange mix of sadness and admiration.

"Good thing, probably, because if you ask me, she's got her work cut out for her. I typed up her contract. She's going to have to go over every line of the script—which you and I both know is nowhere near being done—plus every prop, every set piece, every word of dialogue to make sure it rings true. She's also going to be coaching the actors on how to sound like they're from the South. You probably read in *Variety* that Mr. Gable has refused to fake a Southern accent. Flat-out refused. So she won't be coaching him much, but Leslie Howard and Vivien Leigh— whom I told you back on the night of the fire was going to play Scarlett—and Olivia de Havilland will all need hours and hours of coaching to scrub their voices of their British accents. They're going to keep Susan Myrick hopping. Which means you will be hopping, too."

"Should . . . should I have said no?"

Audrey looked up from the typewriter. "Absolutely not! You are going to be working on the sets of *Gone With the Wind*, Vi! You are going to be right there watching it come to life. You wanted something exciting to happen to you when you came here, didn't you?"

Violet smiled and nodded.

"Well, then. Welcome to the real Hollywood."

• • •

Violet stood a few yards from Selznick's Tara, a house that in the pages of *Gone With the Wind* was nearly a character unto itself but was now merely a corner on the back lot—just two walls that met at right angles. At first glance, it appeared to offer all that a house should: a wide front door to welcome visitors, windows to watch the sun rise or set, and four sides as a defense against the heat, the damp, the cold, and the enemy. But the other side of the facade was completely open, with nothing beyond the front door but Culver City dirt.

The fragmented outside of Tara stood apart from its disjointed inside. Violet had already seen what should be behind the walls—the stairway that Scarlett would descend on her way to evening prayers and also when she shot a Yankee deserter, and the parlor with the green velvet curtains that would one day make a dress— but those interiors had been constructed inside Soundstage Number 3, which she and Miss Myrick had toured earlier that day.

Violet had settled into her new job with relative ease. Miss Myrick was all that she had been rumored to be. Capable, kind, funny, and smart. She was about the same height as Violet at five foot five, neither fat nor skinny, with short curly hair just starting to turn silver. The woman had seemed amused that she'd been given a young Southerner to take down her dictation, as if to ward off homesickness. Miss Myrick had been on the job only a few days and already it seemed she chased the sun one minute and the moon the next.

As Miss Myrick now observed the look and feel of Tara's exterior, Violet dutifully recorded her comments on a steno pad so that she could later send those comments in a memo to David Selznick and the director, George Cukor.

There shouldn't be quite so many dogs on the opening scene on the porch.

Prissy ought not to go barefoot inside the house.

The dirt around the house needs to be redder.

Cotton isn't chopped while dogwoods are in bloom.

Minutes later, as she and Miss Myrick headed toward the minibus that would take them back to the Mansion, a props man with a question stopped them. This had happened at least once an hour that day and also the day before. Everyone had been told they needed to get Miss Myrick's insights on nearly everything they did. Violet waited to see if Miss Myrick wanted her to make a notation of what was being discussed on the fly.

"You can go on back to the office, Violet, and I'll see you tomorrow. I've a coaching session with Mr. Howard after this." Miss Myrick walked away with the props man, their heads bent over his clipboard.

Violet returned to the Mansion and spent the

rest of the afternoon typing notes from the two previous days, sending out several memos, and then monitoring Miss Myrick's phone and answering what questions she could. A few minutes before five she went in search of Audrey for the commute home together.

She found her roommate sitting at her typewriter with an ample pile of dictation in front of her. Most of the other secretaries had finished for the day and were already gone. An understated, steady staccato echoed in the room as the typewriter keys hit their targets.

"Selznick is writing his own damn book on the hell of love and war," Audrey grumbled, nodding toward the thick stack of pages.

"Want to give me some of those?" Violet took a seat at the unoccupied desk next to her.

Audrey handed over a handful of her notes. "Your Miss Myrick went home early?"

"She's off teaching Leslie Howard how to talk like a proper Georgian."

Audrey looked up from her work, regarded Violet for a moment, and then continued tapping away. "You should offer to go with her when she does that so they can get to know you," Audrey said quietly, mindful of the two remaining secretaries in the room. "You could coach on the Southern voice. Doesn't Miss Myrick have more important things to do?"

Violet couldn't imagine asking Miss Myrick

such a thing. "The coaching *is* important. Mr. Cukor and Mr. Selznick trust Miss Myrick. I don't think they want anyone else coaching the cast."

"What they don't want are details getting lost in the maelstrom because they've given that woman too much to do. If they trust her, then they would trust her judgment if she told them you can coach as well as she can."

"I've never coached dialogue before!" Violet exclaimed under her breath.

"And you think she has? How hard can it be? The actors read off a line of dialog; you show them how a Southerner would say it. They practice mimicking you. Simple as that."

"I suppose."

"I just think you have a lot to offer, Violet," Audrey said. "That's all. You should do what you're already good at."

Another ten minutes had passed when Audrey suddenly yanked out the memo she had been working on and slapped it onto her desk. "Let's get out of here and do something fun. I'm tired of this."

"But your dictation . . ."

"I'll come in early tomorrow. No one wants to read his memos, anyway. Come on. Let's go see what Bert's up to. I hear Scarlett's dress for the opening scene is finished. I want to see it."

Violet handed the dictation sheets back to Audrey, who tossed them into the wire basket on her desk.

"Are you sure you want to leave those undone?" Violet asked as they both rose from their chairs.

"Absolutely." Audrey reached for her purse off the back of her chair and smoothed the peplum of her jacket over her skirt. She looked especially pretty in the shade of rose that she was wearing, and Violet wished she had on something more colorful than a featureless gray skirt and white blouse.

They exited the back door of the Mansion and passed a few soundstages and people heading for home after the long workday. They stepped inside the expansive building where the costumes were kept, and Violet marveled at the rows upon rows of waiting racks and shelves. From the many memos she had typed she knew five thousand separate pieces of clothing would be housed there when all the costumes were complete. She also knew that at the moment few were done. Two workers on their way out smiled at Audrey and greeted her by name.

"Bert's in the back," one of the men said.

They found Bert in a staging area, cataloging a load of Confederate uniforms that had just come in but that still needed to be altered to look weathered and worn. His eyes lit up when he saw Audrey.

"Well, hello there," he said, smiling wide. "What brings you two down here?"

"May we see the dress for the opening scene on

the porch?" Audrey looked about the room for the gown. "I heard two of the wardrobe girls in the commissary today, talking about how beautiful it is."

Bert was alone in the room, but he looked around, anyway. When he turned back to face the women, he told them to follow him. He took them to a long rack and accompanying shelves tagged with a placard that read *Scarlett*. The dress slated for the opening shot hung on a padded hanger and was covered in cotton sheeting. It was the sole wardrobe piece hanging on the rack. Bert lifted the billowing white dress out of its protective drape. Even without its hoop, it looked like a cloud. Green sprigs danced across the voluminous skirt, and a velvet, emerald-hued ribbon hung from both sides of the tiny waistband, to be tied in the back. Ruffles of white and green fluffed about the bodice.

"It's gorgeous!" Audrey breathed, her face radiant. She took a step toward Bert and touched his arm.

"There's going to be a hat and a parasol, too," Bert said.

Audrey leaned in close to him. "You're so lucky to be surrounded by such loveliness all day long, Bert," she said. "You really are."

Bert looked down at Audrey's manicured hand on his arm and smiled. "Lucky? I spend my days in a never-ending clothes closet. I'd rather be behind one of the cameras. You know that."

"Well, this is better than being a janitor. You know *that*."

They seemed to be recalling a conversation between the two of them that had taken place long before Violet had moved to California. In those few seconds, Violet felt invisible. "It's such a pretty dress," she chimed in, wanting her companions
to remember she was in the room with them.

Audrey let go of Bert's arm to run her fingertips through the yards of fabric. "Miss Leigh will look stunning in it," she said dreamily, almost as if she was imagining herself wrapped in the folds of the dress Vivien Leigh would wear.

Bert cocked his head and smiled, as if he, too, was imagining Audrey in the gown.

"I didn't know filming was what you really wanted to do," Violet said to Bert.

A couple seconds passed before he turned his head to reply. "Doesn't matter." He shrugged. "It won't ever happen, anyway. There's probably a dozen or more people ahead of me, wanting to train on those cameras. I guess I should be glad I'm not still pushing a broom."

He returned his attention to Audrey, signaling as politely as he could that he really didn't want to continue that conversation. Audrey was holding the gown up to her neck and swishing the fabric so that it sounded like muted applause.

• • •

The following morning when Violet reported to Miss Myrick's little office, she learned they were to spend the first part of the day talking with Mr. Lambert, the wardrobe supervisor.

Violet grabbed a pencil and her steno pad. "I thought Walter Plunkett was in charge of all the costumes for this movie," she said, recalling the dozens of memos she had sent out in recent weeks related to the extensive clothing needs.

"Mr. Plunkett designed the costumes, but it's Mr. Lambert who has to see that all Mr. Plunkett's designs get made, and made properly, and then are properly cared for. And it's my job to make sure they're right for the time period. Let's be off."

They walked under gray skies that hinted of rain, past several soundstages to the wardrobe building, and Violet found herself hoping that she would run into Bert. She wondered if he would be pleased to see her.

When indeed it was Bert who brought out the green-sprigged gown for Miss Myrick's approval, his face registered mild surprise at seeing Violet, but then he cautiously winked at her. Violet knew he meant only to silently acknowledge that he had already shown her this dress in secret, but her face colored nonetheless. The wink felt personal, intimate, and suggestive. She could not remember the last time a man had winked at her.

She replayed the gesture in her mind for the rest of the day.

SIX

Audrey swung open the bungalow's front door, and Valentino, at the threshold, meowed a greeting from the edge of the dark living room.

"Hello, kitty." She stepped inside and reached for the wall switch, and kicked off her shoes as light spilled into the room. She tossed her purse and coat onto the sofa and walked barefoot into the kitchen, the cat at her heels.

Moments later, with the cat munching on his food and a martini in her hand, Audrey contemplated making herself something to eat for dinner. She didn't have much of an appetite, and her skills in the kitchen paled miserably in comparison to Violet's. Filming of *Gone With the Wind* had officially begun that day. She'd wait to see whether Violet arrived home feeling motivated to prepare something for the two of them to eat.

She wandered into her bedroom to change into more comfortable clothes, but once there, she lowered herself to the armchair beside her bed. With Violet working late the past few days, Audrey had more hours for introspection—something that most of the time she was content to avoid.

A month had passed since the holidays and the

trip home, and her thoughts crept backward now.

She had arisen early Christmas morning, leaving Violet to her dreams while she tiptoed from the room. The sun had been peeking over the eastern horizon, and Audrey expected to find the kitchen dark and empty. But a light was on and coffee had been brewed. Her father stood at the window, looking out over the orchard, a cup in his hand.

He hadn't heard her coming and she could have gone back to her room without him knowing she had seen him, but she'd remembered what Violet had said about making the horse thirsty so that he would have no choice but to drink.

"Good morning," she said softly, so as not to surprise him.

Her father startled, anyway, and turned around abruptly. Coffee sloshed out of his cup and onto his hand and the floor.

"I'm sorry." She rushed forward to grab a dish towel.

"It's all right, it's all right." He set his cup down, took the towel, and blotted his hand with it, grimacing slightly.

"Do you need some ice?"

"I'm fine. Don't worry."

He turned to the sink and ran the cold tap over his wrist for a few seconds. Audrey opened a drawer to get a clean dish towel for him but found hot pads and place mats instead.

"She keeps them in the next drawer over," her father said.

Audrey located the towels, handed him one, and watched as he patted his skin dry.

"You're up early," he said.

"So are you."

He shrugged. "It's the usual time for me."

"Guess I'd forgotten."

He hadn't known what to say to this, and she immediately wished she had made no comment that alluded to how long she'd had lived away from home. He picked up his cup.

"I better go let the dogs out."

"I can get dressed quick and come with you if you like," she offered.

A look of doubt or maybe unease wavered across his face. "I'm sure you don't want to do that, Audrey. It's cold and dark."

"I don't mind."

"They'll be anxious for me now. I'd best get out there."

Her father had started to move past her and Audrey reached out to stop him. "Are you really saying you won't wait for me?"

Leon Kluge's gaze was trained on the door. "You should go back to your bed, where it's warm. It's too early. Too dark."

"But I want to come with you."

Her father had half turned toward her. "No, I don't think you do," he had said gently, but there had been a pleading undertone. *Just let me go.*

But she hadn't let him. "Why are you making such a big deal of this?"

He'd looked down at his shoes. "I'm not the one who is making a big deal of this."

Anger and frustration had boiled up within in her. "What is it with you?" she had yelled. "Why can't we talk about this?"

"What is it with *me?*" he shot back. "You really want me to say it?"

"Yes! Tell me!"

He'd hesitated a moment, as though he'd not expected her to answer in the affirmative. He opened his mouth and his silver-gray eyes bored into hers. "I was never good enough. Never." He said the words slowly, as though he'd dredged them out of a dark pit and each one weighed a ton. "This farm, over which I've sweat and bled, was never good enough. All your mother ever wanted was to go back to the city. She didn't want to be here. She didn't want to be here with me."

Audrey's complete surprise at this revelation silenced her only momentarily. "But I'm not her!" she'd shouted.

Her father had paused for only a second before saying quietly, "Yes, you are."

And then he'd left.

Now she sipped from her martini, willing the alcohol to numb the echoes of that morning. She wished she had said nothing to him. She wished she hadn't gone at all. She wished she and Violet had driven to San Diego for Christmas to stay at a beach cottage and eat lobster.

Audrey took another swallow, a longer one. The new year was less than a month old; there was still plenty of time to reassess her situation and chart a plan for 1939. She didn't have to think about home if she didn't want to. Besides, what did anything back home have to do with Audrey Duvall? What had taken place there on Christmas didn't matter. Not even the war in Europe mattered. All that mattered was right here, right now. This time, this place. She needed to focus on finding a way to re-create the magic like when she was eighteen. It had happened once before; it would happen again. That was her only concern.

The previous couple of years hadn't yielded her much in the way of opportunities—a screen test here, an interview there—which meant her current approach needed updating. It was becoming clear that she had tapped out her leads at Selznick International. Mr. Selznick himself had had ample opportunities to screen test her and hadn't, and neither had any of his assistant producers. She had taken dictation for nearly every Selznick executive with even a modicum of influence, gotten them coffee and Danishes, bought birthday presents for their wives, made excuses for them when they were late or unprepared, playfully turned down any sexual advances so that she would always remain wanted, not had.

She knew how this game worked. It was not about getting your résumé into Central Casting and becoming just another pretty girl who wanted to be discovered. It was about being in the right place at the right time.

Her hopes had been raised with all the borrowing of actors for *Gone With the Wind*—Clark Gable from MGM, Olivia de Havilland from Warner—as it had led to many letters of correspondence and phone calls to other studios. But obviously those connections hadn't been enough. She had made no new inroads. And Violet's question—"Is it working?"—on the streetcar on the night they met had been a constant niggle at the back of her mind. Perhaps she wasn't availing herself of the opportunities in play now that MGM was getting more involved with this film. She should ask to work more shifts. Selznick was working twenty-hour days and popping Benzedrine to stay awake. She'd heard he'd been asking for a secretary to be available at all hours, and Mrs. Pope was looking for volunteers. Perhaps working more closely with Selznick would in turn get her closer to MGM and Selznick's father-in-law, Louis B. Mayer. Selznick had not proven to have much use for her, even though he knew who she was and what she had almost been. But MGM's needs might have changed in the four years she'd been gone. They'd likely forgotten about her.

Audrey emptied her glass, set it down on the nightstand, and rose from her chair. She reached for a box marked *Photos* on the bottom shelf of her closet and set it on the bed, lifted the lid, and dumped out the contents.

The publicity shots Stiles had paid for all those years ago lay somewhere near the bottom. Audrey fished through the photos of home and the farm and the ones with Aunt Jo until she found them. She pulled them away from the others, wanting only to remind herself of the name of the photographer who had taken them, but the images held her gaze. She had been so young when these were taken.

The poses were alluring and evocative. Stiles had told her that she had luminous eyes, a rosebud mouth, and a china-doll look as enchanting as that of any silent film star. Her hair, long and luxurious, had the same curl and shine, and her body had been as delicately curved as Mary Pickford's and Lillian Gish's. These pictures and that description were what Stiles had used to pitch Audrey to the studios.

She heard in her head Stiles telling her, "You got the part, Audrey. You're going to be a star."

A star. A star. A star!

Audrey closed her eyes. For several moments she stood still, waiting for the past to recede to its shadows, for the voice to be stilled. But it lingered.

She snapped her eyes open. She needed air in her lungs, air that belonged to the here and now, not yesterday. She turned from the room, went into the kitchen, and then threw open the back door to the patio. The cool blast of a night breeze met her, bracing and welcoming. She breathed it in and then stepped outside to indulge in it. She grabbed a tablecloth from the clothesline that Violet had pinned up earlier that day and wrapped herself in it as she stood on the cold patio stones.

Audrey sat down in a rattan chair, not wanting to go back inside, even though her feet were at once freezing. Valentino jumped onto her lap and she pulled him close for warmth.

She had lost her edge—that was what it was—and the trip home at Christmas had just made it worse. She had lost sight of her goal. And it had taken Violet's "Is it working?" question and the Christmas-morning encounter to wake her up.

Making it as an actress in Hollywood was about the people she met. She'd been putting in her time at Selznick International and getting zero results. She hadn't met the right people, and she had gotten lazy trying to find them. She would not keep making that mistake.

Audrey lifted the cat and held him in her arms as she walked back inside. She tossed the tablecloth onto the back of a kitchen chair and then went into the living room to get a cigarette from her purse. Her shoes, which she had kicked off and left in the middle of the floor, were now nowhere in sight, nor was the coat she had thrown onto the couch.

Violet was home.

Audrey set the cat down. She headed for Violet's room, eager for her roommate's company. But Violet wasn't in her own bedroom. She was in Audrey's, standing beside the bed, looking at the photographs. Audrey's shoes stood side by side, toes pointing toward the closet, on the floor by Violet's feet. The coat was draped neatly on the back of the armchair.

Violet turned suddenly at Audrey's approach and the photo in her hand fluttered to the bed. "Audrey! I didn't know you were home! I thought maybe you were at one of the neighbors'."

"I was out on the patio with the cat."

"I'm . . . I didn't mean to pry. I just brought in your shoes and coat and I saw these pictures on your bed. I wasn't—"

"Don't worry about it. I don't care that you're looking at my photos." She moved to stand next to Violet.

"They're beautiful," Violet said, attempting a more casual tone. "These were your professional ones?" She held up one of the studio glossies.

Audrey nodded and took the photo. "It's a shame I can't use them anymore. They cost a fortune."

"I can see why that talent scout thought you looked like Lillian Gish."

"I guess the world only needs one Lillian Gish." She tossed the photo lightly to the bed. "I was thinking I might have some new ones made. That's why I got these out."

Violet lifted another photograph from the pile, one of a ten-year-old Audrey with pigtails. Her slender mother stood next to her. They were squinting in the sun. Her mother looked thin and weary.

"That picture was taken just a few months before she died."

"Was your mother already sick then?" Violet asked carefully.

"I think she must have been, but I didn't know it yet." Audrey extended her hand and Violet placed the photo in it.

"What disease did she have? Did the doctors know?"

"I don't know if they knew. Aunt Jo told me it must have been some kind of wasting disease. It was like she just started disappearing. A little more of her each day would vanish until there was nothing left. I remember her being so weightless at the end. She didn't even have the strength to put her arms around me."

"I am so very sorry, Audrey," Violet said, after a moment's pause. "I can't imagine losing a mother so young. A child's mother is everything."

They were both quiet for a few seconds.

Audrey placed the photo back in the box and then began to gather the rest. "So, I hear filming began today. I barely saw you at all."

Violet reached for a few of the photos as well. "Mr. Cukor shot the scene on the porch at Tara when the Tarleton twins are talking about war. It was very exciting. But tedious, too. Those two actors aren't twins and neither one is redheaded, so their hair has been dyed and it looks very orange. I guess Mr. Selznick isn't happy with the dye job, and he's thinking of scrapping the porch scene altogether. But they shot it anyway, several times. And then the camera broke down for a while, so we had to wait for that, and then Mr. Cukor wanted to shoot a scene where Scarlett runs out to meet her pa coming home from Twelve Oaks."

Audrey sensed a hunger within her that she had not felt in a while. It had been a long time since she had been on a movie set. Secretaries usually weren't needed there. "Tell me all about it." She sat on the bed and patted the mattress. Violet sat down beside her.

"Every action or bit of dialogue was done at least three times, sometimes more," Violet said. "You wonder how these actors and actresses can keep repeating themselves over and over."

"They're used to it. All the best takes are stitched together in production. The audience never sees the extra ones. What do you think of Mr. Cukor?"

"He was amazing," Violet replied. "At least I was amazed. He took aside the actor who is playing Gerald O'Hara and told him to reach into the soul of his lines when Scarlett confesses to her pa that she wants to marry Ashley, and Pa has to tell her she would never be happy with a man like that. Pa tells Scarlett that she is so young, and Mr. Cukor said the unspoken truth here is that Pa has protected her all this time from the ache of loss. She doesn't know what it is to suffer. She doesn't know that most things do not last, and he tells her that she will learn this in time. Because everybody does."

For a second Audrey could not find her voice. "He said that?" she finally murmured.

Violet nodded. "Miss Myrick heard him say this, too, and she told me that's why he's the highest-paid director there is."

Again there was silence between them.

The phone in the living room jangled.

"I'll get it," Violet offered. She left the room, and Audrey gathered the snippets of a past that had been full of promise and returned them to the box, her mind spinning with a messy weave of thoughts. Then Violet called to her.

She walked into the living room and Violet extended the phone. "It's for you. It's Bert."

Audrey put the receiver to her ear. "Hello, Bert."

"Say, I was thinking maybe we could grab a

bite on Sunset and then look for the nightingale," he said. "What do you say?"

"Tonight?" After all her revelations that evening, Audrey was looking forward to another martini and her pajamas.

"Unless you have other plans . . . ?"

The mild disappointment in his voice was endearing, but she could not see herself heading back out into the city now. She needed this evening to come up with a new strategy. And to get Mr. Cukor's words out of her head. Maybe she would give her friend Vince a call. It had been a while since she'd talked with him, probably not since his engagement party in October. She'd heard he had gotten the new job in publicity at Paramount that she had told him about. He owed her one.

"Can we do it another time, Bert? I've had a long day. I'd be terrible company and would no doubt scare all the birds away." She closed her eyes and tipped her head back a bit; swiveled her neck first one way and then another.

"Oh. Of course. We can go another night."

"You're a peach, Bert. Good night."

After he said good-bye, she set the receiver on its cradle and then turned around. Violet stood just a few feet behind her, staring at the phone.

"Do you know how to make pancakes?" Audrey asked, famished now. "I'd love some pancakes."

Violet slowly raised her gaze from the little table where the phone rested. "Sure," she replied.

SEVEN

February 1939

The women and men costumed in antebellum dresses and period suits crowded the soundstage, simulating a festive mood despite the fact that the dancing sequences for the Atlanta Bazaar scene had been shot more than a dozen times already. The actresses' gowns looked pretty enough to Violet, but only moments earlier she had overheard a wardrobe assistant tell Miss Myrick that Mr. Selznick wasn't happy with them. The dresses were, in his words, "ordinary and cheap-looking." She had gone to tell Mr. Lambert that the gowns in question were actually historically correct. But Mr. Selznick wanted vibrant colors and stunning gowns to stand in stark contrast in the upcoming scenes of war and deprivation. A heated conversation was taking place in the far corner of the building about what was beautiful and what was accurate.

Violet hadn't sat through all of the takes that afternoon, but the long day was beginning to wear on all the hired talent Central Casting had sent. A handful of female extras stood a few yards away from her, rubbing their toes and complaining that the gowns made them hot and that MGM served better refreshments. Violet seriously doubted Audrey would behave like that on any set. Miss Leigh and Mr. Gable, in another corner of the building during the break, were going over dance steps and lines of dialogue with the assistant producer, like the two professionals they were. After five days of filming, Violet had yet to meet either movie star in person, but Miss Leigh had smiled at her earlier that day and Mr. Gable had said, "Good morning," to her the day before.

Violet peered at the nameless actresses fanning themselves with call sheets. Audrey was prettier than any of these women, could dance far better, and would make any one of these so-called ordinary dresses look enchanting merely by putting it on. Audrey should've been in this scene.

Audrey could've been in this scene. . . .

Violet frowned as the obvious suddenly assailed her. Why hadn't she thought of this before? She could have suggested that Audrey be fitted for a costume and made a part of the Atlanta Bazaar scene. She had Miss Myrick's ear all day long, and George Cukor listened intently to everything Miss Myrick said.

It was too late now for the Atlanta Bazaar scene, but the barbecue at Twelve Oaks was coming up in a few weeks and even more extras would be needed for that. She could easily put in a word with Miss Myrick, who could then put in a word with George Cukor.

Audrey had seemed distracted since she'd begun working longer days at the instruction of Mr. Selznick, who wanted a stenographer on duty at all hours. She had arrived home after ten the past two workdays and then spent a long while on the phone both nights with someone named Vince, after Violet had gone to bed. They couldn't have been business calls at that hour, although Violet couldn't be sure. Audrey spoke softly, so as not to keep Violet awake, and her deep voice made every indecipherable word sound provocative and yet anxious.

A chance to be in the most-anticipated film in years would be just the thing to lighten Audrey's mood. It might even lead to the rediscovery Audrey had so long been yearning for.

Violet wanted to ask Miss Myrick about it right then and she turned to see if the advisor was on her way back to her, when Bert was suddenly at her side. Violet had seen him on the set on and off that afternoon but with dozens of extras all in costume, he had been too busy to speak to her. She had hoped she might see him. Violet wanted him to know that if he ever wanted to go looking for that nightingale again, she'd be happy to go with him.

"Do you have a minute?" he asked.

Violet glanced in the direction that Miss Myrick had gone. The woman was now nowhere in sight. She turned back to him and smiled. "It looks like I do."

"I was wondering if you might do something for me." His tone was eager.

Her heart tripped over a beat. "Of course."

"Valentine's Day will be coming up soon and I'd like to surprise Audrey with something. I was hoping you would help me."

A second flicked by before Violet answered that she would be happy to help Bert in any way she could.

"I know it's two weeks away yet, but it's so busy right now. I don't always know when I will see you." Bert reached into his pocket and withdrew a handkerchief-wrapped lump. He opened the folds and pulled out a little porcelain bird, painted in soft browns with the faintest rosy pink at its bosom and sapphire blue eyes. It was perched on a porcelain branch decorated with autumn-toned leaves and its beak was open, as though it would sing to whoever held it.

"It's a nightingale," Bert said, smiling.

"I see you finally found it, then." Violet took the little bird in her hands and touched the cool, smooth surface of its wings.

Bert's grin widened. He liked her little joke. "I was thinking maybe you could leave it at her bedside table while she's sleeping, so that when she wakes up on Valentine's Day she'll see it."

Violet considered Bert's request for a moment. "Audrey is working nights now. Sometimes she comes home after I'm already in bed."

"Yes, but she's still sleeping when you get up, right? You could sneak in there in the morning, put the bird on the nightstand, and then she'll wake up after you're gone and see it." He withdrew from his shirt pocket a small, cream-colored envelope. Audrey's name was written across the front. "Could you set it atop this?"

Violet slowly took the envelope from Bert and pondered what she could say. Audrey would think the bird was sweet and the gesture kind, but whatever Bert had written on a note for Valentine's Day she would surely find trouble-some. Audrey wasn't in love with Bert. She liked him—who didn't like Bert?—but she was not in love with him. Audrey was after only one thing at the moment: stardom. Bert didn't figure into that. Bert would never figure into that. And he had no idea Audrey spoke in sultry tones to a man named Vince at late hours.

Nothing good could come from giving Audrey a Valentine's Day note from Bert.

"Don't you think it will be more fun if she just wakes up and sees the sweet little bird and has to wonder how it got there?" She offered the envelope back to Bert but he didn't take it.

"I don't want her to wonder. I want her to know it was me who gave it to her."

"Yes, but sometimes wondering is more . . . fun," Violet said, careful not to say wondering was more romantic. "It might be . . . better for you if you *don't* leave a note, Bert."

He stared at her for a moment and then his gaze dropped to the envelope in her hand. The reason for Violet's reluctance seemed to dawn on him. "She's not seeing someone, is she?" he finally said.

Violet hesitated only a second. "Maybe."

"Maybe?"

"I'm not sure. She doesn't tell me everything. I've just . . . I've heard her talking to a man on the phone. Late at night."

A long moment passed before Bert took the envelope from Violet and slipped it back into his shirt pocket.

"I still want her to have the nightingale." A mix of emotions laced his words together.

"Of course. It's a sweet little bird, Bert. It really is. Any girl would be thrilled to have it."

He nodded slowly, seemingly unconvinced.

"I know she'll love it."

"And you'll tell her it's from me?"

"Of course."

He handed her the handkerchief that had been around the bird. "Don't worry. It's clean."

Violet laughed lightly, took the handkerchief, and wrapped the bird inside it. She placed it inside the handbag at her feet.

"Miss Myrick is coming back this way." Bert's voice lacked the lift it had moments ago.

Violet pressed her hand on Bert's forearm. "Everything will be all right," she said spontaneously, though she knew those words could sound so empty when it felt like you were losing something you thought was yours. So very empty.

She watched him walk away. The swirling platform that Rhett and Scarlett danced upon was wheeled back into place so that their waltz would seem charming and effortless. And then Violet's gaze fell to the little bird resting just inside her handbag.

Her next move would require some careful thinking. She didn't want anyone to get hurt.

Violet knew all too well what it was like to have your deepest affections returned to you unwanted. It was the most devastating feeling in the world. Franklin hadn't even waited until her stitches turned to scar tissue before telling her he thought they should start seeing other people. He'd told her it had nothing to do with the surgery and her inability to give him sons, but his father's shipping company had been family owned for a century. Violet knew it had mattered to him. Of course it mattered.

To offer your love to someone and then have it declined was the worst blow the human heart could suffer. Audrey didn't love Bert, just like Franklin hadn't loved her.

She needed to act in Bert's best interest. He was a good and kind man who didn't deserve to have his heart trampled on. If she could help him fall out of love with Audrey before it went too far, then it wouldn't hurt him so much. That was the merciful thing to do. It was what she wished someone had done for her. Her parents had initially hoped a change of scenery in Shreveport would lift Violet out of the sadness that had enveloped her following her surgery. But the Louisiana landscape hadn't been the tonic she'd needed. Not even Hollywood had been the salve her soul cried out for. She was finding that time was the only agent that mended a broken heart. Best not to have it broken in the first place.

Violet waited until the day before Valentine's Day.

By then Audrey was working the sundown-to-sunup shift, typing up pages of constantly evolving script, over which Mr. Selznick labored while everyone else slept. In the shared hour between the time Violet arrived home from the studio and Audrey left for it, Violet took the handkerchief out of her purse. She and Audrey were sitting at the kitchen table. Audrey was smoking a cigarette and looking at a magazine. After a very difficult day on set, Violet had just made herself a supper of scrambled eggs.

Mr. Selznick and George Cukor had been at odds. Mr. Cukor was making script and blocking changes without Mr. Selznick's approval, and he had his own ideas about feel and tempo. Mr.

Cukor wanted Melanie's childbirth scene to be tense and frightening, for example, and Mr. Selznick insisted the mood be subtle and quietly oppressive. Mr. Cukor was also unhappy with the new pages of script that showed up every morning and the fact that the actors had no time to memorize the latest lines. There were rumors floating about that Mr. Cukor might resign. Miss Myrick had told Violet she couldn't think of anything more upsetting than to see George Cukor go.

"What's that?" Audrey said, pointing to the little fabric-wrapped lump.

"Bert thought you might like it," Violet said casually, and took a bite of her eggs.

Intrigued, Audrey set her cigarette down in an ashtray and pulled away the folds of the handkerchief.

"It's a nightingale." Violet looked at Audrey, not at the piece of porcelain in her friend's hand.

Audrey's smile widened in precisely the way Violet had hoped it might.

"Oh, dear Bert and his nightingales!" Audrey set the little bird down by the fruit bowl in the center of the table and smiled at it.

"It's pretty, isn't it?" Violet did not take her eyes off Audrey.

"Very sweet," Audrey replied thoughtfully. "So very sweet." And then she slowly picked up her cigarette and returned her attention to her magazine.

Violet took another bite of her dinner as she reached across the table.

Her fingers closed around Bert's handkerchief and she drew it into her lap.

EIGHT

Audrey pulled the silk scarf tight around her head as the car she sat in zoomed down Wilshire Boulevard.

"I told you I could put the top up," Vince said from behind the steering wheel, as she tucked in the fluttering ends of the scarf.

"I like it down. It almost feels like we're flying. Besides, I've heard the windblown look is fashionable."

"Any look on you is fashionable, Audie."

She grinned. "You're engaged," she reminded him.

He laughed. "I'm surprised you could get away for lunch today with all that's going on over at the studio."

"I've been working twelve-hour nights for two weeks. I'd say I'm due a long lunch. And, anyway, we're on a shooting break while Victor Fleming gets up to speed. He and Selznick and some other execs are all headed to Palm Springs to work on the script from hell. It's actually quiet at the studio today. I doubt I'll be missed."

Vince shook his head. "I still can't believe Cukor quit. And Fleming taking over for him? To jump into the Civil War after spending the last few months in Oz? That takes guts."

"What do you bet the two settings aren't so different?" Audrey said. "Every movie seems to be the same these days. Some character desperately wants something and has to go through a world turned upside down to get it."

"I'm thinking it was all a genius publicity stunt, switching directors like that. *Photoplay* loves stuff like this. I bet MGM secretly loves it, too, since they're in this for half the profits."

"Well, stunt or no stunt, it hasn't made for a happy cast. Vivien Leigh loved Cukor."

"But Gable didn't."

Audrey turned to him. "And where did you hear *that?*"

"This is Hollywood, Audie!" He was about to turn into the entrance of the Beverly Wilshire, an imposing structure of Carrara marble and Tuscan stone, when Audrey stopped him.

"Wait! I can't get out of the car with you, Vince!" she exclaimed. "What if Dwyer arrives the same time we do? Let me out up the street and then you double back."

"Right." Vince moved back into traffic. "So, when I see you, you're an old friend from . . . ?"

"I am not an old anything. I'm a good friend. We've both just been busy and we haven't seen

111

each other in a while. You want to catch up. You invite me to join you both for lunch. I decline. You insist. You get Mr. Dwyer to also insist. I pretend to mull it over. You signal a waiter to bring another chair and a glass of whatever you are drinking and then you say you won't take no for an answer."

Vince pulled up to the curb on the next block. "And you're sure you don't want me to say anything about *Pocahontas*?"

Audrey had her hand on the door handle but whirled around. "You have to *promise* me you won't say anything about *Pocahontas*!"

"Audie, you were cast in a major motion picture."

"A major motion picture that was never made. Don't mention it, Vince. Promise me you won't unless I do first."

"All right, all right. So he's supposed to just magically assume you're interested in being a movie star, then."

"Did you not listen to anything I told you on the phone the other night? He's supposed to wonder if I would look good on the screen. If I can be made into a star. If I can make Paramount good money."

"And you think he will?"

"If you ask me the right questions he will. Ask if Selznick tested me for Scarlett, along with half the known world. And when I laugh and say no, ask why not. Mr. Dwyer will wonder if I have star quality because you will have planted the thought. It's as simple as that."

Vince grinned. "You're good at this acting gig. Ever thought of giving it a try?"

"Oh, hush." She stepped out of the car.

"See you in ten?"

"Fifteen."

Vince drove off, signaled a U-turn, and headed toward the hotel. Audrey took her time walking back in the same direction so as not to be winded. At the restaurant's host stand she gave her name and said that she had a reservation for a table for one by a window. As the host showed her to her table she gazed about the rest of the room and was relieved to see that Vince had a table not far from the ladies' powder room, just as they had planned. After she was given a glass of water and a menu, she rose from her chair and began to walk toward the powder-room door. Vince saw her rise. When she was only a few feet away, his eyes widened in mock delight.

"Audrey Duvall!" He sprang to his feet. "What a nice surprise!" He leaned forward to kiss her on the cheek.

"Vince, darling, how wonderful to see you," Audrey replied, employing the smoothest tone to her deep voice.

Vince turned to his tablemate. "Bernard, this is a dear friend of mine, Audrey Duvall. Audrey, Bernard Dwyer."

The man stood. He looked to be her father's age, maybe a year or two older. She had expected this assistant producer to be a little younger.

"How do you do?" he said courteously.

"Pleasure to meet you," she said.

"It's been ages since we've talked. How are you?" Vince went on.

"Very well. And you?"

"Splendid, splendid. Still with Selznick, then?"

Audrey saw a flicker of interest in Bernard Dwyer's eyes. "Yes, I am. Busy time now, as you can imagine."

"No doubt." Vince then seemed to have suddenly come up with an idea "Say. Are you dining alone?"

"Oh. Well, yes."

"You should join us," he said enthusiastically.

"Oh, no. I couldn't."

"We insist, don't we, Bernard?"

Bernard Dwyer had just retaken his seat. He looked up from the menu. "What was that?"

"Audrey should join us, shouldn't she?"

Dwyer blinked at him.

"I wouldn't want to impose," Audrey said, glancing from one man to the other. "You look like you have important things to discuss."

"It's no imposition. I can have the waiter bring us another table setting."

"I actually do have some matters I'd like to talk about, Vince," Dwyer said. "I'm sure we'd just bore this lovely young woman to death were she to stay. It was very nice to meet you, Miss . . . ?"

"Duvall. The pleasure was mine."

Vince had clearly not thought about the fact that Dwyer might say no. He stared at Audrey.

"Another time, Vince?" She leaned toward him to give him a peck on the cheek.

"Sorry," he whispered into her ear.

She pulled away. "Good day, gentlemen." Audrey continued to the ladies' room, entered a stall, and closed the door. She leaned her forehead against the polished wood, willing it to cool the heat of her disappointment.

Vince had spent a week setting up this meeting. This had been his best lead, he told her. Dwyer and his scouts were on the lookout for a new brunette they could groom into greatness.

Audrey resisted the urge to pound her forehead against the door. She had just spent two hundred dollars on new studio photos. And for what? Dwyer hadn't shown a hint of interest, other than when he heard she worked at a competing studio. He hadn't asked what she did there. Hadn't cared what she did.

Vince would call her later tonight to tell her again how sorry he was. That was a phone call she did not want to suffer through. She would invite friends over. Bert. Jim. The new hairdresser on set. A few others. They could play charades and drink cocktails and she wouldn't answer the phone if it rang.

She stepped away from the stall door, reached behind to the commode, and flushed it even though there was nothing in it but water.

Twilight had turned the Hollywood sky an ashen azure, and the first stars studded the canvas of the eastern horizon. Though it was damp and a bit chilly, Audrey suggested she and Violet set up the cocktail party out on the bungalow's patio.

She grabbed a kitchen chair to take outside and asked Violet to do the same. Violet put her hands on the chair back but her gaze was on the fruit bowl on the center of the table. She paused.

"What?" Audrey asked

"I was just . . . I was just thinking I should move the nightingale if it was still on the kitchen table so it wouldn't get broken tonight. But it looks like you already did."

"I put it on that little shelf in the bathroom, the one by the window." Audrey grabbed a second chair. "I thought it would look cute there, like it had just flown in."

Violet lifted the chair and followed Audrey outside with it. "That's a good place. So, did you have a nice lunch out with your friend?"

Audrey set the chairs down. "It was all right."

"Vince, is it?"

"Yes." The less she had to talk about her day the better. "And how were things at your end of the studio? Did you and Miss Myrick find anything to do without the cameras rolling?"

They went back inside for the last two chairs. "She's fit to be tied because no one is working on their Southern accents while we wait for Mr. Selznick and Mr. Fleming to get back. Leslie Howard's drawl is horrific. Mr. Gable still won't fake an accent of any kind. And Miss Leigh is still mad that Mr. Cukor is gone, so she isn't working on her lines at all."

They grabbed the chairs and went back outside with them. "Miss Myrick spent most of today trying to track down the actors to resume their coaching. But Miss Leigh said what was the use, since Mr. Selznick will come back with a whole new script, anyway."

"She's probably right about that."

"Have you . . . have you had a chance to see Bert since he asked me to give the nightingale to you?" Violet asked.

"I saw him this afternoon when I got back to the studio. I went over to wardrobe to invite him over tonight."

"Right. Of course."

"Did you think I wouldn't thank him for it?" Bert had seemed happy that she liked the little nightingale. She had asked where he had found it. *A little gift shop near my mom's place in Santa*

Barbara, he'd said and then promptly changed the subject.

"No. No, of course you would. I just wanted to make sure he knew I had given it to you."

Audrey laughed. Violet was a little odd sometimes. But in a nice way. "You and your Southern good manners never cease to amuse me. If someone asked you to ride a camel for them, backward while wearing a tutu, I've no doubt you'd do it twice, just to be nice. Wouldn't you?"

Violet grinned back and said nothing.

The six guests at the impromptu party were all Selznick International employees and party talk on the patio naturally drifted to Cukor's leaving, the script that everyone and his brother seemed to be writing, and Vivien Leigh's scandalous and supposedly secret love affair with Laurence Olivier.

"No more work talk!" Audrey finally announced, an hour after the get-together began. "Let's play a game."

"And let's move indoors," one of the women said. "It's too chilly out here."

The chairs were brought back into the kitchen, drinks refilled, and everyone began to move into the living room. Audrey noticed Bert wasn't inside.

She went back outside and found him looking up at the branches of the massive jacaranda that kept the little backyard in perpetual shade and sprinkled the patio with lavender confetti every June when its blossoms fell.

"Coming, Bert?" she asked.

He nodded without looking at her. "You've got a pair of mourning doves in that tree."

She looked up into the trees' limbs and saw nothing. "I'll take your word for it."

He turned to her. His features were barely distinguishable in the moonlight. "Are you all right, Audrey? You seem sad tonight."

She looped her arm through his. There would be no talk of life's disappointments.

"I'm fine. Let's go in and you can pour me another drink."

Hollywood
March 9, 2012

Christine pulls into her parents' Bel Air driveway and presses the code for the wrought-iron gate. It slides quietly on oiled rails.

Her mother, Glynnis, answers the doorbell, two long-stemmed goblets in hand. She hands one of the glasses of Chardonnay to her daughter. Then she points to the hatbox, the handle of which is over Christine's arm. "Come on in and let's have a look!"

They enter the expansive kitchen and Christine sets the hatbox on the marble-topped island in the center of the room.

"Your text message was very intriguing," Glynnis says. "You know, I just drove past our old neighborhood the other day. I have a listing up in Hollywood Hills. Right next to the Bela Lugosi house."

"So do you remember the name of the woman next door who babysat me?" Christine sips from her glass.

"Her last name was Redmond, I think. She was a widow—I remember that. And I think she had a daughter who lived in Europe somewhere. I can give you the address of the house we lived in, if you want to swing by on the very slim chance she is still there."

"Slim chance?"

"She was elderly then, Chrissy. And that was twenty-five years ago."

"I suppose you're right."

"Can I see it?" Glynnis says.

Christine pushes back the lid on the box. She lifts out the hat and extends it to her mother, who turns it over to look at its underside and the label.

"So you really think this hat is a costume piece from *Gone With the Wind*?" her mother asks.

"It looks exactly like it. I looked it up on the Internet. The thing is, the hat is supposedly at a university in Texas. I looked that up, too. So now I don't know what to think."

"But the owner very much wants this hat back."

"Yes."

Glynnis walks over to a desk area in the kitchen and takes out a notepad and pen. She sits back down and begins to write.

"This was our address back then. Mrs. Redmond lived on the right as you face the houses across the street."

Christine takes the paper. "Thanks."

"You were pretty smitten with Mrs. Redmond. You liked going over to her house even when your dad and I were home. She always had her television on, which I didn't really care for. And she always had it set to reruns of shows from the fifties and sixties. No wonder you like the vintage look."

Flashes of old black-and-white episodes flutter in Christine's mind. "I do remember that."

"Even after we moved you'd want to watch *I Love Lucy* and *The Dick Van Dyke Show* when you had friends over, instead of *Saved by the Bell* and *Full House.* Drove them all crazy."

They laugh and then finish their wine. Christine leaves a little after seven. She checks her phone as she gets into her car to see if Mr. Garceau has tried to reach her. He hasn't.

On impulse, Christine drives the ten miles to the neighborhood that she hasn't thought about in more than a decade. Starlight shimmers down on her as she pulls up to the curb.

The house she lived in all those years ago has been extensively remodeled and is barely recognizable.

The little bungalow next door looks exactly as Christine remembers it.

But every window is dark.

———◆———

NINE

March 1939

Violet stirred the pot of gumbo as it bubbled on Audrey's stove and breathed in its savory aroma. She lifted the spoon to her mouth and carefully tasted the concoction. Perhaps it wasn't the best gumbo ever made, but she was fairly happy with her first attempt at using her mother's tried-and-true recipe. She'd gotten a hankering for it the previous week—she'd been particularly homesick—and written her mother. The return letter had come yesterday. The search for fresh okra had sent her to three grocery stores, but the finished product would be worth it. Hopefully Audrey wouldn't be too much longer and would have an appetite when she got home. Violet hadn't seen much of her at the studio that day and she'd had to ride the streetcar and bus by herself.

She lowered the flame on the pot and sat down at the kitchen table to wait for her roommate's return. Valentino wound in and out of her legs, and Violet scooped up the cat and set him in her lap. It had been a busy day, a frustrating day. The film was finally back in production and everyone was again going to be working ten-hour days or longer. A new script, this one pounded out by screenwriter Ben Hecht, had been given to the cast that morning, and Miss Myrick had been told it was the last revision there would be. She had whispered to Violet that she'd believe that when she saw pigs fly. Violet had also been introduced to Victor Fleming that day, but he was obviously only concerned with remembering who Susan Myrick was, since she still had to approve every word said and every prop used. Mr. Fleming seemed more direct than Mr. Cukor had been and unlikely to coddle anybody, including the leading ladies.

Scarlett's wedding to Charles Hamilton had been shot that afternoon. Bert had been in charge of making sure the bridal gown was ready for Miss Leigh, and he came to the set at the start of the shoot to ensure everything about the dress was in order.

"This wedding was a rushed affair in the book," Bert had said as they both watched Vivien Leigh position herself under the lights. "Scarlett wore her mother's wedding dress, remember?"

Violet recalled reading that part. Agreeing to Charles Hamilton's proposal had seemed the| most reckless thing Scarlett could have done.

"Plunkett used a dress form with the measurements of the actress playing Scarlett's mother so that the gown would seem big on Miss Leigh. Rather clever."

Bert seemed proud of the dress even though he was merely in charge of its whereabouts. Violet hadn't thought the dress was very pretty; the sleeves were as big as sides of beef and the dozens of silk leaves made the skirt looked tattered.

But she had told him it was a very convincing dress and he was soon called away to attend to another costume need.

During a break to change some light fixtures, Miss Myrick decided to dictate a few notes to Violet regarding the plans for the Twelve Oaks barbecue scene, which was going to be a huge affair shot on location at a park called Busch Gardens. Violet had been hoping to find a way to broach the subject of putting in a good word for Audrey with the new, no-nonsense director and it seemed as though it had just been handed to her. Most of the technical crew had been busy with lighting adjustments, Mr. Fleming had been talking to the camera crew about changing a lens, and a couple of script girls and hairdressers were milling about, waiting for filming to resume.

It had seemed like a good time to mention it.

Violet looked down at the cat as what had happened next replayed itself in her mind. "How was I supposed to know that's not how it works?" she said, and Valentino looked up at her and meowed.

She hadn't known a director can't just put in a new girl as an extra, even if she's a studio employee and as beautiful as any other extra on the set, and had had a leading role offered to her once.

There were contracts and casting protocols and regulations and the blood of a two-headed giraffe to be reckoned with.

"I didn't know," Violet said, leaning down and speaking into Valentino's fur.

Thankfully, Mr. Fleming hadn't been within earshot. It was only Miss Myrick who told her that what she was asking on behalf of her room-mate was completely out of the question. Violet's cheeks had burned crimson nonetheless.

"It's ridiculous, if you ask me." Violet rose to her feet and put the cat down on the floor. She reached into a cupboard and pulled out a tin of cat food. Valentino began to dance around her feet as she opened it. "They are stupid rules."

The cat meowed in response. She set down his dish, stirred the gumbo, and sat down again to wait.

By seven thirty there was still no sign of Audrey.

Violet got out two bowls from the cupboard but filled only one. She took her dinner to the table, wishing now that she'd thought to make corn bread, too. She certainly had had the time to make both.

She lifted a spoonful to her mouth and tested the temperature with the tip of her tongue. The gumbo was blistering hot and she winced. As she lowered the spoon to the bowl, she heard the front door open and close.

Audrey was home at last.

"I've made gumbo!" Violet called from the kitchen.

Audrey rounded the corner and stood in the arched doorway between the living room and kitchen. "What did you do?" Her eyes glittered with what seemed to be bridled anger.

Violet stared at her, openmouthed. "I . . . I made gumbo."

Audrey stepped fully into the room. "What did you do at the *studio* today, Violet?"

Blood rushed to Violet's head and bosom. Audrey must have found out she'd tried to get her into the cast as an extra today. But how? And why was she mad about it? "I tried to help you," Violet said, the sting of Audrey's obvious resentment making her voice sound frail. "I only tried to get you in the movie. Isn't that what you want?"

"No, it's not what I want!" Audrey tossed her purse onto the table. The gumbo in Violet's bowl shuddered.

"How can you *say* that?" Violet nearly choked on the words. "I know that's not true. I know you want it."

Audrey closed her eyes. "You don't know anything."

Violet's own anger, fueled by offense, began to course through her. "I know what you told me! You told me you want your movie career back. You told me you were going to have new photographs taken. You told me it was all about

127

meeting the right people! People who could make things happen!"

Audrey's eyes snapped opened. "I never told you I wanted to be a nameless extra in *Gone With the Wind*."

"And what is so terrible about being an extra? Surely lots of famous actresses started out that way. Do you know how many people write to Miss Myrick all the time, wanting a bit part in this movie?"

Audrey shook her head slowly. "I never *asked* you to get me a bit part in *Gone With the Wind*."

Violet could scarcely believe how her good intentions were being thrown back in her face. And here she'd thought Audrey would've been grateful that Violet had even tried.

"I don't know how you even found out that I asked." Violet fingered away tears that had gathered in her eyes. "I couldn't make it happen."

"Thank God you couldn't."

Violet stared at her, incredulous.

"I found out because a couple of script girls heard you," Audrey said. "And they told a couple of wardrobe girls, and those wardrobe girls told some sound technicians, and the sound technicians told everyone else. You embarrassed me, Violet."

Two more tears pooled at Violet's eyes and they slipped down unchecked. "That's not what I meant to do."

"Now everyone thinks I put you up to it."

"But you didn't! It was my idea!"

Audrey sighed heavily, as though the air in her lungs was weighed down with concrete. "But that's not how it looks. And that's all that matters in this town." She turned for her bedroom.

"I was just trying to help," Violet called after Audrey, her voice breaking.

"I don't need your help," Audrey muttered, loud enough for Violet to hear.

Audrey's bedroom door opened and closed.

Violet looked down at the bowl of gumbo, her stomach a weave of knots.

She rose from the table, poured the soup back into the pot, and turned off the burner.

In the morning Violet expected Audrey to tell her that she needed to find another place to live. But Audrey said nothing as the two of them ate breakfast and got ready for work. Violet apologized and offered to make it right somehow and tell everyone that asking had been all her idea, but that was the last thing Audrey wanted Violet to do.

"There must be some way I can make it better," Violet said.

And Audrey said no, there wasn't.

They rode the streetcar without speaking and went their separate ways when they arrived at the studio. Violet worked late, arriving home after eight to an empty bungalow. She went to bed without seeing Audrey, but was unable to fall asleep until she heard Audrey's key in the lock sometime after midnight.

On the set the following day, she asked Bert what she should do—he, too, had heard about what she'd asked Miss Myrick. They were standing on the Forty by a flowing creek. The stunt double for Gerald O'Hara was preparing to jump a white horse over a fence, and Bert was there to make sure his costume matched perfectly—and stayed clean.

"Just let the matter dry up on its own and soon it will float away," Bert said. "That's what my mother says happens to gossip if you stop spreading it and stop listening to it."

"But everyone thinks Audrey put me up to asking!"

"I'm sure anybody whose opinion Audrey cares about knows she would never ask you to do that. You're new to this; she's not. They all know she's not. It will blow over, Vi. I think it already has. No one is talking about it today."

"She hates me."

"No, she doesn't."

"She's not talking to me!"

"Give her some time, Violet."

Violet felt fresh tears beginning to rim her eyes. She hadn't realized how much Audrey's friendship meant to her until the last few days. There was no one back in Montgomery like Audrey.

Violet's childhood friends were all getting married and having babies. They had nothing in common with Violet anymore and had already begun to drift away from her. She squeezed her eyes shut to force the tears to recede.

"Violet," Bert said, and he waited until she opened her eyes to look at him. "I'm going to tell you the same thing I told her."

"You talked to her about this?"

"She talked to me. She called me the night it happened."

"Oh!" Violet had heard Audrey talking on the phone after she'd put the uneaten gumbo away and gone to bed. She had assumed she'd been talking to the mysterious Vince.

"You were motivated by a desire to do something good for Audrey because you care about her. I think in the end that's what's important. And that's what she will remember."

Gratitude for Bert and his kind heart blossomed inside her, scaring her a little with its intensity. She suddenly remembered the sensation of Bert's strong arm around her waist and his hand in hers when they'd danced weeks before on a floor dusted with shimmering beach sand. A tightening deep within made her shudder slightly.

"All right?" he said.

She smiled and nodded.

"She'll get over it, Violet. Audrey isn't one to carry a grudge."

Bert was summoned then, as he often was when another scene was due to be shot.

As he walked away the stunt double on the horse attempted a practice jump and fell too early off the animal, onto the painted dirt.

The sun had already dipped below the western horizon when Violet made it back to the Mansion to type up the day's memos for Miss Myrick. It would be many more hours before she was finished, but that was the case for just about everyone associated with the film. Half a dozen secretaries were still at their typewriters or on the phone when Violet stepped inside. She had just started on her first memo when Audrey appeared at her desk.

"You going to be here awhile?"

She seemed to be a little less angry with her.

"Probably," Violet answered. "You?"

"An hour or so. Want to get something to eat after? There's something I need to tell you."

A lump instantly formed in Violet's throat. "Are you . . . going to ask me to find a new place to live?"

A tender smile broke across Audrey's face. "No, Violet. I'm not."

"All right, then."

An hour and a half later they were sitting at a booth at the Pig'n Whistle on Hollywood Boulevard, after ordering plates of fish and chips.

"Look," Audrey said, after the waiter had left. "I know you meant well the other day. I do. And I know I didn't handle it gracefully when I first found out. But I know why you did it. And even though I wish you hadn't, I know you wanted to make me happy."

Audrey's words were salve on a wound. "I'm so sorry I embarrassed you, Audrey. I'd give anything to take it all back."

"I'm the one who's sorry. I am sure I hurt you with what I said. And I wish I could take those words back, too. You're a good friend, Vi. I haven't had many of those in my life. Sometimes I forget you are different from most people I know here."

"I am?"

Their drinks arrived—two Coca-Colas with splashes of rum—and they each took a sip.

"Hollywood is full of people with dreams, and most of the time that makes it an exciting place, but it can also make it a lonely place," Audrey said. "In this town, you can be in a room full of beautiful people and still be alone."

"I really had no idea you didn't want to be in this movie," Violet said.

"It's not that I don't want to be in *Gone With the Wind*, Violet. It's . . ." Audrey's voice broke away as she searched for the right words. "It's that I don't want to spoil it."

"Spoil *Gone With the Wind*?"

Audrey smiled. "No. The magic. I don't want

133

to spoil the magic. You don't make serendipity happen. Your friends don't make it happen. It comes to you when you are in the right place at the right time. It happened to me once before, and that's how I know it can happen again. The first time, I was just where I'd been destined to be. It was as if my mother had been looking down on me from heaven that day and moved everything into place for me. I could practically feel her there in the coffee shop when Mr. Stiles discovered me. I don't know how to explain it, but I sense that's how it's going to happen again. I tried it the other way. I had screen tests after I lost the picture. I put myself forward with all those anonymous hopefuls in Central Casting. It didn't work. Don't you see? That way is not in the stars for me. I need to be like I was when I was a teenager."

"A waitress in a coffee shop?"

Audrey laughed at her naïveté. "It's not about the coffee shop, Violet. It's about who goes to the coffee shop expecting to get just coffee."

"So being a secretary at Selznick International instead of an extra is like being a waitress in a coffee shop?"

Audrey lifted her drink to her lips. "Something like that."

"So, what are you thinking will happen?"

Audrey drank from her glass and then set it back down on the table. "I'm thinking what happened before will happen again. If I just do my part, someone with the power to change everything is going to find me, when all they were expecting to find was a cup of coffee."

"I . . . I don't think it works that way for most people who want to be an actress."

"I'm not most people. I'm just me."

"What if it never happens?"

"Aunt Jo told me once that if something's meant to happen, it will."

The waiter arrived with their food and they were quiet for a moment as they began to eat.

"Did you always want to be a Hollywood star?" Violet crunched a french fry.

Audrey paused a moment before answering. "I've never really wanted to be a star. I just want to be wanted the way they are. Do you see how people fight over them? Mr. Selznick simply had to have Clark Gable to play Rhett. *Had* to have him. He was willing to hand over the movie to have him, Violet. That's how badly he wanted him for this film. He gave away half the profits to MGM so that they would release Clark Gable from his contract so that he could play Rhett. Can you imagine being wanted that way? Can you imagine what that must feel like?"

Violet could supply no answer. She couldn't imagine it. But her silent wonder surely led Audrey to believe she could. Audrey nodded as though Violet had answered, *Yes, I can absolutely imagine it. And it's wonderful.*

TEN

April 1939

Audrey doubted they would be able to hear the melodic trills of a songbird over the clatter of the streetcar, honking taxis, and the music floating out through nightclub doors, but Bert was strangely optimistic as he walked just a few feet ahead of her and Violet, his head tilted slightly upward.

The April evening on Sunset Boulevard was warm and fine and alive.

Bert had suggested a nightingale hunt that afternoon at lunch, and this time Audrey had said yes.

"But let's bring Violet," she'd said. "She would enjoy it, I think. And I'd like to do something nice for her."

A month had passed since Violet's awkward meddling. The Twelve Oaks barbecue scene had long since been shot with much studio fanfare and apparently a shortage of pretty girls. Audrey had typed the memo herself. Selznick had been unhappy with the "homely" extras Central Casting had sent him for the barbecue scene. She counted her lucky stars that she hadn't been thrown in with that lot of so-called unattractive women. The rumored homeliness of the female extras hadn't mattered so much for filming the frenzied evacuation of Atlanta, of course, a complex affair as Violet had described it, with explosions and mayhem one minute and then drowsy calm and inactivity the next. The Atlanta Bazaar scene had been reshot, too, Fleming style, with less of an eye toward authenticity and more emphasis on spectacle, but with the same unremarkable extras from Central. Audrey was happy to have missed out on being in all three scenes and wouldn't have wanted to be cast in them if she'd been asked.

Bert was amenable to Violet coming along to hunt for the elusive nightingale, and Violet had been as enthused as a schoolgirl when Audrey asked her on the streetcar bound for home if she wanted to go with them.

"You do know in all likelihood we probably won't find it," Audrey had said.

"I don't care," Violet had answered. "It just sounds like fun. Looking for something that's not supposed to be there."

Audrey was actually glad an impromptu invitation had come up for that evening. Vince, who was still feeling bad about the embarrassing lunch at the Wilshire, had recently met a new talent scout that he thought Audrey should meet. He and his fiancée had been planning a party that Audrey would be invited to, but it had fallen through when Vince was called away to an important meeting in San Francisco. Strolling Sunset, looking for a songbird, was far better than sitting at home, thinking about a hoped-for introduction that wasn't taking place.

Bert turned toward them now, his face beaming. "The first time I heard the nightingale, it was in the fronds of that tree." He pointed to a large potted palm as he approached the corner of Sunset and Wilcox five or six buildings away. "I'm pretty sure I heard it again at the next corner, too."

Audrey linked her arm with Violet's, charmed by the general tone of Bert's delight. His animated wonder was like a tonic, in light of recent events. "So, has Bert told you what the big deal is with this nightingale?" she murmured to Violet.

"They don't live in the United States," Violet replied at full volume, obviously proud she remembered this detail.

"Indeed. They are interlopers just like you and me, Vi. This little thing came a long way to get where it wanted to be. And of all the places to go it came to Hollywood! That's my kind of dreamer."

"Oh, he couldn't have flown here all the way from Europe," Bert said with a laugh, any deeper meaning to Audrey's words lost on him. "Someone had to have brought him over."

"And then they just let him go?" Violet frowned. "That seems a little cruel."

"I can think of worse things than being set free," Audrey said softly.

"The sad thing is," Bert continued, "he won't have anyone to mate with. I think that's why I've heard him singing. The bird's looking for another nightingale. He's singing for her. Calling out to her."

"On Sunset Boulevard?" Violet asked, wide-eyed. "In the middle of a busy street?"

Bert shrugged. "He must have heard something here that sounded like another nightingale, and so he keeps coming back to find that other bird. He doesn't know that he probably won't find it. He just knows that he must keep trying. It's in his nature."

A wisp of a memory fell over Audrey at that moment, vivid and sweet. She suddenly recalled her mother sitting on her bed as she tucked Audrey in, and told her a story.

"Once upon a time there was an emperor who lived far away in China, and in his beautiful garden there was a very ordinary nightingale. . . ."

"My mom told me a story once about an emperor and a nightingale," Audrey said, almost to herself, as the remembered moment swirled about her.

Bert dropped back a step to join Audrey and Violet, pleasure in his eyes. "I know that story. That's a fairy tale by Hans Christian Andersen."

"I think I read that one when I was a child," Violet interjected, but her tone was one of doubt.

"It's about an emperor who learns there is a

plain brown nightingale singing in his garden, and that everyone raves about," Audrey went on. "He commands the bird to his court to sing for him and it does. But then he receives a mechanical bird as a gift, right?"

"Yes." Bert's gaze was only on Audrey. "The mechanical bird is magnificent and sings whenever the emperor turns its key. No one listens to the plain nightingale anymore, even though the mechanical bird can only sing the one song. Everyone is so taken with the jeweled bird, the plain nightingale is banished from court. Years later, the mechanical bird has stopped working and the emperor is dying. Then he hears his old friend the living nightingale singing just outside his window. Her beautiful songs chase death away, and the emperor demands she stay perched at his side always. But she convinces him that she sings only to give pleasure to those who will listen, and she asks for nothing in return except her freedom."

"Yes," Audrey whispered. The single memory of her mother was now fuller somehow, as though Audrey had just remembered a thousand moments with her mother instead of one. "I think my mother loved that story."

"It's . . . it's such a lovely tale. You tell it wonderfully, Bert," Violet said, but a second passed before he seemed to have heard the compliment.

"You've heard a nightingale before, haven't you? In the wild," Audrey said to Bert. "That's how you know what it sounds like. That's how you recognized the one you've heard here."

"I have." Bert's voice was laced with the same kind of remembered tranquillity. "My dad and I spent two weeks in Europe the summer I was thirteen. We heard one singing at twilight in the Black Forest in Germany. The sound of it brought my father to tears."

They were now at the intersection. Bert looked up at a stocky palm planted in a massive clay pot. Its fronds extended from its tall trunk like bizarre windmill blades. People passed the three of them, laughing and talking. Someone was playing a jazz piano in a club across the street.

"I heard the nightingale here," Bert said. "In this tree."

For several long moments they stood, heads bent back a bit, their ears straining to catch the faintest sounds of a songbird's call to its soul mate.

The highest fronds on the tree swayed on the curl of a breeze and were lifted upward. The night sky above was diamond speckled, glittering with a dusting of unearthly brilliance.

"I can almost imagine I hear it," Audrey said as she closed her eyes against the cold beauty of the stars shimmering over Sunset Boulevard.

Many minutes passed before Violet said she

was freezing, and perhaps they could go to a club to get a drink and come back another time.

The image of Audrey's mother had receded back to its dark resting place while they had been listening. That, the absence of the bird, and the failed party at Vince's left Audrey feeling chilled and empty.

"I have a better idea." She waited for a lull in traffic and then led them across the street to a liquor store. Inside she bought whiskey, sweet vermouth, and bitters and placed the bottles inside her oversized purse. They walked back outside and she hailed a cab.

"My treat," she said as they climbed into the vehicle. She instructed the driver to take them to Culver City.

An hour later the three friends were inside the darkened wardrobe building at the studio, drinking slightly mixed Manhattans out of coffee cups as they sat on the floor against the wall, surrounded by ruffled gowns and Confederate war uniforms stained with counterfeit blood.

It had been easy convincing the guard at the gate that they had unfinished duties for the next day's shoot. Pockets of people worked the midnight hours all the time during the height of filming.

Audrey, now on her third cocktail and enamored of the costumes all around them, turned to Bert. "I would love to have your job." Her words sounded slushy in her ears. "I'd take your job over mine in a blink if things were different."

"Different?" Bert mumbled.

"This department wouldn't work for me," she said, the alcohol in her veins making it difficult to gesture in a way that included the entirety of where they sat. "This is not a coffee shop."

"Coffee shop," Bert echoed, a frown on his face.

"Violet knows what I mean, don't you, Vi?"

Violet's head lolled a bit to the side as she leaned against the wall. "And this sure isn't coffee," she said as she stared at her mug.

Audrey stood on unsteady feet and walked toward a display of items that waited in readiness for morning light. She reached for Scarlett O'Hara's feathered, curtain-dress hat on a shelf and set it on her head; it had been used in filming earlier in the day and was still out of its box for the next day's shoot. She fit the strap under her chin and let the gold, fringed tail trail down her right shoulder.

"All these dresses and hats and hoops," she said dreamily. "They take you to another place, another world. They can make you believe in an instant you're not who you've always been."

Bert gazed at the hat on Audrey's head, half admiring how it looked on her and half concerned, perhaps, that it was no longer on its shelf. It was difficult to tell.

"They're just costumes, Audrey," Violet said. The word came out *coshtumes*.

"They are not. Don't be so unimaginative, Violet."

"That hat suits you, Audrey!" Bert said, saluting Audrey with his cup.

Audrey scanned the room for a mirror. There was none. No one tried on clothes in the storage room. "I'll have to take your word for it, Bertie."

He laughed and closed his eyes. "Bertie. My mother used to call me that."

"I like Bertie," Violet said, and then swallowed a sip from her cup.

"You know, sometimes you just have to do what you must to get what you want." Audrey fingered the hat's soft fringe that fell past her collar to her breast and, underneath that, her beating heart. "If you must have the three hundred dollars to pay the taxes on Tara, then you do what you have to. You just do it. Everyone knows that. Even Melanie Hamilton knew that."

Violet looked up at Audrey with a furrowed brow. "Melanie never would have done what Scarlett did. Stealing her sister's fiancé like that."

"Oh, really?" Audrey said, grinning. "Think you know Melanie, do you?"

Violet considered Audrey's question for only a moment. "She wouldn't have done it." Her words slurred off her tongue.

"Is that what you think? She wouldn't marry a

man she didn't love to save her home and all the people in it? You don't think she would have done whatever she had to do to hold on to what she loved?"

Violet swished her head back and forth. "Scarlett was the conniving one; Melanie was the good one."

Bert opened his eyes, interested, it seemed, in the little debate.

Despite the three Manhattans she'd consumed, Audrey felt invigorated with the hat on her head and Violet's challenges before her. "And good people never do false things, eh, Vi?"

"Of course they don't."

"So when Rhett Butler makes up a story that Ashley was at a brothel with him instead of at a raid on Shanty Town, and Melanie not only owns the lie but embellishes it, that's not doing what she has to do, even if it is false?"

Violet struggled to form words. "That . . . that's different. Ashley had been shot and—"

"Ashley was on that raid. It was illegal, what he did. People got killed. And sweet Melanie lied about it."

"To save her husband!"

"So, you agree with me!"

Bert was staring at her now in drunken awe. Violet gazed away into the darkness, a look of puzzlement on her face.

"You see?" Audrey said as she readjusted the

hat on her head. "Sometimes you have to do something drastic to keep what is yours." She leaned over, holding the hat on her head, and lifted her drink up off the floor. She downed the rest of its contents and then studied the empty vessel in her hand.

"Give me your cups," she said to Violet and Bert, as she reached for the whiskey bottle.

And they did.

ELEVEN

When Violet awakened, her first thought was how painfully thirsty she was. With her eyes still closed she groped for the glass of water she usually kept by her bedside, but it wasn't there. Her head was pounding, but she forced her eyes open. The bedside table wasn't there, either.

She wasn't in her bed.

She wasn't in her bedroom. And, for a moment, sleep returned to her.

Then there was a voice, hoarse and anxious at her ear, and a hand on her shoulder, shaking her.

"Wake up, Violet!"

She peered up at the voice. Bert. He was in her living room. She lay sprawled across the sofa.

"Where's Audrey?" he said.

Violet struggled to rise, and Bert helped her to a sitting position.

"Where's Audrey, Violet?"

She reached for her forehead to silence the pounding inside her brain.

"Where is Audrey?"

"I don't know. . . ." Violet muttered as she made an effort to get to her feet. Again Bert assisted her. She looked toward the hallway.

"I've already looked in her bedroom!" Bert said, and then he cursed softly.

Violet had never heard Bert use language like that. She'd never seen him angry.

She suddenly remembered it was Wednesday morning. "What time is it?"

"It's eight thirty. Where's her bag from last night?"

Water and aspirin. Violet had to have them. She was already an hour late for work, but she couldn't even begin to picture herself getting ready to go without either one. And she had no idea where Audrey's purse was or why Bert was asking for it.

"I need water." She tottered toward the kitchen.

"I have to find her!" Bert sounded desperate.

Violet didn't want to hear it. "If she's not in her bedroom, I don't know where she is. I have to get ready for work."

Bert reached out for her. "You have to help me, Violet! She has the hat! She took that hat!"

His hand, tight on her arm, steadied Violet as the scattered memories of the previous night attempted to reassemble themselves in her mind.

"Did she leave for work already?" Violet stumbled into the kitchen. A pot of coffee on the stove was still warm, and there was an open bottle of aspirin on the counter next to it. And a note. Bert snatched up the piece of paper and Violet read it in his hands.

Vi:
Left early. A lot to do today. The coffee's strong!

A.

"I've got to go," Bert said. "I'm sorry I can't wait for you." He turned and dashed out the front door before Violet could say a word.

She poured a glass of water and washed down two aspirin before shuffling to her bedroom to change into fresh clothes and run a comb through her hair. Snippets of the previous night's escapades started to filter back to her and she pushed them away. She didn't want to think about what she had done or said or how much she'd had to drink last night.

Her head was still throbbing, but thankfully less so than when Bert had shaken her awake, as she raced to hail the first taxi she saw.

When she finally reached Miss Myrick on the set, she was more than two hours late and full of apologies for having overslept. The advisor, however, was distracted by another, more pressing detail and didn't seem to care much about Violet's tardiness. The curtain-dress hat was missing and no one in wardrobe knew where it was. Violet scanned the room for Bert, but none of the wardrobe people were on the set. They were all off looking for the hat, which was needed for the day's filming.

An oppressive foreboding enveloped Violet and she ached to speak with Bert to make sure that he hadn't gotten into trouble, that he hadn't been fired. She couldn't remember leaving the studio last night. She couldn't remember how she and Audrey had gotten home. Despite the aspirin and the coffee, her brain still felt as though it were full of cotton. She swallowed two more aspirin with another cup of coffee.

When the hat could not be located, its spare, which wasn't quite finished, had to be compared with footage from the day before to make sure that it would be an exact duplicate. The filming schedule was off now and the shooting of the scene with Scarlett walking down a dusty Atlanta street during Reconstruction had to be rescheduled for another time. Violet at last saw Bert when this announcement was given to the cast and crew. A supervisor was telling him he was damn lucky a spare had been made and that he needed to be more responsible or he would be let go; it was as simple as that. A wardrobe piece didn't just disappear overnight. That hat had been Bert's responsibility.

Clearly, his supervisor didn't know Bert had let two lady friends into the wardrobe building the previous night and then had proceeded to get plastered with them. Audrey should never have suggested they come here and get drunk. It had been a terrible idea. Violet's heart ached for Bert as she watched him stand there and receive the reprimand. And as she kept her eyes on him and the second dose of aspirin began to take effect, bits and pieces of the previous night began to materialize in her head, as if a window shade were being slowly raised and light was spilling in.

Audrey had had the hat on her head when they were arguing about why Scarlett married Frank Kennedy—no, about whether Melanie was just like Scarlett.

Audrey had made them another round of drinks and then she had left to go find a restroom.

Violet and Bert were still sitting on the floor with their backs against the wall and drinks in their hands. His gaze had lingered on the door after Audrey had gone and he'd looked a little sad.

Violet remembered trying to find something to talk about that would cheer him up. So she told him about the time she and a childhood friend had found a nest of abandoned baby cardinals.

Bert had turned his head slowly toward her and said how beautiful cardinals were and how he wished they lived in California. Violet tried to think of the names of some of the other birds that lived back home in Alabama. He had been staring at Violet with an odd look on his face, as if he was trying to figure something out. And then out of the blue he'd said, "You're quite pretty, Violet. You're actually quite pretty."

Just hearing it again in her head made Violet's mouth drop open.

She remembered that he'd spoken as if he had never really noticed her before, because up until then all he could see was Audrey. And now suddenly she wasn't some invisible girl trailing along in Audrey's shadow.

Violet had answered back, "Do you really think so?" He'd brushed away a lock of hair that was resting just on her brow and said, "Absolutely." His fingers on her forehead were as tender as any touch she had ever received from a man.

It had been a long time since anyone had called her pretty. Franklin had been the last, but the surgery to remove the menacing growth inside her had changed the way he looked at her. And it had changed the way she looked at men. She'd been wondering since then if it was possible a man could love her in spite of her damaged body. The way Bert had looked at her when he told her she was pretty made her think that with him, it was possible.

They had clinked their cups together and were drinking from them when Audrey reappeared and said she'd run into a few friends who were working late on the Atlanta mansion staircase, and they'd offered to drive them all home.

The window shade seemed to stall a bit then, and Violet was not sure what had happened after that. She and Audrey had accepted the ride—she recalled that—and she remembered that Bert decided to sleep on the floor in the costume building. He had no doubt awakened early, stiff and sore, and noticed that the hat Audrey had been wearing was missing, and then had dashed to the bungalow in a taxi in his desperate search for it.

Later, at lunch, she sought out Bert.

"Did you find Audrey?" she asked, knowing full well it didn't matter if he had. There was no hat.

"I did. She doesn't remember what she did with it," Bert said tonelessly, plainly aching from more than just a hangover. "She thought she took it off before she left. I can't believe she lost it."

"It's not your fault this happened, Bert. I saw the look on your face when Audrey had that hat on. You wanted her to take it off. You were worried about it even then."

"I just wish I could remember," he muttered, shaking his head.

"Don't you remember anything about last night?" Violet asked gently, wondering if he recalled telling her she was pretty.

"I remember I got smashed. Look, I'd better get back. I'm lucky to still have a job after what Audrey did."

He gathered his tray and rose from the table. Violet reached for his arm. "Maybe the next time we go out to look for your nightingale, it can be just you and me."

Bert studied her for a moment. "You would want to?"

She felt herself blush. "Very much."

Her reaction seemed to surprise him as much as her suggestion did. He had been under Audrey's spell for so long, it seemed he'd forgotten there were other women on the planet. "Sure," he said slowly, as if needing to reorient himself with the idea that someone other than Audrey might win his affections.

Bert left her to head back to the wardrobe department. As he walked away, the shade on the window in her mind began to creep up again and she suddenly remembered that after Bert had passed out on the floor, she and Audrey had tottered over to Stage 11. Crew members that Audrey knew were working late to prepare for the filming of Mammy and Melanie's long and sad walk up the stairs after Bonnie Butler's death. They had offered to drive them home.

Violet remembered Audrey singing "Blue Skies" on the way to the bungalow, and her vomiting onto the sidewalk after the men drove off, and Audrey sashaying into Violet's bedroom, not her own, and insisting it was hers. She remembered Audrey collapsing onto Violet's bed and her big purse and coat falling to the floor next to Violet's slippers. She couldn't remember why she had chosen the couch over Audrey's bed, other than that Audrey's bed was a perpetual mess of unmade sheets and discarded clothes.

But the rest of the night was still a blur.

Violet didn't see Audrey at all that afternoon; her roommate had been summoned to take notes for one of the art directors in another building, and that was where she'd spent the day.

Violet returned home alone, hoping to find that Audrey had arrived ahead of her, but the bungalow was dark when Violet unlocked the door. She fed the cat and then opened a can of tomato soup, hoping that the warm liquid would chase away the last residue of the headache she had fought all day.

She went into her bedroom to change into her pajamas while the soup heated, and frowned at her unmade bed. Violet started to yank the sheets to pull them taut when her toe kicked something that lay under Audrey's coat on the floor. She lifted the coat and her breath caught in her throat.

Peeking just outside of Audrey's oversized purse was a flash of gold fringe and green velvet.

Violet knelt down and gently freed the hat from the purse's confines. She rose quickly and turned toward the bedroom door. Bert would be home now, and she could already imagine the look on his face when she phoned to tell him she'd found Audrey's bag and the hat was inside it. She had taken just one step when she stopped.

Violet stood for several long moments, staring at the hat as other options began to formulate in her head.

Was turning it back over to Bert the wisest thing to do?

What was the kindest thing she could do for Bert?

For herself?

Even for Audrey?

What made the most sense in the great scheme of things?

Valentino wandered into the room and looked at the rooster feathers on the hat with keen interest. The cat meowed.

"Go away." Violet shooed him out of the room and closed the door. Her heart began to pound as she looked for a place to hide the hat while she contemplated the best course of action. Then she saw the box of winter clothes she was planning to send back home because she didn't need them in California.

A solution presented itself as she stared at the box. A terrible, brilliant solution.

Violet pulled out half of the wool sweaters and pants and gently laid the hat atop the remaining clothes. Then she replaced what she had taken out. She taped the box shut, lifted it, and opened the bedroom door.

"Meow?" Valentino sat inches from the door, his tail curled about his front paws.

She hoisted the box in her arms and checked her wristwatch. The post office closed late on Wednesdays. If she called a cab, she'd just make it.

While she waited for the taxi she penned a short note that she would mail separately, letting her mother know she was sending to the house a box of clothes she didn't need in such warm weather and which could be taken directly up to her room to be stored until she came home for a visit.

She sealed the envelope, turned off the flame under the soup, and grabbed her purse.

A minute later she was standing at the curb, waiting for the taxi, telling herself over and over and over that what she was about to do was necessary.

Right.

Good.

Hollywood
March 10, 2012

Elle Garceau awakens to the sound of her granddaughters' laughter and the yipping of a little dog. She turns over in bed to look at her cell phone on the nightstand. It's not quite six a.m., and they were all up past midnight. Elle sighs and half grins. The girls are still acclimating to Pacific Standard Time. It wasn't that long ago that her body clock had to make the same adjustment. It will take time, as many adaptations do.

Another voice, low in tone, is gently shushing the girls as they make their way past Elle's closed door to the condo's kitchen. Her son, Daniel, is also awake.

She rises from bed, grabs a robe, and opens the plantation shutters in her bedroom, letting in the palest predawn light. Observing from ten flights up the arrival of each new day has been helping Elle come to terms with being single after fifty years of marriage, as well as readjusting to life in California, emptying the beloved bungalow, and learning to dream and think in English again.

It has been a long time since she's lived in a Los Angeles high-rise. The past few days spent dismantling the bungalow have reminded her just how long. So many fragments of yesteryear were tucked inside her mother's old house, as well as a secret or two. Elle went to sleep the night before, hopeful that the hat her mother kept hidden away for decades would be found and returned without much notice. It was one of the few things in the bungalow that didn't belong in the blazing light of an ordinary day.

Until recently, Elle had hoped she might be able to continue putting off the emptying of the little house, but her son's job offer with Disney changed all that. The little house will be the perfect place for Daniel, Nicola, and the girls to make a new start in America. The bungalow has always been a good place to begin a new life. She's glad there will be a stretch of time when the rooms inside will again be inhabited by the young.

By the time Elle uses the toilet and runs a comb through her hair, the condo is quiet again. When she enters the kitchen her son regards her apologetically.

"*Je suis désolé,*" he says. "*Nous t'avons réveillés.*"

"Don't worry. I don't mind getting up early," Elle replies in English as she looks about for her granddaughters. "Did you send the girls back to bed?"

"Nicola took them down so the dog can pee." He pours a cup of coffee from a French press carafe and hands it to her. "Oh. I got a voice mail yesterday that I didn't see until this morning. The owner of the resale shop called and said she found that hat. I'll text her that I'll come around today or tomorrow."

Elle looks up from her cup. "I can swing by and get it."

"I'm the one who put it in the car with all the other stuff. Nicola and I will get it."

"But you have so much running around to do today. I don't mind."

Daniel refreshes his own coffee cup. "You'll have the girls and the dog with you today, though. And there's still so much to do at the bungalow. You've got plenty on your plate already."

"Yes, but . . ."

"But what? It's my fault it got mixed up with the wrong pile of boxes. I'll take care of it. It's just a hat, right?"

"Yes." Elle nods as she sips her coffee.

It's just a hat.

———⫸◆⫷———

TWELVE

May 1939

The soldiers in tattered and dirty uniforms lay in row after row on the back Forty. Some raised an arm in supplication as they called out, and some lay still as if asleep or dead. Some weren't men at all, but rather dummies dressed in military garb. When one of these raised an arm, it was because a living man next to it was working a lever with one hand while reaching out for Scarlett O'Hara with the other as she walked through a train yard strewn with wounded and defeated Confederates.

A camera attached to a construction crane borrowed from the Long Beach shipyard was pulled slowly back, more and more and more, as the lens took in the nearly one thousand extras sent over from Central Casting. Audrey had heard Selznick wanted fifteen hundred men, and was sent only nine hundred and seventy-seven because of a pay dispute, hence the nearly seven hundred dummies.

The May sun was bright and brassy, and Audrey blotted away the sweat on her neck with a tissue. She didn't mind being out in the heat of the day. She was glad that filming had picked up to such a frenetic pace that she and several other secretaries in the pool had been tasked with helping the team of assistant directors working six days a week to finish shooting on time. Victor Fleming had collapsed from exhaustion a few weeks earlier and had only recently returned. In his absence a third director, Sam Wood, had been brought in, and because the completion date was just a month way, he had stayed on. Scenes were being shot simultaneously all over the studio grounds and everyone was working ten-hour days, six days a week.

Audrey watched Vivien Leigh as Scarlett O'Hara continue her search for Dr. Meade. She imagined herself in the drab calico dress, wearing a straw hat from happier days, picking her way through a thousand injured soldiers who embodied a thousand crushed dreams. She closed her eyes and could very nearly sense the hands of the dying reaching out to her, to speak of what they had lost.

The sensation was not foreign to her. The past month had been one long reminder that she was surrounded by mementos of what might have been or used to be. Her strained friendship with Bert had been the hardest development to make sense of. For the past five years he had been her closest friend and confidant. Losing that hat had put a wedge between them that she could not budge. She had apologized repeatedly, even though she could not remember having left with it that night. And since it hadn't turned up anywhere outside wardrobe, it seemed more likely to her that it had been lost in the labyrinth of costume shelves. Bert was no longer angry with her, but he seemed distant, as if he'd decided she could not be trusted and he needed to create a wall of protection from her. Bert had been the one constant in her life that had nothing to do with her acting career, or hoped-for second chances or providential assignations. He was just a kind, ordinary man who made her believe ordinary happiness was possible. She had known for quite a while that he was a bit infatuated with her, but she had always been careful not to encourage him in that way. She valued his companionship too much to mess it up with romance. Besides, she did not deserve a man like Bert. But she did deserve his friendship, didn't she? And she missed him. She wished they hadn't come back to the wardrobe building to soak themselves in Manhattans that night. If they had just gone to a club, the hat never would have turned up missing, Bert wouldn't have almost lost his job, and she'd still feel she mattered to him.

The junior director, one of eight who was helping to manage the hundreds of extras and whom she was assisting that day, called her name. Audrey was yanked out of her reverie.

"Take these hats back to the costume tent and have wardrobe dirty them up, for God's sake. These men have been in war, not a garden party."

Audrey took the offered basket of too-clean uniform hats and headed over to one of six costume tents set up on the dirt just outside the make-believe train yard. Bert was standing behind a long table of extra pants, shirts, and tattered jackets as she neared the first tent. She could have gone to one of the other wardrobe assistants but she headed for Bert. He had been tagging clothes but he looked up as she came closer. She thought she detected a smidgeon of old desire in his eyes.

"Hello, Bert."

He smiled cordially as he returned the greeting. "So, how are you?"

"All right." She handed him the box. "I've been instructed to tell you these aren't dirty enough. Do you have any others? Dirtier ones?"

Bert looked inside the box. "All the other hats have been assigned out." He looked up at her. "If you want to come back in a little bit I can do something on the fly."

She smiled. "You going to take them out behind the tent and throw them on the ground and trample them?"

He grinned back. "I am."

"Let's go, then. It sounds like fun."

A few minutes later, the hats had been tossed onto the ground and Audrey kicked at the brims while Bert batted them with the flat edge of a shovel.

"You still mad at me?" she asked.

"I was never mad at you, Audrey. I was mad at

myself. Mad that I got so stinking drunk I couldn't even remember what happened."

She ground a brim with the heel of her shoe. "That was my fault, too."

"Nobody forced me to drink, Audrey. All you did was pour."

They were quiet as they worked to ruin the hats.

"But you're different around me now."

He held the shovel over a hat and looked at her. "I was going to say the same thing."

"Are we changing, Bert?"

"Changing into what?"

She couldn't explain it. She knew only that he was drifting from her and the thought saddened her. "I don't know."

Bert whacked a hat and little clouds of dust swirled about it. "Do you still want it, Audrey? Do you still want to be a star?"

Vince had asked her the same thing a few days earlier. He was still eager to help her but he had seemed in need of confirmation that she still wanted to do it her way, relying on chance for her luck to change.

Tears threatened to spill, and she kicked the hat she had dirtied over to Bert so that he could pound it with the shovel. "I don't know how to want anything else."

That night Violet made fried chicken, mashed potatoes, and succotash for dinner. Several nights had passed since they had eaten together, and Audrey basked in the comforting taste of home-style cooking and her roommate's company.

"Which set were you on today?" Violet asked. "Was it a good day?"

Audrey forked some of the buttered vegetables into her mouth. "I was on the pull-back shot from eight until six. It was a long, hot day. But I think Fleming got what he wanted. I saw Bert."

Violet looked up from her plate. "Did you?"

"I haven't seen him much lately. I was thinking maybe he hadn't forgiven me for losing that hat."

Violet slid her knife back into the chicken breast. "Oh. That was more than a month ago. I'm sure he's gotten over it."

"I suppose he has. I don't know. He seems different these days."

Violet popped the piece of chicken into her mouth. "Did he tell you he's fixing up an old truck he bought?"

"A truck? To drive?"

"When he's done with it, he said he'll come by the bungalow in the mornings on his way to work and take us home at the end of the day. He said he doesn't like it that you and I have to ride the streetcar and bus after dark. Isn't that sweet?"

It seemed odd to Audrey for Violet to tell her something about Bert that she didn't already know. "So, when did he tell you this?"

Violet waved her hand to shoo away any notion

that she'd learned this news via some kind of complex situation. "Oh, we just grabbed a sandwich at Newberry's on Sunday night after he got back from his mother's in Santa Barbara. You were out."

"Oh?"

"He's keeping it at a friend's place while he works on it on weekends. Won't it be nice not to have to ride the bus at night? Bert says it won't be any trouble to pick us up. It's on his way."

Audrey swirled a lima bean in a trail of butter. "It will be very nice, but we're not on his way. He's just being kind. As always."

Violet chewed her food and then swallowed, a perplexed look on her face. "He said he'd be happy to do it."

"Then that will be great, I guess."

A few minutes of silence passed between them.

"You know, Audrey," Violet said, "I've been thinking about what you said when we were at the Pig'n Whistle last month. About how at the coffee shop all those years ago you felt as if your mother somehow orchestrated that event from heaven. It seemed fanciful to me at first, but the more I've thought about it, the more I think maybe you're right. You were discovered through providential timing the first time. Who says it can't happen again that way?"

Audrey couldn't remember the last time someone had affirmed the feeling she had deep inside that her path wasn't going to be like everyone else's. Perhaps no one ever had. "You don't know how wonderful it is to hear you say that. The few people who know what I really want think I'm hopelessly unrealistic. Well, Bert doesn't, I guess. He just thinks I gave up too soon on the conventional way."

Violet considered this for a moment. "Yes, well, he wasn't around when you were discovered the first time, was he?"

Audrey laughed lightly. "No. He was still living at home then."

"There you go."

"I don't want to be known as the has-been who auditions for roles and never gets a part. I couldn't handle that, Vi. I don't want to be the one who wants. I want to be the one who is wanted."

Violet reached across the table to squeeze her arm in a comforting gesture of solidarity. "Of course you do."

THIRTEEN

June 1939

Known simply as the Paddock, it was built to represent the most desolate corner of battle-weary Tara. The somber, decidedly monochromatic set was the backdrop for the scene in which Scarlett O'Hara would finally get the impassioned kiss from Ashley Wilkes that she'd always wanted. The director's instructions to Vivien Leigh and Leslie Howard were that they were to make it seem, for just a fragment of time, as though reckless escape was all that was left to them. But then Ashley, pulling himself away from Scarlett, was to take a firmer hold of the one true thing that ruined survivors of war could still cling to: He was to remind Scarlett that honor still belonged to them. Not only that, but Tara, though beaten down and drained of its beauty, was still hers as well. Ashley was to tell Scarlett that she loved Tara more than him, though she may not know it.

It was a difficult, emotionally electrified scene, and it was not the first time Violet and Miss Myrick had stood just off to the side to watch it being shot. The same scene had been attempted nearly a month earlier. Countless takes had been made over a twelve-hour day, but technical difficulties and Mr. Howard's inability to consistently deliver Ashley's lines resulted in not even one take that was good enough for the production room.

Today, on the twenty-fourth of June, with mere days left to finish shooting the picture, the Paddock was again ready for the Technicolor cameras. Violet and Miss Myrick arrived after the morning rehearsal and the recording of the "wild tracks"—the sounds of the set when it's quiet and also when there's activity, but with no accompanying image. Violet had been told that background sounds shifted as the camera moved and even the light fixtures emitted sound. The wild tracks would help the sound editor make sense of the ambient noise during post-filming editing.

Finally, a bit before three in the afternoon, the first of twenty-seven takes of the Paddock scene was shot. Miss Myrick wasn't needed after the first three or four, and she dismissed Violet to take care of a few memos. But before Violet headed back to the main lot, Miss Myrick handed her a piece of paper with just one paragraph typed in its center.

"I want you to come with me to this." Miss Myrick nodded at the piece of paper. "See you tomorrow." Then she turned to a group of set dressers who needed her opinion on something.

Violet read the piece of paper in her hand:

In gratitude for your suffering efforts and courtesy during the Long Siege of Atlanta, and in celebration of the conclusion of the damned thing, we request the pleasure of your company at a little party to be given on Stage 5 immediately after Tuesday's shooting, June 27th.

It was signed by Vivien Leigh, Olivia de Havilland, Clark Gable, Leslie Howard, and Victor Fleming.

Violet had not been expecting an invitation to the cast party, a festive event after a movie's principal filming that no one from the secretary pool usually went to. Violet wondered if wardrobe would be invited and if Bert would be there. Her heart warmed at the thought that perhaps he would be told he could come as well.

Bert had begun to occupy Violet's every spare mental moment. She could not chase him away from her thoughts, nor did she want to. She was falling for him, harder than she had ever fallen for anyone. The long-ago fascination she'd had for Franklin seemed childish and shallow in comparison, and she could not help but nourish the pull she felt toward Bert, especially after he had opened up to her.

Violet had invited Bert over for ham and redeye gravy a few nights earlier, when Audrey had been at a movie Violet hadn't wanted to see. She had felt a bit guilty about inviting him, knowing he was most likely expecting Audrey to be there, too. It wasn't as if she'd said Audrey would be there when she knew she wouldn't be; she just didn't say it would be the two of them. He had appeared to be only momentarily distracted by Audrey's absence. Violet had asked him to tell her more about the birds he loved and his family, since she could tell these were both close to his heart—the place she wanted to be. She had learned that Bert was the oldest in his family, that his two younger sisters were eighteen and nineteen. She also learned that Bert's father, Henry, had seen such horrible things in the Great War that when he came home after the war ended, he had to find something beautiful to spend his spare thoughts on so that his mind wouldn't return to visions of the men he had killed or the comrades he had seen blown to bits.

"I don't think he'd looked at birds much before then, or even thought about them," Bert had said. "But he'd spent hours watching them from his hospital window while he recovered from shrapnel injuries. And I guess when you're lying in a bed after months of marching and shooting other men and watching friends die, you look for any way you can to reconnect with the person you were before you put on an Army uniform. The birds he saw from that hospital window in Germany were the same ones he saw in California. At least that's how they looked to him. And that had astonished him. He told me it helped him begin to heal, and not just from his physical wounds."

Violet had offered Bert a second helping of ham, and he'd continued.

"I was six when my father finally came home from the war. He got his teaching job back at the

171

high school, and he started watching sandpipers on the beach and cormorants on the cliffs above the sea and the swallows that come to the mission at San Juan Capistrano every year. Everywhere he went, he took me with him. I grew up seeing magic in the way birds live and move and communicate with each other, because he saw it. When I was thirteen, Dad and I went on a bird-watching trip to Europe, so he could make peace with the places he had been to and what he'd had to do there, and he wanted me to be a part of it. He had a heart attack a few months after I graduated from high school. His doctor thought it was caused by shrapnel that over the years had slowly traveled to his heart. I'd just started a job as an errand boy at MGM studios in Hollywood when I got the telegram from my mother."

Tears had sprung to Violet's eyes when he'd shared this.

The studio job hadn't been what Bert wanted to do with the rest of his life, but it had been a place to begin, he'd said. Over a dessert of lemon chiffon pie, Bert had shared with Violet something he hadn't told anyone else yet. Not even Audrey. He'd recently decided he wanted to go to college and study ornithology and then travel to faraway places to photograph birds for professional field guides.

"I don't know how or when I will make it happen," he'd said. "College is expensive, and working eight hours a day doesn't leave me with much free time. But it's always there in the back of my mind. I've always had a longing to do something with my camera besides just take pictures for myself, and I'd like to honor my dad somehow for what he did and who he was to me."

It had been a tender, revealing moment, and Violet had replayed it over and over in her mind because he had shared this new idea of his with no one else but her.

It felt as if he'd kissed her. Passionately.

Violet now walked back to the Mansion, contemplating how her workday would change when Miss Myrick returned to Georgia. She wouldn't be seeing Bert during the day anymore unless it was at the commissary at lunch-time. In fact, nothing about her day would seem very exciting after filming ended and Miss Myrick went home.

The secretary pool was quiet—it was a Saturday, and only those directly involved with the frantic effort to film the last few scenes had been called in to work, plus a few who were already tackling a mountain of correspondence for Selznick's next film, *Rebecca*. Audrey was at her station, typing at a gentle pace. Her hair was pulled into a side ponytail that fell serenely across one shoulder. Her dress, blue polka-dot voile with white trim, drew attention to her perfectly shaped body with a subtlety that seemed childlike and innocent. Violet walked past her own desk and headed for Audrey's with the note about the wrap party still in her hand.

"Shooting all done?" Audrey said effortlessly. She was in a good mood.

"They're still at it. It's the Paddock scene. Again. But they don't need Miss Myrick anymore today."

Audrey typed in silence for a few seconds; then she sensed that Violet was lingering. She looked up from her dictation. "Is that something you need help with?" She nodded to the invitation.

Violet looked down at the piece of paper. "Oh. No. Miss Myrick wants me to come to the wrap party on Tuesday."

"Lucky you," Audrey said, with no detectable hint of envy.

"Think I should go?"

Audrey continued to tap away at the keys. "Of course you should. You've spent a lot of long hours on the—what is it called there?—the damned thing."

"So have you."

Audrey smiled. "Don't you worry about me, Vi. You go for both of us."

"Want me to see if I can invite you, too?"

"I've actually got plans for Tuesday night."

"A date?" Violet asked.

Audrey tipped her head to the side as she typed. "I wouldn't exactly call it a date." But she grinned as she said it.

"With Vince?"

At the mention of the name, Audrey's hands fell silent and she looked up in surprise. "Vince?" she echoed with a laugh, clearly waiting for Violet to explain how she'd come up with that name.

"I . . . I heard you taking calls from him a while back," Violet stammered, heat rising to her cheeks, as it was obvious she'd made a wrong assumption. "I wasn't trying to listen to you. The bungalow is quiet at night. I just heard you say his name a couple times."

Audrey's amused grin deepened. "Vince is just a friend, Violet. We met ages ago when I was at MGM. He works in publicity at Paramount now. He knows everybody in this business. But he's engaged to be married, if you must know. He's helping me get connected to someone who might be able to change things around for me—that's all." Audrey commenced typing again, but she still smiled, at the vision, no doubt, of her friend Vince being romantically interested in her.

"Oh," Violet said numbly.

"Dear Violet, you do brighten my days." Audrey shook her head. "Vince has stealthily put me in contact with someone who scouts for Warner and that's who I am meeting on Tuesday. They're looking to groom some new talent. I've been working on getting this meeting for a long while. I had to do it my way and that takes longer."

"Your way?"

"I had to wait for this man to ask *me* for the meeting, of course."

Violet immediately pictured Audrey at soirees and parties where this man had been present. In her mind's eye, she saw Audrey subtly positioning herself so that Providence—in the form of her mother—could persuade him to look Audrey's way. And perhaps he said to the person next to him, *"Who is that over there with Vince?"*

She pictured that man walking over to Audrey and saying something like, *"Have we met before?"* and Audrey, pretending she didn't know who he was, responding with, *"I don't believe so. I'm Audrey Duvall."*

The man surely would be charmed by Audrey's loveliness and appeal; all men were. Violet wondered if Audrey truly knew how devastatingly beautiful she was. Or if she had considered that this man she would be meeting on Tuesday might have something on his mind other than Audrey's future as a movie star.

"But . . . but does this man think it's a date?" Violet asked tentatively.

Audrey's hands fell still over the keys as she looked up. "Do you think that's the only reason a man like that would ask me out to dinner?"

Violet stiffened. "No. That's not . . . I didn't mean it that way. I just meant—"

"You think I let him come up to me out of the blue and ask me to dinner with absolutely no context at all for it? You think I haven't had him wanting to find a way to get me interested in what's happening at Warner? That I haven't been in complete control of this from the moment he introduced himself to me?"

"Audrey, I . . ." But Violet could not finish her thought.

"What? What are you trying to say?"

"You are just so beautiful and elegant and alluring. Men can be so stupid. And selfish."

Audrey's laugh was musical this time, and she reached out a hand to pat Violet's arm. "It's sweet of you to worry about me. But I promise you that I'm not naïve about any of this, Violet. And I don't want you to ever be naïve about it, either." Audrey leaned forward in her chair and locked her gaze onto Violet's. "Don't ever sleep with a man to get what you want, because you won't get it. He will, but you won't. You get what you want by being smart with what you have, not by giving away what you have. Promise me you won't forget I told you this."

Violet was stunned for a moment by Audrey's profoundly fraternal devotion toward her.

"So you won't forget?" Audrey pressed.

Violet promised she would not give away what she had.

FOURTEEN

Audrey stood in front of her closet, arms folded across the front of her dressing gown, and studied the dresses on their hangers.

The rose-and-ivory linen suit was a possibility.

Or perhaps the ivy challis with its fitted waist and dolman sleeves?

But no. The challis would wrinkle while she sat all day, taking down *Rebecca* dictation notes and then typing them up. There would not be enough time to come all the way back to the bungalow to change before meeting the Warner talent scout at Musso and Frank at six thirty. Whatever she wore to work would be what she wore to dinner. It had to still look perfect at the end of the day.

Maybe the tangerine sheath and matching bolero jacket?

She reached for the orange-hued ensemble, turned toward her vanity mirror, and held it up to her body.

"That looks fabulous on you even with your hair up in a turban."

Audrey caught a glimpse of Violet's reflection in the mirror. Her roommate stood in her nightgown at the open doorway, a cup of coffee in her hands.

"Not so, but you're sweet to say it, Vi." She

tossed the hanger onto the bed and pulled from the closet a lemon yellow fitted dress with ebony trim. "What do you think of this one?"

"It's stunning. I wish I could turn heads the way you do," Violet said.

Audrey turned to her. "Who says you don't?"

"I know I don't."

Audrey turned back to the mirror. "I wouldn't be so sure of that. Anyway. Beauty is all about perception, Vi. Your own perception is right up there with everyone else's. You could turn heads if you wanted to."

Violet shrugged. "I wouldn't know where to begin. Back home it was all about dressing modestly and organizing church bazaars and attending teas with the governor's wife. We weren't supposed to turn heads. We were raised to impress just one good man from one good family and win a proposal from him."

Audrey swung back around. After six months with Violet as her roommate, it seemed she was finally getting a peek into why Violet had gotten on the train that brought her westward. "And you wanted something more?"

Violet was quiet for a second. "It doesn't matter now what I wanted."

Audrey tossed the yellow dress back on the bed. "Of course it matters. If there's something you want, you shouldn't let anything stand in your way, Vi. Or anyone."

She waited for Violet to tell her more, but her roommate sipped her coffee and said nothing else. Audrey sensed a hundred unspoken thoughts in the tiny stretch of seconds.

"What was his name, Vi?" Audrey asked gently.

Violet looked up from her cup. A weak smile tugged at the corners of her mouth. Clearly Violet was relieved she could skip the painful rehashing of the general details. "Franklin."

"Were in you love with him?"

"At the time I was."

"And if you had stayed in Alabama and this Franklin had asked you to marry him, you'd be volunteering at all of Montgomery's white-glove social events right now?"

The little smile curling on Violet's lips broadened. "Probably."

"I'm sure you're meant for more than church bazaars and teas with the governor's wife, Violet."

Violet laugh was short but genuine. "Maybe."

"Assuredly."

Audrey retrieved the dress in the shade of ripe tangerines. This was the one. She peeked at Violet's reflection in the mirror. She was staring off into space. Audrey turned to face her. "Want to wear something of mine to your cast party today?"

Violet slowly turned her head toward her. "Something of yours?"

Audrey reached for a white pencil skirt and periwinkle silk blouse hanging in her closet.

"Here. You'll look dynamite in this shade of blue. And I've got just the shoes for you. I'll do your eyebrows for you, too. And your rouge. You'll turn heads all right."

Violet stood speechless before her. Audrey wondered for a moment if by suggesting such a makeover she had offended Violet. She opened her mouth to apologize but Violet filled the silence before she could say another word.

"Can you do my hair, too?" Violet said.

Audrey grinned and handed her the clothes.

Primping Violet for the last day of shooting *Gone With the Wind* had been exciting; watching heads swivel their way as they strode onto the studio had been enjoyable, too. But the rest of the day slogged on. The studio was abuzz with the energy that accompanies a film's last day of shooting. But Audrey sensed only the tedium of the long day's work.

By five o'clock, she could no longer concentrate on her typing and clocked out, giving herself plenty of time to get to the restaurant.

She took the streetcar to Hollywood Boulevard and stopped first at The Broadway department store to browse the perfume counter and pretend to be an interested customer so that she could be spritzed with the tantalizing scent of Tabu. After a quick trip to the ladies' restroom to fluff her hair and reapply her lipstick, Audrey was ready to meet the scout. She left the store and cast a glance skyward as she began to leisurely walk the three blocks to Musso and Frank. She hoped that through the ruffled clouds, her angel mother was watching over her.

The scout, Woodrow Wallace, had already been seated when Audrey arrived. She had met him at a party Vince had taken her to a few weeks earlier, and she was glad they wouldn't need to waste time on pleasantries. When she was shown to the table he rose and smiled, but Audrey detected the faintest hint of pretense behind it. She sat down.

The man was her age, perhaps a year or two older, newly married for the second time already, and father to a newborn son. Audrey knew Wallace's father had been a silent film star and that he had dabbled in acting himself until he got a taste for working alongside producers and directors to help cast movies. He had confided in Audrey that he hoped to follow in Myron Selznick's footsteps and start his own agency in the not-too-distant future. She had dared to believe that he might want to talk to her that night about becoming his first client.

But as she took her seat, she sensed that nothing about this situation felt like the moment when Stiles had stared at her in that coffee shop and asked her if she wanted to be a star.

"Would you like a drink?" he said politely as he

raised his martini. Too politely. He had bad news to share.

"Am I going to need one?"

Wallace placed his drink on the table. "I got called into a meeting today. Your name came up."

He smiled, but not happily so.

"Did it?"

"I brought it up, actually. The conversation was leading right to what I had told you earlier, about Warner wanting to find their own Joan Crawford– type breakout star. It seemed like perfect timing for me to mention you."

The room felt warm and the splashes of Tabu at her neck suddenly smelled cloying. She said nothing.

"They want someone younger, Audrey. I couldn't get them past the fact that you're turning thirty-one. I showed them your photo. They saw that you don't look a day over twenty-five."

Audrey half grinned at the stabbing compliment. "Then let's just tell them you're bad at math. You added the numbers wrong. I'm only twenty-five."

Wallace smiled. "I wish it was that easy. Some of them remember you."

Audrey winced uncontrollably. There had been a period of time after the failed movie that she wished she could erase. She nearly thought she had. "What do they remember?"

Wallace lifted a shoulder. "I guess they remember how old you are."

Audrey pushed the dark memory away. "What about a screen test? Shouldn't they wait to decide until they've seen a screen test?"

"Yes, they should. But they feel they don't need to. They've already got someone else in mind."

Audrey closed her eyes to keep the room from spinning. "Someone younger."

"Yes."

She kept her eyes closed as she fought to hold on to the trailing edge of heaven. Hadn't she just felt it as she walked down the boulevard? Or had it been a dream? Had it all been a dream?

"I'm so sorry, Audrey. If it was up to me, this would have turned out differently. I think you have potential."

"You there, Mama?" Audrey whispered.

"Pardon me?"

But there was no sound except for the clinking of silverware in the distance and the soft tones of a dozen nearby conversations.

Audrey opened her eyes. "I believe I'll have that drink now."

FIFTEEN

Stage 5, which had recently been dressed to look like Atlanta during the War Between the States, now appeared to have been overrun by time travelers from another era. Men and women were tipping back drinks, Glenn Miller played on a radio that someone had brought in, and there were laughter and noise and other unmistakable signs of the twentieth century.

The mood was relaxed and festive, and even though the mingling of cast and crew wouldn't be out of place, Violet sensed there was still an atmosphere of quiet division between the two, not because one couldn't appreciate the other, but because the Herculean effort to film the monstrous project that was *Gone With the Wind* had ended, thank God, and everyone was ready to slide back into the normal, easy lives they'd had before it had begun.

Violet, standing off to the side, felt very much like the spectator she had been from the beginning. Miss Myrick, comfortable with cast as well as crew, since both had relied on her expertise during filming, moved easily through the small clutches of people, posing for pictures, smiling, and saying her good-byes. She'd told Violet just as the party got under way that she would be leaving Hollywood for a much-deserved vacation before heading back to Atlanta, and she didn't think she'd be needed for any of the post-filming. Violet could only assume that she would have to report back to the secretarial pool in the morning.

She sighed at this thought and shifted her weight from one foot to the other. Audrey's shoes were squeezing her toes, and she allowed herself a grimace before edging out from the wall on which she'd been leaning to again scan the crowd for Bert. This time she was rewarded. He stood among other wardrobe staff, off to the side. He wore his cap and jacket and had the look of one not planning to stay long. Violet tossed her paper cup into the trash bin and headed in his direction, her pained feet protesting every step.

"I hoped I'd see you here," Violet said cheerfully when she was just a few feet from him.

Bert looked at her, taking in the sweep of her hair around her shoulders, the hue of the silk blouse, Audrey's slimming skirt, and even the shiny charcoal gray shoes on her feet.

"Violet." Bert said her name as though he wondered if that's who she really was. The three coworkers he was with were all looking at Violet, too.

A grin tugged at her mouth but she reined it back to a polite smile as she said hello to Bert's companions.

"Hey, Violet," one of them said. "You're looking nice tonight."

"Why, thank you, Teddy," she replied as demurely as she could, mindful that Bert was still staring at her.

"Who's the lucky fella?" said another, winking at her almost as if he could read her thoughts.

"No one!" Violet tried to sound pleased and

playful. "You'd think I'd dyed my hair green instead of just deciding to wear it down today."

Bert's friends laughed.

She turned back to Bert, who seemed less surprised now by her appearance, but he was not laughing with the others. He looked as though he was contemplating something.

"Are you not staying for the party?" she said.

Bert hesitated a second before answering. "I'm . . . I'm picking up my truck at my friend's house tonight."

"You finished it!"

"Almost. I was waiting on a part that came in yesterday. I just have to pop it in."

"Maybe you'd like to bring Violet with you to get it," the one named Teddy said slyly.

Violet pretended she didn't catch the connotation. "I'd love to come with you," she said to Bert.

The men laughed again and eyed one another.

An embarrassed smile pulled at the corner of Bert's mouth. "I'm sure you'd rather be here at the party."

"No, I wouldn't," she said quickly. "I don't really know anybody here except Miss Myrick and she's off saying good-bye to everyone. I've been bored out of my mind."

"But you're all dressed up."

Violet looked down at the milky blue blouse and the white pencil skirt and then raised her gaze to meet his. "They're just work clothes."

187

"What kind of work would that be?" one of the men whispered to Teddy.

Before Violet could even think of a response Bert told the man to shut his trap.

The three friends laughed and stepped away, with one telling Bert to make sure he knew how to drive the thing before he took off down the street in it.

"Sorry," Bert said as his friends moved out of earshot. "They've no manners."

But Violet wasn't pondering the offense. Bert's quick and chivalrous defense of her honor was the only thing reverberating in her head.

"You honestly don't have to come with me," he said, when she didn't reply.

"But I really do want to come."

He studied her for a moment. "Okay."

"I'll be right back. Don't leave without me." Violet rushed away to say good-bye to Miss Myrick. As she returned to Bert she couldn't help but limp a little. A blister on her right heel felt ready to burst. He looked down at her feet as she neared him.

"New shoes," she said, dismissing her pain as if it was nothing.

Bert opened the door for her as they left Stage 5. "Maybe we should stop by your place so you can change?"

Violet was immediately stung by his suggestion. She didn't want to be, but she was. She wanted to respond with, *Don't you realize I went to all this trouble for you?*

Bert saw her veiled displeasure and quickly added, "Not that you don't look great, Violet, because you do. But I'm going to pick up a truck, not a limousine. And those shoes are obviously hurting your feet."

The sting was gone in an instant. "Do you really think I look great?"

"Sure. I mean, it's a different look for you and all, but it's . . . it's a nice look."

A nice look. She wanted to hear him say she looked beautiful. She wanted him to say she was as beautiful as Audrey was.

They walked for a few paces in silence.

"Audrey told me I'd be pretty with my hair down and this makeup on," Violet finally said.

"You . . . you are," Bert said, clearly unskilled in the kind of conversation they were having. "It's just . . . you looked pretty before."

"You think so?"

He averted his gaze. "Of course."

She yearned to hear him say it again. Again and again. That he thought she was pretty. They walked for a few moments in silence.

"Thanks for letting me come with you," Violet finally said as they neared the gatehouse to Selznick International and the streetcar stop that lay beyond it.

"Sure." Bert shrugged her thanks away, as if such gratitude was truly not needed.

When they arrived at the bungalow, Violet was happy to see that Audrey was not home—most likely she was already on her way to her rendez-vous with the talent scout from Warner. Bert also noticed Audrey was not there.

A tiny wave of disappointment seemed to wash over him when he realized he couldn't ask her if she would like to join them to get his new truck.

"Audrey had plans for tonight, Bert," Violet said, wanting him to know she alone saw the contours of his heart.

Bert seemed surprised that she so effortlessly read his mind. "Oh. I . . . I wasn't . . ." But he couldn't get out the words. Lying did not come easily to Bert Redmond. She took a step toward him.

"It's okay, Bert. I know how much you like her. Of course you like her. Who doesn't love Audrey?"

He said nothing.

Violet used his silence to bolster her courage. She longed to tell him the truth about how she felt about him, even though it could change everything between them. Violet felt strangely compelled to tell him, as though she might not get another chance like this one. She moved closer. "I really like you, Bert. I know I'm not Audrey—I will never be as beautiful and glamorous as Audrey is—but I do so very much want to be your friend and perhaps . . . maybe one day more than your friend."

She was only inches from Bert now and she longed to lean forward and kiss him.

"I . . . I like you, too, Violet."

But Violet couldn't tell if he said it merely to be polite or if he meant those words the same way she did.

She stood silent for a moment, waiting to see if he would say something else that could clue her in.

"Do I stand even a chance against her?" Violet whispered.

Bert's eyes widened as he realized the depth of Violet's vulnerability before him. "I . . . I don't know what to say."

"You deserve someone who will put you first, Bert." Violet leaned forward, bent her neck slightly, and pressed her lips gently to his. She waited for him to respond in kind. He didn't, but neither did he pull away.

She stepped back, hoping the kiss would linger as she headed for her bedroom to change into different clothes. She chose a pair of wide-leg slacks, flats, and a blue-checked blouse with eyelet trim. She left the hairdo and makeup undisturbed.

When she came back out a few minutes later, Bert was standing at the open door as the sounds of evening started to filter inside the bungalow. Birdsong filled the air as the day that was ending was lulled to sleep.

Violet braced herself for whatever Bert had been thinking about while she was in the bedroom. "Ready to go?" she said nervously.

He turned slowly. When he spoke, his tone was one of quiet resignation. "I think I've known all along that Audrey was never going to want to be anything more than just friends."

Violet hadn't rehearsed how to respond if Bert were to say something like this. Her mouth dropped open a little but no words came out.

Bert smiled, though it was not a completely happy grin. "I've just been kidding myself. Of course I've been kidding myself. What would someone like Audrey ever see in someone like me?" He looked away.

Violet placed her hand on his arm. "Don't talk that way, Bert. It's not you. It's her. She's just got one thing on her mind—that's all. Her career. It has nothing to do with you. You are a wonderful, kind, good man. I could see that from the moment I met you."

When he turned back to her, the aching look he'd worn a second before seemed to have diminished. He laughed lightly. "I'm apparently not too bright, though."

She squeezed his arm. "Yes, you are."

Bert considered her for a second and then

placed his hand over hers. He looked as though he might kiss her this time.

You are as bright as the stars in the sky, Bert, that are at last, at last, at last smiling down on me.

And then he did kiss her. His lips on hers were light and restrained, a sweet tasting of what could be, what might be, when at last Audrey was expunged from within him. He broke away too soon, but Violet found that she didn't mind. Audrey was still partially wrapped around his thoughts, but the old knots had been loosened. Bert extended his arm and they walked out into the twilight.

"Maybe we can grab a bite after we get the truck?" he said.

And it was as if the world was full of nightingales singing.

Two hours later, after a dinner of Reuben sandwiches and apple pie, Bert pulled up to the bungalow in his fixed-up truck, a nut brown, slightly-worse-for-the-wear Chevy Stovebolt. Violet could see from the passenger's side that the kitchen light was on. Audrey was home.

Bert either didn't notice or chose not to comment on it.

"Thanks for dinner, Bert. It was lovely." They'd had a great time talking and laughing and eating at a popular diner just off Vine.

He seemed surprised that she was saying good-bye, perhaps almost relieved. He would need to take their relationship slowly, and she could easily pretend she understood this. She leaned forward on the seat to kiss him and the leather seat squawked.

Her kiss was soft and nondemanding. "This was fun," she said when she pulled away.

"Maybe . . . maybe we can do it again?" Hi tone was hesitant but hopeful.

"I'd like that very much." She opened the door to climb out.

"So. I'll see you gals tomorrow morning?"

"If you're sure it's not too much trouble."

"Not at all. I'm happy to do it."

Violet felt as though she were floating after Bert drove away. She hoped Audrey had had an equally wonderful night and that they would both go to bed happy.

But when she walked into the kitchen she found her roommate sitting at the table in her bathrobe, her face washed of its makeup, her hair down around her shoulders. A bottle of whiskey and a tumbler sat on the table along with an ashtray full of cigarette butts. As Violet approached Audrey, she saw that her roommate was working at something. She was gluing the little nightingale's wing. Her eyes were red.

"What happened, Audrey?"

She looked up. "I knocked it off the window-sill when I was taking my makeup off. I didn't mean to break it. I . . . I just didn't see it." Her eyes welled with fresh tears.

"I mean, I didn't expect you home so soon. What happened with your meeting?"

Audrey laughed mirthlessly as she set down the bird, pressing on the part of the wing that now bore a tiny fissure and a creamy white seam of glue.

"My meeting," she echoed. "Is that what I called it?"

Violet pulled out a chair and sat down at the table.

Audrey reached for the whiskey bottle and tipped some of its amber liquid into the glass. "What happened, dear Violet, is time. Time happened." She placed the bottle down and raised the glass. "Here's to Father Time!"

She slung back the glass and the whiskey disappeared down her throat. She grimaced as she put the tumbler back down on the table.

"Please tell me what happened!" Violet said.

Audrey's gaze rested on the bird between them. "This is a rotten town to have birthdays in, Violet. Before you know it, you're almost thirty-one and everyone around you is ten years younger than you and ten times prettier. And all the while you've been fooling yourself into thinking no one has noticed that you've gotten older."

"What do you mean? Who told you this?"

But Audrey seemed not to have heard her. A weak laugh escaped her. "And here I thought that I was invisible while I was waiting for my second big break. That people had forgotten all about me. That I could come sneaking back into the spotlight and no one would remember that when was I eighteen I almost had it all."

She laid a finger delicately on the bird's brown head, as if it were a real bird that would fly away if it was startled.

"I'm a fool, Violet," Audrey murmured.

Violet leaned forward and covered Audrey's free hand with hers. "No, you're not. You're beautiful and talented and smart. It's everyone else who's an idiot."

Audrey seemed to think about Violet's response for a moment. "I wish that were true, Violet. I really do. But I'm beginning to think it's Peg Entwistle who was the smart one."

Violet had no idea what Audrey was talking about. "Who's Peg Entwistle?"

Audrey looked up languidly. For a moment she did not answer. Then she rose from her chair. "No one."

She reached for the nightingale and took it gingerly into her hand. Then she turned from Violet, walked to her bedroom, and closed the door gently behind her.

Hollywood
March 10, 2012

The bungalow seems oddly shrunken with most of its contents packed away in boxes. It should look larger, but to Elle, who stands inside the living room with a broom in her hand and a sheen of sweat on her brow, the little house appears smaller without its furnishings.

Her granddaughters run past, chasing the three-year-old shelter dog they named Jacques. The animal was a consolation present from Daniel and Nicola for uprooting the girls from all their friends in France and moving them to the States.

"Careful around all the boxes," Elle says.

The older girl turns back.

"*Nous pouvons le prendre pour faire une promenade?*"

Elle smiles at her granddaughter. "In English, Michelle."

The girl huffs. "May we please take him for a walk?"

"You may only go in the direction of the Hollywood sign and only for ten houses up. Then you turn back. *Oui?*"

"In English, Mamie!" The girl laughs as she

and her sister scoop up the dog and his leash and take him outside into the late-afternoon sunshine.

The bungalow is instantly quiet without the girls. Daniel and Nicola are running errands, and Elle is alone.

She inhales, breathing in the scent of the passage of time. The bungalow is nearly a hundred years old, and while it has been updated in terms of wiring and plumbing, the aura inside is still tangy with nostalgia, as if at any moment strains of Glenn Miller might suddenly fill the room.

Inside her pants pocket her cell phone vibrates. She pulls it out to read a text message from Daniel.

Running late. Will text the resale-shop owner and tell her I'll pick up the hat tomorrow. Traffic is terrible. Can we meet you and the girls back at your condo around 7? We'll get Thai takeout.

Elle is disappointed that the hat will be away from the bungalow another night, despite having nearly forgotten it existed. Her mother had kept it squirreled away in a cedar chest in the attic for decades, hidden from renters during the years they'd all lived abroad.

She had told her mother—a long time ago—that

she could probably sell that hat and get a lot of money.

And her mother said she didn't feel right about selling something that didn't belong to her.

⟫◆⟪

SIXTEEN

August 1939

The moviemakers, half a dozen of them, were seated around a meeting table on the second floor of the Mansion at Selznick International. Cups of hot coffee sent tendrils of steam upward to join a heavier layer of cigarette smoke and the unmistakable atmosphere of fretful purpose. Audrey, taking notes for the art director, William Menzies, was seated just to the right of Selznick's executive secretary, Marcella Rabwin. She was glad when Miss Rabwin leaned over and told her to crack open a window. The men didn't notice when she rose from her chair, set her steno pad down on the seat, and headed to the row of windows. When she raised one a few inches, a welcoming ribbon of morning air wafted into the room and trifled playfully with the weightiness of smoke and decision making.

"The picture's nearly five hours long," one of the men said as Audrey retook her chair. "It's an impossible length. No one will sit for five hours to watch it."

"I'm not going to release a movie that is five hours long," Selznick said easily. "We will edit it down."

The man shook his head as a lopsided grin spread across his face. "You say that like you think it will be easy. What can possibly be cut?"

"We'll find a way." Selznick didn't seem worried in the least from what Audrey could tell.

The talk turned then to updates on the musical score and the sound effects, the painstaking task of matching everything to the Technicolor reels, the making of the prints, and whether it waseven possible to have it all done for an Atlanta premiere in November that could coincide with the seventy-fifth anniversary of the burning of the city.

While the men went over the mounting particulars of the upcoming premiere, Audrey permitted herself a mental break while keeping her pen poised above her notepad.

She'd been relieved beyond words to get away from the monotony of the secretary pool and the scores of letters Selznick still got on a daily basis from those who wrote that *Gone With the Wind* was un-American, reactionary, pro–Ku Klux Klan, pro-slavery, and even pro-Nazi. Audrey had lost count of how many times she had sent the standard letter that was sent to anyone who lodged a concern. She could recite the verbiage in her sleep. . . .

We are in receipt of your letter concerning our imminent production of *Gone With the Wind*. We urge you to believe that we feel as strongly as you do about the presentation to the public of any material that might be prejudicial to the interests of any race or creed, or that might contain any anti-American material. We respectfully suggest you suspend judgment until the completion of the picture, which we can assure you will contain nothing that possibly could be offensive to you. In particular, you may be sure that the treatment of the Negro characters will be with the utmost respect for this race and with the greatest concern for its sensibilities.

The letter was always closed with a tailored response, a sentence or two about the writer's specific grievance.

Violet had told her that she didn't like the way the letters of complaint made her feel, and there was no way to type the needed response without reading them. But Audrey admired the people who had the courage to be honest and state their opinion. She wasn't bothered by their comments. If people couldn't be honest with one another, then life was just fluff and pretense. Audrey had told Violet that she could pass any of those letters on to her if Violet didn't care to respond to them.

Her roommate had seemed distracted during the past few days. Bert, too. Audrey saw him only in the mornings when he came for them in his truck, and then again when they met for the drive home. His department was busy disposing of the massive *Gone With the Wind* wardrobe in preparation for the influx of all new costumes for the filming of *Rebecca*, and for some reason that Audrey couldn't imagine, Violet found that extremely interesting. Most of the conversation in the truck centered on what Bert was doing or not doing in wardrobe. And while it was nice not having to ride the streetcar and bus to work, Bert and Violet seemed separate from her. As if she were being pulled away from everything that used to hold her fast.

She was torn from this reverie when Mr. Menzies said her name, apparently not for the first time.

"I beg your pardon!" Audrey said, her cheeks blooming crimson.

Mr. Menzies rattled off a list of things to be taken care of that afternoon and Audrey dutifully recorded them.

The meeting ended shortly after that and Audrey headed back to her desk, feeling strangely detached from the hum of the activity in the room full of secretaries. She had just begun to type her first memo when the phone at her desk rang.

"You've got a call," the switchboard operator said when Audrey picked up.

"This is Audrey Duvall."

"Audie, it's Vince. Can you be at Paramount at two thirty?" He sounded tense.

"Why? What for?"

"I think I got you a screen test for the role of Mima in *Road to Singapore*."

Audrey heard every word. Her mind refused to embrace their meaning. "What?"

"I said, I think I got you a screen test for *Road to Singapore*! But you have to be here by two thirty. Can you get away?"

A screen test. For a major motion picture.

"Audrey, did you hear me?"

"Yes," she answered.

"Can you make it?"

She willed her pulse to stop its pounding. *Stay calm. Stay focused.* "I can."

"This might be it, Audie!"

Yes.

It might be.

"I'll be there," she said.

Audrey hung up the phone. For several seconds she stared at it, unable to decide what to do first. She looked at her wristwatch. A few minutes before noon. She had to get back to the bungalow and change, redo her hair. She would need to take a taxi there and back again. She had a little over two hours to do it. She rose from her chair and headed for Violet's desk. Her roommate looked up from her typewriter.

"I need to take off early," Audrey murmured. "Can you cover for me?"

"Where are you going?" Violet's hands hovered motionless above the typewriter keys.

"Vince called me. I need to be somewhere in a little bit and I've got to look like a million dollars."

"You already look like a million dollars."

Audrey smiled. "If anyone asks, just tell them I was called out to one of the stages."

Before Violet could respond, Audrey turned from her and headed for the door.

The sun was bright and hot as she stepped outside, warmer than she thought the sense of heaven would feel, but she was sure of its presence just the same. The magic was happening all over again, just like it had before. She had been patient. She had played by the rules of Providence. She had kept her head this time. And now her angel mother was smiling down on her finally, finally.

Finally the tide was turning.

When she raised her hand to signal a taxi she felt as if she could fly.

SEVENTEEN

Violet took the dictation she had been working on that afternoon and readied the memos and letters for the mail room and interoffice mail courier. No one had asked her about Audrey, much to her relief. Everyone apparently had enough on their minds with postproduction for *Gone With the Wind* and preproduction for *Rebecca* to notice. Audrey had seemed excited but also nervous when she stole away. Audrey hadn't ever seemed the type to get nervous, not even when she took Violet home to the farm for Christmas. Violet couldn't imagine what could have called Audrey away in the middle of the workday and so unsteadied her. The oddity of it reminded Violet that a few days earlier, Audrey had mentioned a name Violet hadn't heard before: Peg Entwistle.

What had Audrey said—Peg Entwistle had had the right idea? Violet had forgotten to ask someone else who that woman was. She'd ask Bert on the way home if he knew.

A few minutes after quitting time, she met him at his pickup truck.

"Audrey had somewhere she had to be," Violet said as soon as she was near him and before he could ask.

"She doesn't want us to wait for her?"

Violet was fairly certain he was asking more from politeness than genuine interest. Fairly certain. "No, she snuck away at lunchtime. Something came up." She climbed into the truck.

It was the first time in many days that they had been alone in the truck and Violet wished she didn't feel so awkward. She asked about Bert's day as they pulled onto Ince Street and he returned the favor by asking about hers. But it was all such superficial talk. Violet didn't know how to get back to the place they'd been two weeks ago when he'd kissed her. She was pondering this when Bert cleared his throat.

"Would you like to go get some dinner?"

She wanted to squeal that she would absolutely love to, but managed to smile and accept his invitation with far less volume.

He grinned and Violet scooted nearer him. He looked down at her.

"You don't mind if I sit here, do you?" she asked.

"I don't mind," Bert said easily. "I don't mind at all."

Sitting close to Bert felt natural and right, like they were already a couple and he already loved her. She didn't want to think about what she would have to tell him at some point. Right now it didn't matter. How could it matter right then? It was too soon to talk about something as personal as that. Far too soon. Light conversation was in order, not the intimate details of her flawed body.

"Say, do you know who Peg Entwistle is?" she asked.

Bert crooked an eyebrow and looked away from the road for a second to peer at her. "You don't?"

"No."

"What brings her up?"

"Why? Who is she?"

"You mean who *was* she."

"Oh. So she's deceased, then?"

"I'd say that's putting it lightly."

"What happened to her?"

Bert sighed lightly. "It's very sad what happened to her. Peg Entwistle killed herself."

A slender stab of alarm pierced Violet. "When? Why?"

"A few years back. She was an actress trying to make it here in Hollywood but it wasn't working out for her, I guess. Her last film got such poor reviews that she climbed to the top of the H on the Hollywoodland sign and jumped."

Violet couldn't breathe. Surely Audrey had been joking when she'd said what she did. She had to have been. Had to.

"I was still living at home then," Bert went on. "I didn't get the job at MGM until a couple of years later. Audrey would have been here, though. Peg Entwistle didn't live far from Audrey's bungalow. Her name doesn't come up much anymore. Did someone in the secretary pool mention her?"

But Violet barely heard him. Audrey had been speaking sarcastically, surely.

"Violet?"

"Oh. No. I mean yes. Someone in the pool brought her name up. Just in passing. As a joke. Sort of."

"A joke?'

"Sort of. Never mind. We don't have to talk about her anymore."

It was a name Audrey had mentioned by way of simple exaggeration. That was all.

When Bert brought Violet home a few hours later, the bungalow was dark. He walked her to the door and leaned in to kiss her lightly, tentatively, as though he was still getting acclimated to letting his affections drift to another woman.

Violet listened for Audrey's return as she lay in bed, but Bert's kiss lingered on her lips and lulled her into dreamless sleep.

At seven fifteen the next morning the temperature read eighty degrees and a thin ribbon of sweat circled Violet's neck and forehead as she finished her breakfast. The past few days had been sweltering, like it got in Montgomery, but there was no moisture in the air. It was as if someone had turned on an oven and everyone in Los Angeles was roasting inside it without so much as a tablespoon of sauce for basting.

Violet poured the rest of her coffee down the

sink and dabbed at her moist skin with a tea towel. She looked at her wristwatch, even though she knew what time it was. Bert would be coming for them soon and Audrey still hadn't emerged from her bedroom.

Violet tossed the towel onto the countertop and headed down the hall. She listened at Audrey's door but heard nothing.

"Audrey?" Violet knocked gently.

When there was no response, she knocked again. "Audrey?" she said again, this time louder.

"What is it, Violet?"

The words from beyond the door sounded weighted by more than just the timbre of a sultry voice. Violet turned the knob, slowly cracked open the door, and peeked inside. The room was swathed in rust-colored light created from the closed curtains. Audrey, in her bathrobe, sat in an armchair, smoking a cigarette with the cat on her lap.

"It's getting late. Bert will be coming for us," Violet said.

"I'm not going to work today."

Violet stepped in fully and Audrey looked up at her. Even in her nightgown, with her hair tousled about her shoulders, Audrey looked lovely. But her expression was one of cool disinterest. She brought the cigarette to her mouth and inhaled.

"You're not?" Violet said.

Audrey exhaled and tapped the cigarette on the

ashtray on the bedside table next to her. The little nightingale was on the table, too.

"No. I think a girl should get to do whatever she wants on her birthday."

Violet, surprised by this news, took another step inside the room. "It's your birthday? Why didn't you tell me?"

"I told you when you moved in when my birthday was."

"Audrey, that was ages ago."

"Thanks for reminding me."

Bert hadn't said anything, either, about Audrey's birthday coming up, which meant he likely had overlooked it. They shouldn't have forgotten it. Violet walked over to the armchair. "I'm sorry I didn't remember."

Audrey shrugged and took a drag on her cigarette.

"We can do something fun later," Violet said.

"I like what I'm doing right now."

Violet sat down on the unmade bed, her knees touching Audrey's knees. "Are you sure skipping out on work is a good idea, though?"

Audrey laughed and even with her dark mood it sounded like music. "You do have a way with words, Violet. It is quite possibly a terrible idea." Audrey stroked the cat, and he lifted his head and meowed lazily.

"Then get dressed and come with me."

Audrey put the cigarette to her mouth again.

211

"No," she said when she pulled it away. Smoke wafted out of her pursed lips like it had somewhere to be and was late.

"But what if . . . what if Mrs. Pope—"

"What if she fires me?" Audrey finished for her. "Frankly, my dear, I don't give a damn." She tipped her head back and laughed at her comical reference to Rhett Butler's last line in the current version of the *Gone With the Wind* script. Valentino jumped off her lap and strolled away.

"But, Audrey—"

Audrey leveled her gaze back to meet Violet's. "I honestly don't care, Violet. I've given this studio the best years of my life, and what has it given me?"

"Yes, but—"

"I've ingratiated myself before every assistant producer, director, writer, idea man, and talent scout who's had even a modicum of influence. I've done everything they've asked of me and then some. I may as well have been a fifty-year-old grandmother, for all the good it's done me."

"But maybe . . . maybe they don't know how to see past the fact that you're a secretary. Do any of those people know what you'd really like to do?"

For a second Audrey didn't answer. "You go on to work, little busy bee Violet. Go on," she finally said.

A truck pulled up to the curb outside the house. Audrey heard it, too.

"Go on." Audrey crushed out her cigarette.

Violet stood up. "I'll tell Mrs. Pope you're not feeling well."

"Tell her anything you want."

Violet made one last appeal. "I can tell Bert to wait for us. Or I can tell him to go ahead and you and I will catch the streetcar. I'll help you get ready, Audrey. Come on. Please?"

Audrey smiled at her. "You're a peach. But I need to think. I can't think at work. Go on. Bert's waiting for you." She turned her head to the curtained window where, on the other side of the glass, the truck idled at the curb. "Dear, sweet Bert," she said in a faraway voice that sounded heavy with regret.

At first Violet could only stare at Audrey. "I'll tell Mrs. Pope you have the flu," she said a few seconds later.

"You do that." Audrey leaned back in the chair and rested her head on its rounded back.

Violet walked back out into the main room, grabbed her purse, and headed for the front door.

When she climbed into the truck, Bert looked past her to see if she was alone.

"Where's Audrey?"

"She's . . . she's feeling under the weather." Violet shut the passenger's-side door.

Bert put the truck into gear and pulled away from the curb. "After deciding out of the blue to leave early yesterday? She's going to lose her job if she's not careful."

"I actually don't think she's too keen on staying at Selznick much longer."

"Getting fired from one job is not the way to go looking for another."

"That's pretty much what I told her. She won't listen to me." Violet scooted closer to him. "But I think she's always been the kind of person to do what she wants."

Bert shrugged. "Well, I don't know about that."

The subject of her roommate fell away, and Violet finally relaxed next to the man she was falling in love with. She'd tell Bert later that it was Audrey's birthday and they should take her out for a malt or a movie. If Audrey was even amenable to that.

Half an hour later, when Violet told Mrs. Pope that Audrey had the flu, the woman regarded Violet with unmistakable doubt in her eyes.

"The flu?"

"Yes, ma'am."

"She couldn't call in herself? She's that sick?"

"Oh. I told her I would tell you."

Mrs. Pope cocked her head slightly. "You're a good worker, Violet. One of the best we have here in this office. You do yourself no favors by lying for your roommate."

Blood rushed warm to her face. "But Audrey is—"

"I know exactly what Audrey Duvall is." Mrs. Pope lowered her gaze back to her desk. "She is someone who left without permission yesterday and abandoned a pile of unsent dictation that has caused no small amount of trouble this morning."

Violet sensed that not only was Mrs. Pope aware of Audrey's absence yesterday afternoon, but she also knew why she'd slipped away.

"She just wants a chance!"

"What she wants is to be a star. What she is is a secretary. It's what she was hired to be. Nobody forced her to take up a steno pad."

"Please don't fire her, Mrs. Pope."

"That decision has already been made." Mrs. Pope did not look up. "We're finished here."

Violet returned slowly to her desk, numb with worry and unease. Her wire basket of incoming correspondence was brimming, and she was glad. She didn't want to think about what had just happened and the work would keep her mind from it.

She sought out Bert at lunch and told him the news that as far as she could tell, Audrey had lost her job.

"What do you think she'll do?" she said.

"I don't know. She owns that house and I think she might still have some of the inheritance Aunt Jo left her. I know she's been careful with it."

"But it will be so strange not going to work with her each day."

Bert crumpled up his napkin. "Things are

already strange. Maybe it's time she did something different. She doesn't want to be a secretary, anyway. She's wasting her time here. It's all been a waste." His attitude seemed forced and abrupt.

"Surely it hasn't all been a waste," Violet said, hoping to lighten his mood.

"Maybe." He was quiet for a moment. Then he turned to her, a different look on his face. "So you want to go bowling with me and some friends tonight? We can go out for hamburgers first."

It sounded like a date. She was about to say she'd love to when she remembered it was Audrey's birthday. She pondered for just a moment what to do. Audrey probably wouldn't be in much of a mood to celebrate turning thirty-one. She'd say nothing until Bert took her home to change out of her work clothes. If Audrey was home, she'd ask her to join them.

Before the day was over, Violet was called out to the Forty. The opening scene on the porch with Scarlett and the Tarleton twins was to be shot again, for the fourth time. Miss Leigh was back on the set for it, and Violet was to stand in for Miss Myrick, who was now at home in Georgia. This time, Miss Leigh didn't wear the dress with the green sprigs. She wore the ruffled white dress from the evening prayers scene. Mr. Selznick wanted her to look naïve and innocent when she complains that she doesn't want to hear one more word about some silly war.

EIGHTEEN

Audrey tipped her head as she sat on the divan, her knees curled up under her, and drank from the cocktail in her hand. Her satin dressing gown was tied loosely around her. She pulled at the lapels as across from her in an armchair Vince lifted his own drink to his mouth.

"Does your fiancée know where you are?" she said as she rearranged the bathrobe's folds. Her hair had tumbled out of its pins and fell about her face in fat curls.

"She's the understanding type. She knows I can appreciate all kinds of beauty without getting myself into trouble." He raised his glass. "To your enduring loveliness, Birthday Girl."

"Don't call me that." She took another sip.

"Hey. I think it's high time you got out of there, Audie. I think this is the best thing that could have happened to you. Best birthday present in the world."

"I know what you think."

"And I know what *you* think. You can't wait around for good things to happen to you, darlin'."

She studied the liquid in her glass, shimmering, cool, and bracing. "I wasn't waiting."

"Yes, you were."

Audrey emptied the glass and handed it to him. "Well, I'm done with waiting."

"Good for you."

A truck pulled up alongside the curb outside. From windows that had been opened to let in the cooler, late-August night air, Audrey watched Violet and Bert get out.

"Ah. At last we can have a party." Audrey rose unsteadily to her feet and fluffed up her hair, and tied the sash of her robe tighter. "How do I look?"

"Smashing, as always. Not a day over twenty-five."

"Why do I put up with you?"

Vince laughed as she strode toward the front door and swung it open. "Come in, come in!" she said.

Violet and Bert stood on the welcome mat, facing each other. Bert had his arm around Violet's waist. They both turned their heads in surprise.

For a second, Audrey could only stare at the curl of Bert's arm around Violet's back and how close she stood to him.

"I thought I heard the truck," she said, smiling and reaching out to pull Bert into the house. "Come inside, you two. Vince is making Sidecars."

Bert was three steps into the house before Violet spoke. "Bert was just leaving," she said.

"Nonsense." Audrey tugged Bert fully into the living room and Violet followed. "Vince, this is

218

my dear friend Bert. The first real friend I made here in Hollywood."

Vince smiled and extended a hand. "Pleasure to finally meet you."

"Uh. Likewise," Bert said numbly.

"And here is my sweet little Southern belle roommate, Violet." Audrey reached behind her for Violet. He extended his hand toward her also.

"Ah, Violet. I've heard so much about you."

"So nice to meet you, Vince." Violet shook his hand, an unmistakable "so this is Vince" look in her eyes.

Vince took a seat on the sofa and proceeded to pour Cointreau into a shaker on the coffee table.

"Sit with us!" Audrey said gaily, pulling Violet down on the couch with her. "Take the other armchair, Bert, darling."

Bert hesitated a second. "It's getting late. I should probably go."

Audrey frowned at him. "Since when is midnight late? Don't be a stick in the mud, Bert. Not you."

She didn't wait for him to respond, but leaned forward and took a paring knife from the coffee table next to a trio of limes. She grabbed one of the limes, cut it in two, and handed one of the halves to Vince. He squeezed the fruit into the shaker and liquid squirted out. A tiny jet of lime juice hit Audrey's neck and she squealed in mock alarm. It had felt like a kiss. Bert sat slowly down with an unreadable expression on his face.

Vince put the cover on the shaker and began to shake it.

"Oh!" Audrey exclaimed. "We need two more glasses. I'll get them."

"I don't need one." Bert started to rise. But Audrey, already on her feet, pushed him back onto the chair.

"Yes, you do. We are celebrating."

"Celebrating what?" Bert said.

"It's her b—," Violet began, but Audrey cut her off.

"The end of an era!" Audrey said dramatically as she headed to the kitchen. She returned a moment later with two more tumblers.

She plopped back down next to Violet and set the glasses on the coffee table.

"Wonderful. Here we are," Vince said as he poured.

Audrey extended a tumbler toward Bert. He stared at her for a moment before he took it. It was almost as if he was wondering what he had ever seen in her. *What, indeed?* Audrey raised her own tumbler high and so did Vince.

"Cheers!" she said.

Bert held his glass but did not drink. "What exactly are we toasting?"

"I told you. The end of an era."

"And what era would that be?"

Audrey stared at Bert, a smile plastered to her

face, and didn't reply. She had never seen him so distant from her. So detached. He used to look at her with different eyes.

"Come on, then, Bert," Vince said encouragingly. "Drink up."

Bert ignored him. "What era would that be, Audrey?" he said again, this time with more determination.

Her eyes were suddenly burning with ready tears. "The end of my captivity," she finally answered, still smiling. She brought the drink to her lips and tipped it back, draining the glass.

"You lost your job today," Bert said, in a kinder, gentler tone.

Audrey wiped her mouth with the back of her hand. "I haven't lost anything."

Bert leaned forward in his chair, as if he and she were alone in the room and he was speaking only to her. "Your supervisor let you go, Audrey." His tone now brimmed with disappointment and concern. Maybe even sorrow.

"I let *her* go," Audrey said defiantly, as she extended her glass to Vince. "I'll have another, Vincent."

Vince nodded toward Bert's drink in his hand. "How about it, Bert? The lady wants to celebrate. It's her life."

Bert set his drink down on the table in front of him. "That's right. It is. And we each only get the one. I think I should be going. Good night."

He stood and headed for the front door. Violet jumped up to open it for him.

"Come back, Bert! Don't be a fuddy-duddy!" Audrey called after him.

But Bert didn't turn back or answer her. He stepped outside and Violet followed him, shutting the door behind her.

Vince rose and reached for his sport coat and hat.

Audrey stared up at him. "You're leaving now, too? Doesn't anybody know how to have a good time anymore?"

Vince leaned over her and kissed her forehead. "Even good times must come to an end at some point, Audie. So that there can be more on another day." He stroked her cheek.

Audrey didn't want to dwell on such philosophical thoughts. "Hand me Bert's drink."

As Violet came back inside, Vince obeyed.

"It was very nice to meet you," he said a moment later, as he walked toward Violet. "Take care of her, will you? It's been a rough day," he said in low tones, but Audrey caught every word. He tipped his hat to them both as he let himself out.

Violet turned to her when the front door closed. Audrey took a long swig of Bert's drink.

"How about if I help you get into bed?" Violet said as she took a step toward Audrey.

Audrey looked at Violet over the rim of the

drink. "I can take artifice from just about anybody, but not from Bert and not you."

"What . . . what do you mean?"

"You know what I mean." She closed her eyes and folded one arm lazily over her head, and with her other hand rested the tumbler on her bosom. "Don't treat me like a child, Violet."

When Violet said nothing, Audrey opened her eyes. "For heaven's sake, Violet. Sit down and enjoy your drink."

Violet made her way to the armchair where Bert had been and sat down. She picked up her glass.

"Just please don't patronize me, Violet. Please?"

"I wasn't trying to. I was just—"

"Try the drink. Vince makes a devilishly tangy Sidecar."

Violet lifted the glass to her mouth and sampled the concoction inside. She startled at its invigorating effect.

"Do you ever feel like you are living someone else's life?" Audrey set the tumbler down on the coffee table and reached for her cigarettes and lighter. Droplets of lime juice had spattered the cigarette box. She lowered her arm from above her head and wiped the liquid away with a finger.

"Sometimes."

Audrey nodded as she lit a cigarette. She inhaled deeply and stared up at the ceiling. "If you could be living any kind of life but the one you've been handed, what would it be?"

Violet hesitated a second. "I don't know."

Audrey lowered her gaze to look at Violet. "Sure you do. What is it you want from life, Violet? What have you always wanted?"

Another pause from her roommate. "It doesn't matter what I've always wanted. I can't have it."

Audrey sat up on the couch on her elbows. "Why? Why can't you have it?"

Violet took another drink and lowered the glass to the table as she swallowed. "Because what I've always wanted is to be a mother. Even when I was little, I didn't want to be a teacher or a nurse or a stupid secretary. I wanted to be a wife and mother and have a sweet little house with a white fence and rosebushes and toys in the yard. I wanted to feel a baby growing inside me and then push him or her out into the big world, and then take that child to my breast and sing lullabies. And I wanted to soothe away fevers and fears, kiss away the hurts and doubts, and be that child's very universe. That's what I was raised to be. That's what I wanted to be."

Audrey stared at Violet, her mouth slightly open. "And?"

Violet shrugged. "Something was wrong inside me and I had to have surgery. And now I can't have children."

"That's terrible," Audrey whispered.

"Yes, it is," Violet murmured, and she flicked away a spilled tear.

"Is that why that man named Franklin broke things off with you?"

Violet nodded.

"Lousy scoundrel."

Violet said nothing.

"I just don't get it." Audrey reached for Bert's drink again. "I really don't. You, who would make a great mother, can't get pregnant, and I, who would make a terrible mother, wouldn't have any trouble with that at all."

Violet blinked a second set of tears.

"That just makes no sense," Audrey continued, thoroughly perplexed by the arbitrary unfairness of life. "Why would it be so awful if you got what you wanted and I got what I wanted? You want to be a mother; I want to be a movie star. It's not like we're asking for wings to fly or immortality or to play hopscotch on the moon. Lots of people are mothers. Lots of people are movie stars. I just don't get it."

Violet sighed heavily. "I don't, either."

Silence hung between for them for a moment. "I've been pregnant twice." The confession fell from her lips as though it had bubbled out from the deep with a force of its own.

Violet slowly looked up from her glass. "What?"

"You already know about the first time," Audrey said as the buried year that still felt like it had been someone else's life continued to froth out of her. "After the movie was canceled, Mr. Stiles tried to get me other auditions and screen tests. He did get a few, but no one wanted me, Violet. No one. It was such a . . . such a dark time for me. And then when I got pregnant again I . . ." Audrey's voice fell away.

"You what?" Violet said, her fingers white around the tumbler in her hand.

Audrey pushed away the fragmented images of the parties, the alcohol, the old desire to just disappear the way her mother had. "The father wasn't anyone I truly cared about, and he definitely didn't care about me. I never saw that baby. I . . . They wouldn't let me. I don't even know who adopted it."

"They?" Violet's voice sounded splintered.

"I spent a year away," Audrey said, the multiple cocktails making it easier to speak of the twelve months she did not often mentally revisit.

"*Who* didn't let you see your baby?" Violet sounded insistent.

"The doctors and nurses at the sanitorium."

Violet stared at her, wide-eyed.

"After I lost the movie, no one would hire me for any kind of movie. It was very disheartening and I . . . Well, after a while I didn't care what happened to me," Audrey said. "I went to parties and drank too much and woke up in strange beds, and I didn't care. I fell into such a terrible state of sadness that Aunt Jo convinced me to

226

voluntarily have myself committed so that I could get well. I was pregnant then and didn't even know it yet. I had that baby at the hospital and I never saw it. When I was ready to be released, it was the one time Aunt Jo said maybe I should go home. But I didn't want to go back home to my father, as a failure. That's the way I had felt when I left." As these words tumbled from Audrey's mouth, she remembered the look in her father's face the only time he came to visit her at the sanitorium. He had barely been able to speak to her. She closed her eyes tight to squash that memory and flatten it back into place.

"And they wouldn't let you keep your baby?"

Audrey heard Violet's question but it floated away the second Violet asked it, as if that query belonged to a completely different conversation. "You know, Violet," Audrey continued sleepily, "sometimes I just want to say to hell with all of it. I just want to say to hell with the movie business. There's no one in heaven watching over me. Sometimes I just want to fall in love with a good man like Bert and live an anonymous, ordinary life with that little house you talked about with the toys in the yard. Sometimes that seems like the sweetest dream of all. Can you see me living that life, Violet?"

But Violet didn't answer. And Audrey opened her eyes to see if Violet was still in the room with her.

"Don't give up on your dream, Audrey," Violet finally said, her voice hoarse with emotion. "Don't give up now, after you've come so far. Of course your mother is still watching over you. Show the world you are the star it has been waiting for. She would want you to. She would want you to live the full life she didn't get to live."

"I am so tired of it," Audrey said as she stared at the remnants of Bert's drink in her hand.

Violet said nothing, and Audrey raised her head to look at her roommate. "Did you hear me, Violet? I'm tired."

Violet cleared her throat. "Tired people don't give up, Audrey. Tired people just take a rest. Rest a bit and try again. You don't want to live with regret."

She laughed. "Take a rest. Take a rest from what? I'm not doing anything."

"Take a rest from chasing it. You just need to rest a bit if you're tired. Don't give up now. I know you can make it as a movie star."

"How? How do you know it?"

"Because you have everything all those other famous movie stars have and then some. You're smarter and prettier. And you've wanted it more than they ever did, so you will work harder and shine that much brighter."

"You really think so?"

"I know so."

A slow smile stretched across Audrey's tired face that felt like it began somewhere deep. "You'd make a wonderful mother, Violet. You really would."

Violet's eyes instantly shimmered, and Audrey saw that as much as she wanted stardom, Violet wanted motherhood. Violet was caring for her the way a mother would, the way her mother would have. Should have. Audrey suddenly remembered a snippet of a long-ago conversation at the sanitorium between her and Aunt Jo, long forgotten, never pondered. Aunt Jo had said Audrey's mother had wasted away because she'd chosen to feed only her sadness. Audrey hadn't understood until that moment what Aunt Jo had meant: Unhappiness has an insatiable appetite. It does not care what it might have to kill to feed its cravings.

Audrey reached into the pocket of her robe and pulled out the brown bottle she had placed there earlier that evening. It made a rattling noise as she extended the bottle toward Violet. "Do something with these."

"What are they?"

They had been a ticket. A ticket to her disappearing act. "Sleeping pills," she said. "I was going to take them tonight. All of them."

"What are you saying?" Violet whispered.

Audrey shook the bottle so that Violet would take it from her. "I am saying I want you to take these and get rid of them. Please, Violet. I want them gone. Please? Take them."

Violet uncurled her fingers from the glass she held and set it down on the table.

"Thank you," Audrey whispered, as the bottle was transferred from one woman's hand to the other.

"You're probably the best friend I've ever had, Vi." Audrey locked her gaze on Violet's for a moment, then closed her eyes and laid her head back against the sofa pillow. When sleep overcame her, Violet was still sitting in the chair with the bottle in her hand.

NINETEEN

September 1939

Violet's waking thought on the morning of the tenth of September was the kiss Bert had given her the night before. A smile broke across her lips and she giggled. She felt a little like Scarlett on the morning after an inebriated Rhett carries her up the stairs in a rage fueled more by hurt than alcohol. And in the morning, Scarlett had been giddy with the thought of Rhett having needed her so.

Hours earlier, Bert had taken her in his arms as they said good night on the porch. "Want to go with me to Santa Barbara tomorrow?" he'd whispered into her hair. "I'd like you to meet my mother and sisters. I want them to meet you."

Her heart had felt primed to burst. "Of course!" she'd murmured. *Yes, yes, yes!*

The kiss had been the perfect ending to a perfect evening, which had begun with them going incognito to a theater in Riverside an hour away for a secret screening of *Gone With the Wind*. Stealing away for it had been deliciously deceptive and pleasurable.

Violet had learned via a collection of memos she had typed that the movie was going to be shown at a theater full of unsuspecting patrons who thought they were going to be seeing *Beau Geste*. Selznick wanted a test audience for the film, even though the premiere was many weeks away yet. Violet had whispered the news to Bert at lunch and suggested they take his truck and sneak over to Riverside to be a part of the test audience, fairly certain he would think she was joking, but Bert had surprised her by agreeing they should do it. It was almost as if, like Audrey, he was shaking off an old life. They hadn't told anyone what they were doing, and they'd timed their arrival at the Fox Theater to just mere minutes remained before the newsreel was to start, so that they could slip in without any studio people, including Selznick himself, recognizing them. They sat in the back row in the farthest corner so they could stick to the shadows and be the first to leave when the screening was over.

The moment the announcement was made that instead of *Beau Geste* the seated audience was going to see a three-and-a-half-hour, soon-to-be-released film, the air inside the room became electric. The audience was told there would be only one intermission. No one would be allowed to use the telephone. No one would be allowed to leave the theater once it started. And if someone did leave, they would not be allowed to come back inside. Policemen had been stationed at the doors. When the lights dimmed and the *Gone With the Wind* title began moving across the screen, the crowd roared with delight, and when they saw Clark Gable in his first scene, they cheered for five whole minutes. Nobody left early, even though the movie wasn't over until just before midnight.

Afterward, Violet and Bert were given reaction questionnaires that they were supposed to take home and send back to the studio. They had ducked out before anyone could recognize them and gone out for drinks when they got back to Hollywood, and walked Sunset, listening for the nightingale and talking about the movie.

It had been an exciting evening, and the kiss as Bert said good night had been magical. Bert was fully hers now. Perhaps this should be the morning to tell Audrey that she and Bert were seeing each other.

Bert hadn't asked about Audrey in recent days other than in polite terms. Violet liked to imagine he had been wondering what he had seen in Audrey as a love interest all those years. Violet wanted to believe he had finally realized Audrey wasn't someone to fall in love with, but rather someone to appreciate from a distance.

She had not told him about the pills Audrey had given to her to dispose of. What would have been the point of that? Doing so would only have served to arouse Bert's compassion, which Audrey didn't need. What Audrey needed was confirmation that it was a good thing she had been let go from the studio. Being a secretary had been keeping her from pursuing her true goals rather than helping her meet them. Audrey hadn't been making inroads with influential people because they never thought of her as anything but a lovely girl with a steno pad.

Audrey hadn't brought up the matter of the pills, either. The morning after that disastrous night, Audrey had simply given Violet a cozy, one-armed hug in the kitchen and then headed for the coffee and aspirin bottle. That had been two weeks ago. There had been no more allusions to Peg Entwistle or the handing over of the little brown bottle, or tearful reminders of crushed hopes.

Violet didn't know what Audrey was doing for money or how she was spending her ample supply of free time since her firing. Just as Violet had expected, everything was different now that Audrey no longer worked at the studio. Audrey was usually still asleep when Violet left in the morning and was gone when Violet got home from work. And yet Audrey still had food on her side of the Frigidaire, and Violet had seen a new pair of shoes on the bathroom floor a couple of days ago. When she did see Audrey, she seemed happy or at least determined, and with Audrey that was kind of the same thing. It was apparent to Violet that Audrey was no longer waiting around anymore for her angel mother to set everything in motion.

As she lay in her bed, contemplating last night's kiss, Violet heard movement in the bedroom next door. It was a Sunday morning and still relatively early. Audrey had been out later than Violet the night before, and Violet was surprised Audrey was even awake. Perhaps she would make biscuits and gravy, and she could tell Audrey about last night's screening—and that she and Bert were in love.

Violet rose from the bed, grabbed her robe, and opened her bedroom door. She found Audrey in the kitchen with a cup of coffee in one hand and the questionnaire from last night's screening in the other. The morning newspaper lay unread on the kitchen table.

"What's this?" Audrey asked without looking up from it.

"Oh. Selznick did a surprise screening in Riverside last night. Bert and I drove out for it and snuck in."

Audrey turned to her. "Did you?"

Violet took a coffee cup from the dish drainer and filled it from the coffeepot on the stove. "It was amazing, Audrey. You should've heard the audience cheer when the title came up on the screen. And to finally see all those scenes that I had stood by and watched being filmed? It was marvelous."

She turned back to the table. Audrey was staring at her, waiting for more.

"I think Selznick is going to be very happy with the responses he gets. Of course, Bert and I won't be sending in our questionnaires, since we probably shouldn't have been there in the first place."

Audrey looked down at the response sheet and then back up again. "It's a thrill to do something you aren't supposed to be doing, isn't it? Though I don't suppose you've had much experience with that."

An image of the curtain hat filled Violet's head and she mentally flicked it away. "It's going to be the best film ever," Violet prattled on, pulling out a kitchen chair and sitting down. "Though Mr. Selznick is still not happy with how the movie ends. The Hays Office won't let him use the word 'damn' in Rhett Butler's last line. Right now it's 'Frankly my dear, I just don't care,' and he hates it."

"Not quite the same thing, is it?" Audrey took a sip of coffee.

Violet couldn't read her tone. Something about it unnerved her. "That's not the only trouble Mr. Selznick is having with the end," she continued, keeping her own tone light. "After Rhett Butler leaves, there's poor Scarlett, without the man she truly loves. There's nothing at the end of the book to suggest Scarlett will get Rhett back, and everyone at the studio says audiences won't like that for an ending. So there have been a bunch of different endings that the script people have written, and not one of them has seemed right. Mr. Selznick finally came up with one that I really like, though no one really cares what I think. He thinks Scarlett should say something about how she will just *have* to win Rhett back, and of course the audience will believe her, because, you know, when has Scarlett not gotten what she wanted? But she doesn't yet know how and she doesn't know what to do with herself while she tries to figure it out. And so she's crying on the stairs of her fancy house after Rhett leaves, and then she hears in her mind the voices of the three men who've mattered most to her—Pa, Ashley, and Rhett—and they are telling her that Tara is where she has always gone when life handed her sorrow, and it was at Tara that she was always able to find the strength to overcome whatever opposed her. Home is where she will go to begin again. It's not how Miss Mitchell ends the book, but I like it."

Violet paused for breath.

"Sounds like the perfect ending," Audrey said.

Violet knew Audrey was not talking about the movie anymore.

"Bert and I are seeing each other," Violet said, and she held Audrey's gaze.

"So I've gathered."

"It just happened over time, Audrey. We both realized we love and want the same things. You've been so busy with your career and Vince and meeting new people. I hardly ever see you anymore. I was going to tell you before now."

Audrey seemed to need a second to take this in. "You'll be good to Bert, won't you?" Her resonant voice was thick with neither anger nor resentment, but something closer to longing. "Promise me you will, Violet. He's the kindest man I've ever known. And my first true friend. Promise me you'll be good to him."

"I . . . Of course I promise. I love him."

Audrey closed her eyes just for a moment. When she opened them, a glistening sheen sparkled in both. "I'm so very happy for you both. Really."

They regarded each other for a moment silently.

"You two won't forget about me now, will you?" Audrey finally said, a sad laugh coating her words.

"Never in a million years!" Violet answered quickly. Audrey would forever be within the folds of Violet's soul. She could already feel her weighty presence there. Things were coming together just as Violet had dared to hope they could, but it was as though everything she held was made of gauze and could drift away at the slightest breath of wind. If she wasn't careful she could lose it all. Hadn't she learned that already? Hadn't Audrey's sad life borne witness to this? What you owned one day could be snatched away from you the next if you didn't find a way to hold on tight to it.

Audrey smiled a tired grin, as if Violet's unspoken thoughts had been audible. "I think I might go back to bed for a while."

She lowered the *Gone With the Wind* response sheet to the table, letting it fall onto the newspaper and cover up the headline that a world away, Adolf Hitler had just laid siege on Warsaw.

TWENTY

October 1939

A blanket of predawn mist shrouded the bungalow in ghostly white fog as Audrey slipped her key into the lock. She turned and waved at the man who had brought her home, and was now sitting in his sleek Packard at the curb. Desmond, the aspiring playwright who had wanted her to stay overnight at his place, had been playfully disappointed when she'd declined. They'd spent the evening dancing and drinking at the Trocadero, and then continued with impromptu festivities at a friend of Desmond's whose Beverly Hills mansion easily accommodated the forty people that showed up. Desmond waved back and then sped away.

She liked Desmond. He was ten years older than she was, a confirmed bachelor—so he liked to say—and a gifted writer. Several of his plays had been produced in Los Angeles over the past few years; one had even caught Broadway's eye. Glen Wainwright, Desmond's longtime friend with the Beverly Hills mansion and a passion for live theater, had funded the local productions. Vince had told Audrey weeks ago that Desmond was being courted to write screenplays for several movie studios. He was a good person to know. But what she enjoyed best about Desmond was that he wasn't like the other men in Hollywood with whom she'd been trying to get close. Desmond Hale was hungry for fame, just like she was. He was further along than she in his pursuit of happiness, but he still craved what he didn't yet have. It was of secondary importance to Audrey that Desmond had friends in well-appointed places.

She stepped inside quietly, so as not to wake Violet. Their friendship was different now that Audrey was no longer at Selznick International and Violet and Bert were a couple. She had acclimated to not going into the studio every day far more easily than she'd gotten used to the idea that Violet and Bert were in love with each other. In all the years Audrey had known Bert, he had always had a calming influence on her, and she'd been careful not to lead him on romantically or trample on his obvious affection for her. She had grown fond of his attraction to her and hadn't realized just how much until she had misplaced that costume hat and almost gotten him fired. He had started to look at her differently after that. And then there had been that disastrous evening Bert came to the house after she'd lost her job. The way he had looked at her . . . If Violet hadn't been there after he left, she surely would have swallowed every pill in that bottle. If there was anyone she might have given up her career dreams for, it would have been Bert.

Except that he deserved someone better than her.

And now he had fallen in love with Violet. And she with him. She wondered if he knew Violet could never give him children. It would be just like Bert to love her anyway.

Valentino sidled up to her as she closed the front door and kicked off her shoes. He meowed loudly and she shushed him. She scooped up the cat and lowered her purse and outer wrap onto the sofa as she walked past it. In the little hallway that led to the bedrooms she stopped. Violet's door was open, her bed made.

Instinctively Audrey looked at her watch. Five twenty-two in the morning. Violet hadn't slept in her bed. All night. Half alarmed and half shocked, Audrey set down the cat and walked into the kitchen. The hoped-for note lay propped up against a juice glass.

We will be home on Sunday! Don't worry.
All is well!

Love, Violet

Audrey frowned as she read the note a second time.

We. We will be home on Sunday. Had Violet actually gone with Bert on a trip somewhere? Just the two of them?

Were they sleeping together?

"I don't believe it," Audrey whispered.

"Meow," said Valentino.

She stood there for a few seconds longer, unable to fathom the thought that sweet, innocent Violet was sharing a bed with kindhearted Bert Redmond.

Bert.

When at last she turned for her bedroom, she

tossed the note back toward the table, but it wafted to the floor when she walked away.

Much later, after Audrey had slept a few hours, Desmond called to ask if she wanted to see a play that night. They went back to his place for drinks afterward and he asked her to stay.

She stayed.

Audrey had been home only for a few minutes late Sunday afternoon when she heard Bert's truck pull up just outside the bungalow. From the armchair by the front-room window, she watched Violet get out of the truck. Bert got out, too, reached into the back, and pulled out a small suitcase, which he handed to her.

He said something to Violet and she shook her head, leaned up, and kissed him. Then she started up the short path to the front door. Violet had just opened it when Audrey heard Bert call out, "I'll be back in an hour or two."

"All right!" Violet said.

And then she was in the house, clutching her little suitcase, her cheeks flushed with excitement. And something else. At first Violet didn't see Audrey sitting there with a cup of coffee and the unread Sunday paper in her lap. When she did see her, she jumped.

"Spent the weekend with Bert, did you?" Audrey asked, a knowing tone in her voice.

"Oh my goodness! Audrey! You frightened

me!" Violet laughed like a schoolgirl who did not sound frightened at all. She set down her suitcase and unbuttoned her coat.

"Well, you surprised me." Audrey smiled slyly and put the cup on the coffee table. "What would your sweet Southern mama say if she knew you had spent the weekend with a man?"

Violet giggled and plopped down on the couch. "I already told her."

Audrey laughed. "You *what?*"

"I called home. Yesterday. From the hotel in Las Vegas. I told my parents where I was and who I was with."

Audrey couldn't believe what she was hearing. "Oh, really?"

Violet nodded happily. "Yes, ma'am. I did!"

"And were you sober when you did this?"

Again Violet chuckled. "Well, I'd had some champagne by that time. So not exactly."

Audrey shook her head. "Violet, Violet. And what did your parents say?"

Violet leaned forward on the sofa. Her eyes were bright with mischievous glee. "Mama started crying and Daddy started yelling, and I had to tell them that if they both didn't stop I was going to hang up. They simmered down, and then I told them what a wonderful man Bert is, that he comes from a wonderful family, that I love him very much. Mother kept saying, 'But he's not Southern!' And Daddy kept saying, 'What kind of future does a costume boy have?' That's what he called Bert—a costume boy."

Words failed Audrey. "Violet, I must say, you have taken me completely by surprise. You and Bert both. I hardly know what to even say to you."

Violet's happy grin increased. "Well, how about congratulations?"

Audrey felt the air around her grow still.

Violet thrust her left hand forward. A gold band with a tiny diamond sparkled on Violet's finger and happy tears shimmered in her eyes.

"We got married!"

The moment felt like make-believe, like a line in a script. "Married?" Audrey echoed.

Violet pulled her arm back to admire the ring herself. "It wasn't like we planned it. Not really. We were just cuddling and kissing Friday night, very late, and we both just wanted to be together, you know, in the married way. And we started laughing about how expensive and complicated weddings are when it really is so very simple for two people who love each other to pledge their devotion and sign a paper. So very simple. Right?"

Audrey could neither nod in agreement nor shake her head to the contrary. After a second, Violet went on.

"So we just said, 'Let's do it. Let's elope.' And the next thing you know, we are heading out of Los Angeles in the middle of the night to drive to

Las Vegas. Bert was a little nervous about doing something so spontaneous and he wanted to call his mother to tell her, but he didn't when I said I wasn't going to call mine until after. Once we got there and had breakfast, we bought two very simple rings and some white daisies at a roadside stand. Then we filled out some papers, and next thing you know we're both saying, 'I do!' Bert kept saying, 'I can't believe we just did that!' and I kept saying, 'I know, I know!' Then we found this sweet honeymoon cottage to stay the night in, and, well, you know!" Violet blushed crimson.

"And your parents?" Audrey said, numb with surprise and a strange sense of disappointment. "They are all right with this?"

"Well, Mama was sad that I hadn't been married in a church and that she hadn't been there. I can understand her melancholy about that. But Bert wouldn't have wanted a big Montgomery wedding that would have put him in the center of all that attention. He's a very private person, you know."

Audrey nodded. "Yes, I know."

"We will go home to Montgomery for Christmas—Mama and Daddy are insisting on it. They want to host a wedding reception for us. The premiere of *Gone With the Wind* will have taken place by then, so we won't be so incredibly busy. I am so excited for all my Montgomery friends to meet Bert! He's such a gentleman, everyone will think he was Alabama born and raised!"

"No doubt," Audrey said.

Violet leaned across the table and took Audrey's hands in hers. "You are happy for me, aren't you?"

"I'm happy if you're happy."

Violet closed her eyes and squeezed Audrey's hands. "I'm over-the-moon happy!"

"And you will remember what you promised me?"

Violet nodded. "Not to forget you."

Audrey squeezed Violet's hands in return. "To be good to Bert. You will be good to Bert, won't you?"

Violet hesitated only a second. "Of course! I love Bert, Audrey. I do. And he loves me."

"You got what you wanted," Audrey murmured a second later, as tears stung her eyes. They would be happy together, these two. Life wouldn't always be easy, certainly, but at least they would always have each other to lean on.

"Mostly," Violet whispered in return, her eyes glassy as well.

"The love between you will be enough—I'm sure of that."

Violet nodded, unable to say anything else.

It occurred to Audrey then that Violet would be leaving the bungalow that very night. "I guess I've lost you as a roommate," she said.

"But not as a friend," Violet said quickly. She stood up, reached over, and pulled Audrey up out of her chair and into an embrace. "Thank you for everything, Audrey."

Audrey laughed lightly. "I didn't do anything."

Violet broke away. "You introduced me to Bert! I owe you everything."

Then Violet pulled away and headed to her room to pack her belongings.

TWENTY-ONE

December 1939

Violet awoke before her husband, pulled from sleep by a troubling dream that faded from her memory even as she opened her eyes. She didn't want to remember what had been chasing her while she slept, so she sat up in the bed and leaned back against the headboard so that sleep could not return to her. The pale light of a mid-December daybreak seeped through the blinds of the one narrow window in their bedroom, and she glanced at Bert lying beside her. Violet reached out a hand to gently touch his shoulder, not to awaken him but rather to reassure herself as she had done every morning since he'd married her that he was indeed lying next to her.

She turned her head to look at the clock on the bedside table. Just a few minutes after six. She switched off the alarm so that Bert could sleep a little while longer. It would be quiet at the studio that day; they didn't need to rush. Selznick and his entourage were all in Atlanta for the premiere of *Gone With the Wind*. She rose from bed, slipped on her robe and slippers, and tiptoed out to the main room of their half of the tiny duplex they were renting. The open space tripled as living area, dining room, and kitchen. It was a sweet little place. Not far from the studio but away from the busiest streets. They didn't have much for furnishings or other conveniences but they had managed to come by the necessities at a used furniture store. Her parents had sent a wedding gift of china in an elegant pattern Violet might have liked a year or so ago, but that seemed out of place in their humble quarters. But since it was all they had for dishes, they ate everything off it. Bert's mother, Delores, had put together a box of hand-me-downs from her own kitchen for Violet and Bert to set up housekeeping with, which she seemed happy enough to do after she recovered from the surprise and shock of her son's elopement. When they drove up to Santa Barbara the weekend after they married, Violet had overheard Delores ask Bert in a hushed tone if she was in the family way. After a quick prick of anxiety, Violet had taken comfort in Bert's quick defense of her high morals. Delores seemed to relax after that, at least somewhat. She said more than once how astonished she was, though it did not seem that she was unhappy about Violet being her new daughter-in-law. Just surprised. Delores had now had six weeks to get used to the idea of Bert and Violet being married. Everyone had. It was not so astonishing anymore, surely.

After getting the coffee going, Violet sat down with the morning paper and the unopened mail from yesterday, which included a gas bill and a letter from her mother. She noted with satisfaction that the headline story in the newspaper was the success of last night's premiere in Atlanta. Violet glanced at all the news stories on the front page, even the ones that didn't interest her, until at last she set down the paper. She couldn't put off reading her mother's letter forever. It was the second one since Violet had eloped; the first had arrived ten days after she and Bert had married. Mama had closed that note with how much she and Daddy and everyone else were looking forward to meeting Bert at Christmas, and a PS that read, *You* did *tell him, didn't you?*

Violet hadn't answered that letter. She had been too busy. Too distracted with the details of setting up a house. She reached for the newest one, tore open the flap, and pulled out the single sheet of paper.

Dear Violet,
I've been anxious to hear back from you, and while I've been waiting it has occurred

to me that perhaps you think I stuck my nose in where it doesn't belong. Perhaps you think I shouldn't have asked what I did in my last letter. Maybe I shouldn't have.

Since you have not written me, which is not like you, I cannot help but think I have my answer—you did not tell Bert that you cannot give him children. I so very much hope that I am mistaken. If you love this man as you say you do, surely you agree that he is worthy of knowing the truth.

I will say nothing more of it after this, Violet.

Until we see you at Christmas,
Love, Mama

Violet stared at the letter for several long minutes after she'd read the last word. It wasn't until she heard footfalls behind her that she folded the letter into thirds and slipped it back in its envelope.

A second later Bert's arms were around her and he was kissing the back of her head. "Good morning. Letter from your mother?"

"Yes." She put the letter in her robe pocket with one hand and reached up to touch his face with the other. "She and Daddy can't wait to meet you when we go home next week."

He nuzzled her neck before standing straight

and heading for the coffeepot on the stove. "She and all your friends must be pretty angry with me for denying everyone a fancy wedding to attend."

"The minute they meet you they won't care about any of that. They're going to love you. Just like I do."

Bert poured coffee into two bone china cups and handed her one. "If you say so," he said, grinning.

She took the offered cup. "I know so."

He sipped his coffee and grimaced at its heat. "It will be strange not being with my mother and sisters this Christmas, especially with my mother's health the way it is," he said, almost as if musing aloud to himself.

"We can take turns where we spend our Christmases, darling. Next year we can stay in California, and then maybe the following Christmas we can go back to Alabama."

"Unless we've a little one to make us want to stay close to home." He brought the cup back to his lips as he winked at her.

She laughed despite a slight lurching sensation inside her stomach. "Look," she said a second later. "The premiere went well." She handed him the newspaper as she stood. A corner of the envelope in her pocket was poking her thigh.

Violet moved toward the fridge to get out the carton of eggs and a bottle of milk. Taped to the door was an invitation from Audrey to her Christmas party that evening. Bert wanted to go.

Of course he wanted to go. He had already told Audrey they were coming. Violet had spent little time with Audrey in the past few weeks. It was awkward to be in Audrey's presence now that she and Bert were married. Audrey looked at her differently. Looked at Bert differently. When Violet had started to box up her few kitchen things at Audrey's, she noticed the little nightingale was on the sill above the sink, where Audrey would see it every time she stood and looked out at the world beyond the glass.

Violet closed the fridge door now and turned away from Audrey's invitation. She and Bert were quiet as she whisked eggs and he sat at the table, reading the article about the premiere.

"So the masses weren't horrified after all that Rhett Butler said 'damn,'" Bert said a moment later. "I still can't believe the Hays Office let him say it."

Violet poured a splash of milk into the eggs. "Me, either."

"Well, Selznick ought to be happy." Bert set down the paper on the table. "Hope the rest of the world likes the movie as much as Atlanta apparently did."

"Of course they will," Violet said as she reached for their only frying pan.

Several minutes later they sat down to their meal, and there was no conversation between them at first. Violet was too distracted to notice.

Her mother's letter crinkled in her pocket when she leaned forward in her chair to take a bite of breakfast.

"I need to ask you something, Violet," Bert finally said when his plate was empty.

She nearly dropped her fork. "Yes?"

"I've . . . I've been thinking."

She waited.

"I've been thinking maybe you and I should maybe move home to Santa Barbara. I'd like for us to be closer to my mother. She hasn't said anything, but I can tell the house is getting to be too much for her. I think eventually that house will be ours. So I was thinking, why don't we start helping her with it now?"

Violet's first thought was one of astonished elation. "Move to Santa Barbara?"

Bert mistook her tone for hesitation. "Think about it, Vi. Mr. Selznick wants the studio to take a major break after *Rebecca* is finished. I am likely to be laid off then, anyway. You probably will be, too, since you're one of the last hires in the secretary pool. And with your office skills you could work anywhere. I don't want to be pushing around costumes the rest of my life. I'd like to see if maybe I could go back to school, learn what I need to have the career in ornithology that I want. There's a university right there. And I don't want to raise a family here in Hollywood."

"Raise a family," Violet echoed, toneless.

"Yes. Can you see us trying to raise kids in a place like this?"

She shook her head. No, she could not.

"So you'll think about it?"

But Violet didn't need to think about it.

"I will go anywhere with you, Bert," she said, and the smile that broke wide across her husband's face made her eyes water.

He grabbed her hand across the table and squeezed it. "I love you, Vi. And you won't regret this. I promise you."

Bert started to explain when and how they should make the move, but Violet was not listening. She was pondering.

What Violet had wanted from her new life she had—for the most part. There was really nothing left in Hollywood but reminders of what she'd done to get it.

A few minutes later, after Bert had left the table to shave, Violet pulled Bert's handkerchief from the zippered pocket in her purse, where it had been nestled since the day before Valentine's Day. She brought it to her face, brushed it across her cheek, and kissed it. Then she tossed it atop the rest of Bert's laundry that needed washing.

She would write her mother at lunch and tell her that she need not worry so. All was perfectly well between her and Bert.

Bert adored her and she adored him.

They couldn't have been happier.

1942

TWENTY-TWO

August 1942

Violet sat on the porch step with Bert's letter in her hands. She had already read it twice, but she flattened the paper against her bent knees and read it again just to imagine his voice saying these words to her:

August 4, 1942

Dear Violet,

I am nearly finished with basic training here at Camp Wheeler and am happy to assure you I will be getting a week's leave before I am to report to my duty station. I can't wait to get home and hear the birds singing in the morning again. I never hear birds here, and the heat has been ruthless. I know you warned me what Southern summers are like, but I still cannot understand how air can feel like water.

I also found out that I won't be heading out to any place faraway—at least not soon. I am being assigned to the Fourth Infantry Division, which is posted here in Georgia at Fort Gordon. They are doing training maneuvers in the States. I don't think Fort Gordon is a place where you would want to come, though, and it's definitely not a place to bring Mother. I think the best place for you to be is with her, and she with you. Hopefully this war will be over soon, perhaps even before I go to any place outside of the States. And I can come home to you and we can pick up our lives again as if this war never happened.

I only wish God had seen fit to bless us with a baby by now, so that in my absence you would have a son or a daughter to keep you company and fill these dark days with sunshine. I still pray that someday God will grant us a child. You would be a wonderful mother, Violet.

Time for lights-out, so better sign off. I will be home before the month ends.

Love to Mother, but especially to you.

Bert

Violet traced his handwriting on the paper, missing his touch, the sound of his voice, his warm presence in her bed. Bert had been gone for more than a month already—after having been called up earlier that summer—and was learning how to do what kind souls like Bert should never have to do. In his letters he made it seem like learning to be a soldier wasn't so bad, but Violet could tell he missed her and his little photography business and his classes at the university and even taking care of his ailing mother. She hoped that wherever he was ultimately assigned, it would be somewhere safe. There were still safe places in the world, weren't there?

She had tried to convince Bert to find a way out of enlisting. But since Pearl Harbor, every able-bodied young man in Santa Barbara was looked upon as someone who should've been gone already. He had felt compelled to sign up.

With Bert away it fell to Violet to take care of her mother-in-law, Delores. Bert's two sisters were both married now and living elsewhere, Evelyn in Seattle and Charlene in San Francisco. Delores hadn't been in the best of health when Bert and Violet relocated to Santa Barbara two years ago, and she'd only been getting worse. Violet got along fairly well with Delores, but she knew she wasn't Delores's first choice for a caregiver. She adored Bert, but he was gone. And while both of Delores's daughters had offered her a room at their respective houses, she wouldn't leave the home her husband had built for her and that contained all her memories of him. Charlene was expecting, which Delores was very happy about, and Violet was hopeful that when she finally had a grandchild to cuddle, Delores would rethink the idea of moving to San Francisco. If she moved in with Charlene and her husband, that would leave the house for Bert and Violet, and she wouldn't have minded that at all.

In the meantime, Violet saved her tin cans for the war effort, she prayed for peace, and she tried to make the house as cozy as she could for an ailing woman. She took Delores to the movies sometimes, like *Mrs. Miniver*, which Delores didn't like, and Walt Disney's *Bambi*, which made her cry. Right after Bert left, Violet saw *To Be or Not to Be* with Carole Lombard, which she enjoyed even though she went alone.

Violet often found it hard to believe she had been gone from the studio for two years. Had she and Bert stayed in Hollywood, she didn't know what she would have been doing for work. David Selznick was dissolving his company and she didn't think he even owned *Gone With the Wind* anymore. She'd read in *Variety* that a good friend of his, Jock Whitney, bought the film from him as part of the studio's liquidation.

Sometimes, that year she'd spent in Hollywood seemed like a dream, as if her new life had begun when she and Bert eloped. It had all happened so fast. She hadn't purposely not told Bert that she couldn't get pregnant; a good time to tell him had just never presented itself, and now she didn't know how to bring up the matter.

She and Bert heard from Audrey now and then. She'd been in a few plays, and in April had sent a review of her most recent one, as the critic liked her performance very much. Violet missed Audrey in ways that surprised her, even when Bert had still been home. She had made a few friends in Santa Barbara, but no one like Audrey. And despite what she had done to Audrey to win over Bert, she found herself feeling lonely for her companionship. She often wondered whether Audrey felt the same way.

The screen door behind her squeaked on rusty hinges.

"Is that a letter from Bert?"

Violet turned to nod at her mother-in-law.

"What does he say? How is he?" Delores looked longingly at the letter in Violet's hand.

Violet smiled up at her. "He says he can't wait to get home to see you. He has a week of leave coming to him when he finishes and will be here by the end of August."

"Just a week?"

Violet was only momentarily annoyed at Delores's hunger to see her son, when he was first and foremost Violet's husband. Delores loved Bert as much as she loved Bert. She worried for his safety like Violet did. He wasn't an hour away in glamorous Hollywood anymore. He was three thousand miles away, in a world that suddenly seemed to have turned hostile in every direction. Delores looked pale and her hand trembled as she held open the screen door. The hot afternoon sun slanting across the porch made her forehead glisten.

Violet slipped the letter into her pants pocket and rose to her feet. She took Delores's arm and guided her back inside the house. "Then we will make it a wonderful week, won't we? And guess what he told me? He's not going anywhere far away. He gets to stay in Georgia."

"Really? Is he certain?"

"At least for now. Isn't that wonderful?"

Delores leaned into Violet as they stepped over the threshold. "I don't want him going to where the war is. He can't go there. War killed his father. You know that, don't you? He was never the same after the trenches."

Violet ushered Delores to her favorite arm-chair and settled her into it. "Let's not think about that right now. Ready for some tea?"

Delores sighed audibly, picked up a wooden fan stamped with stenciled palm trees and a flamenco dancer, and began to wave it back and forth. "It's too hot for tea, Violet."

"How about some lemonade, then?"

Delores closed her eyes. "I don't want anything from the kitchen. You get something if you want it."

"Well, I'll just go see what I can make for us for dinner tonight, then." Violet started to walk away.

"So, Bert said he's all right?" Delores called after her.

Violet turned back around and for a moment she considered her answer. She wanted Bert to hear that she took good care of his mother while he was away. She wanted Delores to say to him how wonderful Violet was, so thoughtful and caring. She pulled the letter out of her pants pocket and extended it toward her. "Do you want to read his letter, Delores?" she said kindly. "I don't mind."

Delores's eyes widened. "Oh, surely you don't mean that!"

Violet took a step closer and smiled benevolently. "But I do. I wouldn't offer if I didn't. Truly."

"But he wrote it to you. It's personal. You're . . . you're his wife."

"He wrote nothing in this one that will embarrass either one of us, I promise." Violet laughed.

Delores's anxiety seemed to soften and she smiled at Violet. "Maybe you can read it to me?"

"Sure." Violet began to read aloud. She faltered when she got to Bert's longing for them to have a child and she mentally kicked herself for not skipping ahead when she got to that part. She quickened her pace to get to the line where Bert spoke of his love to his mother.

When Violet was finished she slipped the letter back into her pocket and forced a smile to her lips. She raised her gaze to look at Delores.

The woman was smiling but tears rimmed her

eyes. "It doesn't seem fair that God should with-hold children from Bert and you," she murmured. "Not fair at all."

Violet hesitated only a second before responding. "No. It doesn't."

"Bert's right, you know. You would make a good mother, Violet. You've been taking such good care of me while he's been gone. I know it can't be easy when you probably miss your own mother and father and wish you could spend the time that Bert is away with them."

A stab of equal parts longing and regret poked at Violet and she involuntarily winced. "I wouldn't dream of leaving you here alone, Delores."

Delores dropped the fan in her lap. She reached out her hand toward her daughter-in-law and Violet took a step forward to squeeze it.

The two women were silent for a moment.

Violet broke away first. She turned to head back into the kitchen. "How does bacon and eggs sound?" she called over her shoulder to Delores. "I always liked it when Mama made breakfast for supper."

Before Delores could answer, Violet heard footsteps coming up the walkway to the front door. She turned her head toward the sound, and on the other side of the screen door a woman in heels, a full skirt, and a flowered hat was walking toward her. The visitor was backlit by a brilliant low-lying sun, which made her facial features indistinguishable as she approached.

But Violet would know that silhouette anywhere.

Half a second later Audrey came to a stop at the doorstep.

"Oh, my stars!" Violet reached for the handle on the screen door and swung it open wide.

Even before Audrey was fully inside, she was taking Violet into her arms. "It's so good to see you, Vi. I've missed you so much." Audrey spoke the words over Violet's shoulders.

Out of the corner of her eye, Violet saw that Delores, curious, was staring at the beautiful stranger.

Audrey stepped back and held Violet at arm's length. "Let me look at you."

The request gave Violet a moment to study Audrey as well. She looked as lovely and enchanting as ever. Her hair was a deeper shade of brown than when Violet had last seen her. The lemon yellow, full-skirted dress was not Audrey's usual figure-hugging sheath, but it was nevertheless eye-catching and fashionable, and accented by a boxy, short-sleeved linen jacket. Ample jewelry shimmered golden at her neck, wrists, and ears. Violet was embarrassed by the plain slacks and faded cotton blouse she was wearing, and the old kerchief of Bert's that held her hair off her neck.

"Marriage agrees with you," Audrey said, smiling.

Violet laughed nervously. "I look frightful and you know it."

"You look happy as a clam," Audrey replied, her tone friendly but serious. "I can see how happy you are. It wouldn't matter what you are wearing. I am sure Bert can't wait to get home to you."

Behind them Delores had risen from her chair.

"Delores, this is Audrey Duvall." Violet directed Audrey's attention to her mother-in-law. "Audrey's a good friend of Bert's and mine from Hollywood."

Delores's eyes widened at once at the introduction with an unmistakable look of recognition. Violet couldn't recall mentioning Audrey's name recently to Delores. Had she? Or had she made much mention of Audrey's occasional phone calls to the house? Violet was still pondering the look when Audrey stepped forward to clasp Delores's hands in her own.

"It's so good to finally meet you, Mrs. Redmond. Bert has told me so much about you."

"Please. Call me Delores." The woman's eyes were still wide with wonder. "Very nice to meet you, too."

Audrey looked from Violet to Delores and then back to Violet. There was a sudden desperation in her eyes. "I hope it's all right that I didn't call first before coming to see you."

"Of course it's all right!" Violet replied. "I would have met you at the train station, though." *And changed into something decent to receive a visitor.*

Audrey smiled in relief. "I'm so glad! And I didn't take the train. I actually learned how to drive. I've got a car." She nodded toward the screen door and a light green sedan that was visible across the street. "It's used but it gets me around."

"Oh!" Violet exclaimed. "How exciting."

"Yes," Audrey said, but Violet detected a sudden sad undertone. Something wasn't quite right with Audrey. Whatever it was, it was the reason she was on Violet's doorstep without having called first.

"Can you stay for supper or do you have to rush right back?" Violet asked.

Audrey's gaze was still on her car parked across the street, but as she turned Violet saw a shimmering in Audrey's eyes. She was holding back tears. "I don't have to rush back."

Something was terribly wrong. Audrey was in some kind of trouble. Violet reached out to touch Audrey's arm. "Perhaps you'd like to stay overnight? We've a guest room and we'd be happy to have you. Wouldn't we, Delores?"

"Of course," Delores replied, still a bit taken aback by the afternoon's turn of events.

"Did you bring a suitcase, Audrey?"

Audrey nodded and forced a smile past her pursed lips.

"Here," Violet said, leading Audrey away from the door, Delores, and the view of the little green car that had brought Audrey to her. "I'll show you the guest room, and you can set down your purse and hat."

Audrey followed Violet down the narrow hall to the smallest of the three bedrooms, the one that years ago had been Bert's. Remnants of his childhood still graced the walls and bookshelves—bird-watching guides, a butterfly net, photo albums, and swim-team trophies. Violet had forgotten how many little reminders of Bert's younger years were still scattered about the room. Audrey's gaze lingered on the mementos as she took in the room. She walked slowly to the bed, unpinned her hat, and set it on the mattress.

"I'll just open the window to get some fresh air in here," Violet said, unnerved now by Audrey's demeanor.

"Thank you, Violet."

"No need to thank me. We're glad you're here." Violet tugged on the window, and it shimmied upward.

"I should have called."

"Nonsense. Surprises are fun." She turned back around. Audrey was still standing at the side of the bed.

"I didn't know what else to do."

"What do you mean?"

"I . . . I need to get out of Hollywood for a little while." Audrey's gaze dropped to the hat on the bed.

A dozen questions materialized in Violet's head and she didn't know which one to ask first.

"I can be on my way in the morning if . . . if you need me to leave," Audrey said when Violet had no response.

Violet finally found her voice. "Audrey, what is it? What has happened?"

For a second Audrey said nothing. Then she started to take off the linen jacket and Violet saw the rounded lump at Audrey's waistline.

Audrey tossed the jacket on the bed and turned to face Violet.

"I'm pregnant."

TWENTY-THREE

A grandfather clock was chiming nine o'clock as Audrey watched Violet escort her mother-in-law to her bedroom. Audrey viewed them from the sofa as they made their way with measured steps down the hallway. The tiny life inside her wriggled and she placed a hand over her swelling abdomen. She'd been with Violet and Delores for a little over a week and she couldn't remember when she'd experienced such a tranquil time.

The three of them had gone to the movies, played cards, listened to the radio, read magazines, sipped iced tea, and eaten three square meals a day.

Violet hadn't pressured Audrey to divulge more than she wanted to, which Audrey was grateful for. She hadn't wanted to talk about how she'd managed to get herself into the same situation she had been in twice before, even though it had been different this time. Desmond wasn't like Rafael, and she hadn't been in an emotional abyss like she had been when she got pregnant the second time. She had naïvely hoped that Desmond would marry her even though he joked that he, like Rhett Butler, wasn't the marrying kind. But when Broadway called, Desmond left for New York alone, telling her he would send for her later. The day he left was the day she realized his child was growing inside her. When she arrived in New York she'd planned to surprise him with the news that they were going to be parents, and nervously hoped that he would be happy and would want them to be a family. Violet's life dream of marriage and motherhood had suddenly seemed very attractive and attainable. But two months after Desmond had arrived in Manhattan, he'd sent a telegram telling Audrey he was not going to send for her. He didn't want her to come. He was moving on with his life, and so should she.

Violet had been satisfied for the moment,

knowing that the father of Audrey's child didn't want to be married or carry the responsibilities of parenthood, and didn't even know she was carrying his baby. And Audrey had told Violet that her friends and connections back in Hollywood thought she had gone home to the farm for an extended visit because there was an illness in the family. She wasn't in a play at the moment and didn't have to rush back. Violet had told Audrey she could stay as long as she liked.

"Are all Audrey's stories about Hollywood true?" Delores now said, under the impression she was asking quietly and Audrey couldn't hear her. But Delores's voice carried in the small house.

"Probably." Violet laughed, casting a glance back at Audrey as they turned into the bedroom. "Audrey has led a very interesting life."

"She's different than I imagined she'd be," Delores said thoughtfully. "Bert always made her seem so mysterious. How long do you think she'll stay?"

"Well, I don't really know, Delores," Violet said softly.

And then Audrey heard no more. Violet had shut the door to help Delores put on her nightgown and get into bed. Audrey couldn't imagine what Bert might have told his mother about her, and she worried that Delores's comment might have upset Violet. She would have to find a way to tell Violet that she had no idea Bert had ever mentioned her name to his mother. She needed Violet to be in a good mood. She had something to ask her and it wasn't just any small thing. Audrey drew her knees up onto the sofa and curled her legs underneath her, rehearsing in her mind what she would say. Several minutes later, Violet returned to the living room.

"I think Delores is more impressed that you shared an elevator with Charlie Chaplin than that I once got Clark Gable a cup of coffee," Violet said to Audrey as she sat down in the armchair next to her.

"You're so good with Bert's mother. It must be a tremendous relief for him to have you here."

"Yes, I suppose it is."

"I bet you can't wait to see him again."

"I'm counting the days. We've been apart for almost four months."

Audrey smiled. "No doubt you're wondering how much longer you will have to put up with me."

"Oh! No. Not at all."

Audrey reached across the corner of the coffee table and patted Violet's knee. "You and your sweet Southern hospitality, Vi. You can't even tell me it would be nice to know if I ever plan on leaving." She laughed.

Violet attempted a grin. "Well, maybe."

Audrey withdrew her hand and laid it across her tummy in a gentle caress. "I promise I won't stay in your house a moment longer than you want me to. Honestly. The second you want me to go, I'll go. But there is something I need to ask of you. I've been wanting to since I got here, but it's been so nice just pretending the most troubling thing either of us has to worry about is which movie to go see."

Violet waited for Audrey to continue.

"I want you to know that this time is different. I wasn't being careless or reckless. I had begun to think maybe your dream of marriage and family was one I could have instead of mine. I thought the father of this child would want to marry me, would want us to be a family. But I know no that he doesn't. He never wanted that. Vince thinks I should have . . . should've had this taken care of when I first found out I was pregnant. He knows people who would have done it. But that's not what I wanted, Violet. I didn't want to have this child ripped from me. This one I wanted to keep. I really did."

Violet's gaze dropped to the little mound at Audrey's middle. Her expression was difficult to read.

"But, Violet, I know I can't keep it," Audrey continued. "I've become friends with a man who now has big plans for me. Glen Wainwright has influence. And he has money. He believes in my talent and is convinced he can make a star out of me. But not if I am an unmarried mother. And what kind of life could I ever offer this child? A child needs a mother and a father."

A tear started to slip down Violet's cheek and her chest was heaving slightly as she stared at Audrey's abdomen.

"Violet, I've been thinking maybe . . . maybe you and Bert could take this child. You could adopt it and it would be yours."

Violet lifted her head. "What?"

"I know you and Bert can't have children of your own, but maybe the two of you have considered adoption and were just wondering how to go about it. Wouldn't it be wonderful for all three of us if you and Bert adopted *this* child? My child."

Violet stared at Audrey, wordless. It was not the reaction Audrey had hoped for. There wasn't a sound in the room aside from the ticking of the grandfather clock.

"Have you and Bert not considered adoption? Have you not even discussed it?" Audrey asked a moment later.

Silence.

"Violet?"

Then Audrey inhaled a quick breath as realization sank in. "Oh, my God. You haven't told him."

Violet opened her mouth but no sound emerged.

"I couldn't do it," Violet whispered a second later as two more tears slipped down her cheek.

"I wanted to before we got married—I did. But it happened so fast. One minute we were just on a date, and the next we were eloping."

"You've been married for almost three years! You're telling me he *still* doesn't know?"

"Audrey, please," Violet pleaded, leaning forward in the armchair. "Please don't say anything. He thinks it's the quirky hand of fate that has kept me from getting pregnant. Some couples just can't have children. He doesn't blame me. Please? Please don't tell him. I know I should've been honest from the beginning, but I loved him, Audrey! I didn't want to lose him. Please, please don't tell him."

Audrey could hardly believe what she was hearing. "How have you been able to keep this a secret from him? Doesn't your family know what happened to you?"

"My parents think he knows I can't have children," Violet said in a hushed tone, mindful that Delores was asleep down the hall. "My close friends back home who know the details of my surgery all think he knows."

"But what if they were to say something!" Audrey said, the volume of her voice rising. "What if it should come up in conversation when you're visiting?"

"It hasn't! And it won't!" Violet said in a desperate whisper. "You just don't talk about things like that where I'm from."

Audrey shook her head in wonder and disappointment. "I just can't believe you would keep this from him."

"It's not what I wanted to do or planned to do. It just happened! I don't know what to do about it! How can I tell him now?"

"Do you honestly think Bert's the kind of person to leave you just because you can't give him children?" Audrey's tone was both pleading and stern.

"I don't want him to think he can't trust me!"

"Sooner or later he will find out, Violet. You've got to tell him."

"I don't know how!"

Audrey stared at her friend, miserable and stricken and afraid, her world about to crumble, or so it seemed. "I will help you, Violet. We'll do it together and I'll be right there with you. I'll make sure he knows that fear makes us do stupid things."

"It was because I loved him!" Violet said as she shook with muted sobs.

"Sometimes fear looks like love. But they aren't the same, Violet. You didn't know that then. Now you do. I will make sure he knows this."

The room was quiet again, with just the echoing of the clock and Violet's quiet sobs.

"I will do that for you if you will do this for me," Audrey said a few seconds later, her tone now resolute and controlled. "The baby will be yours and Bert's. I've a lawyer friend who will draw up all the proper papers. And I won't interfere, I promise. I just . . . I just want to be able to visit from time to time and send a birthday present once a year. I can be a good friend who doesn't have any children of her own. I can be the child's Auntie Audrey. He or she never has to know who I am beyond being someone who is fond of him or her, if that's what you want."

Violet wiped away the tears from her face with her bathrobe sleeve.

"Violet?" Audrey continued. "Will you do this for me?"

"Yes," Violet whispered.

"And what if Bert says no?"

Violet shook her head. "He won't."

TWENTY-FOUR

Bert's train pulled into Union Station right on schedule, much to Violet's relief.

It had been Audrey's idea to have him get off in Los Angeles and not transfer to another train for the last leg of the trip home to Santa Barbara.

"You don't need Delores listening in on everything that needs to be said and heard," Audrey had advised. "Tell him you will meet him on the platform. I'll be waiting outside with my car. Then we'll go somewhere private but not too private.

277

I will tell him what I need to say and then you will do the same. Actually, we'll do it at the same time. They kind of go together."

Violet had lost sleep over how to tell Bert she'd not been truthful with him, but now as the time neared for the weight of that deception to be gone, she found she was anxious to have the ordeal over with. At least the part about not being able to get pregnant. She could never tell him about the hat. He wouldn't understand.

Audrey had assured her that Bert would forgive her. People who loved each other did that. And that she would eventually earn back his trust. People who loved each other did that, too.

She scanned the platform as the doors parted and passengers began to disembark, many of them servicemen just like Bert. After a few seconds Violet saw him step down out of a train car and hoist a duffel bag to his shoulder. He was thin and wore a sand-colored Army uniform. She could see none of his usual wavy hair under his cap. She ran toward him, and he dropped the bag and pulled her close.

At first she could only marvel at the sensation of having his arms around her, and hearing him say her name and feeling his kisses on her neck. She began to cry at the beauty of the present moment and the dread of what would follow when they met up with Audrey.

"You can't imagine how good it is to see you

and hold you," he said as they finally broke away.

"I think maybe I can!" she said, laughing a little and wiping her eyes.

He grabbed his bag. "Shall we go home?"

"Actually, Audrey and I thought we'd take you to lunch before we head back."

He blinked at her. "Audrey's here?"

"She is. She can drive now. And she's . . . We've got some news for you."

Bert's happy expression wilted somewhat. "What's happened? What's wrong?"

"Nothing's wrong!" she said quickly, looping her arm through his and leading him away from the belching steam of the train so that she could say the rest of what she and Audrey had rehearsed. "Audrey needs our help with something, Bert. She's expecting."

He turned his head to face her as they walked. "Expecting?"

"Yes. And she needs our help."

Violet could see Bert was working out in his head the ramifications of what she had just told him. She would have written him if Audrey had recently gotten married. He'd already surmised that she was still single.

"And there's something I want to tell you, too. But let's wait until we're all together. All right? Your train ride was okay?"

She peppered him with questions about his travel and boot camp until they reached Audrey's car in the parking lot. She got out, and Violet noticed that Bert's gaze bulleted straight to the mound at her middle.

Audrey went to him and kissed him on the cheek. "So good to see you, Bert."

"And you, too," he said in return, a dozen questions evident in his tone.

Audrey took a deep breath and smiled. "Violet told you?"

"I can see for myself." Bert smiled back politely.

"I know a great little park where we can sit and chat for a bit before we find a place to eat. Shall we?"

They got into the car, and again there was small talk, mostly about Audrey's car and her recent play, until they reached the park off Alvarado Street. Audrey parked and directed them to a table nea the little lake, but under a willow and shaded from the August sun. Children were splashing about in the water while their mothers sat on blankets and entertained toddlers. A hot-dog vendor and balloon man were having an animated conversation about Babe Ruth donning a baseball uniform for the first time in seven years, and a teenage boy was tossing a red rubber ball to a curly-haired dog.

"So," Bert said. "What's all this about?" He looked from Violet to Audrey.

Violet opened her mouth but the rehearsed words hovered at her lips, as if held back by a mighty force.

Audrey took her hand. "Violet has something she needs to tell you, Bert."

Hours later Bert was sitting up in bed when Violet came into their room from the bathroom. Delores, overjoyed to have her son home but baffled by the news that Bert and Violet were seriously considering adopting Audrey's unborn child, had been full of questions but was at last asleep. Audrey, too, had gone to Bert's old bedroom and turned in.

Violet was at last alone with her husband.

His arms were folded loosely across his chest and an issue of *Audubon* magazine lay unopened on his lap. He was staring at the yellow-and-black bird on the cover, but Violet could tell he was not really seeing it. She knew he was pondering what she'd told him that afternoon.

"You've kept this from me? All this time?" he had said, after she'd at last confessed she could bear him no children. His eyes had been shining with an aching anger she'd dreaded for three years. The happy sounds of children playing in the background had seemed cruelly out of place.

True to her word, Audrey had come to Violet's aid when Bert's anguished question left her struggling to continue.

"She wanted to tell you. You can see in her face how much she did, Bert. She just didn't know how."

He had turned on Audrey and glared at her. "And you knew about this?"

Violet had expected Audrey to say that she'd realized only recently that Violet hadn't told Bert the truth. Instead, Audrey left the question unanswered.

"She'd been hurt before by someone she'd given her heart to, Bert. Someone who abandoned her because of this very thing. He wasn't the man you are and Violet knows it, but when your heart is crushed it does things to keep it from ever getting hurt the same way again. It does foolish things prompted by the worst kind of fear. Violet loves you. She didn't want to lose you."

Bert had turned his attention back to Violet, his eyes beseeching her to help him understand. "Did you really think I would leave you over this?"

"I wasn't thinking! I was afraid. And the longer I didn't tell you, the more afraid I became, because I knew how badly you wanted us to have a baby."

It had been at that moment that the edge of his anger had seemed to soften. A few minutes later Audrey had voiced her request. And as Violet had predicted, Bert, though still stunned, was open to the idea of adopting Audrey's baby.

Violet now walked over to Bert's side of the bed and sat down.

Several seconds passed before he looked up at

her. "I'm not angry anymore," he said, but the tone of his voice made Violet tremble.

"But you're *something,*" she said, fresh tears springing to her eyes.

He inhaled slowly. "I don't know what I am. Disillusioned, maybe. Hurt. I don't know."

"Bert, I am so very—"

"I know. You're sorry."

"But I am! I just loved you so much. I still do. I couldn't . . . I just couldn't risk losing you."

"And is this why you wanted to elope? Because you were afraid I'd find out and leave you?"

She stared at him for a second. "Didn't you want to marry me when you did?"

"I did. I just . . . We rushed into marriage so quickly, Violet."

"When I asked if you thought we should get married, you said yes. I was kidding when I said, *'Let's elope.'* I didn't think you would take me up on it. Of course I wanted to marry you right then. You were tired of pining away after Audrey. And you knew I loved you!"

She had said too much. Violet looked away. Another stretch of silent seconds passed, and then Bert tossed the magazine onto the floor. Violet flinched and slowly turned her gaze to him. Bert's hand was extended toward her, though, beckoning her to come into his embrace. She scrambled into his arms.

"I'm so sorry," she whispered.

"Shhhh. Let's not talk about it anymore right now. What's done is done."

They lay quiet in each other's arms for several minutes as Violet's tears abated.

"Are you sure you want to adopt Audrey's child?" he finally said.

She looked up at him. "Aren't you?"

"It will change things between all of us."

"Will it?"

"How can it not? We will be raising her child as our own."

"That's what Audrey wants. And this may be our only chance to have a child."

Bert seemed to be far away in this thoughts. "It just doesn't seem fair to Audrey that the child won't know who she is."

Violet sat up. "She has a career to think about, darling. A child out of wedlock would harm her reputation."

"But she's leaving to us the decision of whether or not the child should be told."

"Yes, but what good would there be in the child knowing? Who wants to grow up thinking his mother thought more of her career than she did of her own child? Would you want to grow up knowing that?"

"I suppose not."

Violet snuggled back into his arms and they were quiet for a moment. "It makes me sad to think you won't get leave again until Christmas.

The baby will already be a month old by then."

"I know. If we're going to do this, you make sure Audrey knows we'll pay for everything. And she can stay here with you and Mom until she delivers, if that's what she wants. If she believes she needs to stay hidden for the next three months, then she should just stay here."

Violet smiled against Bert's chest. She liked the thought of Audrey being there while Bert was away and of the child being born right there in Santa Barbara. "Can we call her Elaine if it's a girl? I've always loved that name. We can call her Lainey for short."

"And if it's a boy?"

"Henry. After your father." Violet looked up at her husband. His eyes were glistening with what were surely conflicting emotions.

"So you forgive me? Please tell me yes," she pleaded.

He hesitated a moment, and her pulse quickened under her skin. "We need to know we can trust each other. We can't have any more secrets like this between us, Violet. We just can't."

She blinked back new tears. "I know we can't."

"Promise me no more after this."

Violet could make that promise. She could easily make it. To suddenly have everything she'd always wanted made her feel light-headed and free.

What she had done in the past—all of it—

would be buried under the pledge she was now making.

No more secrets.

"I promise," she said.

As he took her into his arms, Violet felt as though she were soaring.

She still had to make the call to her parents to tell them she and Bert were adopting Audrey's baby. She knew her parents would likely be concerned about the kind of person Audrey was that she would be in the family way and unmarried.

But Violet didn't want to think about that then. She'd think about it tomorrow.

TWENTY-FIVE

November 1942

The closing credits for *For Me and My Gal* were rolling down the screen but the theater was still dark as the audience started to rise from their seats. Audrey had enjoyed the movie but she'd been distracted by an odd, menacing pressure inside her body that had begun as soon as the houselights went down. She remembered the ache from years before; her body was reminding her that the child wouldn't always be hidden inside her, that a time of emptying was coming.

She had three more weeks before her due date, nearly another month of letting Violet pamper her, of putting puzzles together with Delores, of waking up in Bert's old room, of holding the child as close to her body as a mother could.

Audrey placed her hands over her swollen middle. The sensation was intensifying. Maybe if she could lie down, it would lessen. Or maybe if she just sat there for a few minutes, the tightening would subside.

Violet, sitting in the seat next to her, leaned toward her. "Don't you just love Judy Garland?"

"She's incredible," Audrey replied, with little lilt to her voice.

"Everything all right?"

"Probably. But let's just sit for a minute." Audrey smiled in spite of her discomfort. Violet was going to be a wonderful mother. Her kind attention these past two months had assured her of that. But Audrey knew Violet looked to the end of Audrey's pregnancy with a different kind of expectation. The home she had graciously offered so that Audrey could give birth, concealed from Hollywood's prying eyes, did not bear the look of a house being made ready for a new life. Violet hadn't been able to do anything to prepare a nursery. Audrey slept in the room that would be the baby's, and though she had offered to let Violet do whatever she wished with that room, Violet had declined, saying it could wait. The few baby things Violet had bought she had stuffed on Bert's side of the closet so that, as Violet had said, Audrey wouldn't have to look at them.

A newborn didn't need a crib or even its own room, Violet had told her. In the beginning, a bassinet at the mother's bedside was all that was required, as the baby was so tiny and the mother was up and down at all hours, seeing to its many needs.

The theater was almost empty now and the house-lights came on. "Want to go get ice cream before we head home?" Violet asked.

Another strong contraction rolled across her midsection, and Audrey closed her eyes against its force.

"Or something else, if you're not in the mood for ice cream," Violet added.

"I think . . . I think something is happening, Violet." Audrey opened her eyes as the pain subsided.

Violet instinctively looked down at Audrey's bulging abdomen. "What do you mean? Now? Right now?"

Audrey leaned forward a bit in her seat as a ripple of nausea moved within her, coupled with a feeling of urgency.

"But it's too early!" Violet exclaimed. "You still have three more weeks!"

"I think I might need to go to the hospital." Audrey reached for her purse.

"But it's too early!" Violet said again, as she watched Audrey rise awkwardly to her feet. "You've got three more weeks!"

"Babies come when they want to come."

Violet grabbed her pocketbook as well, sprang to her feet, and followed Audrey into the aisle. "Are you sure you need to go to the hospital?"

"I've done this before, Vi."

"But we didn't bring your car! We walked here!"

They entered the foyer of the theater, now swarming with ticket holders for the next showing of the movie.

Audrey headed for the concession stand, where slick-haired young men in bow ties were selling popcorn and licorice.

"Could you please have someone call us a cab?" Audrey said politely, and then reached out for Violet as a new pain—a more aggressive one—seized her.

One of the young men's eyes grew wide and he dashed for the office in back.

The theater manager was suddenly at their side, ushering them to the big revolving doors. He spoke in gentle tones to Audrey, assuring her that the taxi was on its way. Audrey appreciated his effort to keep her calm, but she felt strangely tranquil. As they started to head outside, the manager called over his shoulder to tell the young man to alert the hospital that a woman in labor was headed their way.

The manager stayed with them until the taxi arrived and he helped Audrey inside.

"Do you have money for the fare?" he asked Violet. She replied in a nervous voice that she didn't know and she began to poke about in her purse for her wallet.

"I have it," Audrey replied between gritted teeth.

Violet got into the cab. Audrey could sense Violet's anxiety. The manager shut the door and the taxi sped away.

"It's going to be okay, Violet." Audrey leaned her head back on the seat.

"I don't know what to do."

"Just hold on to my purse for me and don't let them give me anything to make me sleepy. Promise me you won't let them put me to sleep. I want to be awake."

There was no answer. Violet appeared to have no idea what Audrey was talking about.

Audrey raised her head to look at Violet. "Promise?"

"I promise."

They arrived at the hospital's front entrance in less than ten minutes. A nurse in a starched hat and a white-uniformed orderly stood at the curb next to a wheelchair. Audrey handed Violet her purse.

"Pay the driver before we get out so that you can stay with me."

Violet handed the money across the seat as the

passenger's door on Audrey's side opened and the orderly reached for her.

Violet scrambled out the other side as Audrey was getting settled into the wheelchair.

"Is this your first baby, dear?" the nurse said, smiling wide.

"No," Audrey answered before she doubled over in pain.

"What's her name?" the nurse said to Violet as they turned toward the hospital's front doors.

Violet opened her mouth, but Audrey answered before Violet could get any words past her lips.

"I'm Audrey Kluge."

The nurse bent down toward Audrey as she wheeled her over the hospital's threshold and inside the building. "And can we call Mr. Kluge for you? I take it he wasn't at the movies with you ladies?"

"There is no Mr. Kluge," Audrey said through clenched teeth.

The nurse gave Violet a questioning look. "Oh! Um. He died," Violet said. "In a boating accident. In . . . in May. Very tragic. He was my cousin."

A tiny smile tugged at Audrey's mouth.

"Don't give her anything to make her sleepy," Violet continued, as they rushed Audrey toward double doors that Violet wasn't allowed through. "She doesn't want anything that will make her sleepy. She wants to be awake."

The nurse raised an eyebrow. "That's up to the doctor to decide."

Violet put out her arm to stop the nurse. "She doesn't want anything to make her sleepy. Tell the doctor that."

The nurse frowned at Violet as the orderly parted the double doors. Audrey looked quickly over her shoulder to catch Violet's gaze. *Thank you,* she mouthed.

"I'll be right here," Violet called out after her.

And then the doors closed.

Audrey remembered being terribly afraid when her first child was born. Of her second delivery, she had no memory at all. She wanted to hold on to every bit of the last hours this baby would be hers, even the worst moments. The memory of pain stayed with a person; she already knew this. She didn't want to forget even a snippet of the brief amount of time she would be this child's mother. She was grateful that the doctor had agreed to let her deliver without the mask and its mystifying gas that made a person forget what mattered to her.

The moment her body granted the baby its freedom was as sharp and distinct as a knife blade. She could feel the separation as the baby wriggled away from her into the doctor's waiting hands, eager to take a breath and cry out to the world, *I am here!*

"You have a little girl, Mrs. Kluge," the doctor announced.

For a second the world seemed to cease its spinning. All Audrey was aware of was those five words echoing in her head.

You have a little girl. You have a little girl.

She strained to get a glimpse of the wailing child as the doctor and nurses hovered over her at the foot of the delivery table.

"Is she all right?" Audrey said.

"She's perfect," one of the nurses said. "Small, but perfect. We just want to get her cleaned up a little for you."

She hadn't told the nurses while she labored that she wasn't going to keep the baby. That information could wait until tomorrow. For now, Audrey wanted to hold this baby, shower kisses on her, whisper endearments over her.

"Do you have a name picked out?" a second nurse said.

Audrey could see the baby now in the nurse's arms, as the doctor readied himself for other matters related to Audrey's body that were of no concern to her. She wanted only to hold her little girl.

"Elaine." Audrey whispered the name Violet and Bert had chosen, and tears were suddenly coursing down her cheeks.

"That's a beautiful name," said the nurse closest to Audrey as she patted her arm. "I am sure Mr. Kluge would have loved it. Would you like to hold her before we take her to be weighed?"

Audrey nodded, unable to speak.

The crying child, wrapped in a yellow hospital blanket, was placed in her arms. She seemed as light as a handful of cotton. Her perfect little cherub face was contorted into an unhappy wail.

"There, now, princess," Audrey cooed. "There, now. You are safe. You are safe, my darling."

The baby stopped crying and gazed at Audrey.

"Yes, yes," Audrey whispered. "You know who I am, don't you?" She tasted salt on her tongue from her tears sliding down into her mouth.

"All babies know their mommy's voice," the nurse said cheerfully.

Audrey knew that the nurse would be taking her child to the nursery, and that soon Violet would be told the baby had been born, and the terrible release would slowly begin. She would hold on to this moment for as long as she could. The next time she saw this child, everything would be different.

The nurse turned away to fetch something and Audrey pulled her daughter closer, their eyes still tight on each other. "Don't forget me, my little girl. Don't forget how much I love you."

Time seemed to lose its meaning in those seconds she held her daughter and their gazes were only on each other. And then the baby was lifted out of her arms.

Audrey fell back on the pillows, exhausted by physical exertion and grief.

"Mr. Kluge would have been very proud of you today," the nurse said softly.

Audrey drifted into sleep.

When she awoke, morning light was creeping in through the slats in the blinds covering a window. A wall clock revealed that it was a few minutes after seven in the morning. There were two other beds in the room, but both were empty. The door to the room was half-open and she heard hospital sounds on the other side of it: nurses' shoes on linoleum, a faraway elevator bell, gurney wheels, and a distant moan of pain.

Audrey gingerly rose to a sitting position. She swung her feet over the side of the bed and noticed that her robe from home was lying across the footboard and her slippers were arranged right below it on the floor. A vase of pink tulips was at her bedside. Violet had been there.

She tested her footing and then reached for the robe and put it on. She took a few careful steps and then walked to the door and pushed it open. In one direction was a long hallway lined with doors like hers on either side. In the other were a few more doors, a nurses' station, and a windowed viewing area that Violet was standing in front of.

Audrey made her way slowly to her friend, passing the nurses silently so that she would not be shooed back into bed.

She had nearly reached the nursery window when Violet looked up.

Audrey smiled and laid a finger across her lips.

And then she was at Violet's side. Beyond the glass, her daughter lay sleeping in a bassinet, wrapped in a cloud of blankets. Two other infants were in the room. One slept, and the other was being bottle-fed by a nurse while she sat in a rocker. The nurse looked up at Audrey, smiled, and then returned her attention to the baby in her arms.

"I can't stop looking at her," Violet said, tearful.

Audrey laid her head on her friend's shoulder.

"They made me go home last night after you had her and told me I could come back during visiting hours this afternoon. I couldn't wait." Violet put her arm around Audrey's back. "I told them I was your only family, which I know is a lie. But I just couldn't stay away. They let me put the robe and the flowers in your room when I got here at daybreak. They think I'm nuts."

"You're not nuts. She's enchanting."

"She's so beautiful."

The two friends stood in silence for a few seconds as they stared at the fairylike child.

"I told the nurses her name is Elaine," Audrey said. "You and Bert haven't changed your minds about that, have you?"

"No." Violet whispered the word as if oxygen were in scarce supply.

Audrey looked at Violet with glistening eyes. "That's how I feel when I look at her, too. She nearly takes my breath away. I'm so glad you and Bert get to have her and love her and raise her. So glad."

Violet opened her mouth but no words came out. Her eyes were shimmering now, too.

"Do you want to hold her, Vi?" Audrey said.

Violet hesitated for a moment. "If I hold her now I won't want to let go."

The instant Audrey heard these words she knew she must leave Santa Barbara the second she could. Her breasts would soon be aching to nourish the child that would not be hers. She couldn't be near the baby when the tender agony of that denial began. She needed to get back to Hollywood and her life as Audrey Duvall. Now. Today.

"Where are my clothes from yesterday?" she said.

"In the little closet in your room, I think. Why?"

Audrey pressed her hand against the nursery window and gazed at her daughter. "We're leaving."

"We are?"

"Yes."

Audrey turned from the glass to head to the nurses' station. An older woman in a white cap looked up, surprised to see Audrey out of bed.

"Why, Mrs. Kluge, you should be resting," the nurse said, wide-eyed.

"I prefer to rest at home. We'd like to leave now."

She looked from Violet to Audrey. "But the doctor hasn't made his rounds yet. You just had a baby."

"I had a baby last night. My third. Both of us are fine. So if you could just draw up my discharge papers?"

"Mrs. Kluge, this is highly irregular! And you haven't filled out the form for the birth certificate yet."

"I'd be happy to do that. Give it to me and I will do it right now. And then I want you to draw up my discharge papers."

The nurse stared at Audrey for several seconds before reaching into a file that had already been readied for later and pulling out an official-looking form.

Audrey read the top line: *Certificate of Live Birth, County of Santa Barbara.*

"And a pen?" she said, urgency in her tone.

A pen was handed to her, and Audrey hurried through the form as if she were underwater and couldn't draw breath until she was finished with it.

Father's Name: Bert Redmond.

Mother's Name: Violet Redmond.

She would've run to her room to change into her clothes had her body allowed it.

TWENTY-SIX

Christmas Eve 1942

Violet extracted the gingerbread-men cookie cutters from the cloth bag that Delores had kept them in since Bert was a baby and tossed them into the sink. Delores had so badly wanted Bert to have his favorite gingerbread men for his Christmas homecoming that Violet felt compelled to use the remainder of the month's sugar ration to make them, even though she would've rather been in the living room with Bert and the baby at that moment.

She ran some hot water into the sink to rinse off the cutters and cast a glance over her shoulder into the other room. Delores was sitting in her favorite chair, listening to Christmas carols on the Victrola, while Bert was on the sofa, cuddling his infant daughter. In the far corner of the living room, a Norwegian white pine bought at the Boy Scouts' tree lot had been decorated with ornaments from as far back as Bert's childhood. Presents that would be opened in the morning lay underneath it. Lainey was smiling up at Bert, and he was making silly noises to encourage her grins. Bert had been home for only two days and already Lainey had taken to him as though he had been there for the entire duration of her seven-week existence. It had been nothing short of wonderful having Bert home to share the joy and work of parenting an infant.

Violet had supposed that life took on new meaning when a woman became a mother, but she had no idea just how much. Lainey was a good baby, but she was still a sweet little bundle of demands—morning, noon, and night. And as much as Violet had always wanted to be a mother, she had little experience with infants. She missed not being near her own mother and resented that Delores was so frail that Violet could not leave her to go home to Montgomery. The past seven weeks had almost been like taking care of two helpless people.

And yet she still loved her reinvented life. The only thing her wonderful new universe had lacked was Bert's presence. He wrote every week and called on Sundays, but this was what she had longed for: seeing him cuddling Lainey on the couch and loving the child like Violet did.

She wished it could be just the three of them for Christmas.

Violet turned back to the cutters in the sink, pulling them out a bit savagely and tossing them onto a towel to dry them off. She wished Delores had gone to be with one of her daughters for the holidays and, yes, she wished Audrey wasn't coming. Violet hadn't actually invited Audrey;

she'd just telephoned earlier that month and asked if it wouldn't be too much trouble if she came. She'd said she'd get a hotel room, since with Lainey now sleeping in the nursery, there wasn't an extra bedroom for guests. The sofa in the living room was the only other option and Violet hadn't offered it.

It wasn't that Violet didn't want to see Audrey; it was just that this was their first Christmas, Bert's and hers, as parents. And they hadn't seen each other in weeks. She also didn't think that it was wise for Audrey to be around Lainey right then. It had been so hard for Audrey when she left Lainey with Violet the day after she had given birth to her. Audrey had called a couple of times to see how Violet was and to inquire if she needed anything, and Violet had heard the longing in Audrey's voice when she asked about Lainey. Audrey surely needed more distance. It wasn't like Lainey was going to remember Aunt Audrey had been there, anyway.

But the real reason Violet wished Audrey wasn't coming was that Violet still dreamed from time to time that Audrey had changed her mind and wanted Lainey back. She tried not to dwell on that dreadful thought during her waking hours, but it kept sneaking up on her. Violet already loved Lainey like she was her own flesh and blood.

She couldn't bear it if Audrey were to try to get Lainey back.

Violet forced herself to concentrate on the task at hand: rolling out the gingerbread dough, carefully cutting the shapes, and using a floured spatula to slide them onto the cookie sheet. The dough smelled spicy and sweet as she worked with it, and the aroma teased her into believing it was Christmas and therefore all was well. She opened the oven and put the first dozen inside and then began working on the second batch. As she was carefully cutting the last man for the next tray, Violet heard, from the open window over the sink, a car pulling up outside.

Audrey emerged from the vehicle with shopping bags brimming with beribboned presents. She was wearing a scarlet dress with white trim and shiny black pumps, and her long, coffee brown hair was pulled back with a wide crimson ribbon. She bore no trace of having had a child a little less than two months earlier. The black belt at her waist was cinched tight, and as she moved away from her car and began to walk up the narrow cement path to the front door, she looked like she was stepping out of a *Vogue* photo shoot.

Instinctively, Violet reached up to smooth back the hair from her face and then wiped floured hands on her dark green apron. Ghostlike images of her palms appeared on the fabric.

She moved to the entrance to the living room, and Bert looked up from the cooing baby in his arms.

"Is she here?" he asked.

Violet nodded and Bert got to his feet. She turned and reached for the doorknob, but before she could turn it, three knocks landed on the other side. When Violet opened the door, Audrey was framed in a halo of light, just like she had been the last time she'd arrived from Hollywood in the late afternoon.

"Merry Christmas, Audrey!" Violet said brightly, forcing a happy smile.

Audrey stepped forward across the threshold, plopped the bags down on the floor, and wrapped her arms around Violet. "Oh, Violet. It's so good to be in this house again! Thanks so much for letting me come."

"Of course!"

Audrey broke off the embrace and said a cordial hello to Delores, still sitting in her armchair. Then her gaze traveled to Bert standing behind his wife. Audrey's eyes misted over in an instant at the sight of the infant in his arms.

"Oh, my! Look how big she is!" Audrey whispered, her voice as fragile as lace.

Bert took a few steps forward. He seemed a bit tentative, too, Violet noted, and she was glad of it.

"Hello, Audrey." He leaned forward to plant a gentle kiss on her cheek. Lainey in his arms prevented him from embracing her.

"Bert," Audrey said as she blinked back tears that refused to be quelled. "You look different. I

303

don't know if it's because you're a father now or because someone is trying to make a soldier out of you."

Bert's grin in return was genuine and full. He was happy to see his old friend. Happy to have her in his home. The baby lifted a little fist out from under her blanket as if to say she, too, was happy to welcome Audrey.

The odor of something charred suddenly filled Violet's nostrils.

She turned toward the kitchen. Tendrils of smoke were curling out of the vents in the oven door. Her gingerbread men were burning.

"Oh!" Violet dashed into the kitchen, grabbed two hot pads, and pulled open the oven door. More smoke billowed out. She reached inside for the tray of blackened cookies, yanked them out, and tossed the hot sheet onto the tile counter. She opened the window fully and coaxed the smoke outside with the hot pads. When she finally went back to the living room, only Delores was looking in her direction. Bert and Audrey were gazing at the baby and smiling, completely unaware, or at least undisturbed, by the fiasco in the kitchen.

Violet strode toward Bert, Audrey, and Lainey.

"Did you burn them all?" Delores asked as Violet walked past her armchair.

Violet pretended not to have heard her. She reached Bert, put an arm around his waist, and leaned into him so that the amalgam of father, mother, and child couldn't possibly be missed.

"She's so beautiful," Audrey said, smiling up at Violet.

"Well, of course," Bert replied. "How could she not be beautiful?"

Audrey smiled at the veiled compliment.

Violet was about to ask Audrey if she'd care to sit down and make herself comfortable when Bert asked if she'd like to hold Lainey.

Audrey looked from Bert to Violet to Bert again. "May I?"

Bert waited for Violet to answer. It was almost as if he could tell she was hesitant.

"Of course," Violet said after a moment's pause.

Bert extended the baby toward Audrey. She took Lainey into her arms effortlessly, without the slightest awkward jostle.

"Hello, little angel," Audrey murmured as she walked slowly to the sofa and sat down with the baby close to her chest. "My, how you've grown. And look at you smiling already!"

Bert returned to the couch and sat down next to Audrey. "Violet said she just started doing that a few days ago."

Audrey bent down to snuggle Lainey and Bert laughed.

"Did you burn all the cookies, Violet?" Delores asked again from her armchair.

Violet couldn't stomach much more of the scene on the couch. The sooner she served dinner, the sooner Audrey would go to her hotel for the night. It was only a bit after three now, though. Too soon to get the food on the table.

"Did you put the oven on too high?"

Violet turned to her mother-in-law. "I don't have the oven on too high. I just got sidetracked for a moment. I'm making some more."

She had just started to turn toward the kitchen when she heard Bert tell Audrey that she didn't have to go to a hotel that night if she didn't want to. The sofa was hers if she wanted it.

"The sofa's not comfortable enough to sleep on, Bert." The words flew out of Violet's mouth. "And there's absolutely no privacy."

Audrey gazed at Violet for a second before turning to face Bert. "And you only just got home, Bert. I don't mind sleeping elsewhere tonight."

"It's Christmas Eve," he said insistently. "Do you really want to wake up Christmas morning in a hotel room?"

Audrey was at a loss for what to do; Violet could see that. Her friend looked down at the baby in her arms as a weak smile broke across her face. "I probably outstayed my welcome the last time I was here, Bert. I was here for a *long* time."

"You didn't outstay your welcome," Delores chimed in. "I can sleep on the couch and you can have my bed."

"Oh, I couldn't let you do that, Delores," Audrey said quickly.

"It's just one night, Audrey," Bert said. "We want you here. Don't we, Violet?"

Three sets of eyes were on her. Violet cleared her throat. "Yes. Please do stay here tonight, Audrey," Violet heard herself saying. "Bert's right. You don't want to wake up in a hotel on Christmas. You're coming back to the house in the morning, anyway. If you don't mind the couch, you should just stay here."

Audrey held Violet's gaze for a moment. "If you're sure I won't be in the way."

"You're not in the way," Bert said reassuringly.

"All right."

"Then it's all settled." Bert started to stand. "I'll just go get your suitcase from your car."

Audrey reached out with one hand to stop him. "Actually, Bert, it's just a travel bag, and I don't need it right this minute. Here. Sit back down with your little girl. You'll be having to report back to the Army post before you know it. You don't want to miss out on any cuddle time. And I want to help Violet make the cookies."

She transferred the baby back into Bert's arms and kissed Lainey's forehead just before she stood up.

Audrey crossed the room and linked her arm with Violet's. They turned toward the kitchen.

"I love making cookies at Christmastime," Audrey said, and leaned her head toward Violet's. "My mom and I used to do this together.

It was always such a special time. Just her and me."

"I'm not very good at gingerbread men," Violet said.

"I'm not very good at baking any kind of cookie." Audrey laughed. "But it's not about the cookies, really. It's about the time you spend with the person you make them with."

Violet handed Audrey the apron that Delores used to wear and that Audrey had worn when she was pregnant and living there. Bantam roosters strutted across the front of it.

Even though it had been only been a matter of weeks since Audrey left, it was different having her at the house now. Bert was home, for one thing, and Lainey was no longer hidden from view within Audrey's body. It was almost as if Violet and Audrey had nothing in common anymore. For one fleeting moment, Violet missed the way it was when she first arrived in Hollywood and she and Audrey were just secretaries at a studio. The filming of *Gone With the Wind* had only just begun and everything seemed new and exciting. There was no war, and curly-haired Bert, who hadn't yet held a rifle or been shown how to point it at someone and pull the trigger, had been utterly convinced there was a nightingale on Sunset Boulevard, calling for its lover against a star-studded sky. Back then Violet had longed for what she now had—a husband and a child—yet an ache seized her as she remembered the way things used to be. She handed the apron to Audrey.

Audrey took the apron. The look on her face was one of understanding, as if she was thinking the same thing.

"Thank you, Violet."

She tied the apron around her slim waist.

Hours later, Violet awoke in the middle of the night, surprised that she hadn't heard from Lainey. Then she realized Bert wasn't in bed with her, and she smiled as she pictured him in the nursery in the rocking chair, whispering sweet nonsense to Lainey while she had her bottle. But then she heard voices in the living room.

She got out of bed and tiptoed down the hall. Bert and Audrey were talking in low tones. She couldn't see them from where she stood hidden from view, but she could hear them. And she could hear Lainey. One of them was holding her while she sucked on a bottle. Violet could hear the sweet little sounds the baby made when she drank.

Audrey was telling Bert that she thought the man she was seeing now, Glen Wainwright, was going to ask her to marry him. Audrey had told Violet plenty of things about her new beau, includingthat he was quite a bit older than her, as they'd rolled out the gingerbread dough, but not that she was expecting a proposal from him. Bert had coaxed it out of her somehow and it stung that he had.

"Do you love him? Are you going to say yes?" Bert asked.

Violet couldn't see what Audrey was doing as she contemplated her response, but several seconds passed before she answered. "What does it matter if I love him or not? He loves me. He's good to me. He wants me to go far in my career, and he has the money and the connections to make it happen. There's a lot of comfort in that. Maybe for me, that's what love is. It's being with someone who makes me feel safe and cherished and wanted."

"Maybe that's what love is for all of us," Bert said after a few moments of silence.

It got very quiet then. Violet knew if she so much as moved a toe they'd hear her, so she stood glued to the wall while she pondered if love really was what Bert and Audrey said it was.

She was not ready to hear what Bert said next.

"Are you sure about letting us keep and raise your daughter?"

Violet didn't hear what Audrey said in response because there was suddenly a terrible roaring in her ears as she imagined her responding with, *Yes, I'm having second thoughts, now that you mention it.* But Audrey must have said something like, *But I have nothing to offer Lainey,* because Bert said she had what every mother has to offer her child: herself.

The earth seemed to have tilted off its axis. Violet felt for the wall behind her to steady herself. Then after a few seconds of no words at all between them, Audrey spoke.

"I can tell how much you and Violet love Lainey. I know it would break your hearts not to have her."

"That's exactly why I am asking you if you are, because surely your heart is breaking, too."

Violet had to stop this conversation from continuing. She came forward as if she'd just emerged from the bedroom, and rubbed her eyes as if she hadn't heard a word they'd said.

Audrey was sitting on the sofa with her legs tucked up underneath her and her blankets all askew. Bert, who had pulled Delores's armchair close to the couch, was sitting in it, and he had Lainey over his shoulder as he gently rubbed her back to burp her.

Violet's heart was pounding in her chest but she forced herself to sound relaxed and sweetly cordial. "Bert, you are so thoughtful to get up with Lainey, but you didn't need to feed her here in the living room, where Audrey is trying to sleep."

"I actually hadn't been asleep yet, Vi," Audrey said. "Bert was being as quiet as a mouse in the kitchen, getting her a bottle, and I told him he could bring the baby into the living room while he fed her. I didn't mind."

The room became quiet again. Bert finally got

out of the chair with a sleeping baby over his shoulder. "We should all get to sleep so Santa will come, I guess. Good night, Audrey."

"Good night."

Violet blew Audrey a kiss as Bert took Lainey back to the nursery. Audrey clicked off the light.

TWENTY-SEVEN

March 1943

A breeze toyed with the edges of Lainey's blanket as Violet sat with her daughter on the grass and waited for the mailman to arrive. Bert's letters usually came on Saturdays, and she was eager for news of where he might be posted. His division was gearing up for some kind of move-ment. He didn't know where or when, but it was imminent.

Lainey, on her back with a rattle in her tight little fist, was making happy gurgling noises, pleased with herself that she could produce such sounds. Violet tickled her child on her cheek and Lainey smiled and uttered a monosyllabic response of delight.

It was not quite warm enough to be sitting outside and Violet had to keep replacing the little crocheted shawl over Lainey's legs, as her daughter kept kicking it off. But she had to get away from Delores and her constant commentary on how terrible the war was and how much she wished Bert would come home and how tired she was all the time and how Violet wasn't seeing to her needs like she used to and how much she missed her new grandson.

Their relationship had been tense since her mother-in-law's return from her visit to San Francisco to see Bert's sister's new baby. Delores's health had continued to decline, and she required more help from Violet than she had when Bert had first left for the Army. What with helping Delores in and out of bed and in the bathroom, making all her meals, and doing her laundry, Violet felt as if she had two children to care for. While it was a joy to care for Lainey, jumping through hoops for Delores was wearing Violet out. Plus, Delores's constant reminders that her new grandson was three hundred terrible miles away were just plain annoying.

"But you've got Lainey right here!" Violet had said earlier that day, when Delores had again remarked how frustrating it was that baby Owen was so far from her.

"Well, yes. Yes, that's true," Delores had said, looking down at Lainey lying on a flannel blanket on the living room floor while Violet folded laundry on the sofa.

Violet had stopped smoothing out the clean diaper on her lap. She could tell by the look on her mother-in-law's face that Delores considered Owen to be different from Lainey. Owen was biologically a part of her, an extension of her own life. The new baby also had her beloved dead husband's blood coursing through his infant veins. Lainey did not.

Sweet Lainey was easy to feel affection for, but she wasn't like Owen.

The sheepish look on Delores's face had made it appear as if she'd read Violet's thoughts.

"I just don't like it that I don't get to see him as often as I get to see Lainey," Delores had said.

Then go live with Charlene, Violet had wanted to say.

Again it seemed as though Delores had heard Violet's unspoken words.

"Maybe I should go back up for an extended stay." Delores's brow had crinkled in consternation, revealing that she had already been thinking about a return trip to San Francisco.

"I am sure Charlene and Howard would like that."

"They've prepared a room for me so that I don't have to rush back if I don't want to."

Violet had folded the clean diaper and pressed it across her lap, hoping that Delores was saying what Violet thought she was saying. That maybe she was thinking of returning to San Francisco to stay. "How very nice of them."

"Charlene's a nurse, you know," Delores

continued, more to herself than Violet, as though lecturing herself on good reasons to leave her beloved home and move up north.

"Yes," Violet said.

Delores had inhaled heavily as she looked about the parts of the house visible to her from her armchair. Violet could tell Delores was picturing herself saying good-bye to the home she had shared with Bert's father, and not just for a week or two, but for good.

"I never thought I'd leave this house." Delores's eyes had glistened with ready tears.

"Every memory you made here you can take with you," Violet had replied, willing herself to sound compassionate and not relieved at the thought that Delores might cease to be her responsibility.

"That's true," Delores had said softly as a tear had slipped down her cheek. Violet pretended not to notice.

Now, as Violet sat outside on the blanket with Lainey, she found herself thinking how she might redecorate the kitchen when it was finally hers. When the mailman arrived, Violet jumped to her feet to receive the little collection of envelopes he had for her.

But there was no letter from Bert that day.

Instead there was a note from Audrey. Violet opened the envelope, thinking perhaps Audrey was at last announcing her engagement to Glen

Wainwright. She would have to not let on that she'd overheard in that terrible conversation between Bert and Audrey that Wainwright might propose. But that wasn't what the note was about. It was about coming to visit. Audrey wouldn't be starting rehearsals for her next play until the third week of April. She wanted to know if she could come up to Santa Barbara and spend the weekend after next with them, if it wasn't too much trouble.

Maybe we could get a sitter for Lainey and the three of us could go see No Time for Love *with Claudette Colbert,* Audrey wrote. *And, oh! I found the cutest little striped pinafore for Lainey. With a matching hat.*

Was that all right? Could she come?

Violet crumpled the piece of paper and Lainey cooed happily at the sound. From the living room, Delores called out that she needed to use the toilet.

Violet scooped up her daughter and the blanket and headed inside, the note a wad of paper in her fist.

She set Lainey down in her crib before attending to Delores's needs.

As she helped her mother-in-law get situated on the toilet, she knew she could not continue to live this way. She didn't want to wipe Delores's rear end anymore and endure her many complaints. She didn't want to pretend to be happy about Audrey's frequent intrusions. She didn't want to sleep alone any longer in the bed she'd shared with Bert. She wanted to go home. If she could get Delores safely settled with Charlene and Howard in San Francisco, she could take the train—at last—to Montgomery. There she and Lainey could bask in the love and care of her parents while Bert was away fighting.

She left Delores to give her a few minutes of privacy on the commode. As Violet stood just outside the bathroom, she looked at the crumpled letter in her hand. She hadn't seen her parents for two years and they had never met their granddaughter. When the war was over and Bert returned to them, it would be much easier to get to New York from Montgomery to meet the people Bert wanted to meet at the Audubon Society. Daddy had banking friends in Manhattan. Surely one of them knew someone who knew someone who could help Bert get his foot in the Audubon door. Whatever schooling Bert needed to finish, he could finish back home in Alabama, over in Auburn, maybe. If they stayed with Mama and Daddy after the war, Bert wouldn't have to worry about making a living and providing a home; he could just concentrate on finishing his biology degree. And then the three of them could travel to wherever he wanted to go to photograph his birds. South America or Canada or some island in the Pacific. It would be a great adventure. *Their* great adventure.

But for now, she needed to get out of this house. She wanted to go home. She wanted her mother.

Violet shoved Audrey's letter into her pants pocket as Delores called out that she was finished. A minute or so later, Violet was helping Delores make her way back to the living room.

"Want me to make the call to Charlene, Delores? I'm happy to do it for you." Violet said as the two of them walked slowly down the hall.

"Yes," Delores said, leaning heavily on Violet. "I do. I'm just not happy here anymore."

Violet patted her mother-in-law's arm.

"Leave it to me, Delores. I'll take care of everything."

TWENTY-EIGHT

April 1943

The top was down on Glen's Cadillac Series 62 as Audrey zipped up the coastal highway with one hand on the wheel and the other holding a cigarette. The ends of the gauzy white scarf around her head frolicked behind her as if dancing on the wind. The midmorning sun was warm on her face, even though the sea air was still chilly from the last remnants of morning fog.

On the seat next to her were presents for the baby: darling dresses she hadn't been able to resist, a stuffed giraffe, and a silver cup with

Lainey's initials engraved across it. For the first time in her life Audrey had more money than she knew what to do with. The play she had been cast in would pay a modest salary, but it was Glen's insistent generosity that allowed her to buy whatever she wanted. He didn't seem to care that Audrey doted on Lainey from afar; he actually encouraged her wild spending on the baby.

It made her happy. And Glen loved seeing Audrey happy.

In the past few months he had bought her jewels and furs, dined and danced with her at expensive restaurants and clubs, and taken her sailing on his yacht because that level of attention also made her happy. And he had seen to it that she had at last signed on with a respected agent, and he was already planning a lavish opening night party for when the curtain on the new play was raised. She had a fairly decent role in the new show, and Glen was convinced she was on the cusp of a stellar acting career. He had already told her he was going to see to it that it did happen, just as soon as the war was over and people could go back to having fun and enjoying life instead of killing one another.

Not only that, but Glen wanted to marry her because he wanted to spend the rest of his life finding ways to make her happy.

Glen had proposed on Valentine's Day, after presenting Audrey with a four-carat diamond. She hadn't been completely surprised, and yet she had still trembled at the thought of making such a huge shift. Marrying Glen would surely change how often she could see Lainey. She would not be able to drop everything and hop in a car to go see the child whenever she wanted if she was married. Glen was sympathetic to a point when it came to Lainey. He'd told Audrey he thought she'd done the right thing by hiding her pregnancy and secretly giving up the baby. Her image in Hollywood was being reinvented, and a child out of wedlock would not have been received well by the public. Glen would say she needed to be careful about how much time and attention she lavished on her best friend's little girl, lest anyone begin to have doubts about whose child Lainey really was.

More than anything else, it was this gnawing thought that had kept her from saying yes to Glen. He didn't love Lainey; he had no familial bond with her. He was a widower with two grown children of his own and a new grandson. Audrey could not imagine her life apart from Lainey now, even if it meant turning Glen down. When she had been unable to answer him, he had told her to take all the time she needed, as though he was confident she would ultimately say yes. He offered a life of ease and riches and devotion. He loved her—of that she was certain. And yet she still hadn't been able to tell Glen that she would marry him. Not with Lainey seemingly hanging in the balance.

A few minutes later she was pulling up to Bert and Violet's house, and her heart was pounding with anticipation. Though she had sent little gifts and toys in the mail to Lainey over the past couple months, Audrey hadn't actually seen her since late January, when she'd come up on a Sunday afternoon for an impromptu visit.

She grabbed the gifts off the seat next to her and walked briskly up the path to the front door. Three months was a long time in an infant's first year; Lainey had probably changed so much. Audrey knocked lightly on the door, mindful that the baby could be asleep, and then opened it.

"Yoo-hoo!" she said softly as she poked her head inside. "It's me, Audrey." She stepped inside.

The living room was different. At first Audrey wasn't quite sure in what way. There was less of everything somehow. Fewer photographs in frames, fewer pictures on the wall. The afghan over the couch was gone. Delores's favorite chair was also missing.

A wave of shock roiled across her as she instantly assumed the worst: Delores had died.

She set her packages down with a sense of sadness. And then she heard a door closing and quiet footsteps approaching from down the hall. Violet walked into the room and laid a finger to her lips. She looked serene.

"Lainey just went down for her nap," Violet murmured.

"What's happened? Is Delores is all right?"

"Delores is fine. She is with Charlene and Howard. In San Francisco." Violet closed the distance and put her arms around Audrey, but her embrace seemed loose. Violet was not quite herself. Something was amiss.

"Oh," Audrey said as they separated. She nodded toward the empty space where the armchair had been. "She took her chair?"

"She took everything that was important to her," Violet said, her tone odd. "She is living with them now. Charlene is a nurse. She is better able to help Delores with her medical needs."

"Oh, I see. My goodness. So it's just you and Lainey here, then?"

Violet smiled a half grin. "Yes."

"Are you all right with that? Does Bert know?"

Violet cocked her head. "Does Bert know what? That his mother wanted to be closer to her new grandson? Of course. He thinks it's a great idea, especially with Charlene being a nurse and all. Want some coffee?"

Everything was off. Violet was off. The mood inside the house was off. Something still wasn't right.

"Sure. Can I just peek at Lainey first? I've missed her so much." Audrey took a step toward the hallway and Violet reached out to stop her.

"It will be better for her if you let her sleep. She wakes up so easily now and she needs her nap. It's too hard on her when she misses it. Let's have some coffee first. There's . . . there's something I need to tell you."

Audrey sensed a different kind of quaking in her heart and soul. Something was about to change. Tendrils of fear curled about her as she followed Violet into the kitchen. Violet took out two cups and their saucers and poured coffee that she had obviously already made for this purpose. Audrey pulled out a chair and sat down. The china cups made little rattling noises as Violet brought them to the table.

"Want any cream?" Violet asked.

What I want is for you to tell me what's going on. Audrey shook her head. "No, thanks."

Violet sat down, too. She put her hands around her cup, as if using its heat to power her words. Her gaze was on the steam rising from it. "Lainey and I are going home to Alabama."

The tendrils of fear thickened. "For a visit?"

"Until the war is over. Maybe longer. We're going to be renting out this house."

"Are you telling me Bert wants to live in Alabama after the war, with his mother so ill?" Audrey's voice sounded childlike in her ears.

"Delores may not live to see the end of the war. And Bert has dreams for his life that my parents can help him with. He wants to travel the world and photograph birds. Maybe you didn't know that about him."

Hot tears instantly pooled in Audrey's eyes. An ache she hadn't felt since leaving the hospital after having Lainey swelled up within her. She blinked away the tears and tamped down the dread. "You don't want to be alone here with Bert gone. I get that. Come back with me to Hollywood, Violet. The bungalow's plenty big for two women and a baby. It would be just like old times, only better. We can—"

Violet looked up at her "Audrey."

"What?"

"I want to go home. I want my mother. I want my family. I'm tired of having to do everything by myself."

The tears trickled down Audrey's cheeks, warm and rapid. She had to think of a way to keep Violet and Lainey in California. Had to.

Glen. She could marry Glen.

Glen had a mansion in Beverly Hills with eight bedrooms and a guest suite. Surely he would do his part for the war effort by letting an Army wife and infant daughter come live with them. He'd get to know Lainey that way. He might even begin to love her a little.

"Wait, Violet. Listen. Glen has asked me to marry him. He has this amazing house that is as big as a castle. You would want for nothing there. You and Lainey could have one whole wing all to yourselves. You'd feel like a princess, and he'd give Lainey everything she needed. You could—"

"Audrey, you're not listening to me. I want to be with my family."

"But that's just it. You would be with family. You are like a sister to me. And Lainey? I'm her auntie Audrey." She had to make Violet understand. "You're like family to me, Vi!" she exclaimed.

"But I'm *not* your family, Audrey!" Violet shouted. "I'm not your sister. And Lainey is not your niece!"

"But you and Bert and Lainey are all I have!" Audrey reached across the table for Violet, bumping her cup and sending coffee sloshing out of it.

Violet backed away from her. "We are *not* all you have! You have a family! You have one and you walked away from it!"

Audrey sat back now, too. Stunned. "How can you say that?"

Violet's exasperation seemed to melt into a lesser form of anger. "Because it's true! You have a father and two half brothers and a stepmother and an uncle and aunt, and cousins, too, probably. You have a family. You have one, Audrey. You walked away from it. That's no one's fault but yours."

A cry erupted from the nursery. Their shouting had awakened Lainey.

Violet stood and left the kitchen. Audrey sat numb and stricken in the chair. When Violet returned, Lainey was cuddled against Violet, her angelic face buried in the crook of Violet's neck, fully comforted in the arms of her mother. The image seared itself into Audrey's heart.

"Look, I didn't mean to hurt you. I just—," Violet said as she retook her seat.

"No. You're right. Bert is yours. Lainey is yours. They are your family. Not mine."

Seconds of silence hovered between them. It was inevitable, this tearing. Audrey knew that now. She had pulled herself away from Lainey before and then had made the mistake of sewing the rip back together.

"I'm sorry I woke her," Audrey murmured, fresh tears spilling from her eyes.

Violet gently patted Lainey's back. "She'll be all right."

The two friends sat in silence as the baby in Violet's arms fell back asleep.

"When do you leave?" Audrey asked, steeling her heart for the answer.

"On Friday."

Audrey let the knowledge settle over her. "May I write to you?"

"Of course. And I will write to you."

"And may I . . . may I send her things? Just from time to time?"

Violet hesitated a second. "From time to time."

Audrey wiped her eyes with a napkin.

"You've spilled your coffee," Violet said.

Audrey looked down at the splash of coffee on the table. "I did."

"Here." Violet stood and offered the sleeping child to her. "You hold Lainey while I make a fresh pot. And I'll cut some cake for us. It's the one I used to make at the bungalow that you liked so much. With the sugared pecans."

Audrey set down the tearstained napkin and took the baby carefully, so that her engagement ring would not scrape the child's delicate skin.

Audrey stayed only one night in Santa Barbara, not two.

Sleep eluded her hour after hour as she lay in Delores's old bed, and Audrey decided what she would do after Violet and Lainey left.

After saying a tearful good-bye the next day, she got into Glen's Cadillac and headed north, not south.

She arrived at her father's farm a bit before three. Leon Kluge was bent over a tractor in the nearest shed when her car came up the gravel road. He looked up, shielded his eyes against the sun, and stared at the vehicle that he did not recognize. Audrey parked in front of the house, got out, and walked slowly toward him, her soul feeling as raw and exposed as a newborn child.

Her father wiped his hands on his dungarees as he stepped away from the tractor, an anxious look on his face. He stopped just at the opening of the shed and waited for her to come to him.

When she was a few feet away, she stopped, too.

"Hi, Dad."

He stared at her for a moment. "Audrey. You . . . you drove all the way up from Los Angeles?"

She nodded.

"Everything all right?"

"Maybe," she said, blinking back tears that she could not name.

He continued to stare, so unsure of what to do or say. She saw in his eyes the fear that she knew all too well. His fear had masqueraded as bitterness, indignation, anguish, and resentment. But it was fear, plain and simple. He was just like her. He was afraid of not being wanted just like she was. Her mother hadn't been happy here and had made herself ill because of it. Her mother hadn't been happy with the life he'd made for her.

She had stopped wanting him.

"Why are you here?" he finally asked.

"I'm getting married, Dad."

He waited.

"I'd really like you to walk me down the aisle and give me away."

He looked away, first at his shoes and then at the horizon of budding fruit trees that stretched endlessly in every direction. When he returned his gaze to her, his eyes were shimmering. "If that's really what you want."

"I think it's what I've always wanted. I just didn't know it."

He averted his eyes again and she knew it

would be slow, this reconnecting of unraveled threads between them. Slow was good. Everything else that had happened that weekend had happened too fast. Much too fast.

"If it's not during harvest," he said, his gaze on the trees, not on her.

"Of course."

"That his car?"

Audrey looked back at Glen's gleaming Cadillac and then turned back around. "Yes."

Leon Kluge stared at the car for a moment and then at her. "Is he a good man?"

She nodded and a knot of emotion swelled in her throat at all that lay beneath that question. "He is."

Her father hesitated for only a moment. "Guess we can look at the calendar, then."

They turned for the house. The dogs, who had been off in the groves when she had arrived, bounded toward her now, tails wagging, tongues lolling, welcoming her home.

TWENTY-NINE

November 1943

Violet tied a pink balloon to the grosgrain ribbon she held in her hand and ascended a stepladder to attach it to a chandelier. She heard a voice behind her as she pulled the bow tight.

"Bessie can do that for you, Violet."

Violet turned to see her mother, dressed in a peach-toned linen dress accented by a strand of pearls, standing at the entrance to the formal dining room. At fifty-eight, Mama was still trim, elegant, and very active in Montgomery's social and charitable circles. For Violet, the sweetest aspect of coming home had been finding she was at last seeing shimmers of her own reflection when she looked at Mama, who was a paragon of social graces.

"I don't mind doing it." Violet leaned back a bit to gauge the need to add another balloon to the cluster already dangling from the light fixture. "I've got to keep busy, or I'll go crazy watching the clock."

"Well, don't go falling off that ladder, now. It's a big day and you don't want to spend it with an ice pack on your ankle."

Violet laughed. "I promise I'm being careful." The cluster of pink and yellow balloons looked festive and cheerful. Violet climbed down the ladder. "Do the balloons look all right?"

Her mother nodded. "Very nice. It's going to be a lovely birthday party."

"I guess I can finally start getting ready to go to the train station, then."

Bessie, her parents' housekeeper for the past twenty-five years, appeared at the doorway to the kitchen.

"Let me take that ladder back out to the utility room, Violet." The housekeeper reached for the stepladder and folded it closed. "I'm so glad your Mr. Redmond gets to be here for Miss Lainey's first birthday party."

"Thanks, Bessie. I probably don't have to tell you that I am, too."

Bessie laughed. Her voice was low and resonant, like Audrey's. An ache from a deep place swelled inside. Violet missed Audrey more than she'd ever thought she would. There had been letters and cards over the past seven months, and Audrey had sent a photograph of her May wedding to Glen Wainwright, but those letters and the picture had seemed only to intensify Violet's feelings of sadness at their parting. And yet she did not for a minute want to go back to California right now. Violet shook her head slightly to coax that sad sensation away.

"I so wish he could stay through Thanksgiving and Christmas, though," her mother said. "Seems a shame he's coming right before the holidays and then must head back to New Jersey just as everything else is about to begin."

Violet shrugged. "I guess I'd rather he were here for Lainey's first birthday, which will only happen once, while Christmas will be back around again before we know it."

"I suppose that's true."

The housekeeper started to walk away with the

ladder under her arm. Violet heard the faint sounds of Lainey chattering in her crib upstairs. She had awakened early from her nap. All three women looked toward the stairs beyond the dining room.

"Don't you gals worry none about Little Miss," Bessie said. "I'll get her cleaned up and fed while you ready yourself for the train station, Violet. And I knows you've got to go get the cake and flowers, Mrs. Mayfield."

"Thanks, Bessie. I'll get back as soon as I can," Violet's mother said. "I'm sure you've got all the food yet to prepare for the party."

"No worries, no worries. There's a lot I can take care of in the kitchen while Lainey has her lunch in the high chair. No worries at all."

Violet turned from the decorated room to head upstairs to change and fix her hair. A happy knot was already forming in her stomach at the thought of seeing Bert again after six months.

She ascended the staircase to what had been her oldest brother's bedroom, which she and Mama had redecorated when she'd arrived home. She bypassed the closed door to her old room, which was now Lainey's. Behind the door, her daughter was happily babbling nonsense, but that cheerful chatter wouldn't last. In a moment or two, if no one came for her, Lainey would start to howl for attention.

Sweet girl.

Violet stepped into the bedroom that was hers now and closed the door. She stripped off her party-decorating clothes and picked up a powder puff laden with scented talcum to chase away any unpleasant scents.

The party for Lainey later that day wouldn't be a huge affair; everyone seemed to be doing less entertaining with a war on and rationing to go with it. But her grandparents would be there. Her brothers and their wives and their children. A few of the cousins who still lived in town. Some high school friends and their young ones.

Violet frowned as she pulled on a clean slip. Her friends from her younger years just weren't the same as when they had all been childhood chums. Or maybe since Violet was the one who had lived in California for the past four years, she was the one who had changed while everyone in Montgomery had stayed exactly the same. She could tell just how much they had drifted apart when she'd moved back home seven months ago. Their easy camaraderie had thinned; their affection for one another now was one of Southern politeness. Her high school friends had forged new friendships with other young mothers at her church and at the different charitable organizations for whom they now volunteered. Violet still had some work to do to get back into that little universe, even with her mother's help reintroducing her into local society.

Violet now started for her closet and nearly tripped over a box on the floor that had arrived in the mail the day before. It was for Lainey from Audrey, and she had meant to open it earlier and had forgotten. She picked up the box, wondering what she should do with it. It felt heavy. There were probably several presents inside. It would be a little odd to add Audrey's presents to the growing pile of gifts downstairs that would be opened during the party. Audrey had surely signed her card *Love, Auntie Audrey.* And since her brothers' wives—Lainey's actual aunts—would be at the party, that might be thorny. Perhaps she could open it tomorrow, after all the hullabaloo. But in the meantime, it was in the way. If she left the box in their bedroom, Bert would see it and ask what it was. He might not understand the awkwardness of trying to explain to a roomful of people who Auntie Audrey was.

Still wearing only her slip, Violet opened the bedroom door and peeked out to make sure her father hadn't come inside the house. Across the hall, Lainey's door was open and there was no sound coming from it. Bessie had her downstairs.

Violet dashed across the hall into Lainey's room and opened its closet doors. The left side was full of Lainey's clothes and toys. The other side contained boxes and books and trinkets that| had been Violet's when this room had been hers. She rearranged a few of the items to make room for Audrey's package until she could decide when to open it.

Her hands touched a box she had missed seeing when she had put Lainey's things inside the closet. It had a California postmark and the mailing label was in her handwriting. The return address was that of the bungalow that Violet had shared with Audrey.

Violet hadn't thought about the contents of that box in a long time. A very long time.

She put Audrey's gifts down and knelt by the unopened box that she had sent home four years earlier.

Clothes not needed in California was what she had told her mother were inside.

Violet stared at the box for a minute before running her fingernail under packing tape that had lost much of its sticking power. It came away easily. She opened the flaps, pulled out three wool sweaters, and placed them on the floor. She reached in again and her fingers touched the tips of feathers and then braided cord and velvet. She put her hands around the hat—Scarlett #13—and lifted it out of the box. Her mind took her back to the night she and Audrey and Bert got drunk in the wardrobe building, the night Audrey put this hat on her head, and the night Bert told her she was pretty.

The spell had broken that night. Audrey's merciless hold on Bert's affections had been wrested from her when that hat turned up missing. He had finally begun to see that loving Audrey Duvall would bring him only unhappiness.

Audrey had been careless with what mattered to him.

That was what Violet had let him think; it was what she'd needed him to think.

He had almost lost his job and he'd believed it was all Audrey's fault. What would Bert think of Violet now if he knew why she had this hat? Would he forgive her as he'd forgiven her for not telling him before they married that she couldn't have children?

He had understood that she had lied because she loved him and didn't want to lose him.

But this. This was different. She'd lied this time not to keep him loving her but to get him to stop loving someone else.

An irritating pang of remorse started to shoot through her and she tamped it down.

Everything was as it should be. Everything.

Bert was meant to be with her, not Audrey. Audrey was meant to be with Glen.

What she had done was all for everyone's ultimate benefit. Sometimes a person had to do something drastic, like rip apart beautiful curtains to make a dress and hat, to bring about the better good.

It had taken courage to do what she had done, just as it had taken courage for Scarlett to do what she had done. Even Melanie had understood that.

Melanie had understood every harsh thing Scarlett did.

The hat both condemned and commended Violet, just as it had for its fictional owner. Violet couldn't risk Bert seeing it and she couldn't just toss the hat away. The movie was still being talked about four years later. Anyone who saw the hat would recognize it, especially with the label on its underside. And the thought of taking it downstairs to the fireplace and burning it seemed wrong somehow.

Violet reached up to the top shelf of her old childhood closet and pulled an old sewing basket toward her. Inside were hats from her high school days that she no longer wore but were special to her. She dropped Scarlett #13 inside, replaced the flannel sheeting over all the hats, and lowered the lid. She hoisted the sewing basket onto her arm by its black leather handle, lifted Audrey's package into her hands, and then went back to her bed-room. She set the two containers on her bed while she put on a bathrobe over her slip for the quick trip up the attic stairs.

She grabbed the sewing basket.

A blast of chilly air met her as she opened the little attic door and ducked inside. The long, narrow, and low-ceilinged room was filled with crates of Christmas decorations that would soon be coming downstairs, plus old dress forms and extra dining-room chairs and an old phonograph and picture frames. She walked to the little window that provided the only light and opened the steamer trunk beneath it. The trunk had a broken lock but it was a good place to store things, as it kept the bugs and moths out. Violet had long kept in it her dolls and diaries and special memorabilia from years past. She lowered the sewing basket inside and let the lid fall shut.

Violet headed back to her room. She took off the bathrobe and slipped into the new dress she had bought to meet Bert at the train station. It was salmon colored with ivory trim, and her mother had said she looked like a movie star in it. Violet pinned on the dress's lapel the little rhinestone hummingbird that Bert had given her on her last birthday. She fluffed her hair and reapplied her lipstick. In the mirror she saw Audrey's package still on the bed. She turned and pondered it for a moment.

She could take Audrey's gifts downstairs and put them with the other presents on her way out the door. Of course she could. She was making more of the situation than she needed to. How hard would it be to explain to the other guests that Auntie Audrey was Violet's very good friend in Hollywood who didn't have any children of her own?

That wouldn't be hard at all.

Because it was the truth.

E lle, her granddaughters, and the dog are out on the balcony when Daniel and Nicola finally make it back to the bungalow a few minutes before eight. In their arms are In-N-Out burger bags. The girls squeal with delight, and Jacques yips as they all make their way inside.

Daniel rolls his eyes when Elle good-naturedly says she didn't know cheeseburgers were now considered Thai cuisine. "After an hour stuck in traffic, we just went with something fast and easy that didn't involve a bottlenecked freeway," he says.

Nicola sets one of the bags down on the kitchen counter. "And I thought traffic in Paris was bad." Having been raised in Italy, Nicola has an accent that adds an *a* sound to the end of nearly every word. "That was insane."

Elle starts to get out plates.

"Tell your mother about the woman at the shop!" Nicola says to her husband as she withdraws paper-wrapped burgers from a white bag.

Elle turns to her son, a rivulet of disquiet zippering through her. "Something up with the hat?"

"Not really. The shop owner says she lived

next door to Grandma when she was little. She recognized the hat."

"You're kidding."

"It's true!" Nicola says. "Show her the texts."

Daniel pulls his phone out of his pocket. "So I texted her—her name is Christine McAllister— and told her I would be stopping by her shop sometime tomorrow, and this is what she said." He hands the phone to Elle. "She knew Grandma's last name and the street the bungalow is on. At first I thought maybe one of the boxes I took over there had an old mailing label on it, but that wasn't it."

Elle takes the phone and reads the exchange of messages:

> **Christine:** May I ask if the house where all these things came from is on Beechwood? Is the last name Redmond a family name, by chance?
>
> **Daniel:** Yes! That house was my grand-mother's. Violet Redmond. How did you know?
>
> **Christine:** I used to live next door. Your grandmother babysat me when I was six. I'm happy to bring the hat by that house tomorrow, if that's where you will be. I know right where it is.
>
> **Daniel:** That's too kind. You don't have to do that.

Christine: I'd be happy to. Around 4 p.m. okay?

Daniel: If you're sure it's not too much trouble. My mother, Elle Garceau, will be there if I am not. We're still in the process of emptying it. I'm sure she'd love to meet you.

Christine: And I would love to meet her. Your grandmother was a wonderful baby-sitter. She let me try on this hat once.

Daniel: Small world, right?

Christine: Small and lovely. I will have the estimate of your other items ready by then.

Daniel: No rush. Thanks for bringing the hat by.

Christine: My pleasure.

The string of messages ends and Elle looks up from the phone.

"Isn't that amazing?" Nicola says.

"Very," Elle murmurs as she hands the phone back to her son. She wonders if this Christine McAllister is aware that the headpiece she will return tomorrow isn't some ordinary accessory that just happens to smell of cedar and lost years. Surely she knows what it really is. Daniel said it himself.

She recognized the hat.

$\Longrightarrow\!\cdot\!\diamond\!\cdot\!\Longleftarrow$

1962

THIRTY

July 1962

Violet pulled the Plymouth into the driveway of the Santa Barbara house, happy to see Bert was home early from his lecture in San Luis Obispo. Perhaps Lainey was home, too, and the three of them could actually have dinner together—a rarity lately. Lainey's part-time job at the record store was only one of the reasons. Their nineteen-year-old daughter was eager for change, to spread her wings and fly. She had recently applied for a transfer to UCLA and spent most evenings at the beach with friends, imagining a future that would take place far beyond the Santa Barbara horizon.

Bert kept telling Violet that was what baby birds did. Eventually they flew.

And Violet kept reminding him that learning to fly didn't have to mean flying away.

She set the brake, opened the car door, and reached for the grocery sack on the backseat. The bracelet Lainey had made for her when she was eight jangled at her wrist as she lifted the sack. The Peruvian beads and the image of Lainey running alongside little girls with long black braids and coffee brown skin made her smile and her heart ache a little.

Violet missed the years when Bert traveled regularly to South America to take photographs for the Audubon field guides. They'd had such happy times, just the three of them, and the beautiful and exotic locales had been especially therapeutic for Bert after the war. The march across France to liberate it from the Nazis had left him longing to reconnect with the beauty of the earth and its birds, just as his father had done after the First World War. Bert had returned in the summer of 1945, whole but hungry for a repurposed life. The GI Bill had allowed him to finish his degree with a specialty in ornithology and complete his training in photography, and her father's New York connections had indeed helped him get in with the Audubon Society. They had then spent the next six years in a charming Brooklyn brownstone, whenever they weren't traveling the western side of the southern hemisphere to photograph and study birds.

They'd returned to Santa Barbara primarily because Bert wanted ten-year-old Lainey to have a normal education, but also because his health had not been the same after returning from the battlefield. The long last winter of the war, which he spent in frozen foxholes, had been hard on his lungs and heart. Hearing of his mother's death while his regiment chased the Germans across France and Belgium hadn't been easy, either.

They had been back in Santa Barbara for nine

years, and Bert had settled in as a field agent for the U.S. Fish and Wildlife Service. He still spent the majority of the day outside, looking at birds or for birds.

Audrey had been wildly happy about their return to the United States. Her career had at last taken off with the advent of television, just as Glen Wainwright had said it would. She had visited them in the field twice in the years they were away, once in Brazil and once in New York. But as the popularity of television grew and she was more and more in demand—usually, and ironically, to portray someone's mother—she had less time for visits. Anytime a television show needed a woman in her forties with a deep, sultry voice, it was Audrey Wainwright they wanted. Audrey Duvall was all but forgotten.

The return to Santa Barbara had made it easy for Audrey to see them again at holidays, and to invite Lainey, who had become starstruck of late, down to Beverly Hills for long weekends. Lainey adored Audrey and was far too enamored with her auntie's Hollywood lifestyle, in Violet's estimation.

Lainey had assumed what Violet had wanted her to assume about Audrey: She was her mother's childless best friend who lavished on Lainey what she might have on her own children, had she been blessed with any. As to the whereabouts of her true biological mother, Violet had told

Lainey early on—with Bert's somewhat reluctant consent—that her mother had been a single woman in a bad situation who couldn't raise Lainey but who loved her enough to give her to two people who could. For most of her childhood, Lainey had been satisfied with that answer. It wasn't until her early teen years that she'd starting asking questions about who her real mother was and how to find her. She'd even gone to Audrey to enlist her help in convincing Violet and Bert to help her in her quest. Violet had learned that Audrey had told Lainey to just keep trusting that people who had loved her when she was born loved her still and had done what they thought was best for her. Bert had been ready at that point to let Lainey know the truth, but Violet had assured him nothing good would come from that.

And yet with each passing year, Lainey grew to look more and more like her beautiful birth mother. Violet often wondered if it was truly possible to keep Lainey protected from the truth when it seemed so obvious, especially when Audrey and Lainey were together, which these days was painfully often.

Violet shut the car door and hoisted the grocery bag to her hip. Lainey's adoration of Audrey coupled with Audrey's mutual feelings for Lainey were a constant thorn that Violet had tried for years to pluck. She was envious of the affection that Audrey lavished on Lainey, and equally jealous of her daughter's devotion toward Audrey. She hated feeling that way but she did not know how to slay her resentment. The older Lainey got and the more she set her sights south toward Los Angeles, the more it festered.

Violet made her way into the house, stepping into a living room that bore little resemblance to its former appearance when the house was Delores's. Framed photographs of macaws and caracaras and yellow-billed jacamars accented the modern furniture. Vibrant rugs, pottery, and artwork from their many travels to South America decorated the walls and floor. Field guides and coffee-table books that Bert had written or had provided photographs for were displayed on the end tables. A bronze agami heron stood in the far corner of the room where Delores's armchair used to be.

It was a room that shouted that the world was a big place begging to be discovered. Violet hadn't realized just how loudly until that moment, as her gaze was drawn to an opened letter on the small table just inside the door. The table was the stopping place for their car keys and the mail and other little things that spoke of the world outside the house.

The letter from UCLA lay on top of the rest of the mail, its envelope—bearing signs that it had been hurriedly opened—beneath it. Violet set the grocery bag down on the floor by her feet and picked up the piece of paper. The letter congratulated Elaine Redmond for being accepted as a transfer student for UCLA's fall 1962 semester.

For a few seconds Violet could only stand and stare at the words on the page. Then she was aware that Bert was behind her. He put his arm around her waist.

"You should've heard her shout when she opened it," he said.

No, I shouldn't have.

"I suppose she was overjoyed," Violet said tonelessly instead.

"That's putting it mildly. She took off to tell her friends. I'm guessing we will be eating alone tonight."

"So what else is new?" The words tasted bitter in her mouth.

"She wants this, Vi. You can't blame her."

Violet let the letter fall back onto the table. "What does that even mean? That I can't blame her? What does blame have to do with it?"

She snatched up the grocery bag and strode into the kitchen. Bert followed her.

"We can't expect Lainey to live with us the rest of her life," Bert said, a light laugh escaping him.

"She's only nineteen." Violet withdrew a bag of carrots and slapped it to the counter.

"Violet." Bert was at her side again.

She tossed a bag of rice next to the carrots. "What?"

"Lainey wants to follow her dreams, just like any normal young person does. You followed yours. I followed mine. It's what we do."

Violet put her hands on the counter as if to draw strength from the hard ceramic tile. She thought of the choices she had made, the things she had done when she had been chasing after dreams that often seemed elusive. "It's such a big, cruel world."

Bert pulled her close. "It's big, but it's not always cruel. Not always, Vi. And it's not like she's taking off for New York or somewhere else faraway. It's only Los Angeles. Just down the road, really. And Audrey will be right there."

Violet stiffened in his arms as if he'd pierced her with a blade.

When Lainey had first started talking about changing her major from communications to theater and transferring to UCLA, Violet had phoned Audrey to ask for help in getting Lainey to see reason. She'd asked Audrey if she really wanted Lainey to go into acting, when she—of all people—knew what kind of life that would mean. And Audrey had answered that the best thing they could do for Lainey was to let her know they trusted her and loved her and would stand with her no matter what she decided to do.

What that really had meant was Audrey was tickled pink that if Lainey was at UCLA, she would be only a taxi ride away.

Audrey would then have what she'd wanted since she'd tossed Lainey away: to have her back.

Violet spun from Bert and dashed for the hallway and their bedroom. Bert was not far behind.

She sat down hard on their bed as hot tears of anger slid down her cheeks. "She's our daughter! Ours!"

Bert sat down next to her. "Of course she's ours!"

"Audrey's always wanted to steal Lainey's affection away from us!"

Bert took her hand. "That's not true. You're just upset at the thought of Lainey moving away. You're—"

She snatched her hand away. "Stop telling me what I am! I know what I am! And I know what Audrey is!"

"Violet. Look at me."

Several seconds passed before she turned her head to face him.

"You can't expect Audrey not to have feelings for Lainey that are going to rub up against yours. You had to know it was going to be like this. Audrey is your best friend, not some stranger you never saw or never knew."

For a fraction of a second Violet wished Audrey was some stranger she had never seen again. But the black thought skittered away, back to the dark place where it belonged. She could not entertain that dreadful image.

"Audrey doesn't deserve her," she said, her voice like a child's. "She gave Lainey away."

Bert wrapped an arm around her. "She gave her to *us*. Because she loves us and she knew we would love Lainey. Maybe . . ."

She looked up at him. "Maybe what?"

"Maybe it's time Lainey knew the truth. That we all love her and we always have."

Violet stared at him. What he was suggesting was a terrible idea. "She already knows that."

"You know what I mean."

The sound of the front door being opened pulled their attention away from each other. Violet stood and wiped her eyes. She did not want Lainey to see that she had been crying. "She already knows what she needs to know, Bert."

A voice called out. "Anybody home? Mom? Are you here?"

"I'm here!" Violet turned to Bert and offered her hand. He took it as he rose from the bed.

THIRTY-ONE

November 1962

Audrey sipped from a Limoges coffee cup on her patio as she perused the script that her agent had sent over that morning. She had told Rodney on the phone that she had a busy day ahead, with Lainey's twentieth birthday party to host, but he'd been adamant that CBS needed an answer right away. The role called for her to play the mother of a murdered twenty-eight-year-old librarian, and filming was to start next week.

"A twenty-eight-year-old? I'm only fifty-two!" Audrey had growled.

"Don't look at it that way," Rodney had said. "Hair and makeup can have you looking as old or as young as they want. You know that."

"I'd rather play the twenty-eight-year-old, then."

Rodney had laughed and told her to get back to him by noon.

Audrey had lost count of how many times she'd portrayed someone's mother, beginning with the first television role she'd landed, a cameo on *The Lone Ranger* in 1949. In the past decade she'd become the woman every TV-show director wanted when they needed a medium-profile actress to play the lead's mother, or the lead's lover's mother, or the lead's enemy's mother, or the lead's best friend's mother. She'd been in episodes of everything from *Gunsmoke* to *The Twilight Zone* to *Dennis the Menace*. She was never cast in the lead, never given a role that lasted for longer than a season, but yet she was always having to choose among scripts. It was strange the way the directors competed for her. They all wanted her, but only for minor parts. At first she had resisted, preferring to hold out for lead roles, but Rodney and Glen had both told her she excelled at what she did and that was why they all asked for her.

"Playing a mother?" she had said.

"You're good at it," Rodney, who knew nothing of her past, had repeated.

And because being sought after was what she had always desired, she had stayed the course.

But she had been feeling restless of late. Perhaps it was time to think about getting out while she was still in demand. The last thing she wanted was to start getting scripts to play someone's grandmother. Maybe she needed to seriously think about taking her bows while she still felt she had control of her career. It was better to be wanted than to have been wanted. Better to decline a role than to beg for one.

She would have more time for Lainey if she wasn't so busy all the time. It had been so wonderful having her just a short drive away at UCLA the past couple months. Lainey had already spent several weekends with her and Glen, had brought over for dinner her new boyfriend—a French exchange student named Marc—and had been asking Audrey for advice on everything from romance to how to care for cashmere.

Having more free time for Lainey—and Glen— would be wonderful, actually.

Hollywood was different now, and had been

since right after America's troops came home. When the dust of war settled and people returned again to pursuits of happiness, television became the new form of entertainment. The golden age of Hollywood had come to an end while the war was being won, and no one was truly ready for the change.

MGM's Sam Goldwyn had said back in 1949 that just as in the early days of motion-picture history, it would now take brains instead of just money to make films, and that a great many people who had been enjoying a free ride on the Hollywood carousel would now find themselves flung off of it. People wouldn't pay to see poorly made movies when they could stay home and watch something that was no worse. Newsreels and cartoons and short films, which used to be shown before and between movies at the theater, migrated to television. To draw the audience back to the theaters, moviemakers started crafting longer, better-acted, more expensive films, which meant fewer were being made.

Rodney had told Audrey time and time again that she was lucky she had gotten in with television from the start instead of languishing in the wings with the hundreds of nameless film actresses who could no longer get work.

All of her old Hollywood friends, including Vince, had either moved on to become part of the entertainment revolution that was television, or had been forced to fight for a toehold in the thinned-out, more selective studio system. Some tried their luck at independent studios that finally had a chance after the big five studios were forced by a court order to sell off their theater chains. And of those, some succeeded. Some did not.

Glen, who had amassed his wealth in real estate long before the war, simply went on with life as he had before. The changes in the entertainment industry had not affected, impressed, or annoyed him. He simply kept buying the next television set, writing checks to keep live theater functioning in Los Angeles, and spending money on whatever made Audrey happy. His health had begun to diminish since his seventy-fifth birthday a few months earlier. It was hard for Audrey to see him age so suddenly.

He stepped onto the patio now, looking wan. "Who was that at the door?"

"Darling, have a seat." Audrey pulled out a chair and moved her coffee cup.

"You promised you wouldn't fuss over me today," he scolded, but he sat down anyway.

"I'm not fussing. I just want you to feel well for the party later. You said you were going back upstairs to rest."

"I did rest." He leaned back in the chair. "I got bored. Who was that at the door?"

"Messenger service. Rodney sent over a script."

"Like it?"

Audrey tossed the thin sheaf of papers to the patio table. "Maybe. I don't know."

"Then don't do it." He pulled her bare feet into his lap and started to massage her toes.

"It's *Perry Mason*, though."

He shrugged. "Make them beg for you."

She smiled at him. Audrey had never known anyone as genuinely good and kind as Glen, with the possible exception of Bert Redmond. It had not taken her long to love her husband. In fact, she liked the fact that she had fallen in love with Glen after they married. It seemed more romantic somehow. She didn't regret agreeing to marry Glen after Violet announced she was moving back to Alabama and taking Lainey with her. Glen's devotion to her was what got her through the first year Violet and Lainey were gone. Her father hadn't liked it that Glen was so much older than Audrey—only three years younger than he was—and while Audrey didn't like to dwell on the fact that Glen would likely fly away to heaven well before she did, it had warmed her heart that her father was worried she'd end up alone. It had taken a few years after her wedding for Audrey and her dad to fully reconnect, but in the end she had learned that her father expressed his love in understatement. A person would miss it if she was not careful, but that did not mean his love was not ardent. He had been fragile inside, as she was, and he protected what had been broken in the past, just as she did.

Leon Kluge had passed away in his sleep two years earlier, and Audrey still missed him.

And now as she looked at Glen, an ache filled her soul to realize that he was weakening before her eyes, just as her father had.

"We could always have the party at Chasen's instead of here," she said impulsively.

He frowned. "Nonsense. You've already paid the caterer. I want the suckling pig on a spit."

She laughed. "I went for the pulled pork in a pan. Less show-offy."

"Same thing."

Inside the house, the phone rang. She pulled her legs away to stand.

"Let Beatriz get it," Glen said.

Audrey touched his shoulder. His white hair, like fine gauze, wisped as she moved past him. "It will be Rodney."

As she walked away, Audrey decided she would take the part. It was *Perry Mason*, after all.

By eight o'clock, the house and patio, which had been decorated with garlands of plumeria and flickering tiki torches, were filled with Lainey's new UCLA friends; a few old chums from Santa Barbara; the new boyfriend, Marc; and Bert and Violet. A long banquet table of Hawaiian-themed food had satisfied the guests, and now there was a break between the main course and the cake. The young people played billiards, cards, and Yahtzee in the giant game room on the first floor.

Audrey could tell as Glen mixed drinks for the four of them that Violet was not happy. She hadn't been truly happy since Lainey had transferred to UCLA three months earlier—a development for which Audrey had secretly cheered. Lainey was finally living close to her and outside of Violet's intensely watchful eye. Audrey had spent the past twenty years agonizing over the distance she was beholden to keep between herself and Lainey, and it hadn't been easy. Lainey was clearly fond of her, and while she quietly basked in that affection, she knew it rankled Violet, even though Violet tried to pretend it didn't.

But there was something else on Violet's mind as Glen handed out the martinis, something else besides Lainey's recent move to Los Angeles. Audrey had a feeling she knew what it was.

For her birthday, Lainey had asked Audrey for a plane ticket to Paris for the coming summer, after Marc graduated and returned home. Violet had given Audrey a stern look earlier that evening when Lainey had opened Audrey's gift and then squealed with delight at the promise of airfare to France come June.

Violet crossed the expansive living room now with her drink in hand and asked if she could have a moment with Audrey.

"Of course," Audrey said, and then turned to Glen. "We'll be right back."

They went into Glen's study, a richly paneled room with shiny leather couches and built-in bookshelves. French doors looked out onto the pool and patio area, dark now except for the light of the tiki torches.

"Do you want to sit?" Audrey motioned to one of the sofas.

Violet nodded, her lips pursed together. They both sat down and the couches squawked hello. Violet sipped her drink and then set the glass down on the coffee table in front of them.

"This has been a very lovely party for Lainey," Violet said, a strained smile on her lips. "You shouldn't have gone to so much trouble."

Audrey smiled back. "It wasn't any trouble. Glen and I were happy to do it. We love Lainey. You know that."

"Yes. Well . . ." Violet seemed to search the Persian carpet at their feet for the words she wanted next. "I know for you it wasn't any trouble to throw this party and have all these special luau decorations put up and such, but Lainey is used to a simpler life. You've been giving her too much, too soon, since she's moved down here. You are overwhelming her with too much generosity."

A thinly veiled reprimand lay beneath Violet's words; it was a lecture that was wholly unneeded.

If anything, Audrey had exercised tremendous restraint.

"We really haven't given her that much, Vi. And she seems fine to me," she said politely.

Violet bristled; Audrey had inadvertently struck a nerve. "But you don't know her like I do," Violet said coolly. "You *have* given her too much. First all those new clothes you bought her for school, and this party, and then that ridiculous promise of a plane ticket to Paris—"

"Excuse me?" Audrey interjected. "She asked for that plane ticket. It is the only thing she asked me for."

"But that doesn't mean you had to give it to her."

Audrey set down her own drink. It was clear Violet had been harboring these thoughts for a while. Audrey wondered how long. She wondered, too, if Violet knew Audrey had her own pent-up emotions when it came to Lainey. The conversation would get ugly if they were not careful.

"Violet," she continued in a gentler tone. "Lainey just wants to go to Paris this summer. It is no trouble for Glen and me to help her get there. It's our pleasure to help her."

"Just because it's easy for you to do something doesn't mean you should do it. You should have asked Bert and me first, for one thing."

"She's twenty years old."

Violet reacted as if Audrey had slapped her.

"You don't have to tell me how old my daughter is," she said evenly.

This was nuts. Violet was inflating every word Audrey said. "Why are you taking this personally? It has nothing to do with you. It's just a plane ticket to Paris, for God's sake!"

Violet's chest was now rhythmically heaving in short little bursts. "Really? Is that really all it is?"

Audrey now saw envy, desire, and resentment in Violet's eyes—three old friends she realized she knew very well, especially with regard to Lainey. Violet was jealous.

"It's not my fault she likes being here in Los Angeles, Vi. It's not my fault she likes being here at this house."

Violet narrowed her eyes. "Of course it's your fault. You wanted her to transfer. You wanted her to be here in Los Angeles, close to you and away from me."

"That is not true."

"You know it's true. You wanted her here so you could spoil her with things Bert and I could never give her."

A pall seemed to drop over the room, as if a black curtain had fallen and the deepest, darkest longings of their souls were now slithering out of their hiding places. What Violet was saying was ugly, heavy, and yet not completely untrue.

"Violet—"

But Violet's eyes were glistening with angry tears of determination. "Are you forgetting who gave Lainey a home these past twenty years? Have you forgotten that? Have you forgotten who held her when she cried and when fever ravaged her body and when nightmares woke her? Have you forgotten who taught her to swim and ride a bicycle and sew a button and make a cake? Have you forgotten who stayed up waiting for her to get home at night and who dried her tears when friends betrayed her and when boys broke her heart? Have you forgotten who took her in when you tossed her away like she was a dog you didn't want?"

The blade found its home in Audrey's chest and she flinched as the accusation sliced through. For a second she could say nothing.

"I can't believe you said that," Audrey finally whispered.

Violet looked petrified, as if she couldn't believe she had said it, either. No words came out of her mouth.

"It killed me to give her away," Audrey said. "Even to you. You know it did."

"How did you even do it?" Violet said, her voice now coated with disgust. "How *could* you even do it?"

"I had nothing to offer her! Nothing!" Audrey shouted, tears now streaming down her face as well.

"You had what all mothers have to give! You had love! And you gave her away!"

"It was because I loved her that I did! How can you not know that? You, of all people, know how much I loved her and how much I love her still."

Violet's gaze was livid. "And now you're trying to buy her love in return when you could have had it from the beginning."

Fury raged inside Audrey's chest and pounded against her ribs. "You've never wanted me to love her and you didn't want her loving me. I've played by your rules, Violet. For twenty long years I've played by your rules. And now *you* accuse *me* of being unfair? She was the only beautiful thing I've ever managed to create with my life, and you won't even let me stand back and admire her."

Violet opened her mouth to respond but there was suddenly a third voice in the room.

"How could you do this?"

The voice was Lainey's. The question—Audrey did not know to whom it was directed. Lainey stood at the doorway behind them, her face pale with shock and anger.

"Oh, God!" Violet whispered.

"Lainey—," Audrey began, but she turned from them and left the open doorway.

"Wait! Lainey!" Violet wailed as she sprang from the sofa to run after her.

Audrey sped after them both.

"Please let me explain!" Violet said to Lainey's retreating back.

"Marc!" Lainey yelled, storming past the living room and the surprised faces of Bert and Glen, who were standing at its wide entrance.

"Lainey!" Violet chased after her.

"What's happened?" Glen called out as Audrey bolted past them. "She just wanted to know when we could have the cake! I told her to ask you."

Lainey spun around, and Violet and Audrey nearly crashed into her. But her gaze was on Bert. "I'll tell you what happened! I *know*. I know what you have all been keeping from me!"

Then she turned on her heel and headed for the marble staircase that led to the downstairs game room. "Marc!" she yelled from the top step. "Tell everyone we're leaving."

"*Comment dit?*" Marc's voice wafted up the stairs.

"We're leaving!" Lainey turned back toward her stunned parents and Audrey. She said nothing, but grabbed her purse off the massive entry table that separated the marble staircase from the living room.

She strode for the door as Marc and Lainey's friends ascended the stairs with surprised faces.

"What has happened?" Marc said to Audrey, his musical French accent making his question sound lovely in spite of the situation. Lainey was out the door and the rest of the party was milling toward it, clearly astounded.

"Don't let her be alone," Audrey answered him. "Bring her back here if she will allow it. She has a right to be angry. But she has a right to an explanation, too."

"Lainey!" Violet called out after her daughter. She started for the door and Bert held her back.

"Let her go, Vi. I don't think she wants to talk to us right now."

She whirled on him. "I don't know how much she heard!"

"I think it's pretty obvious how much she heard!" Audrey shouted.

Glen moved to the front door to escort the rest of the guests out. A couple of them thanked him for the food and the leis and the nice party.

"What happened?" Bert said to Audrey, as the last guest stepped over the threshold and Glen started to shut the door.

But Audrey could not find the words to tell him what had happened in Glen's study when the dark curtain fell.

"She knows," was all Audrey said.

Violet collapsed to her knees, sobbing and calling out her daughter's name.

THIRTY-TWO

June 1963

Violet surveyed the living room with her hands on her hips and then grabbed and fluffed the sofa pillows. She started to straighten the books on the coffee table but the sound of a car outside made her freeze, and she didn't resume her task until the vehicle continued on its way down the street. She checked her watch for the fifth time in the past hour. And then straightened the books again.

"She's not going to care about the way the living room looks." Bert was suddenly behind her. His voice was gentle but tired-sounding, as though he was not also counting down the minutes to Lainey's visit. How could he not be anticipating this day after seven months of silence?

Then again, it hadn't exactly been seven months of silence for him. He'd spoken to Lainey on the phone a few times since that terrible night. Violet had listened at the study door when he'd called Lainey and she'd agreed to speak with him. Violet had only heard Bert's voice, of course, but she could tell by his responses and questions that Lainey was all right. She had moved in with Audrey and Glen. She didn't need anything. She was not ready yet to talk to Violet.

From the awful things Violet had said to Audrey the night of the birthday party—for which she later had apologized to Audrey profusely—and from Bert's own honest answers, Lainey had been able to surmise it was Violet who had insisted year after year that she not be told the truth. Lainey's anger at Bert and Audrey had subsided for the most part, but not her resentment toward Violet. Until now. Lainey was coming to the house today. It would be the first time Violet had seen or talked to her daughter since November.

"I need to keep busy or I will go crazy waiting for them," Violet said.

She wanted Bert to come put his arms around her and hold her close and tell her it was all going to work out fine, that today was going to be the day she and Lainey at last mended their broken relationship.

But he turned from her to head into the kitchen.

The rift between Lainey and the two of them had spilled over into their marriage. For the first few weeks after the party, Bert had blamed himself for not insisting that they at least consider telling Lainey the truth when she first started showing an interest in knowing who her birth mother was.

"Every time she asked about it, we lied to her," he had said on the way home the night of the birthday party.

And Violet had said they hadn't lied; they'd been vague. To protect Lainey.

"Protect her from what?"

And she'd had no answer for him.

Christmas had been especially hard. Lainey had spent it in Manhattan with Marc and his parents, who were visiting the States from Paris. Lainey had called Bert at his field office to tell him where she would be for the holidays, because she hadn't wanted to call home and have Violet answer.

It wasn't until after the first of the year that Lainey reconnected with Audrey, and nearly February before she was ready to have a longer phone conversation with Bert.

"I'm afraid she will never forgive me," Violet had said to Audrey by phone the day she let Violet know that Lainey had moved in with her and Glen.

"Give her time," Audrey had said.

"Give her time for what? What does time do?" Violet had responded in exasperation.

"Time gives us the opportunity to learn to live with a new reality, Violet. We can't expect her to happily embrace a complex situation that we've had twenty years to become familiar with."

"But she's moved in with *you!*" Violet had whined, unable to rid her voice of the envy that dripped from it.

"Lainey is forgiving each one of us in her own

way, Vi. And I'd rather she mentally worked this out here in this house, where there are people who love her, than in her dorm room. Don't you agree?"

"It's so unfair. It's not like this was all my fault. I didn't hold a gun to your head or Bert's. You could have told her if you'd really wanted to," Violet had exclaimed, and then immediately wished she hadn't. It was Audrey's and Bert's loyalty to a promise they'd made that had kept them quiet. "I'm sorry. I shouldn't have said that."

"You're right. It is not all your fault. She has projected all her hurt and disappointment onto you. I'm sorry about that, Violet."

"Do you wish you'd never given her to us?" Violet had said a moment or two later, whispering the words through her tears.

Audrey had paused for only a moment. "If you're asking me if I wish I had kept her, yes, I wish I had. But I didn't. That's not what I did. And, no, I don't wish I had never given her to you."

As jealous as Violet was when Lainey moved in with Audrey, she'd been grateful that she could now find out how Lainey was, especially as her bitterness toward Violet started to mellow. Lainey was leaving the next day for her long-awaited trip to Paris. Audrey had convinced her to drive up with her to Santa Barbara and patch things up with Violet before she left. Audrey had said they would be there by two. It was now a few minutes before.

Violet followed Bert into the kitchen. He was standing at the open fridge, pulling out a pitcher of iced tea.

"That's for dinner tonight!" Violet said.

Bert sighed and put the pitcher back, and grabbed a bottle of Pepsi instead. "You need to relax, Vi."

"I can't relax."

He shut the fridge door. "Well, you need to. Lainey deserves normal for a change. This is not normal." He popped the cap and tossed it into the trash.

The sound of an idling motor outside riveted Violet's attention to the window. She sprang for it and looked out. A brown truck had pulled up in front of the house.

"It's just the UPS man," she growled. "Did you order something?"

Bert shook his head.

Violet went to the front door and swung it open. The UPS man was setting a large box onto a hand truck. Then he was wheeling it toward her.

"Are you sure that's for us?" she called out as he approached. "We're not expecting anything."

"If you're Violet Redmond, this is yours. You know anyone in Montgomery, Alabama?"

Violet looked at the return label. "What on earth is Mama sending in a box so big?" Violet said more to herself than anyone else.

The UPS man asked where she wanted the box,

and Violet frowned and told him he could bring it into the kitchen. This was not a good time for a surprise delivery, not with Audrey and Lainey due any minute. She would find out what was inside and then have Bert move the box to his study. She was still secretly hoping Audrey and Lainey might stay the night. She wanted to keep the guest room free of clutter.

"What is that?" Bert asked as he looked down at the box.

"I have no idea." Violet signed the UPS man's paperwork, and he left.

She grabbed a pair of scissors and slid one blade down the packaging tape. Inside the box were—at first glance—a myriad of old, friendly things: dolls she'd had as a child and that Lainey had also played with when they'd visited Montgomery, books, a jewelry box and other trinkets, and much more. A letter lay on top. Violet opened the flap on the envelope and withdrew the letter.

Dear Violet:
So sorry that things with you and Lainey are still jumbled. I am sure in time Lainey will come to see she has two wonderful mother figures in her life who love her. Most of us only have one, and some not even that.

Your father and I have decided to sell the house, like I told you we might, and retire to Florida. I've been going through closets and such and I found many old things of yours you might want, and I thought perhaps you could share them with Lainey as a way to reconnect with her. One thing mothers do is pass on what we love to our children. I was thinking she might enjoy having some of these things that used to be yours. It could be a start to gaining back the close relationship with her that you've lost for right now.

And even if she doesn't want these old things, know that resentment is a hard companion to have around. She will tire of it, Violet. Don't give up. Mothers never do.

I'll call you next week sometime,
Love, Mama

Violet wasn't aware that Bert was reading over her shoulder until she felt his arm around her waist.

"That was a nice thing for her to do," he said.

Violet wiped her wet cheeks. "It was."

She had just started to kneel at the box when through the open window she heard the sound of a car door closing just outside. They had been so intrigued by the box and the letter, neither one of them had heard a car pull up.

"They're here!" Violet tossed the letter to the

box and stood. She pivoted and made for the front door, which was still slightly ajar. She flung it the rest of the way open. Audrey was coming up the walkway alone.

Lainey wasn't with her.

Audrey looked beautiful in turquoise pants and a matching top. Her long hair was pulled back from her face with a wide black headband. She carried an oversized woven bag dotted with large fabric daisies.

Words escaped Violet as Audrey closed the distance to them. They wordlessly exchanged embraces.

"She decided not to come?" Bert said, his voice polite but weighted with disappointment.

Audrey pulled off her white-framed sunglasses. "I'm so sorry. She . . . she changed her mind at the last minute." Then she turned to Violet. "She did give me this to bring to you." Audrey reached into the woven bag and withdrew an envelope. Written across the front was one word.

Mom.

Violet began to shake with tears she desperately wanted to rein in and knew she would not be able to. The word looked so beautiful, so tender, but the letter was in place of Lainey herself. She clasped the envelope to her chest and looked up at Audrey, willing her to tell her what she might expect to read on the pages inside.

Audrey seemed to know Violet wanted assurance

that the contents would not destroy her. She said nothing. Audrey didn't know what the letter said.

"Come on inside, Audrey," Bert said.

Audrey stepped into the house and put her hand on Violet's arm. "She doesn't hate you, Violet."

The tears slid down steadily now.

Bert's arm was at her back. "You want to read it alone in the bedroom, Vi?"

Violet shook her head. She did not want to be alone. She turned to him. "I don't think I can read it!"

His eyes were misted, too.

Violet turned to Audrey and handed her the letter. Audrey silently took it. She sat down in one of the armchairs, and Bert and Violet moved to the couch and sat down, too. They sat forward on the cushions, and Violet was glad to have Bert's hand in hers.

Audrey took out the letter and began to read:

Dear Mom,

I'm sorry I am not there with Audrey right now. There will be a time when I can look at you and not be angry, but that time hasn't come yet. I've lived long enough to know that when someone you love hurts you, it takes longer to heal. And I do still love you. But my heart feels tattered right now, and I can't trust you.

I know why Audrey gave me up. I know

why she wanted you and Dad to take me. What I don't understand is why you made them promise not to tell me the truth, especially when I wanted to know where I came from. When I was a teenager, I asked Audrey once if she knew who my birth mother was. She told me that was a question for you and Dad. When I asked Dad if he knew who she was, he just said he knew that she had loved me and wanted me to be happy. But when I asked you if you knew who she was, you said you didn't. When I asked you if you knew what her name was, you said no.

Audrey says you did what you thought was best for everyone, not just for me, but for her and for you. But she also told me, because I insisted on her honesty, that she never demanded of you and Daddy that I not be told. Not telling me was your idea. I don't understand what terrible tragedy you were attempting to prevent. You knew how much I wanted to know who my birth mother was.

Year after year you let me think "Auntie" Audrey was just a good friend who couldn't have children and that my birth mother was some troubled, unwed girl in need of rescue. Audrey insists you did rescue her—and me—and that she had been in a desperate situation. But she wasn't some nameless stranger. She was the person you always told me was your best friend.

You were always such a good mother to me. And this—all of this—doesn't seem like something you would have done.

I am leaving for France tomorrow, as you know. And I think this trip is coming at a good time. Perhaps when I am far, far away from everything and everyone I thought I knew, I can make sense of this. Or at least learn to live with it.

I'm sorry I can't just let this go like none of it matters. I know you want me to. But that's not how you raised me.

Lainey

When Audrey was finished, the room was silent. After a few moments, Audrey handed the letter back to Violet.

She took the letter and folded it with a shaking hand. Bert put his arm around her and pulled her close. His touch in that way was exquisite and yet piercing. Love had such sharp edges.

"I never wanted it to be like this," Violet whispered as she held the letter's words, folded from view, in her hand.

"Of course you didn't," Bert said, stroking her shoulder. "None of us did. Lainey will come around."

Violet wiped away her tears and looked up at Audrey. "I'm sorry I told her I didn't know your name or who you were. I hated lying to her. But she kept pressing me. I . . . I wanted her to stop."

Audrey looked down at her empty hands. "We've all made choices we might've handled differently if we knew then what we know now. Bert's right. She'll come around."

The three of them were quiet again for a few moments.

"Can you stay for dinner? Bert is grilling steaks," Violet said.

Audrey shook her head. "I'm going to head back before too long. Glen's not well and I don't like being two hours away."

"So sorry to hear that," Bert said.

"Yes, so sorry," Violet whispered.

"But I can stay for a little while and we can visit and catch up."

Audrey told them that her most recent role on *The Twilight Zone* was going to be her last for a while, maybe for good. She wanted to spend more time with Glen and was actually looking forward to retirement.

Violet couldn't believe what she was hearing. This was not the Audrey she knew. "But all your life you wanted to be a star and now you are one. And you want to quit?"

Audrey smiled lightly. "I wanted to be wanted. And for the past dozen years I've known first-hand what it's like to be sought after. It's funny how when you get what you've always longed for, sometimes the reason you wanted it no longer exists."

She went on to talk about the different philanthropic ventures she and Glen were involved in, and that they were planning to spend the autumn months at a Tuscan villa they had just bought in Italy.

"Maybe you two could come visit us for a week or two this fall," Audrey said.

"What about Lainey?" Violet replied.

"What about her? She can come if she wants to."

"But she'll be in school."

"Then she can come some other time."

Audrey seemed to be suggesting that it was time for the three of them to start living without Lainey at the center of their universe.

Easy for Audrey to look at it that way; she had Lainey's forgiveness.

Audrey turned to Bert. "There are lots of birds to photograph in Tuscany."

He smiled. "That reminds me. I wanted to give Lainey one of my cameras for her trip to Paris. I'll be right back."

Bert left the room. The women watched him leave.

"Are you two all right? With each other, I mean?" Audrey asked in a low voice.

Violet's first response was to tell Audrey that of

course they were all right, but she was feeling alone and vulnerable and very much in need of her friend's companionship.

"I hope so. I think so."

"Bert's a good man. And he loves you."

Violet turned to face Audrey. "Does he?" The two words spilled out of her heart as well as her mouth, surprising them both.

"Of course he does," Audrey said with gentle force.

"He's disappointed in me."

Audrey leaned forward and took Violet's hand. "He's just disappointed in the general state of things."

Violet sighed. "I wish I could fix it. I wish I could just kiss the wound and make it all better."

Audrey squeezed her hand and let go. "Spoken like a true mother."

Violet looked up at her friend. Sometimes, as at that moment, Violet could see Audrey in her mind's eye, sitting on the little cement bench at the studio commissary the first day she met her and the two of them were both young and full of dreams. They'd both managed to seize what they had so desperately wanted. And yet here they were, all these many years later, and it seemed as if what she had so determinedly clutched to her chest was struggling to free itself from her grasp.

Audrey stood and pulled the handles of her

woven bag over her shoulder. "I should probably start heading back."

Violet stood as well. She suddenly decided she wanted Audrey to take something for Lainey, too. As a peace offering of sorts. She'd look for something in the box her mother had sent.

"I'd also like you to give something to Lainey. From me," she said.

Violet went into the kitchen and Audrey followed. Violet bent over the box.

"My mother sent me a box of things that were mine when I was young that she and Daddy have kept at the house for me," she said as she began to sift through the contents. "They're moving and emptying closets and such. I was thinking maybe one of my old dolls would cheer Lainey up."

"How wonderful that your mother saved all these things for you," Audrey said in an astonished voice. She leaned over the box, too, her gaze taking in all the saved pieces of Violet's childhood.

"I have this one doll from France. A cancan dancer," Violet went on. She uncovered a muslin-wrapped bundle. "If it's in here, you can—"

But Violet didn't finish. Her words froze in her mouth as the fabric fell away, exposing at first folds of green velvet, then gold braid, and the iridescent tail feathers from a farmyard rooster.

Audrey gasped next to her.

Lying on the unfolded muslin was the curtain hat from *Gone With the Wind*.

"Oh . . ." Violet breathed.

"How in the world did your mother get that hat?" Audrey said, incredulous.

The room seemed to spin, and heat flared to Violet's cheeks.

"That is the hat, isn't it?" Audrey seemed happily dumbfounded.

Violet could only nod.

"How did she get it?"

"I sent it to her," Violet whispered.

"When? When did you find it?"

"The day after you took it."

The curious smile on Audrey's face slowly morphed into a doubtful grin.

"What are you saying, Vi? That you had it this whole time?"

Violet slowly nodded.

"Why?" Audrey asked, her expression one of bewilderment, not anger. After what the truth had done to her relationship with Lainey, Violet had no desire to repeat that situation. Perhaps this was just a little thing; perhaps Audrey would laugh about it. Perhaps Bert would, too. But she wasn't sure. She wasn't sure of anything anymore. She knew only that this hat had been the beginning of every deceitful thing she had done to win her heart's desires.

"Don't ask me that, Audrey."

Audrey stared at her, her gaze betraying that she was puzzling over what would have motivated Violet to hide the hat all those years ago. "Does Bert know you have it?"

Two tears that had formed at the corners of Violet's eyes spilled out and slid down her cheekbones. "No."

Audrey opened her mouth to say something else, but Bert's voice called out to them from the hallway. He was asking Violet if she knew where his lens cleaner was. He was coming their way.

In an instant Audrey had the hat and its muslin covering in her hands and was slipping it into her woven bag. When Bert rounded the corner with a Leica camera in his hands, the hat was nowhere in sight.

He looked with concern at Violet. "You all right?"

Violet could only nod as she wiped her eyes.

"She was looking for one of her old dolls to send home with me to Lainey," Audrey said quickly. "But it wasn't in the box." Audrey reached out her hand to pat Violet's arm. "Maybe your mother doesn't have it anymore?"

Violet nodded. "Maybe not."

Audrey looked at the camera in Bert's hands. "That the one you want me to take to her?"

"Yes. I just wanted to clean up the lens a little."

"I saw the bottle of lens cleaner on your

dresser last night," Violet said, unable to take her eyes off Audrey's woven bag.

"Oh. Right." Bert spun away, back down the hall.

"What do you want me to do with it?" Audrey said as soon as Bert was gone, softly but with no emotion. Violet could not read her friend's thoughts.

"I've never known the answer to that," Violet whispered back.

The two of them stared at each other for a moment.

"You know, I always liked that hat," Audrey said a moment later, her deep voice low and rich. "I've always admired what it was made from. It scared me a little, too, what it was made from."

"It still scares me."

Bert was coming back. The women fell silent. He had placed the camera in a leather bag and was dropping the lens cleaner inside it as he came back into the kitchen. "Lainey knows how to use it. This camera was her favorite when she was a teenager. Give it to her with our love?" Bert offered the bag to Audrey and she took it.

"I will."

Bert put his arm around Violet's waist. "From both of us?"

Audrey smiled. "Of course."

She turned to leave, and Violet found she could not put words together to say good-bye.

"We're so sorry you can't stay for dinner," Bert said, when she said nothing. "And we'll keep Glen in our prayers."

"Thank you. That means a lot to me."

The three of them walked to the front door. Bert hugged Audrey and kissed her on the cheek. "Thank you for all you are doing for Lainey right now."

"Of course. Good-bye, Bert." Audrey turned to Violet and pulled her into an embrace. "Think about what I said?"

"What you said?" Violet replied, trembling.

Audrey pulled away. "About you and Bert coming to Italy this fall. It would be nice to just sit and talk without having to rush off somewhere. We barely got to talk about anything today."

Violet licked her lips. "Yes. That would be nice."

"Kiss Lainey for us!" Bert said as Audrey started to walk toward her car.

"I will."

Violet watched as Audrey strode confidently toward her silver Thunderbird.

"She has a new car," Bert said.

But Violet barely heard him. Her eyes were on the woven bag with the fat, floppy daisies running riot across it.

"Tell me you love me, Bert," she murmured as Audrey drove off.

Bert looked at her. "You know I love you, Vi."

"Why? Why do you love me?"

He laughed. "Do we have to have reasons?"

"Don't we?"

He leaned over and kissed her cheek. "No. We don't. I don't think it's love if there are reasons. Reasons are for why you like someone."

Audrey's car was getting smaller in the distance. "Do you ever wish you had married someone else?"

"What? No! Do you?"

She turned to him. "Never. You are the only one for me. You always have been. Always will be."

He cupped her face in his hand. "That's reason enough if I needed one. And you are the only woman for me. Where is all this doubt coming from?"

Violet put a hand to her heart. "From here."

Bert took her hand and kissed it. "We're going to be okay. Lainey isn't the glue that keeps us together. We are. We're the glue. Okay?"

She nodded and they went back into the house, where she spent the rest of the afternoon going through the box her mother had sent and remembering the time of her innocence.

Two months later, on a blazing-hot August afternoon, a trans-Atlantic phone call came to the house. Bert answered it and he yelled for Violet, who was hanging up undergarments to dry in the bathroom.

"It's Lainey!" Bert yelled. "She's calling from Paris!"

Violet dropped the hosiery and ran to where Bert stood with the telephone receiver in his hand. Bert held it so they both could hear.

"I'm here, Lainey!" Violet said excitedly. "I'm right here!"

Lainey's voice sounded remarkably clear considering how far away she was.

She sounded like she was just next door when she told Violet and Bert that she and Marc Garceau had just eloped in Marseille.

THIRTY-THREE

September 1963

G len hadn't wanted anyone to wear black to his funeral, and although some of the guests on the patio hadn't gotten the message, most were clad in shades of yellow, red, and gold. Autumn hues. The colors of change. Audrey had chosen a fitted dress of crimson lace that had been one of Glen's favorites. He had often told her she looked like Scarlett on the day of Ashley Wilkes's birthday party, only without the guilt, when she wore that red dress.

Audrey moved about the patio now, thanking people for coming, for sharing the day with her, and even for having happy little conversations as they ate catered hors d'oeuvres off china plates. Glen's two children and their spouses were making the rounds, too, greeting their father's friends and family. Glen's sole grandchild, a quiet college student named Roland, was sitting by the pool, talking with Bert about photography.

The afternoon had been a calm, clear one with barely a hint of chill in the breeze; Glen's favorite kind of day. It was almost as if he'd paid for it and had it waiting for the day his life would be celebrated. The memorial at Hollywood Presbyterian had been attended by hundreds. Glen had lived a life of benevolence, and those who'd been touched by his generosity had turned out in droves to mourn his death and pay their respects. The reception afterward at the house had been a private one, but still attended by more than one hundred people.

Glen had left Audrey quickly, while asleep next to her; one of myriad, end-of-life kindnesses he had been able to show her. Others included having taken care of all the complex arrangements related to death and dying, including the disposition of his estate. Audrey didn't care that Glen had left the Beverly Hills house to his children. It was only right that they should jointly own the home they had been raised in. Besides, she could not imagine living in the house now that Glen was gone. She still had her bungalow, although her portion of Glen's estate and her own earnings had made her a wealthy woman.

She was glad that he'd left her the villa in Italy, though. He had bought it as a twentieth-wedding-anniversary gift, and due to his health, they hadn't been able to visit it yet. Up until a week earlier, they had hoped he would soon feel well enough to travel so that they could have the Italian autumn they'd dreamed about. Glen had even extracted a promise from Audrey that she would go alone if anything should happen. The thought of traveling there solo had at first filled with her sadness, but as she mentally began to prepare to leave the mansion in the days after Glen's death, she found herself looking more and more forward to discovering all of the villa's lovely secrets. And perhaps staying there past the autumn. She had more than enough money to live on her own. The bungalow was being rented out by a kind, childless couple in their forties who would take good care of it.

And she'd be relatively close to Lainey in France.

Lainey.

That girl was so like her and Violet. First in her response to the wounding by those she loved most, and then in her spontaneous move to elope. So like them both.

When Violet had called Audrey in tears to tell her Lainey had married Marc Garceau, remarking over and over, "How could Lainey do such a thing?" Audrey had not been able to conceal her amusement.

"How can you laugh at a time like this?" Violet had railed. "She got married! Without telling anyone!"

"So did you!"

There had been a couple seconds of silence.

"But I didn't marry a Frenchman! Who lives in Paris!"

"You married the man you loved. I am sure Lainey did the same thing."

"But . . . but she's so young! How does she know what she wants?"

At this, the smile that had been on Audrey's face thinned to a thoughtful grin. "How do any of us at that age, Violet?"

On the other end of the phone, Audrey had heard Violet sniffle.

"What am I going to do?" Violet finally said.

"You already know what to do."

"I do?"

"You and Bert will send a lovely card and wedding gift, and you will welcome your new son-in-law into the family. And then you will let them know you'd love to come see them whenever they are ready for a visit. And then when the invitation comes, you will go, and you will say only how happy you are for them. That is what she wants to hear from you. From all of us. That we love her and trust her. You already know this."

"Is that what you're going to do?" Violet had asked, the tiniest undercurrent of contempt in her voice.

Glen had needed her at that moment, and she was glad to tell Violet that she had to hang up. She'd had her own feelings over the news of Lainey's elopement to wrestle with. Part of her was glad, glad, glad that a married Lainey living in a foreign country was no longer Violet's responsibility. That seemed childish and ugly and she hadn't wanted to think about it then. She still didn't.

Violet appeared now on the patio, a tea towel on her arm as she gathered plates that funeral guests had left behind.

"You don't have to do that," Audrey said. "The catering staff will take care of it."

"I want to do it. I need to feel useful," Violet answered as she fisted a used napkin in her hand and used it to brush crumbs off a tablecloth.

Audrey half smiled. "I know you do."

Violet stopped for a moment and looked toward Glen's grandson and Bert. "Those two have been talking for over an hour."

"Roland is an aspiring photographer. And he's a shy person. Having Bert to talk to today has been perfect for him."

"I suppose he and his parents are moving in here?"

Audrey shrugged. "I don't really know what the children are going to do with this house."

"You aren't sad about having to leave it?"

"This always felt like Glen's house to me. I was happy here. But it was never my house."

"So you really are going to the villa alone, then?"

Audrey nodded.

"For how long?"

"I don't know."

They were quiet for a moment.

"I still have your hat," Audrey said.

Violet stiffened. "It's not mine. It was never mine." A pained look had crept across Violet's face.

"Does that mean you don't want it back?"

Violet shook her head.

"Are you ever going to tell me why you hid it all these years?"

Violet turned to her, her eyes pleading. "Can't you just get rid of it? Please?"

"Get rid of it? As in 'throw it away'? You can't be serious. It's from *Gone With the Wind.*"

"Shhh!" Violet said. "I mean I don't want to see it anymore."

"Are you giving it to me, then?"

Violet cast a glance toward Bert. "What will you do with it?"

Audrey followed her gaze. "I've put it in the bungalow. I have renters there who don't have a key to the attic. It will be safe there."

Violet chewed her bottom lip and nodded once.

"Do you really think Bert would care that it was you who took the hat?" Audrey asked. "It was so long ago."

"I really don't want to talk about it."

Audrey studied her friend for a moment. "I can have it destroyed if that's really what you want."

Violet grimaced, as if the image was painful to contemplate. "No," she murmured.

Several moments of silence hung between them.

Violet breathed in deep and looked out over the landscaped yard, the towering cypress trees, bougainvillaea and stately palms. "Bert's been invited back to South America to work on a research project on birds that migrate to the Amazon. He's wanted there by the first of January. He wants us to go. It would be for at least a year."

Audrey sensed a tugging in her chest, and the faintest pull of regret that she had her own secrets. She closed her eyes for a second against the idea that it could be a very long time before she saw Violet again. "Think you will do it?"

Violet looked down at the crumpled napkin in her hand. "Bert says we should. It's different now with Lainey married and so far away. Bert says she has her own life to live now and we can't forget we still have ours, too."

"He's right," Audrey said.

"We're hoping to see her and Marc before we

go. We've asked her if they would like to come home to the States for Christmas. We'll pay for them to come. I don't know how we will, but we will."

"So, things are good again between you and Lainey?"

Violet inhaled deeply. "I guess that's the best word for it. It's not perfect or wonderful. But it's good. It's so expensive to call. So we've been writing, and that's probably best. Writing gives us a chance to see what we're going to say before we say it. What she wanted to know more than anything was why I wouldn't tell her who you were."

"And what did you tell her?" Audrey asked.

Violet locked eyes with Audrey. "I told her the truth. That I didn't want her to stop needing me because she had you." Then she laughed as she looked away, off into the trees again. "And here she is, thousands of miles away now, married. She doesn't need you or me."

"That's not exactly true. I know how much a young woman needs a mother."

But Violet hadn't seemed to have heard her. When she spoke again, she seemed far away in thought. "Everything is changing, Audrey, and nothing is turning out the way I thought it would."

"How did you think it would be?"

Violet tossed her gaze back to Bert by the pool and the hopeful young man he was talking to. "I don't know. I guess I thought I would feel it had all been worth it. But instead I feel like . . ."

Violet paused and Audrey waited expectantly for Violet to finish.

"I feel that everything I've ever held close is being torn from me," Violet finally said. "Like a cage door has opened and all my little birds are flying away on the wind, and everything that matters to me is disappearing."

For a moment there was only this spoken thought hovering between them. And then Audrey heard someone say her name, and she turned from the heaviness of Violet's observations. It was the first time that day that she'd felt the full weight of Glen's absence, and she now embraced the interruption like one seeing an oasis in the desert. She was wanted in the house.

Audrey touched Violet on the shoulder and went inside.

THIRTY-FOUR

November 1963

Violet stood at the open double doors and looked over undulating hills in shades of mossy green and the tiny thousand-year-old Tuscan village of Adine off in the distance. In her hands was a cup of frothy cappuccino—her first—

and at her right, Audrey had laid out a breakfast table with jam-filled cornettos and orange slices. Bert was walking off the hours they had spent sitting the day before; first the flight from Los Angeles to New York, then New York to Rome, and then the train from Rome to Siena. They had arrived at Audrey's villa tired and sore, but the beauty of the Italian countryside was charming away their little discomforts.

It had been Audrey's idea for Violet and Bert to spend a week with her before they all flew to Paris to see Lainey and Marc. Marc was a new hire at an investment firm in Paris's financial district. Lainey was taking language classes so that she could continue her college education at a French university, now as a literature major. While it hadn't been feasible for the newlyweds to hop on a plane back to California for Christmas, they had both been amenable to a visit from the three of them before the holidays—Marc especially so. He didn't like the friction between Lainey and her *deux mamans*, as he described them. Her two mothers.

Audrey had made all the arrangements with, what seemed to Violet, a sense of urgency, as though she and Violet had unfinished business between them.

Violet had sensed it, too. Since the day of Glen's funeral when she'd told Audrey that it felt as if everything that mattered to her was poised to take flight, she had known that she owed Audrey an explanation. She had owed her one for twenty-three years, not just about the hat, but about a lot of things. For the past eight weeks, this debt had weighed on her more than it had during the previous two decades. The tugging of all that she held dear also seemed to apply to everything else that she held, including her secrets.

Audrey came into the room at that moment with her own cappuccino, and Violet startled as if Audrey had heard her unspoken thoughts.

"Bert out for a stroll?" Audrey said.

Violet nodded. "He's on the lookout for a zitting cisticola."

"That's survivable, I hope."

Violet smiled. "It's a warbler of some kind."

"How's the cappuccino?"

"Divine. As is your view. It's so beautiful and peaceful here."

"It is. Glen bought this place for us based on photographs. He would have loved it."

Several seconds of silence passed between them.

"Want some breakfast?" Audrey nodded to the little table laden with food.

"Actually, I need to tell you something before Bert gets back," Violet said, not daring to raise her eyes to meet Audrey's. "Something I should have told you long ago. And, surprisingly enough, I have the courage to tell you now, which I've never had before."

Audrey laughed, but nervously. "I actually have something to tell you, too."

Violet looked up. "You do?"

"Maybe we should sit."

Audrey led her to a little room just off the kitchen, with a large picture window cracked open a few inches to let in the morning air, and which looked out over the Tuscan hills. Two plump armchairs faced the glass. Bookshelves lined the walls, and a mariner's chest served as a coffee table. They sat down.

Audrey took a sip from her cup and then set it down on a tiled table between the two chairs. "I've had a lot of time to think since I got here. It's really all I've done. I barely know any Italian, and I've no nearby neighbors. And the nearest village has only a handful of people living in it, so I've had many hours to myself here. I feel like I've been given a second chance to live the rest of my life, Violet. I don't know what I am going to do with it yet, but I want to start it with no dark spots. I need to make things right between us."

For several seconds Violet could only gape at her. Audrey had it all wrong. "I'm the one who needs to make things right," Violet said. "If that is even possible. I did something terrible to you. And not only you."

"What are you talking about?"

Violet studied Audrey's face, beautiful even with the artistry of the years beginning to crisscross her skin in every direction. "I . . . I have wanted to tell you this for a long time, but I was afraid you would hate me. And I was too young to have you hate me for the rest of your life."

Audrey's brow crinkled with puzzlement. "If this is about the hat . . ."

"It's not just about the hat. I feel like I've . . . like I've altered Bert's life, ruined it, maybe, and Lainey's, too. And I think I may have ruined yours, even though you don't know it."

Audrey stared at her. Violet closed her eyes against the rush of guilt. "It started with that hat but it didn't end there. That day that it came up missing I wanted Bert to think you'd taken it and lost it. I wanted him to think you were someone he couldn't trust. I wanted to break the spell."

"The spell?"

"The spell you had over him."

Audrey looked baffled.

"That night we got drunk in the wardrobe department, you staggered into my bed, thinking it was yours. Bert came to the cottage looking for you the next morning because the hat was missing, remember? Because you were the last one to have it. But you weren't in your bed when he came; you had already left. And it didn't occur to me until later that you hadn't slept in your bedroom; you had slept in mine. You had tossed your big bag onto the floor in *my* room and that's where the hat was. I knew as soon as I saw it that you had put it in your bag by mistake because you were drunk, but I let Bert think you had lost it so that he would be mad at you. He almost lost his job over it, and I wanted him to blame you for that. So I wrapped the hat up in clothes I didn't need and sent it home to Alabama so you wouldn't find it in the bungalow."

Audrey stared at Violet, incredulous. "Because . . . because you were in love with him?"

The rest of Violet's confession bubbled out of her like poison she was spitting out of her mouth. "Because he was in love with you! And I wanted him to love me instead. I wanted him to be mad at you for nearly costing him his job. And he was. He started to see you differently after that. And then after the hat went missing, I let him think you were seeing Vince when I knew he was only a friend who was engaged to someone else. I gave you that little porcelain nightingale the day before Valentine's Day instead of on Valentine's Day, like Bert asked me to, because I didn't want you to know just how crazy he was about you. He was in love with you, not me. He loved you, Audrey. You were the one he wanted."

Violet turned away. She wished Audrey would say something, anything. But her friend was silent beside her. "I made a mess of everything, Audrey. If Bert had been with you instead of me, Lainey would have been yours and his. And there could have been more children. You could

401

have given him the son he wanted and that I couldn't give him. I made a mess of everything first because I wanted Bert, and then because I wanted Lainey to be mine, not yours. I can't help feeling that I ruined everything."

Sobs gathered thick in her throat. Violet had thought a confession would somehow lessen the burden of her old offenses, but she felt worse, not better.

"You didn't ruin everything, Violet," Audrey finally said.

Violet couldn't believe she heard Audrey correctly. She turned her head slightly. "What?"

"I said, you didn't ruin everything."

"But I did! Bert loved you."

"Maybe he was in love with me at one time, a very long time ago, but he loved you after me. I know he did. He still does. And who can say he would've been happy with me?"

"Of course he would've been happy with you."

"You don't know that! None of us knows that. And I wasn't in love with him."

"But when things started going badly for you, you talked like you wished you could just run off with Bert and forget all about Hollywood. You were starting to think that way."

"Because Bert was such a good man. And I was envious of *your* dream. Violet, he chose you."

"Because I made choosing you seem like a disastrous idea. Sometimes I wish I'd never gotten on that train to California. I can't help thinking that if I'd never come, you and Bert could've had a long and happy life together. But I came and ruined it all because I was so insanely jealous of you. I wish I'd never come."

"Don't say that."

"It's true. I wish I hadn't."

In an instant Audrey was kneeling before Violet, clasping her hands. "Listen to me! Don't ever wish that you and I had never met. I wouldn't be here if it wasn't for you. I wouldn't have met Glen. I wouldn't have reconciled with my father. I wouldn't even have Lainey if it wasn't for you."

"Yes, you would've."

"No! No, I wouldn't, because I'd be dead. Do you hear me? If it wasn't for you, I'd be dead!"

Audrey paused and released Violet's hands, willing Violet to look at her.

When Violet raised her head, Audrey continued.

"Do you remember the night I gave you those sleeping pills and told you to throw them away? Do you remember that night?"

Violet nodded. She remembered.

"That was the night I was going to end my life, Violet. I really was. You convinced me not to. Do you remember what you told me?"

Violet could only remember desperately trying to convince Audrey to focus on her career so that she'd be too preoccupied to shift her focus onto Bert. She shook her head.

"You told me that my mother was still watching over me and that she would want me to keep reaching for my dreams, even though I was so tired of fighting for them. You said tired people don't give up. Tired people just take a rest. Rest a bit and try again. You told me that I didn't want to live with regret."

Violet could barely recall those words, and yet as soon as she heard them she remembered saying them.

"You saved my life, Violet."

"I did it for me," Violet murmured.

"It doesn't matter why you did it. It only matters that you did. You saved my life. And because you saved mine, you saved Lainey's. And were it not for you and Bert raising her, I would not have the pleasure of having her in my life. And it's this reason that I wanted you here to confess to you what *I* did."

"I already told you. You did nothing. I'm the one who messed everything up."

"No, Violet. We both made mistakes. I was jealous, too. Jealous and angry. I was jealous that Lainey was yours, and I was angry that you wouldn't allow her to know I was her real mother. When she found out that I was, I wanted her to prefer me over you. I wanted her to want to be with me instead of you. I should have told her from the very moment she learned the truth about me that were it not for you, I would be dead and she would have never been born. But I didn't. So you see? We've both done things for all the wrong reasons."

An ache like none she had ever suffered was pounding in Violet's chest as she searched for a response. "Are you saying this makes us even?" she finally said.

"No!" Audrey answered quickly. "It shows how fragile we are. We were both shattered. We were broken people who longed to be whole. We thought it was love that was driving us to do what we did. But it wasn't love. It was fear. We were both too afraid of ending up unwanted and unneeded."

Several seconds of silence passed.

"Do you remember the night the three of us were on Sunset Boulevard, looking for that nightingale?" Audrey said, a moment later.

Violet remembered. There had been no nightingale. Only a sky full of stars, distant, glittering and cold. "It was never there."

"I choose to believe it was."

"But we never found it."

"But we did. We did find what we were looking for. Do you remember the story of the emperor and the nightingale?"

Violet shook her head. She couldn't.

"The emperor loved the plain brown nightingale that sang in his garden, but then he received a beautiful, mechanical bird as a gift and he sent the real one away. But then, many years later, the emperor was dying and the mechanical bird had long stopped working. He heard his old friend the real nightingale singing just outside his window. Her beautiful songs made him well again, and the emperor demanded she stay at his side always. But she told him she sang only to give pleasure to those who would listen, and she asked for nothing in return except her freedom. Remember?"

Violet nodded. A tear dropped from her eyes and landed on her folded hands.

"We held too tightly to what we were afraid we would lose," Audrey continued. "I don't want to live that way anymore. It's not too late. You were right. We don't want to live with regret."

Violet knew in that moment that she would always be a mother to her daughter, no matter what came between them, and that she was bound to her marriage not just by love but by the vows she had taken. But she could have stepped away from Audrey's friendship whenever she wanted and there wouldn't have been a judge or jury to call her back, and Audrey had always been free to do the same.

Yet they had both chosen, despite their colliding desires, to hold on to the love between them. Year after year after year.

Some things Violet did need to let go.

But others she would choose—always—to keep.

A distant figure appeared on the horizon outside the window. Bert was returning to the villa.

"And what should we do with that hat back home in the bungalow?" Violet asked as she watched her husband move toward them, his gaze on the sky.

Audrey smiled. "We'll keep it, secretly, to remind us of what we promised each other this morning."

"That hat is the color of envy and greed," Violet murmured.

"Not always. Not today." Audrey took her hand in a gesture of solidarity. "Today green is the color of life springing up out of the earth, Violet. Today it's the color of new beginnings."

Hollywood
March 10, 2012

Christine rings the bungalow's doorbell and the front door opens. The woman standing in front of her is pretty and seventyish. Her silver hair is fashionably cut, and there is a lilt to her voice that sounds like a foreign accent but it is too subtle for Christine to be sure.

She is not Mrs. Redmond.

"How very kind of you to return the hat," the woman says. "Please come in. I hear you used to live next door when you were a child. How remarkable."

Christine steps inside and hands over the pink-striped box. "Yes, I did. A long time ago. It was just for a year."

The woman smiles wide as she stretches out her hand. "Elaine Garceau. Friends call me Elle."

"Christine McAllister."

"So very nice to meet you, Christine. Please have a seat. While I still have one to offer you."

They sit down on the sofa. All around them are boxes. Some are full; some are not. Some are taped shut and ready for whatever is to happen next.

"So, you were six when you and my mother were neighbors?" Elle asks.

"Yes. During first grade. We moved to Laurel Canyon when I was seven and then to Bel Air. Your mother made the long hours my parents worked back then enjoyable. She would bake something wonderful and then we'd sit and watch old TV shows while she told me about all the places in the world she had been to. I think there was an actress on those old shows who was her favorite. Your mother always liked it when one of her episodes came on."

"Audrey Wainwright?"

Christine didn't know the name. "Maybe."

"They were lifelong best friends, my mother and Audrey Wainwright. They met on the set of *Gone With the Wind*. They were both studio secretaries back then."

"Oh!" Christine looks down at the hatbox.

Elle follows her gaze. "They stole that hat from wardrobe. Lucky for them, there was a spare for the rest of the filming."

"So that really is Scarlett O'Hara's hat from the movie?"

"It really is." Elle reaches into a cardboard box near the couch that is half-full of pictures and artwork. She pulls out a framed black-and-white photograph and hands it to Christine. Two women are standing arm in arm. One of the women is Mrs. Redmond long before Christine knew her. Their clothes are 1940s style.

"I have some dresses just like these in my shop," Christine says.

"Cute, aren't they? My dad took this picture. He was a wildlife photographer. Birds, mostly. That's Audrey Wainwright before she was a TV star. Wasn't she beautiful? And that's my mother. All three of them worked on the set of *Gone With the Wind.* My father was employed in the wardrobe department, hence access to the hat. But he apparently wasn't an accessory to the crime. He didn't know they'd made off with it. I'm not sure he ever knew." Elle laughs lightly.

Christine hands the photograph back to her. "Did your mother ever tell you what made them take it?"

"She told me it was just a silly thing they did one night when they'd had too much to drink. I think the real reason was just between them. A secret thing between friends." Elle places the photograph back in the box. "Audrey died ten years ago. Her passing was very hard on my mother. It was hard on all of us. We were all very close to her."

"I'm so sorry. And when did your mother pass away?"

Elle looks up from the box, surprise etched on her face. "My mother isn't dead."

Christine is wholly unprepared for such news. "She's . . . she's not?"

"No. She just celebrated her ninety-sixth birthday a few months ago here in this house. Just before I moved her out of it. She lives in West Hollywood now, in an assisted-care facility, probably not very far from your boutique."

For a second Christine is too stunned to speak. "She's been here in this house all this time?"

"Mom moved in right after my dad died, almost thirty years ago. It was Audrey Wainwright's bungalow, but she let my mother live here and then left it to her in her will. Mom was able to manage on her own until just recently. I've held off emptying it until now because it was rather sad having to move her out. She loved this house. Her age finally caught up with her, I'm afraid."

"Oh."

Christine is about to ask if it would be possible to visit Mrs. Redmond when Elle speaks.

"Christine, would you like to come with me and my granddaughters to see her right now? I told her I'd bring the hat by when it was returned to us. She's been anxious to see it again. I'm afraid she may not remember you, but you never know. Would you like to join us?"

"Very much."

Half an hour later Christine is following Elle and her granddaughters down a carpeted hallway in a facility that looks and feels more like a Mediterranean resort than a nursing home. The textured walls are painted a creamy shade of pumpkin, and an aroma of citrus, clove, and sandalwood tumbles about them as they walk.

Elle looks back at Christine. "By the way, Mom still calls me Lainey, even though I haven't gone by that nickname in fifty years."

"My mom still calls me Chrissy."

The two women share a smile as Elle stops at the second-to-the-last door. She knocks once, opens the door, and pokes her head in.

"Mom, it's Lainey. Are you dressed? We've brought the hat. And a guest."

Christine follows Elle and the granddaughters inside.

On one side of the room is a large picture window, an armchair, a TV, a tiny kitchen area, and a mirrored closet. The other is dominated by a hospital bed; a second, smaller window; and, in the bed, propped up with pillows, a fragment of an old woman.

Her paper white skin and hair are thin. Even her bones appear to be thin. She looks as if she might be able to fly away if she could lift her delicate arms and move them up and down. The only part of her that doesn't look ancient and decrepit are her gray-blue eyes.

Christine knows those eyes. "Hello, Mrs. Redmond," she says.

"Who are you?"

A slight Southern drawl coats the woman's words.

"Mom, this Christine McAllister. You babysat her many years ago when you came back to Hollywood to live in the bungalow."

"Christine who?" She frowns.

Christine moves closer to her. "Christine McAllister. I lived in the house next door, Mrs. Redmond."

Mrs. Redmond stares at her, ancient brows puckered. "Just call me Violet. You make me sound like an old woman when you call me| Mrs. Redmond. How do I know you again?"

Christine breaks into a wide smile. "You used to watch me after school."

Violet narrows her eyes. "Christine. You liked macaroons."

"Yes! You baked wonderful things but the macaroons were the best."

"Christine owns a vintage-clothing shop, and that's where the hat ended up. Isn't that amazing?" Elle says.

Violet cocks her head in wonderment and gawks at Christine. "You had the hat?"

"No, Mom. It just got sent there by accident with all those old clothes you had at the bungalow. Christine brought it back and told me she knew you. You let her try on the hat once. She remembered it."

"Is Audrey with you?"

"Audrey's in heaven, Mom."

Violet swivels her head toward Christine. "Audrey runs a home for unwed mothers out of her villa in Italy. Did you know that?"

"I didn't," Christine says.

"Bert and I came out every summer to help her. And then it was just me who came out. Is Bert here?"

Christine casts a glance at Elle. She is opening the box and withdrawing the hat. Then she places it on her mother's lap. "Here's the hat, Mom. Has it been a while since you've seen it?"

The old woman looks at the hat. "A long while."

"*Je peux l'essayer, Grandmère?*" one of the granddaughters asks.

"In English, Michelle," Elle says.

"Grandmother, may I try on the hat?"

But Violet has a distant look in her eyes. "Do you know what Mammy said to Scarlett before she yanked down those curtains?"

"Mom?"

"She said, 'You been brave so long, Miss Scarlett. You just gotta go on bein' brave.' That's what we did, didn't we, Audrey? We learned to be brave when it was easier to be afraid."

The room is quiet.

"Mom? You all right?"

Violet looks up from the hat on her lap and her

gaze travels to her great-granddaughters. "Which one of you wants to wear this hat?"

"I do!" both girls say.

Violet reaches with a shaking hand for her bedside table and a pair of cuticle scissors. She turns the hat over in her lap and begins to snip away the label that reads *Scarlett #13*.

Christine, shocked, is slow to react. "Mrs. Redmond, are you sure you want to do that?"

But even as she asks, the little label flutters to the carpet.

"Here you go." Violet extends the hat toward the girls. The younger one takes it gleefully. "Go play now," she says.

The girls take the hat and scamper to the mirrored closet door on the far end of the room.

Christine bends down to pick up the faded tag.

"Mom, do you really want the girls to play with that hat?" Elle asks.

"I would have given it to them sooner but I had forgotten where I put it."

Christine extends the label toward Elle.

"No, no. You can keep that," Violet says to Christine. "They don't need that. You take it."

Christine hesitates but Elle nods, and she drops the label into her purse.

"Now open the window there, Lainey. I like to have it open when the sun goes down and the stars come out."

Elle opens the window nearest the bed, and the late-afternoon air is full of birdsong.

Violet turns her head toward the sound.

"Do you hear that?" she says to Christine.

"The birds?"

"That's a nightingale. Did you know a man shipped one hundred nightingales to California from England for a gentleman's park? In 1887. Did you know that?"

"I didn't," Christine replies.

"That man just opened the cages and let them go free. One hundred of them! Bert found out about it when he was preparing to teach a class at the university. You would have thought he'd won a million dollars that day."

Violet leans forward in her bed. "Do you hear it? Isn't that the most beautiful sound in the world?"

She waits expectantly for Christine to answer, her eyes shining with anticipation and delight. Behind them the little girls are laughing and posing at the mirror, pretending they are famous.

"Do you hear it, Audrey?" Violet says.

Christine nods. "I hear it."

⟨⟩⬥⟨⟩

ACKNOWLEDGMENTS

My deepest thanks to:

Ellen Edwards and Kendra Harpster at NAL and my agent, Elisabeth Weed, for expert guidance, insights, and advice; author friends Rene Gutteridge and Susan May Warren for encouragement along the way, and James Scott Bell for all the Old Hollywood particulars and the best pastrami sandwich ever at Langer's Deli on Alvarado; Annette Hubbell and Skot and Amy McCoy for the most amazing research day in Hollywoodland; Becca Peterson and Steve Auer of the Culver Studios for helping me imagine the long-ago Selznick International days and allowing me to walk the lots; Culver City historian Julie Lago Cerra, and Marc Wanamaker from Bison Archives for assisting me with nailing down the little details; Jim Bunte and Steve Crise of the Pacific Electric Railway Historical Society; Robert Houston and Gwyn Houston at Joyride Vintage in the Orange Circle; Steve Wilson, Curator of the Film Collection at the Harry Ransom Center at the University of Texas, and coauthor of the beautifully designed book *The Making of Gone With the Wind*; Susan Lindsley for compiling the diaries and letters of her aunt,

Susan Myrick, so that the rest of the world can peek in on them; Siri Mitchell and Mary Demuth for the French phrases; my mother, Judy Horning, for her careful proofreading; God for giving me a love for story and the inspiration and confidence to tackle the blank page, every day, over and over; and to you, dear reader, for allowing me literary license here and there as I took the facts I gleaned from many of these wonderful people mentioned above and crafted a story that begins with truth, but onto which I imposed the question *What if?*

A CONVERSATION WITH SUSAN MEISSNER

Spoiler alert—A Conversation with Susan Meissner and the Questions for Discussion that follow tell more about what happens in the book than you might want to know until you read it.

Q. What inspired you to use Scarlett's hat from Gone With the Wind *to tell a story about female friendship?*

A. I've long been a fan of *Gone With the Wind.* I've read the book only once, but I'd probably seen the movie a dozen or more times before I decided to write *Stars over Sunset Boulevard.* Margaret Mitchell's legendary novel is not often described as being about friendship, but the more I've watched the film, the more I've seen how incredibly deep and complex Scarlett O'Hara and Melanie Hamilton's relationship is. I wanted to explore the layers of their friendship as depicted in the movie, and I especially wanted to study how these two literary characters at first glance seem to be polar opposites but are actually both fiercely loyal and unafraid of making hard choices to protect what and whom they love. Scarlett's curtain-dress hat is to me emblematic of what dire circumstances can lead someone to do when what she loves most is in danger of being ripped out of her hands. I knew I could use Scarlett and Melanie's fictional friendship as a template for telling a story about two studio secretaries who, like Scarlett and Melanie, are not as different from each other as we might first think, especially when their separate longings collide.

Q. By the end of the novel, I was deeply moved by all that Violet and Audrey have come to mean to each other. I wanted to immediately contact all my best friends in person to tell them how grateful I am for their presence in my life. Is the novel, in part, your tribute to your own friends?

A. It is first a tribute to friendship itself. It is the most remarkable of human relationships because it is completely voluntary. Violet muses late in the book on this very thought: that we are bound by blood and vows to other deeply close relationships, but we get to choose to keep loving our friends, day after day. Or to stop loving them. There is no civil code that demands we stay friends—no pledge is given; no papers are signed; no vows are spoken. And yet most of us have friends whom we love as deeply as those people we are legally and morally bound to. I know I have friends like that. I love writing novels about relationships, and there is no relationship quite like friendship.

Q. What do you find especially appealing about Hollywood during its golden age, and the films that were made then?

A. There was a magical quality about Hollywood in its golden years. It was a dream factory in the 1930s and '40s, a place that produced in fantasy what people imagined life could be like as they stoically moved on from the horrors of the First World War and then the demoralizing years of the Depression. The golden age of Hollywood was a chance to indulge again in beauty and wonderment after death and then deprivation. This era also interests me because Hollywood's golden years ended so suddenly and without any warning. After World War Two, most in Hollywood thought they could just pick up where they left off before the war started. But the advent of television just a few years later would change everything. The beginning of World War Two was actually the beginning of the end of the golden age and no one really saw it coming.

Q. Where did you find such detailed information about the making of Gone With the Wind? *Did anything you discovered particularly surprise you?*

A. Every day that I spent in research I found new details that amazed me. The filming began in January 1939 and the movie premiered just eleven months later; that detail floors me. The fact that the script kept changing up until the last few weeks of shooting, that five thousand separate wardrobe pieces were made, that it is still the most iconic film ever produced, are just a few of the myriad fascinating particulars about *Gone With the Wind*. There were a number of little things I learned about the film that didn't make it into my novel, such as Scarlett's first wedding night scene, which was edited out, in which she makes Charles Hamilton sleep in a chair across the room, and the scene in which Ashley's father, John Wilkes, dies in her arms. The book that was most helpful to me was Steve Wilson's *The Making of Gone With the Wind*. It is a beautifully composed book with wonderful photos and text, published by the University of Texas at Austin. The university's Harry Ransom Center owns much of David O. Selznick's studio archives and a number of *Gone With the Wind* costume pieces, including the curtain dress and its hat.

Q. Where did the idea to include the nightingale spring from? Is it true that one hundred nightingales were shipped to California from England in 1887, as Violet says late in the book?

A. Hans Christian Anderson's story "The Nightingale" was a favorite of mine as a child, so I've wanted for some time to incorporate that fable into the story threads of a novel. I love the idea from the story that the magnificent mechanical bird can satisfy the emperor for only a limited time. In the end, it is the plain brown nightingale that the emperor loves most and longest, and that bird is always meant to be free.

It's quite possible that a hundred nightingales did make it to California in 1887. I found an answer to a query in a 1902 edition of the avian-themed periodical *The Condor* that states a bill of lading existed for one hundred nightingales shipped out of Southampton, England, and bound for New York. The nightingales were reputedly ordered by a man who wanted them for a gentleman's park in Santa Barbara. Did those birds arrive in California? Were they released? Did they survive and multiply? I don't know. But I had the wonderful opportunity as a novelist to imagine in the pages of *Stars over Sunset Boulevard* that they did.

Q. What do you hope readers will take away from the novel and remember long after they've finished reading?

A. I hope the theme that will resonate most is that love and fear can sometimes feel the same, but each will lead a person to take different actions. When a decision has to be made, fear usually motivates me to choose what is best for me, whereas love motivates me to choose what is best for another person. Fear urges me to hang on, white-knuckled, to what is mine, while love can actually lead me to let go. My hoped-for takeaway is the notion that when you hold something you love tightly to your chest for fear of losing it, you actually risk crushing it against you.

Q. Readers are often deeply moved by your stories, and quote liberally from them. Is there something unique about your writing process that results in this emotional reaction to your work?

A. I want my readers to remember a book of mine after they've turned the last page, partly so they will want to read more from me, but also because I want them to feel that reading it was well worth their time. I guess I want a book that I write to be more than entertainment that is enjoyable for the moment but forgettable as the months go by. I don't make a conscious effort to craft quotable prose when I write, but I do endeavor to pose questions and suggest insights that speak across the pages into a reader's life. For me, that translates into a good reason for having read the book. I always remember a book more fully and longer if I've been so emotionally tugged that I find myself highlighting phrases I don't want to forget. And I usually can't wait for that author's next book! Khaled Hosseini's books are always like that for me.

Q. Is this your first novel set in your home state of California? Did that proximity affect your writing?

A. I set two of my older titles in my hometown of San Diego, but this was the first one set in Los Angeles against the glamorous backdrop of Old Hollywood. The geographical proximity made physical research far easier than with my previous book, *Secrets of a Charmed Life*, which was set in England. But as is the case with all historical settings, time has marched on. You can't revisit former years; you can only look at the relics and archives that remain from them. When I visited the Culver Studios, which seventy years ago was the site of Selznick International, I entered the iconic Thomas Ince mansion, stood inside what was David Selznick's office, and peeked at the same sound stages where many *Gone With the Wind* scenes were filmed. But the famed back lot is long gone, as are all the sets, the costumes, and almost everyone who worked on the film. Even so, being able to plant my feet in the very spot where history was made always has an invigorating effect on me. I can more easily imagine what an event was like if I am standing in the place where it happened, closing my eyes, and picturing it all in my head.

Q. A section of Stars over Sunset Boulevard *is set during World War Two. Can you tell us more about how people on the "home front" experienced the war, especially in California?*

A. From what I can gather, the most difficult aspect of World War Two for Californians, especially for those living in larger coastal cities such as Los Angeles, San Francisco, and San Diego, was the fear of attack by Japanese forces from across the Pacific. For Japanese-Americans living in California, life was incredibly hard. Most, including children and second-generation transplants who didn't speak a word of Japanese, were forced off their properties and housed in internment camps for the duration of the war. Interestingly enough, I've read that within days of the bombing of Pearl Harbor, President Roosevelt commissioned Hollywood to strengthen public awareness and morale, and to support the war effort by continuing to make motion pictures. Hollywood made significant movie-making advances during the years of the war despite limitations related to restrictions and shortages, and pretty much perfected the genre of combat films during that time. Plus, Hollywood worked with the war department and the army to distribute its films, free of charge, to soldiers in combat areas. The movies were delivered by boat, jeep, parachute, and any other mode of transportation available.

Q. You're a voracious reader. Have you read anything lately that you particularly recommend?

A. I've always got a towering stack of books on my bedside table. Some of my most recent favorites have been *Girl on a Train* by Paula Hawkins, *The Nightingale* by Kristin Hannah, *All the Light We Cannot See* by Anthony Doerr, and *The Goldfinch* by Donna Tartt. All of these books were superbly written, but none is what I would call a light read. The books I enjoy the most are usually fairly infused with angst and moral dilemmas. It's not that I can't appreciate a lighter read, but those books typically aren't the ones I remember. The books that stay with me are the ones in which ordinary, flawed but likable people have been thrust into extraordinary circumstances that have truly taken them to the mat. Even in *Where'd You Go, Bernadette*, a hilarious read that I loved, there is a complex, deep story underneath the witty writing and the laughs. As I write this, I am eagerly awaiting Kate Morton's newest, *The Lake House*, and Geraldine Brooks's *The Secret Chord.*

Q. Can you give us a hint about your next novel?

A. The nutshell of the story I am writing next is this: Three war brides on their way to the United States in 1946—a British telephone operator who fears the open water, a French Resistance fighter's daughter emotionally scarred by the loss of her family at the hands of the Nazis, and a German ballet dancer who feels despised by everyone she meets—form unlikely bonds of friendship on the famed HMS *Queen Mary* as it transports 1,500 American GI brides and their children from Southampton to New York. The dovetailed contemporary story is about a woman with extrasensory gifts she has never felt comfortable having who boards the supposedly haunted *Queen Mary* with a task she hesitantly undertakes as a favor to an old flame— now a widower—and his young daughter. I live just two hours away from the *Queen Mary*, and I can tell you that stepping onto her deck is like walking into a time machine. This historic and majestic Cunard ship was first a luxury ocean liner, then a WWII troop carrier and bearer of GI war brides to America, and she is now a floating hotel moored in Long Beach, California. Many people insist she is haunted, but I plan to consider not which ghosts allegedly haunt which deck, but rather what stays behind in a place that has seen so much human history. Think of all those who walked the *Queen Mary*'s decks: kings and queens, prime ministers and presidents, millionaires, immigrants, soldiers, prisoners of war, vacationers, happy newlyweds, gray-haired spinsters, and innocent children. The *Queen Mary* is a character unto herself, and if there are echoes of the past aboard her, I want to consider what those echoes might mean. When the story of my three young war brides intersects with my reluctant current-day researcher, I will explore thematically how sometimes a person must bravely cross the unknown to begin a new life when the old one is gone. I can't wait to start writing it.

QUESTIONS FOR DISCUSSION

1. What aspect of the novel had the strongest emotional impact on you?

2. Who did you like more—Violet or Audrey? Which woman is most like you?

3. Who is your best friend? Did this person ever save your life? What do you think is the most remarkable quality about friendship?

4. The novel suggests that Melanie in *Gone With the Wind* is as capable of deceit as Scarlett is, if deceit is required to get what she wants. Do you agree? How do Violet and Audrey compare to Scarlett and Melanie?

5. Have you ever stolen your friend's significant other?

6. Are you keeping a secret from your partner and/or friend because the truth would reflect poorly on you?

7. In Chapter Twenty-nine, Violet tells herself that "Sometimes a person had to do something drastic, like rip apart beautiful curtains

to make a dress and hat, to bring about the better good." How does Violet use this analogy to rationalize her actions?

8. How would the characters' lives have been different if Violet had told Lainey the truth about her mother when she first began to ask?

9. It has been said that there are only two basic emotions, love and fear, and that all the other emotions are variations of these. Do you agree? How are fear and love the same? How are they different?

10. Are you a fan of *Gone With the Wind*—the book and the film? Tell us how you felt and what you thought when you first read the book or saw the movie. Has your opinion changed over time?

11. Have you heard stories or read depictions about what life was like in the U.S. during World War Two? How do they compare to Violet's experiences?

12. What do the nightingales represent in the novel? Have you ever looked for something beautiful that might not exist?

A native of San Diego, **Susan Meissner** is a former managing editor of a weekly newspaper and an award-winning columnist. She has published twenty novels with Penguin Random House and Harvest House. She lives in San Diego with her husband and has four grown children.

Center Point Large Print
600 Brooks Road / PO Box 1
Thorndike, ME 04986-0001 USA

(207) 568-3717

US & Canada:
1 800 929-9108
www.centerpointlargeprint.com

6-16